WHEN I'M TEMPTED

A PROMISES OF GOD NOVEL

KIM CASH TATE

WHEN I'M TEMPTED

A Promises of God Novel

Kim Cash Tate

Cover Design: Jenny Zemanek at Seedlings Design Studio

Scripture quotations are taken from the NEW AMERICAN STANDARD BIBLE ®, Copyright © 1960, 1962, 1963,

1968, 1971, 1972, 1973, 1975, 1977, 1995 by The Lockman Foundation. Used by permission. (www.Lockman.org)

Tate, Kimberly Cash.

When I'm Tempted / Kim Cash Tate.

ISBN 978-1-946336-02-6

1. African American women—Fiction. 2. Christian fiction.

ALSO BY KIM CASH TATE

Heavenly Places

Faithful

Cherished

Hope Springs

The Color of Hope

Hidden Blessings

Though I Stumble

If I Believe

If You're With Me

and

Cling: Choosing a Lifestyle of Intimacy with God

No temptation has overtaken you but such as is common to man; and God is faithful, who will not allow you to be tempted beyond what you are able, but with the temptation will provide the way of escape also, so that you will be able to endure it.

1 CORINTHIANS 10:13

CHAPTER 1

*C*yd London strode across campus coatless and shivering in the dead of winter, a victim of St. Louis's schizophrenic weather. Temps bordered on seventy much of the weekend. At church this morning she'd even spotted sandals. But when she left her office to grab a latte from the student union, the winds had shifted. On her way back now, her hands clutched the warmth of her coffee cup—and a flyer she'd just seen posted. Instead of getting back to work, she had a different mission—to throttle professor Micah Daniels.

A wintry gust blew, whipping Cyd's shoulder length curls and rattling the flyer. She looked at it again. *How dare he?* Bad enough he'd belittled her faith and challenged her to an open debate. She'd prayed about it and accepted the parameters—a small setting with students from within their department. Still, she'd been holed up in her office for days preparing. And seemed the more she prepared, the more ill-prepared she felt. She wasn't some skilled defender of the faith. Had never formally debated a soul in her life. She'd been counting down the days till this Thursday, when it would be over and done with.

Now he'd made flyers and posted them in the Union? She eyed it again as she walked into her building—"Dr. Micah Daniels and Dr. Cydney London debate 'Who Was Jesus?' at Washington University in St. Louis..."

Cyd had seen his door opened earlier and avoided him. Now she made her way directly there.

Behind his desk, feet kicked up, Micah had his nose in a book. Cyd gave two courtesy knocks and continued in.

"What's the meaning of this?" she said, waving the flyer.

Micah peered overtop his book. "I'm not sure I'm following."

Cyd moved closer to his desk. "I agreed to a small debate in an intimate setting with a pre-determined audience. You took it upon yourself to move it to a larger lecture hall and *advertise* it?"

"A meaningful debate such as this begs for a larger audience." Micah laid down his book and moved his feet to the floor. "I would think you'd welcome it. Isn't that the nature of what you believe? 'Spreading the good news?'" His tone was matter-of-fact. "And how often do you see two black professors engaging in this way? That dynamic alone is inviting."

"This is about what *you* believe in—notoriety." Cyd put the flyer on his desk. "I didn't sign up for this. I'm pulling out of the debate." She turned, heading out the door.

"What are you afraid of, Cyd?" Micah stood, came around to the front of his desk and leaned against it. "That your Jesus can't stand up to scrutiny?"

Cyd turned in the doorway, her coffee sloshing a little. "It won't work, Micah. I'm not moved by your comments. You're about building a platform, which is fine. Do that. But you won't get any more help from me."

"Any *more* help?"

"Oh, you've forgotten?" She eyed him. "When you were 'desperate'—your word—to move from your dead-end position and join the faculty here, where you could have a higher profile?" She came closer. "I helped you get here, and all you've done these last few months is make life difficult."

"You did help me," Micah said, "and I apologize for suggesting otherwise." He folded his arms. "But we have fundamental differences about a central issue. This isn't about notoriety. It's about debunking the mythological Jesus. I think you do yourself and others a disservice if you back out."

Cyd turned and walked a few feet down the hall and into her office, kicking her door to a close. She didn't have time for this. She had academic papers to write. Classes for which to prepare. Students to advise. Not to mention all the work with launching the new women's ministry. This debate had demanded too much of her focus, and this was her chance to be done with it.

And yet . . .

She set her latte down and plopped in her office chair, replaying his words.

What are you afraid of, Cyd?

She stared at the books and papers that covered her desk, the Bible prominent among them. For twenty years this campus had been her home, and she loved her job. She could immerse herself in the history, culture, and languages of ancient Greece, Rome, and Israel. She'd been able to carve out a niche in New Testament Studies and earn respect among her colleagues, even if most didn't believe what she believed.

But this debate would put her on new territory. She'd be forced to say it—that she believed Jesus was Lord and Savior, the only way to heaven . . . which would surely alienate students and colleagues alike. A smaller setting would have been tough enough. No telling what his little promo effort would bring.

I know, Lord. She could sense the nudging already, same nudging she'd felt at first. She couldn't run from an opportunity to share truth that could save someone's soul. Micah had his own motives. But she had to trust that the Lord would use this—even if it came with a lot of personal downside.

Cyd sighed, looking at the piles on her desk once again. She'd planned to get coffee and work another couple of hours before the Oscar party at their house. But in this mood she'd get nothing done.

She packed up, closed the door, and inserted the key to lock up.

Micah came out of his office. "I need to know if this is still a go."

Cyd pulled out the key and dropped it into her bag. *Only because the Lord says so.* "I'll do it," she said.

"I get the impression you're taking this personally," Micah said. "It's not personal, Cyd."

She started toward him, on her way out. "Have a good evening, Micah."

~

"I should've never advocated for him to come here." Cyd removed golden brown chicken wings from the oven and began dousing them with barbecue sauce.

"He's right about one thing." Cedric cut sweet potatoes into fries. "You're taking this personally." He turned to his wife. "You know none of this is about you, sweetheart. God's clearly at work."

"I keep telling myself that," Cyd said, "but it's still vexing."

"How did you know him before he got here?" Her sister Stephanie sliced celery for a veggie tray.

"Academia is a small world." Cyd turned the wings with tongs, dousing some more. "And if you're talking classics professors— and narrow that to minorities in the field—it's infinitely smaller. We met years ago at one of those mixers at the annual meeting, and I'd see him year to year."

4

"And he'd never given you a hard time about your faith," Stephanie said, "till now?"

"He knew what kind of research I did," Cyd said, "and that I focused on the New Testament. But when he got here and found out it wasn't purely academic—that I actually believed it—it threw him." She looked at her sister. "Even asked why I wasn't at a seminary instead."

"Girl, what?" Stephanie said.

"I feel like he's calling all the shots," Cyd said. "Got me backed into a corner."

"Cyd, come on." Cedric looked at her. "He's not calling a single thing. This is all God. You're praying for him, right?"

Cyd turned, putting the barbecued wings back into the oven.

"Wow, babe." Cedric moved closer to her. "You're used to 'nice' ministry, where you get to teach the Bible to people who want to hear what you have to say. This is a different setting, but it's still ministry. I can't wait to see what God does—"

"Hey, is everybody in the kitchen?"

Their dog Reese hopped up from her resting spot, barking at the intruder.

"We're in here, Faith," Stephanie called out. "You got your other half with you?"

Faith walked in with Reggie, who had a bundled Zoe in his arms.

"Come here, pumpkin," Stephanie said, taking Zoe and pulling off her coat.

"I can't get over you two." Cyd hugged them both. "So cute. Let me see that ring again, girl."

Faith beamed, holding out her hand. "It's only been a couple weeks, so I'm not over it myself."

"Are y'all looking at dates yet?" Stephanie said.

"I'm #TeamAlonzoandCinda," Reggie said. "Elope and be done with it."

"I could go either way," Faith said, "but part of me wants a

5

small wedding. We'll see. I've already got a lot with graduation in May. Oh, Cyd"—she pulled a paper from her purse—"Why didn't I know about this? You're debating Professor Daniels about Jesus?"

"Where did you get that?" Cyd said.

"Campus library."

Cyd sighed. "Incredible."

"We need to show up on Thursday to support," Stephanie said.

"Definitely," Faith said. "Reg and I already said we're going."

Cyd looked at them. "That would mean a lot, just knowing you all are there."

"I bet it'll be crowded," Faith said. "More than a few students have a crush on the new professor, talking about how handsome he is."

"Oh, really." Stephanie gave her sister a look. "You ain't say all that, Cyd."

"There's nothing cute about that ego of his," Cyd said.

The doorbell rang, setting off the dog again.

"Hello?" a voice said.

"We're in here, Jordyn," Cyd said.

Cyd's six-year-old son Chase came bolting from the family room, tugging on Jordyn before she could get to the kitchen.

"The video game's on," Chase said. "Let's go play."

"You're ready to beat up on me already?" Jordyn smiled. "Okay, let me say hello to people first." She stopped to chat with Faith and Reggie.

Stephanie looked at Cyd. "How does Chase know Jordyn so well?"

"Jordyn started watching him after school for us about a month ago," Cyd said. "Date nights too. I didn't tell you?"

"Had no idea," Stephanie said.

Jordyn came over, hugging them both. "Thanks for inviting me, Cyd."

"Of course," Cyd said. "I was hoping Jade would come too." She elbowed her sister when Stephanie slipped her a look.

"To be honest," Jordyn said, "she wanted me to stay and watch with her at the apartment, since she doesn't really know you all." She shrugged. "But she's got no love for Cinda and Alonzo, and I didn't feel like hearing all that."

"Have you talked to Cinda?" Cyd started chopping broccoli. "How are she and Alonzo feeling?"

"I talked to her maybe a week ago," Jordyn said, "but only briefly. They were on the way to some pre-Oscar luncheon. She's been super busy getting him ready for everything, but loving it."

Faith stole a carrot from the platter. "I talked to her this morning before church. She said Alonzo's a little anxious."

"And I talked to Alonzo," Reggie said. "Says he's cool, of course. But yeah, he's anxious."

"And he's got to wait all night," Stephanie said. "The Best Actor award is one of the last ones they give out."

"The red carpet is what I can't wait to see," Jordyn said. "Cinda wouldn't tell me what she's wearing."

"Me either," Faith said. "Little stinker."

"I'm looking forward to the entire evening," Cyd said. "I still can't believe Randall's movie was nominated for several Academy Awards. That's all I want to focus on—awards, pretty dresses, and—"

Cyd's phone vibrated and she took a look—a tweet by Micah Daniels with her name in it. He'd taken his promotion to social media.

CHAPTER 2

"*B*abe, you ready to go?" Treva Alexander looked up as her husband entered the bedroom. "I'd say little man is finally done eating." She smiled down at the baby, asleep in her bosom. "Cyd just texted and—what's wrong?"

"I don't know." Lance glanced at the phone in his hand. "That was Pastor Lyles. He wants to meet this week."

Treva rocked gently in the chair. "You meet with Pastor Lyles all the time."

"I know, but . . ." Lance stared vaguely. "Something in his voice, and the way he's been operating lately. Doing a whole lot, like the way he fast-tracked Cecil's hire."

"But babe, you know that was all God." Treva covered Wes with a small blanket. "As much as I'd been telling Jillian they needed to move to St. Louis—never thinking it could actually happen. Then a door opens up? That was like a Christmas miracle."

"No doubt," Lance said. "Still, Living Word's got so many committee levels and interview stages, it takes forever to bring people into full time ministry positions. Cecil got the youth pastor spot in a month and a half. The new pastor over missions—

same thing." He leaned against the dresser. "Now Pastor Lyles is turning his attention to Living Hope. He wants to see where we are with Randall's replacement as elder, among other things."

"So what's bothering you about all this?"

"Pastor Lyles is nearly seventy," Lance said. "I think he's tying up loose ends, setting the stage for retirement."

"Sounds like you wouldn't be thrilled about it, though."

Lance sighed. "He's guided me for twenty years, babe," he said. "Preached life into my soul when I was in jail. Helped me get a job when I got out. Taught me the Scriptures and discipled me himself." He drifted a moment, remembering. "He saw things in me I couldn't see in myself. If it weren't for him, I wouldn't have become a youth pastor, definitely wouldn't be pastor of Living Hope. And honestly? A big reason I did both was because I knew he'd be there."

Treva looked at Lance. "You know how much I love Pastor Lyles. His Ephesians study literally changed my life, and for years after that, I devoured one study of his after another. And that was from afar. You've been able to glean from him in a deeply personal way—"

"Exactly," Lance said, "even in practical things like running a church and dealing with people. I couldn't tell you how many times we met leading up to Living Hope's first service—how many questions I had, all the concerns, how many times I tried to back out." He shook his head. "Living Hope celebrates three years in May. And now that I *really* know all the challenges in being a pastor, I look to him even more. If he leaves . . ."

"The dynamic will shift, and you'll feel the void," Treva said. "But I know for a fact that you look to God more than you look to anyone. And *He's* not going anywhere."

"I know. Still . . ."

"Who gave you that sermon this morning," Treva said, "the one that had me about to run around the building when you broke down Romans 6. Did Pastor Lyles email it to you?"

Lance only looked at her, knowing she'd seen him studying all week.

Treva moved the baby to the bassinet. "You don't realize the strength and wisdom you operate in *in Christ*. Not just with your sermons, but every day, the way you lead, the way you *live*. Pastor Lyles would tell you himself it's not about him." She moved closer to him. "Babe, the Spirit of God is *real* in you, and powerful. You can trust that—you can trust *Him*—no matter what."

Lance pulled her close with a long sigh. "You have no idea how much I needed to hear that."

"I don't know if you know, but I married an amazing man of God." Treva eyed him. "And there's nothing sexier than a man who follows hard after Jesus."

"Who told you that bit of wisdom?" Lance said.

"Nobody had to tell me," Treva said. "I can see for myself. Except, it helps that you *are* actually sexy."

"All afternoon you've been saying you want to get to Cyd and Cedric's early." His arms wound tighter around her. "You sure you want to keep talking like that?"

"I'm just realizing . . ." Treva kissed him. "The baby's asleep. The girls are gone. And we said we'd be intentional about grabbing that one-another focus." She checked her watch. "Plus, I've still got time till Cinda hits the red carpet in her dress."

Lance gave her a look. "That's why we're rushing over there, to see a dress? I thought this was about Randall's movie."

"Babe, it's the whole experience"—Treva moved to check her phone as it rang—"oh, shoot, it's Jill, I forgot to call her, one sec." She clicked on. "So, I made it to three open houses after church, two looked promising, but—"

"Two looked promising, and you didn't call right away?" Jillian said.

"I had to get Hope to a friend's house, and—anyway, turned out both had a bidding war going on, which wasn't surprising, given—"

"A bidding war? We'd never stand a chance. What about the smaller one that was farther out—three bedrooms, one-and-a-half baths."

"That's one of the ones I'm talking about"—Treva paused, distracted as Lance hugged her from behind—"Jill, I need to call you—"

"I don't even know what we're supposed to do at this point," Jillian said. "We keep adjusting our search, but everything's out of reach. I'm still disappointed about that one I really wanted . . ."

Treva turned toward him as her sister went on. "I shouldn't have answered," she whispered.

Lance kissed her lightly. "Clearly."

"Jill, I'm sorry, I'm in the middle—I'll have to call you back. Won't be long, promise."

"You sure about that?" Lance said.

"We need to talk about next steps, though," Jillian said. "You do know the time crunch we're under, right?"

"Absolutely," Treva said.

"We're loading furniture and other things to give away, so if I miss your call—"

"Okay, gotcha."

Treva tossed the phone across the bed as a cry sounded from the bassinet.

They peered over, holding their breath. Seconds later, Wes quieted and settled back to sleep.

Treva got her phone again and silenced it, then held up his. "I know you like to be available."

"Turn it off," Lance said. "There's nothing sexier than a woman determined to be with her man."

CHAPTER 3

"This has to be the most radical thing we've done." Jillian Mason moved quickly from the house to the rented truck, the wind against her cheek and a sea green Schwinn in her grip. "Are we sure we haven't lost our minds?"

"I wondered that myself when I officially resigned this week." Her husband Cecil toted an end table a few feet ahead. "Everything's happening so fast."

"Who knew the house would sell the first weekend?" Jillian set the bike at the curb as Cecil arranged items inside the truck. "And of course we'd get a buyer who wants to kick us out ASAP." She could feel the stress. "I still don't see how we'll get everything packed in time. And what if we can't find a house?"

"I think we need to secure a rental at this point," Cecil said. "We've only got two weeks."

"Two weeks . . ." Jillian shook her head. "I almost wish we hadn't taken the first offer we got, since they wouldn't budge on the move-in date. We thought it would take two or three months at least to sell the house. Time to sort through all the changes. Time to find someplace to live in St. Louis. Time for the kids to finish out the school year."

"I thought that was one of the advantages of homeschooling, the flexibility." Cecil brought the bike up.

"Not like when they were younger," Jillian said. "Their favorite classes are math, science, and history, which they do through the co-op. It's not easy cutting that off, especially the friendships they've developed over the years. Plus they're losing friends at church and in the neighborhood. I heard them commiserating last night."

Cecil sighed as they walked back to the house. "What if we got this all wrong, Jill?"

"As much as I'm stressing and saying this is crazy," Jillian said, "three things keep me moving forward."

"What's that?"

"We prayed and fasted about this," Jillian said, heading inside and to the kitchen. "And you said you've never sensed God's direction so clearly."

Cecil nodded, grabbing water from the fridge and giving Jillian one. "I kept trying to tell myself this *wasn't* what I was hearing. But I couldn't shake it."

"Also," Jillian said, "I'm still in awe how it all unfolded. We weren't even supposed to be in St. Louis for Christmas—we drove out last minute." She took a sip. "*And* we said we were hitting the road early that last morning to head back home."

Cecil chuckled. "The look on your face when Lance pulled out those playing cards."

"I *knew* we'd be delayed. *Hours.*" She chuckled a little herself. "I was so frustrated with you. Then Pastor Lyles drops by, and in two hours our lives are changed. It's all we talked about on the long drive home. We couldn't shake that either."

"And what's the third thing?" Cecil said.

Jillian thought a moment. "It's no coincidence that this happened a month after Treva was in intensive care, fighting for her life. I kept thinking, what if I lose her? These past few years we've grown tighter than we ever were. So to be in the same city again?" She nodded. "I'm with you. I sense God's leading all over this, even if I'm having a fit in the process."

Cecil moved into the living area. "We're getting a lot done, actually." He lifted an arm chair. "Once we drop off this truckload we're giving away, we can focus on packing what we're taking with us."

Jillian moved to get the door for him. "Aren't your buddies on the way to help? Why are you tackling the heavy stuff?"

"I just want to get it done," Cecil said.

"Mom, Dad . . ." Their daughter Sophia walked up with her younger brothers. "Can we have a family meeting?"

Jillian and Cecil looked at one another.

"You mean, right now?" Cecil set the chair down. "I thought you guys were sorting everything in your rooms, boxing up clothes, books, and what not to give away."

"We are," David said, "but this was the only time Courtenay could meet."

"Courtenay's in on this too?" Jillian said.

Sophia held up her phone. "I'm FaceTiming her when we're ready."

"Let's do it then," Cecil said. "We want to hear what's on your mind."

They settled downstairs in the family room as Sophia called her sister.

"We're all here," Sophia said, looking into the phone. "You can start."

Cecil moved forward in his chair. "How about we start with, Hello, oldest child of mine who doesn't return calls nearly as much as she should?"

"Hey, Dad," Courtenay said, a smile in her voice. "Sorry. It's all this studying. I'm about to go to the library right after this."

Cecil chuckled a little. "Same old story, huh? And it better be true."

"What else could I be doing with my time?" Courtenay said.

"Okay, so I've been appointed the ambassador since I'm the one least impacted by this move, and thus, somewhat impartial."

"Sounds like a list of demands is forthcoming," Cecil said.

"Actually," Courtenay said, "first I have to say, being in St. Louis for Christmas, seeing how it all happened, you'd have to be blind not to see God at work."

"I thought you were on our side," David said.

"I'm conceding the obvious," Courtenay said. "We understand that Mom and Dad are doing what they feel led to do. So we're not proposing that they back out—"

"That actually *is* my proposal," Sophia said. "I'm the one with the most to lose. I'm coming up on senior year. I'll miss everything I've been looking forward to for years."

"But we've come up with what we feel is a compromise," Courtenay said.

"I'm intrigued," Jillian said. "Let's hear it."

"Sophie, David, and Trevor get to stay and finish out the school year," Courtenay said, "and join you in St. Louis in late May. Grandma Patsy said she'd be delighted to have them stay with her."

"You've already talked to Momma?" Jillian said. "I'm sure she doesn't realize she'd be doing way more than having you as guests. She'd be shuttling you to classes, practices, and who knows what else. And what about the subjects I do with each of you? And the daily barrage of things that needs to be dealt with? Half the time I can't go five minutes without you all needing something." She paused, shaking her head. "I'm not liking this idea."

"It's only three months, Mom," David said. "I've already thought about the school stuff. English, for example. Why can't we have our literature discussions over the phone? And you already edit my papers in Google docs."

"And Grandma Patsy said I could drive her car wherever we need to go," Sophia said. "Mom, Dad, *please*. We'll be fine. And this way I get to go to junior prom with Devin."

"What're your thoughts, Cecil?" Jillian said. "Although, I know we'll need to talk more in private."

"I'm willing to consider it," he said. "Patsy's disappointed that the kids are leaving, so I know she'd love to have extended time with them. It's just figuring all the logistics."

Trevor pumped his fist. "That's how Dad sounds when he's about to say yes."

"Except, I haven't said yes." Cecil gave him a look. "As I think about it, though, your mom and I benefit more from this arrangement than you all do."

David frowned. "How?"

"Three months kid-free?" Cecil said. "My wife all to myself? Date nights every night? I should have paid you guys to come up with this."

Jillian chuckled. "I hadn't thought about it that way."

"All right," Cecil said, standing. "Your mom and I will let you know what we decide. You all need to get back to work so we can get this truck loaded." He looked at the phone. "Let me say goodbye to my daughter who does nothing but study."

Sophia snickered as she handed him the phone. "Mom," she said, turning to Jillian, "with everything going on, don't forget the Academy Awards tonight. We're watching, right?"

"Wouldn't miss it," Jillian said. "I want to see Cinda."

"Cinda who?"

"Alonzo Coles's wife," Jillian said.

"Oh, yeah, I saw them in that *Essence* spread," Sophia said. "You said that like you know her, though."

"Well, I don't *know* her, but when Treva got sick last November and I flew out there, I met her in Treva's Bible study. Then she and Alonzo came to the hospital—"

"Wait, wait, hold it." Sophia cocked her head a little. "You're telling me you met Alonzo Coles and never mentioned it?"

"It wasn't a high priority," Jillian said. "My focus was on my sister."

"So Aunt Treva, Faith, all of them—they know Alonzo and Cinda, and no one mentioned it at Christmas?"

"Girl, they don't sit around with Alonzo and Cinda on the brain," Jillian said. "Although, that might be the case today." She chuckled.

"I can't believe this," Sophia said, taking her phone back from her dad. "I'm calling Joy right now."

"As long as you're multi-tasking," Cecil said.

Jillian hugged her husband as Sophia went upstairs. "I love you."

Cecil looked at her. "What's that for?"

"In the midst of all this crazy, you saw a way that we could benefit as a couple." Jillian kissed him. "You're always mindful of us."

"I wish that were true," Cecil said. "I'll never forget how much I hurt you." He kissed her back. "God is the One who's mindful of us. If this entire move is about us getting three months to devote to one another, I'm all for the crazy."

"But it's about so much more," Jillian said. "I remember when we first got married, you used to talk about one day working in ministry full time, discipling the youth."

"Which seemed more and more unrealistic as we raised our own four kids," Cecil said.

"But God brought it back around when you least expected it," Jillian said.

"I definitely didn't expect it," Cecil said. "When our marriage was in trouble, I thought I was done with ministry."

"I never knew that," Jillian said.

"I didn't talk about it," Cecil said, "but I struggled a lot at church during that time. It was hard on Sundays, serving in youth ministry, but especially at the summer sports camp. Whenever I encouraged kids to live for Christ, I felt like a fraud."

Jillian listened, remembering what that season was like, with Cecil falling for another woman.

"I was ready to step down," Cecil said. "But as I began praying to re-commit fully to you and to God, I felt God moving me to recommit to the ministry He'd called me to." His eyes showed an earnestness even now. "But I thought that was the extent of it, to keep doing what I was doing—serving part-time in youth ministry. I'd almost forgotten what He'd put in my heart years ago."

"He sent Pastor Lyles to remind you," Jillian said, "and to encourage you. He didn't even know he was speaking directly to you at first, and the whole time I had goose bumps."

"Yeah," Cecil said, "when Pastor Lyles said we tell ourselves God's plans are unrealistic or they've somehow faded with time or they've been re-called because of things we've done— God had my attention." He shook his head. "It was like He wanted me to know, despite my failures, He really does love me unconditionally."

"Wow . . ." Jillian took a breath as she thought about that. "Right now I couldn't complain about the challenges with this move if I tried." She put her arms around Cecil's waist. "And let's take the bonus—I'm all for this three-month-long, second honeymoon."

"Amen," Cecil said, hugging her. "All of a sudden, two weeks seems like a long while to wait."

CHAPTER 4

"*S*houldn't you be enjoying the biggest day of your life?" Cinda Coles took a white gold stud and buttoned her husband's crisp white tuxedo shirt. "You've been stressing since you woke up."

"Eloping four months ago was the biggest day of my life." Alonzo lifted her chin and kissed her. "And I'm not stressing."

Cinda took the next stud and inserted into the buttonhole. "Then why are you checking online chatter?" She eyed the phone in his hand. "You never do that."

"I thought I was checking headline news," Alonzo said. "But a 'top story' predicted who will win tonight, which made me curious about predictions on other sites." He navigated to one even now. "Everyone's talking about this horse race between Bradley and me for best actor—and watch, someone completely unexpected will win. But every site's got me or him, and most predict it'll be him—see, look at this—'Bradley's Golden Globe win gives him the edge in the Oscar race—'" He looked up. "What are you doing?"

"Taking your phone."

"You can't take my phone." Alonzo's eyes followed it as she set it on the nightstand in the hotel suite. "There's too much going on."

"When you need it, you'll get it," Cinda said, back to work on his shirt. "We've prayed and the Academy has voted. Who cares about predictions?" She looked up at him. "No worrying. We have too much to be thankful for."

Alonzo sighed. "You're right. It's still surreal, several Oscar nominations for *Bonds of Time*." He nodded. "We're honoring Randall today. That's what I want to focus on."

Cinda added diamond cuff links to the shirt and stood back. "I'm glad I had them taper the arms. It looks good." Her eyes traveled from the shirt down the length of the black trousers, loving the taper there as well. "*You* look good."

Alonzo pulled her close again with his fingers in hers. "Not as good as you."

"I haven't changed into my dress yet."

He kissed her. "You're killing in this leopard print robe, though."

She eyed him, frowning slightly. "What is that wild hair in your eyebrows? I need my tweezers."

"You do realize it's not just the cleaning," Alonzo called after her. "You can't help being extra. It's in your blood."

She returned, took the tweezers to his brow, and plucked, smoothing the rest into place.

"Not a single person would've noticed that micro hair," he said.

His manager's ringtone sounded. Alonzo reached over and put her on speaker.

"You're on your way up?" he said.

"Not yet," Beverly said. "Somebody's got me stuck in this bakery line picking up chocolate croissants."

"He needs that chocolate to de-stress," Cinda said.

"I'm not stressing."

"Check out *Essence* online," Beverly said. "Killer piece on Cinda styling you for awards season."

"Seriously?" Cinda said. "First the cover, then this?"

Cinda had enjoyed styling the two of them for the February cover story—"Alonzo Coles: The Hollywood Heartthrob on Marriage & his Second Oscar Nomination." They'd done a photo session, included in a double page spread.

"It's a follow-up to the cover feature," Beverly said. "Pics of what he's worn and why it worked. Cinda, congrats, my dear. All right, jumping off. See you in a few."

"Ooh, Zee, let's pull it up." Cinda handed him his phone.

"Oh, now I can have it," Alonzo said, chuckling. He went to the site. "'One of Our Faves Ups His Style Game—Thanks to His Wife.'"

"They said that?" Cinda looked at it with him. "Their favorite look was the Globes, with that white Gucci dinner jacket." She kept skimming. "Wow, midnight blue tux at the SAG awards was 'impeccable'. . ."

Alonzo lowered his phone. "I'm waiting."

"For what?" Cinda said.

"'Baby, you were right.'" Alonzo's voice went up an octave. "'This is what I was made to do. I can't believe I had all those doubts and even told you no.'"

Cinda gave him a smirk. "I don't call you 'baby'." She slipped her arms around him. "But yes, you were right about a lot of things. Like us." She kissed him. "And I still have doubts—especially when I read about other stylists and all their education and experience. But I can't believe I said no at first. My job is to make my man look good—how can I not love that?" She kissed him again, his arms pulling her closer.

"Warning," Alonzo said. "Kiss me one more time and I'll be working these buttons in reverse."

Cinda leaned in smiling as if she might. "Okay, staying focused," she said. "I've got more work to do on you, then on me, and before you know it, the team will be here." She moved to find the lint brush.

"Baby," he said, pulling her back, "I want you to know I really am proud of you. And it's dope that others are seeing what I saw in you." He played with the twists in her hair. "Pretty soon I won't be your only client, but I better be the priority."

"Well, if I have more than one client, and their needs are more pressing, you'll just have to get in line."

"Oh, it's like that?" Alonzo pressed his lips against hers and let it linger.

"That's unfair influence," Cinda said. "And what happened to the warning?"

"Maybe I do need to de-stress," he said, "and kissing is better than chocolate."

Alonzo's phone rang again, and he smiled, seeing a FaceTime call from Lance. "Wow," Alonzo said. "Room full of people. Y'all are partying without us?"

Cinda looked at the phone with him.

"Heyyy," rang out and arms waved as Lance panned the room.

"We had to let you know we're all here," Lance said, "ready for the big night. Big prayers going up."

Cinda looked at Alonzo when she didn't hear a response.

"I'm um . . ." Alonzo blew out a sigh. "I didn't realize how much I missed y'all." He looked vaguely into the distance for a moment. "Man, I love y'all."

"Don't get us all emotional in here, Alonzo."

Cinda smiled, hearing Stephanie's voice.

"And if you miss us so much," Stephanie said, "both of you need to get your tail on a plane to St. Louis. It's been three months —way too long."

"Already got a plan," Alonzo said. "Next month. We'll get you the exact dates so you can reserve us a room.'

"Did I see Cinda in the background?" Faith said. "Girl, you dressed yet? We want to see."

Cinda moved her face into the phone. "Nowhere near ready yet."

"Somebody doing your hair and makeup?" Jordyn said.

"Yep," Cinda said. "Me."

"Faith and them need their own FaceTime with Cinda." Reggie showed his face in the screen. "Bruh, from the guys—we got you. Represent! Big excited for you, man."

Alonzo gave a nod, looking emotional again. "I needed this. My fam. Y'all mean the world to us."

"We love you!" several voices said.

"We love you, too!" Cinda smiled into the phone, her arm around Alonzo. "Talk to you soon."

The call ended, and Alonzo walked across the room. "Wow, it's been three months."

"Hard to believe," Cinda said. "I talk to Faith and Jordyn pretty regularly, but it's not the same as seeing all of them."

"I was just thinking, though . . ." Alonzo looked at her. "That means it's been three months since we've been to church."

"We keep saying we need to visit churches," Cinda said. "Awards season made life crazy, but that's over after tonight." She got sand paper and started scuffing the bottom of his shoes.

"I hope we don't have to visit a dozen churches to find the teaching we want, plus the fellowship," Alonzo said. "I basically want an LA version of Living Hope."

"Ha," Cinda said. "That would be awesome. One thing that's been nice, though—listening to Lance's sermons online."

Alonzo sighed. "He hits on something I need every time."

Cinda looked at him a moment, then put down the sandpaper. "I think I'll go get ready, then do the final touches on you. Before the team gets here..." She got his phone and headphones and handed them to him. "Lance's sermon from this morning is probably uploaded. Even better than kisses or chocolate."

CHAPTER 5

*J*ordyn Rogers could feel her heartbeat accelerate. She didn't know he'd be here, even as she told herself it didn't matter. Except, her ripped jeans would've been cuter, and a slimmer fitting shirt instead of this bulky sweater. And her hair. She'd thrown it into a messy bun after church, but would've kept the curls—

"Hey, good to see you," Jordyn said.

She returned the quick hug Jesse gave as he passed through the family room, stopping at his little girl Zoe, whom he scooped up.

"Jordyn, can you get me some more lemonade?" Chase handed her his empty cup.

"Did your mom say you could have more?" Jordyn said.

"She didn't say I couldn't."

Jordyn chuckled. "Cyd?" she said, holding up the cup.

Cyd nodded from a few feet across the room. "It's fine," she said. "Thanks, Jordyn."

She walked with Chase to the kitchen and opened the fridge, taking out the lemonade.

"So how you been, Jordyn?"

She turned as Jesse walked in, headed for the food.

"Pretty good," Jordyn said, pouring.

Jesse put wings on a plate. "Still got the YouTube thing going, hair and makeup and what not?"

"Still at it," Jordyn said. She'd mentioned it in light chit-chat after church one day. "What about you? How's school?"

"A grind," he said. "I keep reminding myself it'll all be over in May."

Jordyn had reminded herself as well. He'd be graduated and gone, which kept her thoughts in check. That and the fact that he'd been in a relationship with Faith. Jordyn didn't know the details, just that it had been complicated, and of course, that they had a daughter.

Chase opened the fridge again and searched inside, producing a green apple. "Can you cut this up for me?" he said.

"I sure can," Jordyn said. She glanced over at Jesse. "Do you know yet where you're headed after graduation?"

"Nothing definite," Jesse said, "Pursuing different options." He added fries. "You must be pumped about tonight, with your dad's movie up for these awards."

"Definitely pumped," Jordyn said, "but it's also bittersweet."

Faith came in and grabbed a small plate. "Zoe is loving these sweet potato fries. She ate all of mine."

"So congratulations are in order?" Jesse spoke in a low tone, eyeing her finger. "Thanks for telling me."

Jordyn angled herself away from them, cutting Chase's apple.

"It hasn't even been two weeks," Faith said. "And I haven't seen you. Weren't you at a conference or something? Anyway you knew the deal with Reggie and me."

"I didn't know there was *that* much deal. Getting married? Already?"

"We've been close for a year now, Jesse."

Jordyn's phone buzzed in her pocket, and she looked at it. Jade
— **I'm at the door.**

She sighed inside. Why had Jade come? If her mouth didn't get something going by the end of the night, it would be a miracle.

Jordyn moved toward the door and opened it, and Jade walked in with the very look Jordyn wished she had—ripped jeans, leather jacket, and a tight fitting top, head full of curls from a fresh braid-out. They had similar features and body type—mahogany brown skin, medium height, can't-miss curves—but somehow Jade always wore it better.

"I ubered here," Jade said, "so I'll just ride back . . ." She looked as Faith and Jesse walked by.

"Faith, Jesse," Jordyn said, "this is my sister Jade."

"We met briefly once," Faith said, "at your birthday party last summer. Good to see you again."

"You too," Jade said.

"Nice to meet you," Jesse said, his hands full with a plate and drink.

Jade eyed him. "Nice to meet you too."

Jordyn turned to her sister once they'd gone. "I thought you didn't want to come."

"I was bored in that apartment," Jade said. "And I'm glad I changed my mind. Who was *that*? Girl, he's cute."

"Hey, Jordyn, red carpet coverage is starting," Faith called.

The twins walked into the family room, and Cyd hopped up when she saw them.

"Jade, I'm Cyd London," she said. "Randall talked so much about his girls. It's good to see you again, in better circumstances." She hugged her.

Jordyn wondered when they'd met before, then remembered. It would have been Randall's funeral.

"Thanks for having me," Jade said.

"Hey, everybody," Cyd said, "This is Jordyn's sister Jade." She looked back at Jade. "There's no way you'll remember all these names, but I promise, they're friendly folk. You'll get to know them."

"Hey, there they are," Faith said, moving to the television. "Ohhh, wow, look at Cinda. She's beautiful."

The women stood, crowding near the flat screen on the wall.

"Cinda, girl, you betta work," Jordyn said. "Why does she look like she was made for this?" Jordyn couldn't stop smiling, checking every detail of the sparkling champagne colored gown. "And did she color her hair?"

"It's definitely lighter," Stephanie said. "Perfect complement to that gown. That girl is stunning."

"Wait, can we turn it up?" Faith said. "They're about to interview Alonzo."

Cyd aimed the remote, increasing the volume.

Jordyn watched as one of the red carpet hosts asked Alonzo the typical questions on his thoughts about the night.

"And your wife is dazzling tonight," the host said. "But she's not only your wife; she's your stylist also. Cinda, how did you get into this line of work? Is this something you've been training toward?"

"Ooh, help her, Lord," Treva said. "This is exactly where she's self-conscious."

Cinda smiled at the woman. "It's a lifelong passion," she said. "I'm blessed to be able to dabble in what I love. I couldn't ask for a better job."

"She's not dabbling," Alonzo said. "My wife gives one hundred ten percent to whatever she puts her hand to. I'm the one who's blessed."

"A-lon-zo!" Stephanie clapped out each syllable. "You better say that."

"And finally," the host said, "this is a special night for both of you, with *Bonds of Time* nominated for five awards. Alonzo, tell us about the pin you're wearing."

"I had it specially made." Alonzo fingered it. "It says 'Phil. 4:4,' which was Randall Rogers's favorite Bible verse—'Rejoice in the

Lord always; again, I will say, rejoice.'" He put an arm around Cinda. "I wanted those words on my heart today."

"Thank you, Alonzo," she said. "We wish you all the best tonight."

"Why do I have tears in my eyes from a red carpet interview?" Treva said.

"Sometimes I just miss Randall more intensely," Lance said. "This is one of those times."

Jordyn nodded, feeling a sadness herself as she was only now beginning to appreciate her father's faith. She glanced around, having lost sight of her sister. Didn't take long to spot her— squeezed next to Jesse on the sofa, engaged in conversation.

CHAPTER 6

*C*yd's stomach churned as another Twitter notification glowed on her phone. Micah's initial tweet announcing Thursday's debate had spawned endless retweets and comments. Most simply expressed interest in the debate topic, but this one was different.

"Looks like @CydLondon is a real zealot. She says the bible is true. Check her article here . . ."

She followed the link to a post she'd written on the Living Word site more than two years ago, encouraging believers to stand on the truth of God's word.

"Best Adapted Screenplay is up," Jordyn said, moving forward in her seat.

Cheers sounded in the family room as the presenters named *Bonds of Time* as one of the nominees.

"Why do they feel the need to show Alonzo and Cinda every five minutes?" Jade said.

Jordyn looked at her sister. "He did actually star in the film."

Jade cut her eyes. "He didn't write the screenplay."

Cyd sighed as a second tweet came from that same individual:

"Are talking donkeys real @CydLondon? U believe 'sinners' should still be stoned? Ppl like u are dangerous."

Cyd's phone lit up every other second now as others retweeted and piled on. She'd opened a Twitter account for ministry reasons, interacting with women about Living Word's Bible studies. But if this was what it would devolve to, she'd certainly deactivate.

A groan sounded in the room when another movie snagged the Best Adapted Screenplay award.

"*Bonds of Time* hasn't won a single category yet," Faith said. "Three down, two more to go. I'm getting nervous."

The doorbell rang and Cyd put down her phone, glad for the distraction.

"Hey, about time you got here," Cyd said, opening the door.

Tommy walked in. "I didn't think I'd make it at all. The concert ended earlier than I thought."

"Must be tough," Cyd said, "getting paid to attend all these shows."

"It's a hard life," Tommy said, "but somebody's got to do it."

Cyd smiled. "We're all in here," she said, leading the way to the family room. "Where's Allison?"

"Still out of town," Tommy said. He stood at the entrance to the family room, surveying the scene. "Y'all must be real serious about these awards. No card table or nothing, huh?"

"I tried to get it going," Cedric said, "but Lindell doesn't play Bid Whist, then Reggie said it wasn't fair for Lance and me to be partners. It never got off the ground."

"I love Bid Whist," Jade said. "Our dad taught us. Do you all give the girls a chance to play?"

Tommy took a spot near Reggie. "They've just never expressed an interest." He smiled. "But that's pretty cool. Sounds like Randall."

Jade looked to her left. "You play, Jesse?"

Jesse nodded. "I do."

"We should be partners." Jade looked at the guys. "Is it too late to get a game going?"

The guys looked at one another.

"Wes and I are good to go," Lance said, holding his baby boy.

"Let's go then, partner," Cedric said. "So we've got Jade and Jesse, and Tommy and Reggie?" When they nodded, he stood. "Cool. Lance and I will get comfortable while y'all rise and fly."

Cyd looked at her husband. "What does that mean?"

"Losing team has to get up and make room for the next set of players," Cedric said.

"Just so we're clear," Jade said. "You'll be able to handle it when you have to rise and fly in your own house?"

"Ohh, okay," Cedric said, getting the folded table and chairs from the closet with Tommy's help. "A trash talker. I love it. Zero guilt when we show no mercy."

Cyd's phone lit up again, her pulse quickening at Micah's latest tweet: **"Stay tuned . . . Looking into setting up a live-stream of Thursday's debate."**

Treva got the baby from Lance and sat beside Cyd. "You okay?" she said.

Cyd leaned her head over. "I told you at church this morning about the debate this professor goaded me into?"

Treva nodded, leaning in as voices swirled around them.

"This afternoon I found out he posted flyers around campus," Cyd said. "Tonight he's tweeting about it and just said it might be live-streamed." She shook her head at the thought. "I am so livid right now."

"So he wants this to be a huge event?" Treva said.

"He's a crass opportunist," Cyd said. "I almost backed out this afternoon, but at this point, I'm there." She opened the email app. "I'm sending nothing more than the subject line—'The debate is off.' Let him tweet *that*."

"But help me understand why you're so upset," Treva said. "Seems to me he's just opening the door wide for you to break down who Jesus is. Girl, do you know what kind of impact you can have? Let him go wild with Twitter, live-streaming, and whatever else. We'll go wild with prayers for the Lord to show up and show out."

"But this is not some evangelistic crusade," Cyd said. "It's my job. And I can't ignore the realities of my workplace." She rolled her eyes at another tweet. "Every time I think about the potential fallout—all because of this one man and his ego."

"Let's back up," Treva said. "Didn't you say you felt God was leading you to do this?"

"That's the only reason I agreed," Cyd said.

"So God said to do it, but that was before He knew the professor would make it into a huge thing?"

Cyd gave her a look.

"And He didn't quite understand the realities of your workplace?"

"Between you and Cedric—see, look at this." Cyd showed her several notifications that had just showed up. "Because of Daniels, people are scouring the Living Word site and posting 'proof' that I'm a Bible fanatic."

"You're just gonna *let* the enemy drive you crazy?" Treva said. "Girl, if you don't turn off those notifications."

Voices rose from across the room.

"I think this means you need to rise and fly," Jade said.

Cedric stared at the cards on the table. "I'm trying to figure out how that happened."

"It's not hard," Jade said. "They call it 'skills'."

Cyd and Treva watched as their husbands rose from the table.

"It's just one game," Lance said. "They call it a 'fluke'."

Tommy took Lance's seat. "Whatever they call it, you two taking an 'L' is a beautiful sight." He looked at Jade. "But don't get comfortable. You and Jesse are about to bounce."

Jade looked across the table at her partner. "Wouldn't be an entirely bad thing."

"Mommy, I can't sleep." Chase wandered into the family room and over to Cyd, rubbing his eyes.

"Aw, I put you to bed almost two hours ago." Cyd hugged her son. "Too much happening down here, huh? You have to go back to bed, though, sweetie. You've got school in the morning."

"Can I have some milk?" Chase said.

"'I'll get it," Cedric said, moving toward him. "Then I'll walk you back up."

"Can Jordyn do it?" Chase said.

Cedric looked at him. "Jordyn's not here tonight to take care of you, Chase-man. She's watching the awards show."

"I don't mind." Jordyn hopped up, glancing at the card table. "There's nothing happening right now that I want to see anyway."

CHAPTER 7

*J*esse tried to focus on the cards in his hand and the ones being played on the table—not on Faith snuggled up with Reggie.

"So why are you playing that one?" Faith had a chair beside Reggie, arm draped around his shoulder. She leaned in as he whispered his strategy.

"Quiet as it's kept," Tommy said, "I don't know if my little brother's the best one to school you, Faith. You might want to scoot your chair to this side."

Faith chuckled. "Don't be talking about my man. I'm fine right here."

Jesse looked at the card Reggie laid down and trumped it, winning the book.

Jade smiled. "Meanwhile, Jesse's schooling all of y'all."

Jesse looked as Zoe toddled over to him. She'd been flitting from person to person all night. Now she lifted her arms for Jesse to pick her up. But soon as she hit his lap, she squiggled down again, moving around the table to Reggie.

"You're having a good time tonight, aren't you?" Reggie lifted her. "Waaay past your bedtime."

"So. Question." Jade looked between the two guys. "Faith is Zoe's mom—obviously. But which one of you is her dad?"

"I'm Zoe's father," Jesse said.

"Really?" Jade glanced at Faith. "Interesting."

"What's interesting about it?" Faith said.

"The way y'all are all here, hanging," Jade said. "Like one big cozy family."

"We're all church family," Reggie said.

"Now I'm really confused," Jade said. "You're at the same church, hooking up with different people? If I had known church was like that . . ."

"Jade, you need to stop." Jordyn had returned moments before. "You know it's not like that."

"I'm simply asking," Jade said. "I'm not up on church life."

"Listen . . ." Jesse leaned in, eyes on Jade. "People aren't hooking up and acting crazy at Living Hope Church. Whatever you see that doesn't look right about this picture, it's all on me."

Jesse played his next card, wishing for the umpteenth time he hadn't come. He'd declined when Lance asked, then Cedric invited him, saying they hadn't seen Jesse in a while, other than at church. He'd gone home to Maryland for the holidays and spent three weeks with his mom and little brother. And over the past month, he'd been busy with school and preparing to graduate—a good busy, since it meant he didn't have time to think about all the ways he'd messed up with Faith. Except, somehow he thought about it still. And seeing her tonight with a ring on her finger . . .

Jesse glanced at Jade as she racked up the next book, all but sealing the win. She'd been flirting all night, and no doubt about it, she looked good. If he had to guess, she was what he typically preferred—someone who wouldn't expect an ounce of commitment. But that's not where his mind—

"Finally," Faith said, looking at the flat screen. "Best Actor time."

The room got quiet as each nominee's movie clip showed on the screen.

"I can't believe this is the one they're showing for Alonzo," Jordyn said.

Jesse watched, remembering the riveting scene, Alonzo's character coming to the end of himself and raising his voice to the heavens:

"What do You *want* from me? Why do You keep taking—and taking, and *taking*? Is that what You want—to leave me with nothing? I'm here, Lord! Out of options." The character broke down in tears. "It's Your move."

The audience applauded as the camera showed Cinda whispering into his ear, then the next nominee came on screen.

Seconds later the presenter said, "And the Oscar goes to . . ." She opened the envelope and read the card silently.

"Dadadada," Zoe said, breaking the silence.

Faith picked her up, moving closer to the screen.

The presenter smiled as she looked out at the audience. "Alonzo Coles."

Cheers erupted in the room as they watched Alonzo stand and bring Cinda to her feet, embracing her. He held onto her, clearly overcome, until she prodded him to get up there.

"I can't believe this boy got me in tears," Stephanie said.

Treva was wiping hers. "You and me both, Steph."

"Send up a prayer for him," Faith said. "He didn't prepare a speech. Cinda said the mere thought made him anxious."

Jesse watched as Zoe squirmed out of Faith's arms—and Faith moved into Reggie's.

"I'm a little speechless right now," Alonzo said, holding the statue, looking out at everyone.

"Ha. Literally," Stephanie said.

"This is about so much more than an award." Alonzo looked down a moment. "Because of this movie, I got to meet an incredible man who impacted my life deeply." He looked upward, tears glazing his eyes. "Randall Rogers, I can't wait to see you again and talk about everything you set in motion in my life."

The camera moved to Cinda who had a tissue to her eyes.

"Because of this movie," Alonzo continued, "I got to meet my beautiful wife." He looked down at her. "Cinda, you are God's gift to me. I'll love you forever, and it won't be long enough."

Jesse felt a surge of emotion. Something in Alonzo's words. Alonzo cherished the love of his life. He *married* the love of his life. Yet, Jesse had done nothing but hurt the one person he'd ever truly loved.

Jesse listened vaguely as Alonzo thanked his mother, the director, producers, and others.

"Shout out to my church fam in St. Louis," Alonzo said, "and my pastor and friend, Lance Alexander."

The room erupted again.

"He's really off the cuff," Lance said. "Somebody make a note—Alonzo is officially on the membership rolls now." He chuckled.

"And last but certainly not least, I give thanks and praise to my Lord and Savior, Jesus Christ." Alonzo looked upward again, holding the statue high. "I'm here, Lord. Your move. Always."

"So okay, that speech was everything." Reggie wrapped his arms tighter around Faith. "I'm ready to elope and start our forever right now."

"I thought it already started." Faith leaned in and kissed him.

Jesse got up. With all the buzz about the win, it was a good time to slip out, even if it meant he couldn't give Zoe a goodbye hug. He'd have her tomorrow, though, while Faith was in class.

"You're leaving?" Jade said. "We're not even finished our game."

Jesse turned as he neared the front door. "Yeah," he said. "I need to head out. Early morning."

"You mind giving me a ride home?" Jade said. "I don't know when Jordyn's leaving, and I'm ready to go myself."

He shrugged. "That's fine, I can take you."

Jade moved past him and opened the door. "We can talk about options on the way."

"Options for what?" Jesse said.

Jade walked with him out the door, closing it behind them. "What to do once we get there."

CHAPTER 8

"I guess your Dad was serious about moving everything out of his office at school tonight." Jillian clicked off the television. "Sounded like a good idea to get it done after Sunday night basketball with the guys. But the awards are over, and he and the boys are still up there."

"Yeah, soon as you two started talking second honeymoon, Daddy kicked into another gear." Sophia gave her mom a look. "I can't believe you two are happy to get rid of us."

Jillian chuckled. "Hey, you're the ones who proposed it." She eyed a cabinet across the room and went to open it. "We missed this," she said. "Look at all these old DVDs down here—wow, even some Nickelodeon kid shows on VHS. We should go through this stuff right now."

Sophia joined her on the floor and pulled out a stack. "So I told Devin I'd be here for prom after all."

"And he said it was too late, that he'd already asked someone else?"

"Mom, I would've died," Sophia said. "Completely."

Jillian threw three more onto a VHS pile. "Even though this is the same Devin you were in tears over after the homecoming dance?"

"Because he acted totally different around his school friends than he does at church," Sophia said. "But that was four months ago. Forever, basically."

Jillian started another pile, movies they never watched. "So what happens when you move to St. Louis?"

"I don't even want to think about it," Sophia said. "But UCLA is at the top of his wish list for next year, and he says I should go for a visit. Can we?"

"I thought you were looking at HBCU's, focused on the east coast."

"Spelman is still a top choice," Sophia said. "But UCLA with Devin—can you even imagine? On the same campus together?"

"Since college visits aren't till summer," Jillian said, "let's see where the two of you are when the next forever has passed."

"But Mom, he's just the sweetest," Sophia said. "At church this morning—"

"Wait, this is your dad," Jillian said, checking her phone as it rang. "Hey, babe, you all finally done?"

"Mom! Something's wrong with Daddy he was shooting a basket and he just collapsed on the floor and we called 9-1-1 but we don't know what to do and—"

"What?" Jillian's heart jammed in her throat. Her fourteen-year-old had never sounded like this. "David, slow down. Are the paramedics there? You're saying he just *collapsed?*" She walked as she talked, heading upstairs to put on her boots.

"What's going on?" Sophia said, following.

"Put your shoes and coat on," Jillian told her. "David, I said are the paramedics there?"

"*No.*" Tears sounded in his voice. "I just called them before I called you."

Jillian felt the panic inside. "I thought the basketball game ended hours ago," she said, searching for keys. "Weren't you all moving his things?"

"We were finished moving everything, and Dad said it'd be his last time in the gym, and Trevor said we should play one last—"

"Why are you blaming me?" Trevor said.

"I'm not *blaming* you, Trevor, and you have to go back and stand by the door so you can see when they get here."

"I'm staying right here by Dad," Trevor said.

She could hear the tears in her youngest son's voice as well.

"Fine, I'll go," David said.

Jillian fought for calm. Maybe it wasn't as bad as it seemed. "Can he talk? Is he moving? What is he doing, David?"

"He's just lying there, Mom. He's just *lying* there."

She gripped the counter, taking a breath. What if this was cardiac arrest? Something she'd seen had said that with every passing minute, there was a ten percent less chance of survival. *Lord God, please help my husband. Please Lord, lay Your healing hand on Cecil—*

"I hear the ambulance," David said.

Jillian looked up. *Thank You, Lord. Help Him, Lord.* She found her keys and grabbed her purse. "Come on, Sophie, we need to go," she called. "David, stay on the phone. I need a play-by-play of what's going on."

Jillian hurried alongside someone from the emergency room staff to a waiting area, thankful for immediate assistance. "So they're working on my husband, he's with the medical team right now?"

"Yes, ma'am," the young woman said, "but I don't know anything more than that."

"But he'll be okay?" Sophia said.

The young woman's expression remained even. "I only know

that he arrived with the paramedics and was given immediate attention."

They turned into the waiting area, and Jillian spotted her sons easily in the sparse crowd. They rushed to her the moment they saw her.

"Oh, guys, are you all right?" Jillian hugged them hard.

"I've been praying, Mom," David said. He'd stayed on the phone with her, giving updates on the way. "But he didn't wake up once. I'm really scared." Tears streamed his face.

"And nobody's telling us anything," Trevor said.

"I do know they're working on him," Jillian said. "Thank God for you two and the way you handled this. Calling 9-1-1 right away was key."

"No, we don't know anything else." Sophia had her older sister on the phone. "I'll call when we get an update."

Jillian sighed, checking her watch as she paced a little. Almost one in the morning. Barely an hour since they'd first called, and it seemed like twenty-four. She just needed to see Cecil. And hear his voice.

Her phone vibrated, and she looked at it. Cecil's mom Elaine. Sophia had called both grandmothers on the ride over, while Jillian stayed on the phone with David. Jillian moved to a quiet corner of the waiting room and answered.

"Hi Elaine, we just got to the hospital," Jillian said.

"I'm getting in the car right now," Elaine said, "ready to drive down. What's the latest update?"

"They're working on him," Jillian said. "I'm believing no news is good news."

"Amen," Elaine said. "I've got the saints praying here in Jersey . . ."

Jillian groaned inside. She hadn't had a moment to call any of their church family. She hadn't even called Treva.

"I refuse to let my mind call up those memories," Cecil's mom was saying. "It's making me too anxious."

"I'm sorry, what memories?" Jillian said.

"When Cecil's father had a heart attack," she said. "But he was overweight and wouldn't eat right, no matter how much I badgered him. Cecil is trim and works out. I never thought something like this could happen."

"Neither did I," Jillian said. And neither did Cecil. Part of his motivation for working out was to stay out of the danger zone.

"Call me the moment you hear anything," Elaine said.

"You know I will," Jillian said. "Drive safely."

Jillian clicked off and dialed her sister.

"I feel awful I didn't call you back," Treva said, "but I've already got a plan to look at houses tomorrow—"

"I think Cecil had a heart attack," Jillian said. "We're at the hospital and—"

"What?" Treva said. "What do you mean, you think? What are they saying?"

"Mrs. Mason?"

Jillian turned. A black man in scrubs stood before her.

"I have to go, Treva," Jillian said, hanging up. She tried to search the man's eyes. "Yes?"

"I'm Dr. Stanley," he said, pausing as the kids joined to hear. "Ma'am, your husband was in cardiac arrest when the paramedics arrived. They started resuscitation procedures in the ambulance, which efforts continued here for forty minutes." He paused again. "We were unable to restart his heart."

"I'm sorry, what?" Jillian said. "You're saying his heart stopped . . ." She could feel herself shaking. "You're saying all this time you've been working on him, he was already *gone*?"

"Ma'am, with a cardiac event such as this, an electrical malfunction occurs," Dr. Stanley said, "and the heart stops effectively pumping blood to the brain, lungs, and other organs. The patient—"

"My husband."

"Yes," the doctor said, "your husband would have lost

consciousness at that point. And every minute that passed without intervention—CPR, defibrillator—decreased the likelihood of survival." He looked into their faces. "So, yes, his heart had stopped when the paramedics arrived. Ma'am, I'm really sorry."

The four of them stood silent, a waiting room television droning in the background.

A sob sounded from Sophia. David and Trevor walked off in separate directions.

"Can I see him?" Jillian said.

She was sure she didn't want to, not like this. But she needed something tangible. Because right now she could still see his eyes, bright and lively, looking into hers. She could still hear his voice, planning their extended second honeymoon. She could still feel his kiss before he walked out the door this evening. Right now there was no way her heart and mind could comprehend a different reality. There was no way her husband could be gone.

CHAPTER 9

$\mathcal{C}$inda felt arms around her waist and lips against her neck.

"Baby, you doing okay?" Alonzo turned her around. "Sorry I keep getting pulled away."

"Don't be silly." Cinda spoke above the music and chatter at the Vanity Fair party. "It's your night. Soak up the interviews, the pictures, all of it. I'm fine. Shane's cracking me up with all his stories."

"I told her about the first movie I directed you in," Shane said, "your second movie overall. How respectful you were—listening, taking direction."

Alonzo smiled at the remembrance. "True. I had mad respect for Shane. He was coming off of *The Course of Nature*, which had been critically acclaimed. And he was serious. Like, don't show up on my set unprepared."

"The next movie we did," Shane said, "you thought you knew a little something. Tried to tell me how to do *my* job."

"Here's where the tale goes left," Alonzo said.

"Now that you've got your shiny statue," Shane said, "you'll be all the way out the box. 'I'll just direct myself.'"

"This from the man who keeps telling me I need to step out and direct."

"And you better," Shane said, "but you know I have to give you a hard time. Keep him humble, Cinda," he said, turning toward her. "Make him do chores, clean the house."

Alonzo gave Shane a look. "You have no idea. If I *try* to clean, she'll tell me to back away slowly."

Cinda spied Simone coming toward them. They'd run into her twice since they'd gotten married, and both times, she'd acted as if Cinda's presence meant nothing.

Beautiful in a navy strapless gown, Simone went directly to Alonzo. "Congratulations, babe," she said, slipping her arms around Alonzo's waist. "I couldn't be more thrilled for you." She turned to Cinda. "I still remember how we celebrated when he got that part."

Alonzo had backed away before she finished. "Simone, come on." He brought Cinda close. "I can't let you disrespect my wife like that."

Cinda eyed Simone. "I just feel bad that you only have old memories to dwell on." She wrapped her arms around Alonzo. "Because that won't compare to the way my husband and I celebrate *tonight* when we get home."

Cinda put her lips to Alonzo's, and they let the kiss linger. When they looked again, Simone was gone.

"Really?" Shane was looking at Cinda. "I didn't know the Midwest girl had it in her."

"Bruh." Alonzo shook his head. "When she activates the warrior princess . . ."

"I hate that she irritates me the way she does," Cinda said. "All your other old flames have been cool tonight—Amber, Noelle LeGrande . . ."

Alonzo frowned. "What?"

"Oh, we've been having a ball over here," Shane said.

"And for the record," Alonzo said, "I told you Noelle wasn't—"

"Alonzo"—a guy extended his hand—"*E-News* online mag. We'd love to get a moment of your time. And first, a picture with your lovely wife?"

Cinda posed with Alonzo as the magazine's photographer moved into place.

"Oh," Cinda said, extending her phone, "would you mind?"

"Not at all," the photographer said. He snapped a few with his camera, then more with Cinda's phone.

Cinda checked them as Alonzo moved to talk with the interviewer. "I'm terrible at this Instagram stuff," she said, glancing at Shane.

She'd uploaded a picture of Alonzo in the hotel room, previewing his look for the evening, and one of the two of them on the red carpet. But she'd forgotten to capture the moment of his win. And she'd meant to get an after-party pic at the first after party.

"After that dope feature you got today," Shane said, "you better think of it as part of your business plan."

"That's what Alonzo's been saying," Cinda said.

Two women approached Shane, hugging and chatting with him. Cinda opened the Instagram app to upload the picture. With her notifications turned off she hadn't seen the thousands of "likes" and new followers she'd gotten in only a few hours.

"Have you met Cinda Coles?" Shane was saying.

"She's the main reason I came over here," one of the women said. She shook Cinda's hand. "I'm Kelsey Vaughn, and I've been stalking you."

"Me?" Cinda said. "As boring as I am?"

"That's what I love about you," Kelsey said. "No pretenses. I first heard about you when that 'shocking' story broke about you being a maid—and you were like, 'And proud of it.'" She chuckled. "But you were *really* like, 'Oh, but watch . . . I'm about to slay this style game.'"

Cinda's eyes widened a little. "I wasn't thinking that at all," she said. "It's been nerve-wracking. I had to hit the ground running, and I'm still trying to catch my breath. The learning curve is steep."

"All I want to know," Kelsey said, "is if you're in this for Alonzo only—or are you willing to work with other clients? I might finally be at a point in my career where I need a stylist."

"Kelsey is the woman right now," Shane said. "Starring in a television show that's blowing up. We met when I directed one of the episodes."

"Not *starring*," Kelsey said, "but thankful to have a part." She turned to Cinda. "But that's the thing. Full disclosure—I approached a couple different stylists over the past month and got turned down because I'm not an A-list actor. But honestly, I think it was a blessing. It's good to know you're a sister in Christ as well."

"We should meet this week, if that works for you," Cinda said. "I'd like to learn more about you and what you've got going on."

"Does that mean you're willing to work with me?" Kelsey said.

"Definitely," Cinda said. "Excited even."

"Aye," Kelsey said, her shoulders dancing.

"Hey, do you know Alonzo?" Cinda tugged his fingers closer as he walked up.

"We've never met, no." She extended her hand. "Kelsey Vaughn. It's good to meet you. And you *better* had won. Lots of folk rooting for you. Congrats."

Alonzo smiled. "Definitely appreciate that. You look familiar, though. And now it's bugging me—"

Eastside," Shane said.

"That's it," Alonzo said. "I watched the episode Shane directed and loved what you did with your character. You're a natural with comedy."

"Hey, definitely appreciate *that*," Kelsey said.

"We need to binge-watch the show," Cinda said, "because"—she gestured to Kelsey—"meet my first real client."

"Seriously? That's dope." Alonzo nudged Cinda. "You out here making moves, huh? But what's up with, 'my first *real* client'?"

Cinda elbowed him. "You know what I mean."

"Right." Kelsey laughed. "The 'real' client is the non-Oscar-winning one? Hey," she said, pulling out her phone, "can we get a picture on Oscar night?"

Cinda stepped aside and reached for Kelsey's phone. "I can take it," she said.

"Girl, I'm talking about a picture of you and me," Kelsey said. "I'm showing off my new stylist."

Cinda skirted back over and, after the picture, exchanged info with Kelsey.

"We're headed to find food," Shane said, taking both women with him.

Alonzo leaned into Cinda's ear. "It's past two in the morning, and there's only one problem with this amazing day."

"What's that?" she said.

Alonzo pulled Cinda into the shadows. "It's been so busy I haven't had enough of these . . ." He kissed her. "And did I hear you mention a celebration when we get home?"

Cinda looked into his eyes. "It's ready and waiting."

"But you didn't know I would win."

"We were celebrating either way."

"So . . ." Alonzo had his arms around her. "What's waiting for us exactly?"

"Well, it's my job to get you out of these cuff links." Cinda ran a finger down the length of his shirt. "Unbutton these gold studs."

He kissed her again. "All part of a day's work, huh?"

"And though you're awfully handsome in this tux"—she tugged the lapel of the jacket—"we need to free you of that too."

Alonzo traced the strap on her shoulder. "But it wouldn't be right if you're still encumbered with this sparkly dress."

"Oh, I bought a little something new to slip into," Cinda said. "I won't give all the details, but let's just say the night involves a plush blanket by the fireplace, chocolate-dipped strawberries . . ."

"Okay, yeah, it's time to go."

Alonzo took Cinda's hand and led her past pockets of conversation, pausing briefly for hellos and goodbyes. Steps from the door, a woman spotted him and moved to head him off.

"Mr. Coles," she said, "I was hoping you hadn't left. Can we get a quick picture and comment?"

Cinda could feel his sigh as he hesitated. "Go on," she whispered. "She said it'd be quick."

Alonzo turned back to the woman. "Sure," he said.

"I'd love to get your comment on a news story released moments ago," the woman said. "The headline reads—'Is Alonzo Coles Becoming Too Christian?'"

CHAPTER 10

*J*ordyn lay across her bed, tears soaking the pillow as her room filled with early morning light. She'd gotten home from Cyd's hours ago and had yet to fall asleep. Too much cycling through her mind. Her dad, for one. The ache had grown worse over time. So much Randall had wanted to give her, teach her, show her—faith things that mattered—and she'd rejected every overture. Seeing him celebrated last night, in their own gathering and even from the Oscar stage, felt good. But she couldn't bear all the things she now wanted to say to him and receive from him—and couldn't.

Then there was her mother, with her gleeful marriage announcement a week ago. She wanted Jordyn and Jade to drive to Chicago for the nuptials this spring. Jade flat refused. Jordyn gave a "maybe," with no intention of going. Whenever she thought about the fact that her mother was having an affair at the time of Randall's death . . .

But then, how was Jordyn any better?

More tears fell as she thought about her own affair with a married man. For months it lasted. And the worst part was that she hadn't wanted it to end. If Kelvin hadn't broken it off, who knows if she would have had the strength to do it herself. Even now she still thought about him. Hated herself for missing him. If she didn't feel so utterly alone . . .

She lifted her head a little, hearing footsteps in Jade's room. Jade's door had been closed when Jordyn got home last night, but Jordyn couldn't wait to have a few words with her. She wished Jade hadn't come to Cyd's, since she didn't know when to shut up and—

Jordyn hopped up when Jade's door opened. No time like the present. She opened her own door and stepped out—and her heart lurched at the sight of Jesse walking toward the front door. He turned and looked at her, both of them frozen in place. Jordyn couldn't have looked worse—hair all over her head, ratty sweatpants—but she didn't care. He was actually there, in her apartment. With her sister. He broke the stare, opening the door. A moment later he was gone.

Jordyn walked straight into Jade's room.

"Can you knock?" Jade spoke from under the cover.

"I can't believe you." Jordyn stood at her bedside. "You come to a gathering of my *church* family, run your mouth nonstop, openly flirt, then Jesse ends up in your bed?"

"How are they your church family?" Jade rolled over and looked at her. "I thought you hadn't joined yet."

"I'm there every week, so they're *like* family." Jordyn shook her head. "Why would you do that? You don't even know him."

"Do I need to remind you of the guys you've slept with and hardly knew?"

"This is totally different," Jordyn said.

"How is it—" Jade came up on an elbow. "You like Jesse."

"That's got nothing to do with it."

"It's got everything to do with you storming through the door like I shot somebody," Jade said. "You should've told me you liked him. Better yet, you could've told him."

"It's complicated," Jordyn said. "*Was* complicated. You just made it simple. He's all yours, Jade."

"Girl, calm down." Jade let her head fall back on the pillow. "I don't even want him like that. You know I'm still seeing Rick."

Jordyn felt the sting of fresh tears. "You don't even care that any chance I could have had with him is gone."

"Jordyn . . ." Jade looked at her. "If you'd *had* a chance, you would've taken it. Obviously he wasn't feeling you."

Jordyn walked out, slamming Jade's door, then slamming her own. She flopped across her bed again, stewing over every word exchanged. But the words that spoke loudest were the ones she wanted to ignore—*Do I need to remind you of the guys you've slept with and hardly knew?*

Her breath stuttered, the truth of it hitting hard. After showing up for some of Treva's Bible study last year and hearing Lance's sermons each week, Jordyn had been forced to face the ugliest parts of her past. Not that her *present* was any better, except, no man was in it. She'd been telling herself that was a good thing. She could focus on getting her life together, deal with whatever was stopping her from making a real commitment—to church, to Jesus. Yet here she was, deep down wishing Jesse had been in her bed instead of Jade's.

That truth hit even harder.

Tears stained her pillow once more. Who was she to tear into Jade like that, when she might have done the same if given the chance? Jade wasn't Jordyn's problem. Jordyn was Jordyn's problem.

And despite her tactless manner, Jade had been right—Jesse wasn't feeling Jordyn. He hardly looked at her. And what did Jordyn see in him anyway? It wasn't just that Jade had been quick to sleep with Jesse—he'd been quick to sleep with Jade. And he'd basically admitted last night to messing things up with Faith. *This* was the man Jordyn just flew into a tirade over?

Jordyn turned, hearing a rap at the door. "What."

"See how I knocked?" Jade walked in, looking at her phone. "We need to talk about our video production schedule this week." She looked up. "You're not still upset, are you?"

"Because two minutes was enough to get over it?" Jordyn said. "Anyway, I thought we already talked about this week—I've got two makeup vids, you've got a hair styling vid and one on fave products . . ."

"We need to add another," Jade said. "An 'Alonzo Watch.'"

"What?" Jordyn said. "We haven't done one of those since the St. Louis premiere last summer, when he fell for Cinda and suddenly you couldn't stand him."

"Oh, I was by myself?"

"I was jealous, I admit it," Jordyn said. "But you never let it go."

"Anyway," Jade said, "We have to weigh in on this article. And I totally agree with it—Alonzo 2.0 is way over the top."

"What's Alonzo 2.0?"

"Mr. Super Christian," Jade said. "You heard him last night with that speech."

"Because he thanked Jesus?" Jordyn said. "People do that all the time."

"And, 'I'm here, Lord' and all that," Jade said.

"Which was from the script," Jordyn said, "which came from Dad's words in the book."

"Alonzo worked Jesus into that *Essence* interview too," Jade said, "but it's not just that. Apparently he turned down a big movie deal because he didn't like the sex scenes."

"Wow, seriously?" Jordyn said. "I remember when he first got that tagline, 'sex scenes that sizzle.'"

"Exactly," Jade said. "Alonzo was a lot more captivating when we could feast on his real life exploits, swoon over his fineness, and hyperventilate over those love scenes."

"Well, you can still swoon over his fineness."

"Whatever," Jade said. "Bottom line, this article asks, 'Is Alonzo

Coles Becoming Too Christian?' And the answer is 'yes.' We'd be crazy not to dish about it."

"Is this where I remind you that his wife happens to be our sister?" Jordyn said. "Not to mention my good friend."

"You can take his side," Jade said.

"While you tear him down," Jordyn said. "No way would I be part of anything like that."

"Then I'll do it by myself," Jade said. "This article raises the question and lays out the case, but I'm willing to say it outright—Alonzo's a fool for blowing everything he's gained. Think about how his star has been rising. Two Oscar nominations and a win for Best Actor? Who *does* that at his age? Now he's restricting the types of roles he'll play, as if there's no difference between what he does in real life and what he does on screen?" She made a face that said it was ridiculous. "If that's what it means to follow Jesus, then it's just dumb."

"You honestly don't care who you hurt, do you?" Jordyn said. "You didn't care if you hurt Faith last night, with your little comment about hooking up with different people. You've never cared how you treated Cinda. Now you want to tear down Alonzo for loving Jesus? What about our *father*? Do you know how much *he* loved Jesus?" Jordyn flicked tears from her eyes.

"Are you hormonal?" Jade said. "Why is every little thing upsetting you?"

Jordyn looked away. *Was* she hormonal? It certainly felt like her emotions had gone haywire. "This actually means something to me," she said, looking back at Jade. "I don't want our channel to be about mocking people for following Jesus. I wish I *could* live like Dad did, or like Alonzo's doing."

"Whatever. Okay." Jade headed for the door.

"I'm asking you not to do this," Jordyn said.

"And I already said I'm doing it."

Jade pulled the door to a hard close, and Jordyn got up to go after her. Tell her, *fine*—she'd start her own channel. But what sense did that make? She'd worked hard to build the channel they had, which now earned thousands each month. And she had a cosmetics contract solely because of her channel. She'd be hurting no one but herself if she separated, and might even get sued. Jade could do what she wanted with their channel—and there was nothing Jordyn could do about it.

CHAPTER 11

"This is absolutely heartbreaking." Cyd paused in the middle of her kitchen floor, looking at her sister. "We just saw Cecil when they were here for Christmas. And seems like just yesterday we were in Hawaii for Lance and Treva's wedding." She stared off a moment. "He was so *young*. Jillian must be devastated."

"I tried to call her," Stephanie said, "but wasn't surprised it went to voicemail. I can't even imagine what she's going through." She took off her coat and draped it over a chair at the kitchen table. "You know Jillian and I have had this praying wives' call every week for a year and a half. I've seen God do so much in their marriage. I just keep thinking, *why?*" She sighed. "I cried when Treva told me this morning. She's on a flight to Maryland right now."

"Just last night," Cyd said, "I was giving Treva ideas about where Jillian and Cecil could look for a house. They were supposed to *be* here in a couple weeks, joining the Living Word family."

Stephanie nodded. "Lindell was looking forward to having Cecil in their guys' fellowship. They really connected." She got a coffee mug and poured a cup. "I'm waiting to hear about the arrangements. With B and B guests coming this weekend, I'll have to figure something out. But I really want to fly out there."

"Maybe we can travel together," Cyd said, "but I don't know if this debate on Thursday will present a conflict. Although, I wouldn't mind having a real reason to back out." She added, "Can't help but have a different perspective, though. I could be dealing with a lot worse things than a debate."

"Mom, this homework is *stupid*." Chase came down the stairs. "How am I supposed to figure out all these math problems?"

"You had all weekend," Cyd said, "and you wait till an hour before school?"

"But where's Dad?" Chase said. "I thought he could help me."

"He had an early morning meeting," Cyd said. "And I'm headed to one as well. Aunt Stephy's taking you to school."

"Can you help with my homework, Aunt Stephy?" Chase handed it to her.

"I don't know if I can handle math problems at your level." Stephanie took the paper. "Just kidding. Slightly. Let me take a look."

"Sweetheart, you need to go get dressed while she's looking at it," Cyd said. "Give me a hug first." She squeezed him tight. "Jordyn's picking you up today. I'll be home a little late from work."

"Awesome," Chase said. "I love when Jordyn's here."

Stephanie looked at her sister as Chase hustled back upstairs. "Interesting arrangement you've got going," she said.

Cyd turned to her. "What, Jordyn? What's interesting about it?"

"I like Jordyn, don't get me wrong," Stephanie said. "But clearly she's a cute young woman, curvy, and loves clothes that show those curves—and before you say it, I know. That was me all day." She looked at her sister. "You don't have a problem with her being here when Cedric's home—and you're not?"

"Jordyn leaves when Cedric gets home," Cyd said. "The whole point is for her to watch Chase *until* one of us gets home."

"Okay then, cool," Stephanie said. "As long as—"

"And anyway, Cedric is old enough to be her father."

"See, now you're confused," Stephanie said. "Cedric is the same tall, dark, and handsome brother *you* fell for. And you really don't know Jordyn that well. I'm not saying anybody's out to do anything. But things happen, given the right time and space." She gave Cyd a look. "Stick to—Cedric pulls into the driveway; Jordyn backs out."

Cyd slung a purse and a messenger bag over her shoulder then grabbed her briefcase. "You do realize you're suspicious by nature."

"And it has served me well." Stephanie took a sip of coffee. "So what's your meeting with Pastor Lyles about? I heard he didn't preach again yesterday, and people are buzzing. I figure if he's about to retire, you'll be one of the first to know."

"Why me?" Cyd said.

"It's no secret Pastor Lyles has two adopted children," Stephanie said. "You and Lance."

Cyd couldn't deny that. Pastor Lyles had said as much after spearheading the Living Hope church plant. He'd encouraged Lance to pastor the church, and when Cyd said her family might go join him, Pastor Lyles didn't hesitate to give his blessing. "It would be like two of my birds leaving the nest," he'd said, "yet flying together." It helped that they were only miles down the road and still very much part of the Living Word family.

"Mom and Dad would know the pastor's plans before I would," Cyd said. "I'm meeting with him for debate prep. I told him the other day I didn't feel ready. He suggested we go over arguments I might encounter and how to respond."

"How are you not ready when this is what you do all day every day?" Stephanie said.

"Debating is different," Cyd said. "I don't know what Micah

Daniels might say, yet I have to be ready. He's got the advantage—my playbook is the Bible."

Stephanie looked at her. "Daniels isn't a believer, right?"

"Right," Cyd said. "That's the point—non-believer debating a believer."

"So," Stephanie said, "I know you're more steeped in this stuff than I am. But are you telling me, you've got the Spirit of God, the power of God, the grace of God, and the wisdom of God—but Daniels has the advantage?"

"Okay, Cedric," Cyd said, heading out the door.

"Huh?" Stephanie said.

~

"You're better prepared than you think you are." Pastor Lyles's words came across his desk. "You've been steeped in the Scriptures, as well as the historical, cultural, and even archeological underpinnings for decades. Frankly, it doesn't matter what debate points this professor might win. You're armed with truth, and God will use that truth to penetrate hearts."

Cyd sighed as his words penetrated her own heart. "I should be honest with you," she said. "I'm struggling with obeying God in this. I almost canceled last night, and it's on my mind still." She paused. "I'm concerned about the impact this may have on my career. And for what? So this arrogant professor can build a platform?"

"What if a soul is saved because of your obedience?" the pastor said.

"That's not exactly a fair question," Cyd said. "God doesn't need a debate circus to save someone's soul."

The pastor focused on her. "So your issue isn't preparing content for this debate. It's preparing your heart. Your issue, Cydney, is fear of man."

Cyd stared across the desk at the man who'd known her since

she was a young teen, when her family moved to St. Louis and joined Living Word, a young church that met in a school building. He was the one who'd seen a teaching gift in her and encouraged her to pursue her love of the Bible, history, and ancient languages through a doctorate degree. And he'd never shied away from saying what she needed to hear, often using her given name in his fatherly tone.

"I don't know if it's *fear.*" Cyd felt convicted even as she said it, since God had already called her on it. "You know how it is on campus. Political correctness is part of the fabric. We have to respect all positions. I can just see Professor Daniels asking me straight out whether I believe Jesus is the only way to heaven—so he can set off a gazillion alarms."

"Well, let's go with that," the pastor said. "Assume there are consequences on the job as a result of this, to whatever degree. Aren't we called to suffer for the sake of Christ, and even to rejoice in it?"

Cyd could feel herself tense up. "Not when it's because some professor is backing me into a corner."

"What if it's God backing you into a corner?" Pastor Lyles said. "What if He wants to see what's in your heart—or more to the point, wants *you* to see?"

Cyd gave a hard sigh. "How do *you* do it? Seems like whenever God moves in your heart, you just do it. It's not hard."

"Now you're being ridiculous," Pastor Lyles said. "It's been one hard thing after another, for decades. You're just not the one who hears me ranting. But God hears it. Your father hears some of it too." He paused, looking out of the window, his fingers steepled. "I'm going through a hard thing right now. Wasn't planning to share this today—only the elders, immediate family, and a couple friends know." He turned back to her. "I'll be stepping down."

It took Cyd a moment to respond. "So the rumors are true. Pastor, I have to say—that makes me really sad. You started this church, and I knew you couldn't lead it forever, but . . ." Her mind started processing all that this would mean. "And it's not just the church. You've built an entire ministry. Are you stepping down from that too?"

"Cyd, I didn't build anything," he said. "'Unless *the Lord* builds the house . . .' Dusty fellows like me come and go. The Lord will continue His work."

His assistant walked in. "Pastor, Lance is on the line."

Cyd stood and motioned for him to take it. She knew Lance would be calling about Cecil. "I need to get to work," she said, moving to the door.

"Cydney," Pastor Lyles said.

She turned.

"I'm praying for you."

She nodded. Those words, coming from the pastor, she'd never taken lightly.

CHAPTER 12

*C*ars filled the driveway and extended down both sides of the street as Treva and her mother pulled up to Jillian's house Monday morning.

Treva looked at her mom. "Were all these people here when you left to pick me up from the airport?"

"Not at all," Patsy said, backing the car to find a spot. "I hope they understand. Jillian really doesn't want to see anyone right now."

Treva looked toward the house, her heart hurting for her sister. She'd called Jillian before she boarded the plane, after she'd landed, and on the drive from the airport, but Jillian's phone had gone straight to voicemail. Treva hadn't talked to Jillian since she'd called to tell her—briefly, almost inaudibly—that Cecil was gone. Treva had called Sophia to learn more, then booked her plane ticket before bed.

Treva got out once Patsy had parked, and opened the back door. Wes's bright eyes stared back at her, his little legs kicking with delight.

"Aww, look at you, sweet boy." Treva kissed his cheek, something in the moment giving her pause. Life. Death. Joy. Sadness. How could they mingle so closely?

Treva lifted the car seat from its base and started down the sidewalk toward the house. "I'll get my bags later," she said, glancing over her shoulder.

Patsy followed just behind. "Now, Treva, don't be taken aback if Jillian isn't ready to see you," she said. "I told you, she's been holed up in that room for hours. Wouldn't open the door even for Darlene. We have to give her time."

"I was the same way when Hezekiah died," Treva said. "And Jillian wouldn't leave me alone. Told me I could stay holed up for days if I wanted, but she would be right there with me."

Treva walked in and heard the crackle of bacon frying plus voices in the kitchen and downstairs, people she undoubtedly knew and loved. Her mother-in-law Darlene, surely the one cooking. And friends from Jillian's church, which had been Treva's church for years. Treva needed to see and hug the whole lot of them, especially her nieces and nephews. But not before she saw Jillian.

"Mother, can you take Wes?" Treva set the car seat down in the living room and lifted him out, removing his coat.

"Of course." Patsy took her grandson and held him close. "Just the kind of sweetness I need right now."

Treva put her own coat in the hall closet and walked upstairs, to the closed door at the end of the hallway. She gave a light knock. "Jill"—she tried the door—"it's me."

Treva waited a few seconds and hearing nothing, knocked again. "Jill, sweetie, you know I know." Her voice broke. "I'm not going anywhere. Remember? You can stay in there for days, but I'll be right with you. Open up."

Silence met her again, and Treva suddenly felt bad. If Jillian had been able to drift to sleep, she shouldn't try to wake her. She turned and headed for the stairs—and the door came open.

Jillian was climbing back into bed as Treva walked in.

"Close the door back and lock it," Jillian mumbled.

Treva obliged and started toward her, then stopped, struck by the sight of Cecil's pants on the bed. Sneakers by the bathroom. A shirt hung outside the closet door. Just twenty-four hours ago he'd been here. Walking, talking, making plans. Her eyes fell on a watch and billfold on the dresser. Had Jillian gotten that from the hospital?

Treva looked at her sister, curled in the bed, turned away from her. She climbed in herself, sitting with her back against the headboard, as tears filled her eyes.

"I hurt for you, Jill. This *sucks.*" Treva reached a hand over and stroked Jillian's hair. "And I won't lie to you—this road is not easy. But you'd better know you're not walking it alone." Her voice was shaky but determined. "You've got Jesus who will never leave you —I can testify to that. And you've got a sister who *gets* it when you want to cry, get angry, fight, even give up—which I'd never let you, but I get it, because I've been there." Tears spilled from her eyes. "I'm here for you, whatever you need. You're my favorite sister in the whole world."

Jillian's head lifted at the words she'd so often said to Treva growing up. She moved slightly, resting her head on Treva's lap. Her body curled even more as she began sobbing aloud.

Treva wept with her. "I know," she said, rubbing her back. "I know."

"I can't . . . do this." Jillian spoke between sobs. "I don't want to see people. There's no way I can plan my husband's *funeral.* I can't even be a *mother* right now."

"It's okay," Treva whispered. "I promise you, it's okay." She grabbed tissues from the nightstand for her. "Everything that needs to be done will be done."

"I loved Cecil . . . so much." Jillian took a tissue and held it. "I think I loved him more this past year and a half than the past twenty. It was like we fell in love again, after all the junk we went through. But more deeply." She looked at Treva. "Why?

Why would God bring us through that, only to take Cecil away?"

Treva stared downward. "I have the same question, Jill. Still got a million *Why's* from Hezekiah's death. It'll never make sense to me. *This* will never make sense to me."

They sat in silence a few minutes, Treva praying over her sister.

"Who'd you fly out with?" Jillian said.

"Just the baby and me," Treva said. "Lance and the girls are driving out on Wednesday."

A knock sounded at the door. "Jillian," Patsy said, "there's a realtor here to see you, with a husband and wife and a contractor. They're saying they have an appointment. I wasn't sure what to tell them."

"Oh, God . . ." Jillian sat up with a sigh. "The people buying our house. They wanted their contractor to take a look at work they want to do." She looked at Treva. "I have no idea what I'm supposed to do. After next week we're basically homeless."

Treva made her way through the pots and pans on the stove and the roaster on the counter, filling her plate. "I feel bad," she said. "People have been dropping food by the house all day, and I'm only focusing on Darlene's."

"How could you not?" Patsy had Wes in her lap. "She's been cooking since early this morning. And you already know it's good."

"And if I have a choice between Darlene's food and anyone else's—including my own—it's Darlene every time." Treva kissed her mother-in-law's cheek. "Thank you for doing all this today."

"You don't have to thank me." Darlene was still at it, mixing batter for a cake. "Cooking helps get me through, and this is a tough one. I still remember when Jillian told me about some guy she was dating named Cecil."

Treva looked at Darlene. "I remember when you invited Jillian and Cecil to dinner, to get to know him. And Hezekiah and I were there—Faith may have been a baby. And Jillian was so nervous . . ." She set her fork down. "That snuck up on me." Tears clouded her eyes. "Thinking about Cecil and Hez . . . being here in this house, where we gathered so often . . ."

Darlene nodded. "Hezekiah has been on my mind a lot today," she said. "I love the Lord, I really do. But it just plain *hurts* sometimes, the things He takes us through. I had to bury my *son*. And now Cecil's mom has to bury hers." She shook her head then looked over at Patsy. "God was using you today, Patsy. The way you got us praying."

"You know I'm not totally comfortable with that," Patsy said. "But Elaine was trying to talk to all the people stopping by, and I could tell she was falling apart. I thought it would be good to pull her away and pray with her. But I needed you to do the praying."

"You needed no such thing," Darlene said. "But that wasn't the time to tell you. Next time, though . . ." She winked at her. "I'm glad Elaine's siblings were able to fly into town this evening. Lifted her spirits for sure."

"Same with Courtenay's arrival," Treva said. "The kids had stayed in their rooms most of the day. At least now they're all in Jillian's room together."

"We need to help Jillian solidify these arrangements," Patsy said. "It's looking like Friday is the best option."

"She's got so much pressing in on her," Treva said. "We've got to help her figure out a housing arrangement too. I hadn't realized how dire things were till she said they're about to be homeless."

"What is Jillian talking about?" Patsy said. "The kids were already going to stay with me. Now Jillian can stay too."

"That was the temporary plan when we thought we were

moving to St. Louis." Jillian walked into the kitchen. "We can't stay there indefinitely."

"I don't know why not," Patsy said. "And no matter what, there's no way you'd be homeless."

"Honestly, that's what it feels like," Jillian said, "when you have no actual place to live and no actual income."

"Let me fix you a plate, Jillian." Darlene got one from the cabinet. "Lord knows I wish you didn't have to deal with this house situation. On top of everything else? It's too much." She shook her head. "Lord Jesus, help."

"Darlene, I'm okay," Jillian said as Darlene headed for the food. "I don't want anything."

"I didn't ask if you wanted anything, sugar." Darlene added roasted chicken. "You haven't eaten all day. I'm getting you a plate."

"I'd be dealing with a house situation either way," Jillian said. "We lived on one income, a teacher's salary. Not a whole lot in savings. And we've got life insurance, but not enough to pay off the mortgage. We would've had to move anyway."

"But not *next week*," Darlene said.

"I need to get a job, pretty quickly." Jillian stared vaguely at the table. "And I haven't worked since, I don't even know when. I have zero skills." She massaged her temples. "I feel like my head's about to explode."

"You have skills you take for granted," Treva said. "We'll sit down and figure out what'll be good to pursue. But I'm with Darlene. It's too much to be thinking about right now."

"As if I have the luxury of thinking about things when I feel like it?" Jillian glanced at the plate Darlene set down. "My life has been snatched out from under me. And you know what—anyone else wondering why God would let our house sell, knowing this would happen? Anybody else thinking what a cruel joke that is?"

Patsy rose from the table, Wes in her arms. "This is another one of those times," she said. "I think we need to pray. Right now." She walked to the middle of the floor.

Darlene left her mixing bowl and joined her, placing a hand on Patsy's shoulder. Treva took Darlene's other hand and stretched one toward Jillian.

Jillian got up and looked at them. "You all go ahead," she said. And headed back upstairs.

CHAPTER 13

*J*illian lay across her bed, a reality program booming in the background. She'd never watched the show, but when she'd aimed the remote at the screen, that's what popped on. And it served its purpose—she could drift in and out of sleep as she liked, the white noise drowning incessant knocks at the door.

It was Wednesday evening and she didn't feel like seeing people. Still. Didn't want to answer her phone. Didn't care if she ate, showered, or brushed her teeth. And didn't care who was alarmed by it. At least she'd done what she had to do—finalized arrangements for Cecil's service on Friday.

Well. She'd okay'd the date and time and chosen a casket and a suit, enough to zap what energy she had. Others were doing the rest, for which she was grateful.

She looked over at the television, where a fight was escalating between two women. She turned, landing on something about baby seals, which was cute until it was about baby seals separated from their mommas. Why was everything so depressing? She turned again, to some show—

A knock sounded. Jillian gave it a quick glance, focusing again on the television.

Another one sounded, louder, at which Jillian rolled her eyes.

"Jilli-Jill, open the door."

She sat up. "Tommy? What are you doing here?"

"I told you I was coming," he said, "in at least three voicemails."

"I'm not really seeing people right now, though."

"So I've heard," Tommy said. "Good thing I'm not 'people'. Open the door, Jill."

Jillian sighed as she walked over and opened it, then sat back on the bed, changing channels with the remote.

Tommy took it from her and turned off the television. "It's time to get up, Jill."

Jillian gave him a look. "When did you get here?"

"About an hour ago," he said. "We hit the road before dawn."

"Shouldn't you be at your mom's house?" she said. "Or your sister's?"

"Anywhere except bothering you, right?" His eyes held hers. "You can't do this, Jill. I know you're hurting. I know your world is caving in. But now is not the time to distance yourself from people who love you. Definitely not the time to pull away from God."

"Nice." Jillian rolled her eyes. "Y'all had a little meeting about me down there?"

"Come on, Jill," Tommy said, "you wouldn't let your pastor pray with you?"

"That's not what happened," Jillian said. "I just generally didn't want to go downstairs."

He looked at her. "In college, what did we do every time something happened that caused you to shut down?"

"You act like it was a regular occurrence," Jillian said. "Two or three times at most." She stared at the bedding. "Went for a walk on South Hill."

"Something about getting up and out," Tommy said, "taking in the fresh air. And I haven't been on campus in years. Let's go."

"What? No. It's cold outside."

"Get your biggest coat," Tommy said. "And put on some gloves and a hat. Your hair is messed up anyway."

"I really cannot stand you."

"Five minutes, Jill," he said, walking out.

"Do you not have any sympathy for what I'm going through?" she called after him.

Tommy glanced back at her. "More than you know."

Jillian hugged herself against the cold as she walked with Tommy along a bricked pathway on the University of Maryland's campus. Students moved briskly past, backpacks shouldered. Jillian found herself plotting their course—to a library, a dorm, someplace to eat—and imagining their frame of mind. Who was stressed? Hurting? Feeling depressed? She'd felt all those things at one time or another on this campus. And nine times out of ten, only one person knew—Tommy.

"Jill," Tommy said, looking over at her, "I was so shocked when I heard what happened. I am so sorry. It's absolutely devastating."

She stared downward as they walked. "Then you should've understood, and let me stay devastated in my bed."

"You want to *stay* devastated?" Tommy said. "Because what, God has no power?"

Jillian cut her eyes away.

"Now is when you run to God," Tommy said, "not away from Him."

Jillian walked in silence a few moments. "Remember almost two years ago, when I found out at the women's conference that Cecil was falling for another woman?"

Tommy nodded, listening.

"At the time," Jillian said, "*that* was devastating. And I wanted to run from God. Well, I did for a minute."

"Right," Tommy said. "You shut down then too."

"Anyway," Jillian said, "the messages about running the race strengthened me to fight for my marriage. And I *did*. And God blessed our marriage in ways I couldn't have imagined." She paused. "So I go through all of that for God to turn around and take him?" She threw up her hands. "What did I fight for?"

Tommy stopped and looked at her. "Are you serious? I know you're not saying you would've been better off watching Cecil walk away. You got to experience God's healing power, the depths of His love and faithfulness, His ability to make all things new—all of which you should be standing on *right now*." He looked away. "I'm still waiting to see God work like that in my marriage."

Jillian looked at him. "What do you mean?"

Tommy started walking. "Nothing I need to get into."

"But you and Allison are okay, right?" Jillian walked alongside. "You rushed me out of the house so fast I didn't get a chance to say hello, but—"

"Allison's not here," Tommy said. "I guess she's still in Cape Town. Or wherever. I haven't seen or heard from her in three weeks."

"I'm sorry, Tommy, I didn't know," Jillian said. "So who'd you drive out here with?"

"Faith and Reggie," he said. "Reggie's taking her to meet Mom, Dad, and everybody while they're in town."

"My niece and your brother," Jillian said. "We never would have thought they'd wind up together. I think Reggie was a baby when we were in college. Faith hadn't been born."

"In some ways they remind me of how we used to be," Tommy said. "Might bicker like crazy but know they've got each other's back."

Jillian nodded. "You were my best friend. There for me even

when I didn't want you to be." She cut her eyes over at him. "Like today. I wanted to punch you in the nose."

"I know you did," Tommy said. "And I know you know how much my heart aches for you and the kids, and how much I've been praying for you." He stopped again, looking at her. "I would think something was wrong if you didn't feel this kind of pain, Jill. And if you didn't have all these questions." His eyes held a softness. "But you've got to work it out with God. You *know* Him. How you gon' act like a television is your refuge?"

Jillian looked away a moment, his words stirring within. "So your pain and your questions," she said. "You're taking them to God?"

"I didn't say I had pain and questions."

She gave him a look.

"What you're dealing with is way bigger than mine," Tommy said. "Let's just stay over there."

"I don't know . . ." Jillian took a breath as a fresh wave of grief came. ". . . how I'm going to get through this week, burying Cecil, or next week . . . with all the moving . . . and finding a job . . ." The tears came faster than she could swipe. "It's too much."

Tommy hugged her. "Answer that yourself, Jill. How are you going to get through all this?"

Her shoulders heaved as tears fell onto his. "God."

"Say it like you believe it."

"God will do it." She drew a firm breath. "He'll get me through this."

CHAPTER 14

MARCH

"So now I'm the one who's been stalking you." Cinda sat across from Kelsey in a lunch spot in downtown LA. "I googled and studied your looks at different events."

"Girl, you said, 'studied'." Kelsey sat up straighter, an easy smile on her face. "Let me brace myself. What did you see?" She chuckled a little. "That sounds weird—as if I don't know what I wore."

"Here's the thing," Cinda said. "You looked good in everything, from casual to glam. But way more attitude and confidence in the casual street looks—that's where you come alive."

"Yep." Kelsey kicked a Converse-clad foot out from under the table. "Definitely my go-to. I grew up in small-town Iowa. I can count on one hand the number of times I wore a dress and heels. Then I move out here to pursue acting, and suddenly I need to be this fashion icon, which is so not me." She tossed her eyes. "It actually stresses me out."

Cinda raised a hand partway. "Wisconsin girl here. And I'm sure I'd worn a dress and heels less times than you."

"But I saw pictures of the two of you during awards season," Kelsey said. "You owned every bit of your look. And today you walked in here basically casual—slouchy white tee, denim pencil skirt—I want that, by the way—but with such a presence that heads turned." She cocked her head. "How'd you make that transition?"

Cinda smiled a little. "Prayer."

The server approached with their Caesar salads. Cinda had added salmon, Kelsey chicken. They both prayed silently.

"Okay, you need to elaborate on that," Kelsey said, digging into her salad.

"Like you said, coming out here—it's a different world," Cinda said. "And I had to jump right in, despite doubts I had about nearly everything. So I started praying to have a godly confidence in what God was calling me to do." She tossed her salad, mixing the dressing. "I even prayed to look like I belonged at those events —because I totally felt like I didn't."

"I wouldn't have thought to ask God for something like that," Kelsey said.

"I was around some praying women last year," Cinda said. "They taught me to take any and everything to God."

"So I've got a prayer-warrior-stylist?" Kelsey said. "Add me to those prayers for godly confidence and looking like I belong."

"I'm nowhere near a prayer warrior," Cinda said. "But I'll definitely pray for you. And seriously—when you're in character, you *completely* own it. I've watched every episode now, and you're amazing." She paused to eat some of her salad. "We just need you to carry that same confidence everywhere else. And you will— when we create the right look."

"A few people have told me it's time to grow up. Ditch the t-shirts and Converse, learn to love silk and stilettos." Kelsey sighed. "I just hate that I have to lose myself."

"You don't," Cinda said. "My goal is for you to feel like yourself —elevated. And I love that your next event is the Luxe & Shine Grand Opening. Perfect time to showcase a new look, red carpet and all."

"Why perfect?" Kelsey said.

"Invitation-only celebrity event," Cinda said, "and highly anticipated, so lots of eyes will be on you."

"That's not a plus," Kelsey said. "I'm good with low-key. I was planning to skip the red carpet part."

"You'll do no such thing," Cinda said. "It's essentially a block party, and it'll be everything from couture to ripped jeans. That's your plus—no pressure to look a certain way." She smiled. "But trust me, you're gonna kill it."

"So I'm going casual, right?" Kelsey said.

"I've already got some looks in mind—"

Kelsey's phone vibrated. "It's my manager," she said. "You mind if I get this?"

"No, go ahead."

Cinda checked her own phone while Kelsey stepped away.

"Excuse me, I hope I'm not bothering you." A young woman walked up to the table. "You're Alonzo Coles's wife, aren't you?"

She nodded, extending her hand. "Cinda Coles. And you are?"

"I'm Abby," she said, smiling. "Not trying to be weird, but I follow you and Alonzo on Instagram. And I've been seeing the chatter about Alonzo being 'too Christian'—there was one video put out by your sister, I think?"

Cinda tried not to roll her eyes. First time Jade had claimed her as a sister, so she could then claim Alonzo as a brother-in-law, only to slam him. In no time the video had gone viral. She pressed her lips into a thin smile, waiting for Abby to continue.

"As a young actress," Abby said, "I just wanted to say I'm inspired by how Alonzo's living out his faith. Even how he said in that *Essence* article that marrying you was a reflection of his love for Jesus—that he wanted to love you the right way." She covered her heart. "So beautiful, even if it made me and my girls jealous." She paused. "Sorry. That was probably rude."

Cinda smiled. "No worries."

"Anyway," Abby said, seeing Kelsey return, "please tell Alonzo a lot of us are thanking God for what he's doing. I'm praying for you two."

Cinda stood and gave her a hug. "Thank you for that," she said.

Kelsey was beaming when Cinda sat back down.

"Good news?" Cinda said.

"Awesome news," Kelsey said. "*Breakthrough Magazine* wants me to be part of a cover feature with two other actresses, shooting right here in LA. Cinda, I'm hoping you're available. You have to style me for it."

Cinda picked up her phone. "When is it?"

"In April," Kelsey said. She showed Cinda the date in her calendar.

Cinda scanned hers, thankful Alonzo didn't have any engagements. Then she remembered why—that was the week they'd planned to be in St. Louis.

She sighed to herself. How could she tell Kelsey no? She was a new client, and a cover feature was a big deal.

Cinda looked at her. "I can do it."

∽

Cinda pulled into the gated Hollywood Hills property she now called home and parked behind Alonzo's SUV in the circular drive. She still wasn't used to this—the house, her new car, the LA scene, her job. Even being married was surreal still. Although, hearing Alonzo refer to her as "my wife" might never get old.

She lifted several garment bags from the trunk and carried them to the house, eager for Alonzo to try on pieces she'd pulled. He'd had appearances all week to talk about his Oscar win and several more yet, alternating between morning programs and late-night shows. After the black-tie formal of awards season, she'd had fun switching to looks that were laid back.

Cinda walked inside and through the spacious entryway, a throwback R&B groove playing throughout the house.

"Cin, in the kitchen," Alonzo called.

"Ooh, must be Mexican," Cinda said, the aroma wafting her way. "Your mom would be too through if she knew we were doing all this take-out." She missed his mom, who'd decided to stay in Chicago after learning over Christmas that her own mom wasn't doing well.

"We should start cooking together," Alonzo said. "That'd be motivation to—" He turned as she walked in. "That's how you've been looking all day, and I'm just now seeing?"

Cinda smiled as she laid the garment bags across a counter. "I had a client meeting," she said, walking toward him. "I'll have to tell you about it, but I want to hear about your meeting with the publicist—and oh, Zee, I need you to try on this one pair of pants like *now* because I can't wait to see how they look. Don't balk at the color, just—"

"Baby," he said, taking her into his arms. "What's first?"

Cinda took a breath, looking into his eyes. "This." She leaned into him, and they kissed, slow and sweet.

"Why am I always the one who breaks the rule?" she said.

"You love what you do." Alonzo brushed her curls from her eyes and kissed her again. "And you'll grind twenty-four-seven. First it was cleaning, now it's styling. And I know I'm the same way. That's why we have to make sure we put our marriage—"

"You just reminded me, though," Cinda said. "I'm trying to like this cleaning service, but do you see this?" She lowered herself next to the wall and showed him. "They're ignoring the base boards. And I know they didn't touch the backsplash." She moved now to inspect it. "It's like, hello? If you can't do more than wipe the counters—"

"Wow, look at that." Alonzo pointed vaguely as the streaming station played one of his old school jams. "See what God just did?"

"Oh, that was God, huh?"

"He knew we weren't done with the 'first' thing." Alonzo took her hand and pulled her close again. "Unless—were *you* done?"

"Now that you mention it . . ." Cinda's senses filled with him as they swayed to the beat. "No, I don't think we were done."

Alonzo took her hands and they moved in and out, rocking to the sultry groove. "For one thing, I was about to tell you—you look beautiful." He spun her slowly around. "And sexy."

She turned, dancing with her back against him. "In a plain tee and denim skirt that hits the knee?"

"It's what you always say—fit is everything." Alonzo backed up a little, eyeing her as he danced. "Yeah. It's definitely *fitting.*"

Cinda turned to face him again, locking her arms around his neck. "I don't know if you've noticed—once we get going with the 'first' thing, it's hard to stop."

"After the day I had," he said, "I've got no problem with that. You have no idea how much I needed this."

She looked at him. "Zee, what happened? You mean the morning show?"

Almost every interviewer this week had asked about the movie he turned down and the "too Christian" buzz. But this morning's interviewer had played a clip from Jade's video and asked him to respond.

Alonzo sighed, leaning against the counter. "That was just the beginning," he said. "You know I was supposed to meet with my publicist today. The entire team showed up, concerned about the negative coverage I'm getting in a week that's supposed to be all celebration. 'Your next movie roles are critical . . . Tone down the Jesus talk . . .'"

"They said that?" Cinda said.

"And of course they circled back to the movie I turned down

last year," Alonzo said, "to make sure I understood what a strategic mistake that was."

Cinda put her arms around him. "You have people cheering for you," she said. "A young actress approached me at lunch to tell me how much your faith inspired her. And nobody's cheering for you more than I am."

"It just felt like I was taking blow after blow today." Alonzo sighed into her hair. "I'll tell you what—I'm counting down the days when we can take a break from all this and spend time in St. Louis. I couldn't be more ready to go."

Cinda's heart skipped. "Um . . . about that . . ." She brought her eyes to his. "I have to work. Kelsey has a cover shoot that week. But St. Louis should be fairly easy to reschedule."

"I know you know what the calendar looks like," Alonzo said. "It was hard to schedule that trip."

"But I'm working too, Zee," Cinda said. "And a cover shoot is a big deal."

"I thought prior plans were a big deal," he said. "Plans we talked about, got excited about. So whenever we book a trip, if something else comes along, you'll just toss it aside?"

"I honestly didn't think the timing was that crucial," Cinda said. "At least, until what you shared just now." She looked at him. "Why don't you just go without me?"

"Why would I—" Alonzo sighed. "I'm not hashing out a plan B right now." He got two plates from the cabinet. "Let's just eat."

Cinda walked up behind him and slipped her arms around his waist. "You're upset with me," she said. "What's first?"

It took him a moment to turn around. "This." Alonzo gave her a kiss, a quick one.

Cinda took his face into her hands and lengthened it.

"Zee, I'm sorry," she said. "I really am. Kelsey got the news while I was with her, and I saw the conflict, but I just couldn't see turning it down. I should've at least talked to you about it." She sighed. "Clearly I'm still learning, but you were right—we can't lose sight of *us* in all the work." She looked into his eyes. "And since this is my fault, I'll pray hard for God to give us an awesome plan B."

Alonzo gave her a look. "You know what I want to say."

Cinda nodded. "He'd already given us an awesome plan A."

"Exactly."

"But you won't say it," Cinda said, "because you're bigger than that."

"Not really."

She stared at him with a slight smile. "When your jaw sets like that, and you get that crease in your brow"—she ran a finger along it—"with the brooding eyes—you are so doggone fine."

Alonzo let those eyes rest on her. "Maybe I'll keep my attitude then."

"No, we need to work on that." Cinda took his hand, leading him out.

"Where are we going?" he said.

"Outdoors by the fire pit," she said. "Taking 'first' a little deeper."

CHAPTER 15

*T*he front door opened and Chase and Reese scurried from the family room to meet Cedric. Jordyn paused the game they'd been playing as Chase's voice got animated, telling his dad about his day. She straightened the room, putting books back on the shelf and picking up cups and empty snack bags. She carried the trash to the kitchen, where Cedric was asking Chase about his homework.

"It's all done," Chase said. "Right, Jordyn?"

"He finished it," Jordyn said. "I told him he couldn't play video games until it was done. And we read a couple of books first too."

"Awesome," Cedric said. He turned more toward her. "Jordyn, Cyd reminded you about staying a little later tonight, right? Her debate is this evening, and I'll be headed up there after a quick bite."

"It probably slipped her mind," Jordyn said, "knowing how busy she's been. But it's cool, I can stay."

"We really appreciate it." Cedric dug into the carryout bags he'd brought in. "I picked up some Pei Wei. Lots of different entrees, so hopefully there's something you like."

"I'm sure," Jordyn said. "I like Pei Wei. Thank you."

"Dad, I'm not real hungry," Chase said, "and I *just* started the video after all the homework. Can I go play?"

"Why aren't you hungry?" Cedric said.

Chase gave a shrug.

Jordyn looked sheepish. "Probably too many snacks. Sorry."

"Oh, I know how relentless he can be about those snacks." Cedric looked at his son. "You know the deal, Chase. After school you get one snack that *you* want. After that, fruit and veggies."

Chase turned up his nose.

"Then we'll go with fruit and veggies only."

"No, I like the first option better," Chase said.

Cedric chuckled, shaking his head.

"So I can go play?"

"Go ahead," Cedric said, watching as he and Reese went scurrying back to the family room. He turned back to the carryout bags, emptying them.

"I have to be firmer about saying no," Jordyn said. "I've got it down now for the video games. It's harder for juice and snacks, probably because I can overdose on juice and snacks myself."

"If that's the biggest worry, then I'm not worried." Cedric got a couple of plates and handed her one. "We're thankful for all you do with Chase. Our jobs can get pretty demanding. Having you here is invaluable."

"I know Cyd's a professor." Jordyn spooned up some of the Mongolian beef. "What do you do exactly?"

Cedric went for the sesame chicken. "I'm a partner in an executive search firm. I help corporations find candidates for key positions."

"So that's like—"

"A headhunter," they both said.

"I don't think I've ever met anyone with that job." Jordyn added honey seared chicken. "How did you get into that?"

Cedric took his plate to the kitchen table. "I had a mentor in the business who said, 'Hey, you're a people person, driven, highly competitive. This could be a good fit for you.' Been doing it now for over twenty years. Finding the perfect person for a position *and* that person thinks it's perfect for him or her—nothing like it." He went to the refrigerator. "Bottled water?"—wry smile —"or juice?"

"Cranberry," Jordyn said, taking a seat at the table. "Thank you."

Cedric returned with the beverages. "Let's pray," he said, lowering his head. "Lord, thank You for this food we're about to eat, we pray you bless it. And You know, Lord, my wife is heavy on my mind. I ask a special blessing upon her as she goes into this debate tonight. Anoint her words, sharpen her mind. Use her mightily, Lord. In Jesus' name. Amen."

"Amen." Jordyn looked at him. "My dad was that way—people person, driven, competitive. I admired that about him."

"That was Randall, for sure. That's why we had fun going at it when we played cards." Cedric seemed to sink into a remembrance. "He and I started attending Living Word around the same time. Both of us in the new believers class at one point. We were instant friends."

"I didn't realize that," Jordyn said. "I remember when Dad started going, because of all the tension in the house on Sundays." Her brow knit. "I assumed you were a Christian forever, like Cyd."

"Forever, huh?" Cedric chuckled a little. "Cyd led me to the Lord, actually. Although, I'd have to call it a long and winding road. I may have been a handful."

"I can't even picture that," Jordyn said, "you being a handful. Gives me hope."

Cedric went for more food. "So how's the transition going, with your mom selling the house and you and your sister moving to an apartment?"

"Terrible."

"Okay, wow," Cedric said.

"I can't even sugarcoat it," Jordyn said. "I'm tired of Jade—

living with her and working with her. I wish I'd moved to Chicago with my mom, and that's saying a lot."

"The working part, that's the video stuff?" Cedric started into his second helping.

Jordyn nodded. "We built our channel together, and it's our primary source of income. But she's off the deep end—you heard about her video bashing Alonzo?"

Cedric shook his head. "No, I didn't hear about it."

"And not only bashing Alonzo, but Christianity as well." Jordyn tossed her eyes. "It went viral—entertainment media even got hold of it—so of course she's about to do another one. And she doesn't care that I'm adamantly against it." She sighed. "And that's just one issue."

Cedric nodded. "And if you separate it's a problem because revenue is still coming to the channel, which you contributed to."

"Exactly," Jordyn said. "Plus I've got a cosmetics contract, so I can't go anywhere."

Cedric shook his head. "That's a complete mess."

"Thanks for that diagnosis."

"If it were me?" Cedric said. "I'd do some counter-programming. There'd be like ten Christian videos uploaded to the channel overnight."

"Oh, man, I'm loving that," Jordyn said, laughing. "Just the thought of Jade's face."

"And you'd *have* to do a counter video to the one that bashes Christianity—ten reasons why you shouldn't touch God's anointed." Cedric was chuckling himself as he took his plate to the sink.

"See, and I thought you were kind of mean," Jordyn said. "You're hilarious."

"You thought I was mean?" Cedric rinsed the plate and put it in the dishwasher.

"Well, not *mean*. Just, all business. Super serious."

Cedric seemed to think about that a moment. "Depends on

who I'm around. The guys know I can be crazy. But you're right, around most women, I'm more . . . reserved."

"So it's a conscious decision?" Jordyn said.

"Absolutely," Cedric said. "But that messy channel of yours drew me out." He chuckled. "I need to change out of this suit and get going," he said, heading upstairs.

Jordyn rinsed her plate as well and put it away, then covered the food and headed back to the family room.

"Look at my score," Chase said, his fingers working the controls. "I'm destroying *everything*."

Jordyn slid onto the floor beside him. "But you know you've gotta switch back to two players."

Cedric walked in a few minutes later, changed into khakis and a light sweater. "Put it on pause, buddy, and give me a goodnight hug."

Chase got up and hugged him.

"Only a few more minutes of screen time," Cedric said. "You need to eat, and don't forget the reading Mom wants you to do before bed. Love you."

"Love you too, Dad."

Chase hopped back on the remote, and Cedric looked at Jordyn.

"I'm not certain how long this debate will last," he said, "or what will be happening after. But I'll make sure Cyd sends you a text afterward with an update."

"No problem," Jordyn said. "We'll be fine."

"Wait, Dad, who's taking me to school?" Chase said. "Isn't Mom leaving town in the morning?"

"Oh, the funeral, that's right," Cedric said. "I'll take you, and we'll get the bagels you like on the way. It's you and me tomorrow, Chase-man."

"And Jordyn," Chase said. "She's picking me up, right?"

Cedric looked at Jordyn. "We're good for tomorrow?"

"Yes, I'll be there," Jordyn said.

"All right, let me get out of here," Cedric said, turning to leave.

Chase bumped her a couple seconds later. "Jordyn, go. It's your turn."

"Oh. Okay." Jordyn shifted. She hadn't realized she'd been eyeing Cedric as he walked out.

CHAPTER 16

*C*yd checked her watch as a student made his way to the microphone. They'd done opening statements, an extended period of rebuttal, and more rebuttal as students asked questions. Only a few minutes more and this farce of a debate would be over. Cyd couldn't wait to tell Micah what she couldn't say in this forum—that whatever respect she'd had for him as a colleague had dissipated in two hours.

"This question is for Professor Daniels," the student said. "First, thank you for your willingness to boldly state that the idea of Jesus Christ as an actual historic person is a myth." He waited as applause sounded from a cohort that had been in Daniels's corner all night. "My question is, given that, how is it possible that Christianity has persisted for two millennia?"

"Great question." Micah looked out from his podium. "You need to understand that the Bible is expertly crafted." He took the microphone from its stand and moved closer to the audience. "You've got fiction within an historical context. Actual places— Jerusalem and Egypt. Actual civilizations—the Babylonians and Romans. Even actual leaders of these civilizations." He focused on the student a moment. "The historical backdrop is meant to lend credence to the stories—and I admit the stories capture the imagination. Take the story of Jesus himself."

Cyd watched him pause as he walked to another part of the stage, ready to tell 'the story' to not only the audience but everyone watching the live stream. *Lord, I know this man is lost, but it grieves me every time he refers to Your word as 'fiction'. Open his eyes to the truth. And thank You for the words You've given me tonight. I pray You give me words to respond to this as well.*

"It begins with his birth," Micah was saying. "God supposedly impregnates a woman so he can be born a human. Why he couldn't just appear as a fully developed human—that's conveniently sidestepped. Nevertheless, the tale includes, as it must, all the so-called signs that this baby is 'the chosen one'—star in the sky, *angels*. And of course, you have to make him sympathetic—no room at the inn, born in a lowly manger. Genius. Story's been sold so well, I can't get so much as a haircut on December 25th."

Laughter sounded in the auditorium, and Cyd worked to keep an even expression. Micah had been doing this all night—cracking his little jokes. Would've been more fitting to have the debate at his barbershop.

"And we know what these fictional writers came up with next," Micah continued. "As the fable goes, Jesus grows up, gets his band of followers, preaches, performs 'miracles'—again, let's sidestep the fact that if he's truly God, he'd rid the world of war, poverty, and natural disaster."

Applause rang out, and Micah motioned for quiet as if he weren't reveling in it.

"But wait," Micah said, "here's the good part. Jesus supposedly dies this horrible death to save horrible people like you and me—don't forget, we're 'sinners'. Then *ta-da!* He's suddenly alive again. And he *loves* you. If you'll just believe in him, you can bypass a fiery hell and float on cloud nine forever." Micah shook his head. "It's no surprise that so many have bought into the fairytale for so long. It appeals to their emotions. The sacrificial hero who loves you? Powerful narrative. Fear that you could end up in a so-called hell if you don't believe? That's powerful too. Just 'give your life to Jesus' and he'll fix everything." He walked back to the podium. "I honestly wonder if those who came up with this story thought in their wildest dreams that it would persist this long. But then, so have other epic tales we know and love."

Cyd took the microphone and waited for applause to die down as she prepared to respond. She smoothed her pantsuit jacket, took a quick sip of water, and approached the student who was still standing at the microphone up front. "You asked how it's possible that Christianity has persisted for two thousand years. And Professor Daniels pointed you to the Bible, specifically, to accounts that bear on the life of Jesus—the gospels in the New Testament. He calls these writings a fiction, with no evidentiary basis. And that's because he knows the evidence points to exactly the opposite." She glanced over at Micah. "I said it earlier, and it bears repeating—virtually every credible New Testament scholar rejects the view that there was no historical Jesus. Why? Because credible scholars and historians understand that if we apply the same tests of historical accuracy to the New Testament that we apply to other ancient writings—the New Testament is in a class by itself. In fact, noted atheists and agnostics in the field have called the position Professor Daniels has taken tonight—silly."

Cyd waited for a smatter of laughter to die down. "The fiction being sold this evening is Professor Daniels's. You heard him admit earlier that in his own academic writings, he's acknowledged the reality of Jesus as an historical figure. Suddenly tonight, he's taken up this new idea, popular among an Internet fringe, that Jesus is a myth. I have to wonder if he has a lucrative book deal in the works."

Micah looked over at her, smug in his dark colored suit.

"I do want to respond specifically to the question," Cyd said. "How has Christianity persisted for two thousand years?" She looked out at the crowd populated with not only students but professors from various departments, and felt a stab of fear. She took a breath. *Help me, Lord.*

"And since Professor Daniels presented his answer with a story," Cyd said, "I'd like to do the same. Except, the story of Jesus doesn't begin with his birth. The Gospel of John tells us Jesus always was, from the beginning. Christians believe He is God, from eternity. And at a point in actual history, He stepped into time and became human. Yes, born of a virgin by the Holy Spirit, because He needed to be a perfect sacrifice. Yes, attested to by a star and heralded by angels—He'd created them both. But He came to earth, not for stars or angels, but for the crown jewel of His creation—mankind. And He preached the good news, healed the sick, performed miracles—all of this affirmed by eyewitnesses —and yes, He died a horrible death, on a cross. Because sin demands a price, and He paid it, for us all."

Cyd vaguely heard the moderator tell her time was up, but no way could she stop there, at His death. "And yes," she said, "Jesus rose from the dead and ascended back to heaven. And that band of followers He had? They weren't looking to say *anything* about Jesus, let alone create some tale about Him. Jesus was hated among the Jews. He'd just been *crucified*. His followers went into *hiding*."

Cyd gave a quick glance to the moderator, who didn't seem poised to stop her, and went on. "It wasn't until God sent His very Spirit that these followers began spreading the good news of salvation through Jesus Christ." She knew many wouldn't under-stand what she was saying. But it was so heavy on her heart, someone needed to hear it. "And more and more believed and *they* spread the good news—the gospel. Because it's more than believ-ing; it's being transformed on the inside. And you can't keep it to yourself. The gospel of Jesus Christ is power and life. *That's* how Christianity has persisted for two thousand years. That's why it will last forever."

Cyd was surprised to see pockets of people standing

throughout the auditorium, clapping. She turned to go back to her podium—

"A follow-up question, if I may," Micah said.

"Our time is up," the moderator said. "I was about to give closing—"

"Just a very quick question," Micah said. "I'm certain it's on the minds of many."

The moderator nodded. "Go on."

"Professor London," Micah said, turning to Cyd, "do you contend that there are ramifications for those who do *not* believe what you believe?" He paused. "In other words, do you contend that Jesus is the only way to heaven?"

Cyd looked out at the sea of faces staring back at her, convinced the room hadn't been this quiet all night. "It's not a matter of what I contend," she said. "It's what Jesus Himself said. 'I am the way, and the truth, and the life; no one comes to the Father but through Me.'"

"And you believe that?" Micah said.

Cyd looked him in the eye. "I believe that."

The moderator gave his closing remarks, but Cyd heard none of them. Her ears filled with the clamor in the audience, which grew once the event had ended and people rose from their seats. She looked as several people approached Micah, smiling and shaking his hand.

Cedric and Stephanie had sat near the front and made their way to her now.

"I'm so proud of you, sweetheart." Cedric hugged her tight. "You were *amazing*. I kept thanking God—you brought it every time. God was glorified in a big way."

Stephanie hugged her next. "Girl, that breakdown you did between the Greek New Testament manuscripts and other ancient whatever, and all the reasons why the New Testament was more reliable . . ." She shook her head. "I couldn't even keep up, but I was like, my sister's an actual scholar."

"Oh, I thought you knew," Cedric said. "My wife is the real deal."

"She was my sister before she was your wife," Stephanie said. "So I knew before you knew."

"This is just the kind of silliness I need right now," Cyd said. "For real." She saw Jesse approaching. "Hey, Jesse, I didn't know you were here."

"I've never been to anything like this," Jesse said, "so I didn't know what to expect. But you weren't playing. You brought the serious scholarship—I was taking notes—then you said, let me keep it one-hundred and bring the gospel. I was so rocked by that."

"I appreciate that, Jesse," Cyd said. "It means a lot." She glanced over at the people forming a line to talk to her, who didn't look especially friendly. "Looks like a lot of other people were rocked, but in a different way."

"You shouldn't feel any pressure to make yourself available to them," Cedric said. "It's been a long night, and I know you're drained."

"Right," Stephanie said. "The last thing you need is people coming at you crazy. That professor-what's-his-name was enough. Let *me* go talk to those people."

Cyd looked at Cedric. "Please take my sister somewhere. She has no sense."

"At all." Cedric elbowed Stephanie. "I kind of like that suggestion, though, Steph."

"Might as well head over there," Cyd said. "This is only the beginning. The line will be outside my office next."

She moved toward the stairs on the platform as Micah headed her way, his hand outstretched.

"Cyd, thank you for the vigorous debate."

She shook his hand. "It was enlightening, Micah, that's for sure."

"Indeed," he said. "You're a true believer."

"And I'm confused as to who you truly are," Cyd said. "You said you wanted to come to Wash U to be taken seriously as a scholar. Now you've abandoned scholarship in favor of petty theories."

"I haven't abandoned serious scholarship," Micah said. "But there's only so much to be gained from academic talks and university presses. Coming here boosted my credentials, such that my agent could secure a book deal in the trade press." He nodded slightly. "You were right, about that part anyway."

"Wow," Cyd said. "So you really were using this debate to build a platform for yourself, ultimately to sell books. There's no telling what you truly believe."

"I truly *don't* believe Jesus is the Son of God," he said. "In case you're wondering."

"How would you really know, though?" Cyd said.

Micah frowned slightly. "Excuse me?"

"During the debate, I mentioned the Greek construction of Jesus' 'I am' statements in the gospel of John. And you didn't seem familiar with it."

"My academic focus has primarily centered around Greek literature," he said. "It shouldn't be surprising that the gospels aren't foremost in my mind."

"But for whatever reason," Cyd said, "you've taken up an interest in the New Testament. And you were fired up about debating Jesus. Surely you've engaged the New Testament directly, in its original language."

"I've read pertinent parts of the gospels and Paul's letters," Micah said.

"I'm curious, though," Cyd said. "Have you read the gospel of John in its entirety?"

"What is your fascination with that particular book?"

"You're the one who's fascinated," Cyd said, "with declaring that Jesus isn't the Son of God, that He didn't even exist. Yet, you haven't read the gospel in which He Himself states plainly who He is?"

"I'm confident I've read what's necessary to arrive at my own beliefs."

"Then you shouldn't be afraid of a little more reading, right?" Cyd started toward the ever growing line. "You challenged me to a debate. I challenge you to read that gospel."

CHAPTER 17

*T*ommy's eyes rested vaguely on the people walking up the aisle, filing slowly past Cecil's coffin, then hugging Jillian and members of the family. He'd been there close to an hour, arriving at Jillian's church a little after ten this morning, when he too had gone up to view the body. He'd stood there longer than he'd expected, staring at the navy suit and red tie. Cecil had probably bought the suit for some event, maybe for church—*regular* church on Sunday. He could've never thought he'd wear it for this. And it had brought tears to Tommy's eyes— the irony of it. Of loving a wife with whom he wouldn't grow old. Of making family plans for a future he wouldn't see. Tommy was convinced—life could be downright rotten.

He sat near the back now, end of the row, as people milled about the sanctuary, talking softly. The funeral was set to start in thirty minutes, but he wasn't sure he would stay. Not sure he *could* stay, without coming undone.

Tommy looked as Cyd and Stephanie walked in and headed toward the front. Moments later Jillian's head was buried in Stephanie's arms, her shoulders heaving as she sobbed silently. She'd broken down a couple of times this morning, and each time it triggered something in Tommy—the sadness he'd done a decent job of pushing down over the past month. He took a breath, stuffing it again by praying for Jillian, their four kids, Cecil's mom, and others. It was why he wanted to stay, to pray. Jillian had said she needed prayer more than anything—today in particular. He was determined to keep his friend lifted.

Tommy's phone vibrated, his heart lurching a little as he pulled it from his suit pocket. *Wife* appeared on the screen with a brief text message—**Yes, came to get a few things.**

He got up to find a quiet spot outside the sanctuary and dialed. Allison answered on the fifth ring.

"Tommy, we're not doing this over the phone," Allison said.

"Then we have a problem," Tommy said, "because we can't do it in person either, since you won't come home—until you know I'm gone." He leaned into the phone. "That's where we are now? I let you know I'm headed to Maryland—despite the fact that I don't know where you've been—and you run home? When did you get back from overseas?"

"I haven't been home because I'm trying to get my head together," Allison said. "And I can't do that when you're asking me endless questions I don't know the answers to."

"You don't know when you got back from overseas?"

"You know what?" Allison said. "This is part of the problem. Your need to keep track of my coming and going. I don't have to file a report of my itinerary with you, Tommy."

"I don't even know why you see it that way." Tommy struggled to keep his voice low. "I wasn't filing a report when I told you I was coming to Maryland. You're my wife. Should you not know what state—or country—I'm in?"

"It's stifling," Allison said. "I was on my own for almost twenty years. And I enjoyed doing what I wanted to do, going where I wanted to go. I thought marriage was the one thing I lacked. I thought it would enhance my life . . . not trample everything that was already good about it. "

"What do you want exactly?" Tommy said. "Should we treat each other like roommates? You do your thing, I do mine, and when we feel like it, we intersect the two?"

"I don't know what I want," Allison said. "That's what I keep saying. I just don't know."

"So, meanwhile—what? We're not even trying to work on this. Have you given any more thought to seeing a counselor?"

"Oh, someone from church who thinks like you do?" Allison said. "I have no interest in listening to someone validate everything you say."

"You pick the counselor," Tommy said. "It's not about validating my position. I just want us to hear each other's heart. I want us to work it out. Allison, I love you."

Silence met him on the other end.

"I have to go," Allison said.

"So you'll be gone when I get back?" Tommy said.

"Like I said, I just came to get a few things."

"And you won't tell me where you're going."

"It's just . . . how I need to handle this right now," Allison said.

"Does any of this involve someone else, Allison?" Tommy said.

"This isn't about anyone else," Allison said. "It's something I'm working out within myself." She paused. "I promise we'll talk soon."

Tommy kept a silent phone in his hand, staring at the pattern in the carpet. *What is it with me, Lord? How did I get this marriage thing wrong again? Was I really too stifling? Was I—*

"Tommy, you okay?" Lance put a hand to his shoulder. "You're standing here like you're in another world."

He looked at Lance. "Guess who's at the house?"

It only took a beat. "Allison?" Lance said. "You talked to her?"

"Got a notification that the house alarm was deactivated, right after I got here this morning, so I texted her," Tommy said. "When she texted back, I was hopeful. I called, and she actually answered."

"And what happened?"

Tommy looked away a moment. "She still doesn't know what she wants to do about our marriage. Still doesn't want to see a counselor. And still staying wherever, as long as it's not home."

Lance sighed. "I don't get how Allison thinks this is helpful—staying gone, not talking it out."

"She doesn't care," Tommy said.

"I don't think you can go that far—"

"If you could hear her, you'd know—she literally doesn't care." Tommy shook his head. "Haven't been married a year, and my wife is *whatever* about the marriage." He focused on Lance. "What is my problem? My first wife left me for another man, now this. I mean, did you see this coming? Because you did the marriage counseling. Did you see I wasn't ready, that I would mess up my marriage, but you didn't want to tell me?"

"And I wouldn't have told you, because what?" Lance said. "I didn't want to hurt your feelings? Tommy, you know that's not what I saw in you."

"I'm just trying to figure it out, man." Tommy could feel his eyes filling. "I'm just trying to figure it out."

Tommy walked away, down a corridor, through the lobby, and out the door. In the car he started the engine and let his head fall back against the headrest with a stream of tears.

What am I supposed to do, Lord? Stop caring? Stop calling my own wife, asking what she's doing, whether she's coming home?

He closed his eyes, swiping tears with his hand, hearing what he'd heard many times lately.

It'd be nice, Lord, if You'd stop giving me Ephesians 5. That's my problem—I love my wife. How about giving her some Bible verses? How about letting her feel some conviction? You convicted me when I didn't want to tell her I was coming to Maryland, but she gets to gallivant around the world without a word. At least let me change the alarm code, so she can't be sneaking in—

The passenger door opened and Reggie got in.

Tommy looked at him and closed his eyes again.

"Lance said you talked to Allison," Reggie said.

Tommy gave a slight nod, sinking back into his thoughts a moment. "I keep trying to retrace everything," he said. "Figure out where it went wrong." He looked over at Reggie. "When did you start seeing a problem?"

Reggie thought a second. "Maybe last fall, around the time Allison was planning that trip to Amsterdam. I remember the two of you arguing."

Tommy nodded. "She told me she was going, and I said we should go together. Never been to Amsterdam." He shook his head. "She'd already booked the trip with a couple girlfriends. So I said, okay, that's what you used to do before we got married, but it'd be nice to know your plans beforehand—even nicer to be included. And it touched off this big thing."

"Yeah, when I walked into the kitchen," Reggie said, "Allison told me, 'When you get married, be the same person you were when you were dating.'"

"That's what she kept saying," Tommy said, "that I did a bait and switch." He lapsed into thought. "I guess I just assumed certain things change when you get married. She did do a lot of traveling when we were dating, and I never asked to go because I didn't want to put us in a compromising position. And I didn't expect her to run her plans by me. But once we were husband and wife . . ." He nodded softly. "Definitely started with the travel and branched out from there."

"I was sure you'd work it out, though," Reggie said. "It didn't seem like *that* big a deal."

"That's because I wasn't telling you everything," Tommy said. "Allison told me she wasn't happy before Christmas. But like you said, I figured we'd work it out, no problem. Until this month."

"So what happened exactly?" Reggie said. "Allison left for South Africa, supposed to be back in a week. Which became two, then three. Meanwhile, you're clearly going through and not wanting to talk about it."

"It was the same thing," Tommy said. "Allison told me she was going to Cape Town, after the trip was booked." He shrugged. "I didn't even say anything. Didn't want to argue. Then right before she left, she said she'd be contemplating next steps with respect to our marriage."

"Seriously?" Reggie said.

"I told her we needed to talk it out together," Tommy said, "that we needed counseling. But she said she needed time to herself. I didn't even know she was back until this morning."

"So what'd she say just now?" Reggie said.

Tommy looked away. "She still doesn't know what she wants."

"I still think you'll work it out," Reggie said. "I've been praying."

Tommy watched as a couple of people walked into the church, then looked at the time.

"The service is about to start," Reggie said. "We should get back inside."

Tommy stared forward, still unsure whether he was staying or going. Part of him just wanted to sit somewhere alone and sulk. But would he really not be there for his oldest friend?

He sighed, turning off the engine, and made his way back inside.

CHAPTER 18

*P*ast midnight Treva leaned against Lance on the sofa in Jillian's family room, baby Wes in her arms. The day had been as long and hard as they all knew it would be, especially at the gravesite, when Trevor lingered long after many had gone, in tears by the casket. Yet now, late into the night, the kids were finding comfort in stories about their dad. Treva smiled as David enhanced his with an imitation. "David, you've got Cecil's voice down," she said.

"And when he said it in the form of a question, you knew you were in trouble." David sat up with a stern look. "'So that's the choice you're making right now? You really want to talk to me like that?'"

"Those were the questions *you* got," Courtenay, their oldest, said, "'cause you're always acting up. I remember when I started getting the 'boy' questions—'Does he love Jesus? And don't just tell me he goes to church—where's the fruit?'"

Faith sat next to her, Zoe asleep in her lap. "That one guy you dated in high school lasted a hot minute. Uncle Cecil was like, 'Yeah, no . . . not even happening.'"

"Girl, he tried to walk up in here and tell my dad, 'I'm not into formal religion.'" Courtenay looked amused even now. "Dad said, 'Neither am I. I just want to know if you and Jesus are tight.'"

"I'm using that," Lance said. "Joy, whoever you bring home better be ready. My list is getting long."

Joy let her head fall against the sofa. "It's hopeless. No one will survive that."

Treva chuckled. "You need to have your own questions. Be selective, girl."

"I keep thinking about the questions Cecil was asking over the past couple of months."

Treva looked at her sister, who'd been mostly quiet this evening. "What kind of questions, Jill?"

"Questions like, 'When was the last time we stepped out in faith?' and 'What do we know we can't do—that we're trusting God for?' and 'What big prayers are we praying?'" Jillian's voice was bare. "All day those questions have been ringing in my ears. And I've been asking God why." She paused. "I think I know what He's saying to me."

Courtenay looked at her. "What's that, Mom?"

Jillian looked at her daughter. "To continue with the plan. To move to St. Louis."

"What?" sounded around the room.

"But how does that make sense?" Sophia perked up, having already said she was glad they wouldn't be leaving. "We were moving because Dad had a job out there. There's no reason to go now."

"I just don't think we're meant to abandon the journey," Jillian said. "Your dad and I prayed and fasted, and he said he'd never felt more strongly about a decision. We put the house on the market— boom, it sold." She thought a moment. "I was mad about that at first, feeling like God had pulled the rug out from under us. But what if it was so we wouldn't turn back?"

Patsy perked up as well, looking over at her daughter. "But how would you afford a place to live? If you stay here, you and the kids can move in with me, at least until you find a job. Treva and Lance have a full house. You'd go out there with no job, no housing, nothing?"

"That's the faith part," Jillian said. "*What if* I prayed big prayers, asking God to provide? I've been so upset with God this week, but today as these thoughts swirled in my mind, it felt like He was leading me, like He hadn't abandoned me."

"I don't know," Patsy said. "Everything I've read says that at a time like this, you shouldn't be making any major life changes."

"Momma," Jillian said, "a major change has been made *for* me. The house is sold. The question is where to go from here. Should I not go with what I believe God is saying?"

"And we can definitely make room," Lance said. "We've got a free bedroom in the lower level, Wes can move into our room, the girls and Sophie can—"

"But, wait," Sophia said, "if we do this, Mom, can the three of us still stay with Grandma Patsy till the end of May? If I wanted to do that before, I *really* want to do it now. Losing Dad, moving across country . . . It's too much. Plus I still want to finish out the school year here."

"Ditto," David said. "I actually think it'll be good for you, Mom, to be with Aunt Treva. But the plan should stay the same."

Jillian was shaking her head. "It was one thing for Cecil and me to head to St. Louis first," she said. "But breaking up the family right now . . . I don't feel good about that at all. We need each other."

"But Mom," Courtenay said, "doesn't that make it easier for you to stay with Aunt Treva while you find a job? You could have everything in place by end of May."

"It's not about what's easier," Jillian said. "I'm not leaving you all behind. It'll be like you're losing both of us." She shook her head again.

"Jillian, I've always said you're a tad too overprotective—"

"Momma, really?" Jillian said. "This has nothing to do with being over—"

"If I may finish," Patsy said. "It's not as if Sophia, David, and Trevor will be orphaned. They've got me as well as Darlene close by. And three months will pass quickly." She spread her hands. "This move is happening *next week*. It's reasonable to give them more of a transition than that."

"What if we tried it for a couple weeks, Mom?" Trevor said. "I know you'll be calling and FaceTiming us every day—"

"Several times a day," David said.

"And you can see how you think it's going," Trevor said.

"Wow, Trev," Sophia said. "That was smart—I mean, nice compromise."

Jillian looked at Trevor, then the rest of her children. "I see where you're coming from, I do," she said. "I still don't like it, though." She sighed. "Let me pray about it."

∾

Treva walked up from the lower level and into the kitchen, past three groups of men carrying furniture to the moving truck. "Now that's teamwork," she said. "Hard to believe it only came together this morning."

"I can't believe it didn't dawn on me until late last night." Jillian taped up a big box with pots and pans. "The blessing was right here—all these hands available to help. No point waiting till a week from now to be out of here."

"And I'm glad our flight isn't till this evening." Stephanie wrapped glassware. "At the rate we're going, we'll be done with the kitchen soon and moving to the next thing."

"So we're not setting aside any of the dishware, right?" Cyd had emptied the cabinets, ready to roll with the packing.

"Right," Jillian said. "I'm taking the bare minimum to St. Louis, and the kids are taking only what they need to my mom's. Almost everything is going to the storage facility here—which will then need to be moved to St. Louis once we've got a place, and who knows how we'll do all that."

"You didn't know how you'd do *this* till a few hours ago." Treva wore baby West as she joined Cyd in packing dishes.

Jillian nodded. "Didn't even know what state I'd be living in until a few hours ago. And still not sure I made the right decision about the kids."

"You only agreed to the compromise," Treva said. "Think of it as two weeks at Grandma's, and keep assessing from there."

Jillian looked at Treva. "You were unusually quiet when we talked about all that last night. I wondered what you were thinking."

"I wanted you to be sure you were hearing from God," Treva said, "with no input from me. Because going forward with the move was exactly what I hoped would happen."

"I hate what you're going through," Stephanie said, "but I have to say . . . I was really looking forward to us living in the same city, so I'm glad you're still coming. Girl, you're like a sister after all these prayer calls."

"It made me sad," Jillian said, "when I realized I wouldn't be doing anymore 'wives prayer calls'."

"We'll just change the name," Stephanie said. "Make it broader. And now that you'll be in town, we can even meet in person."

"Jill, we need you in the basement for a minute." Tommy came into the kitchen. "Not sure which things are being tossed and which are being moved."

Jillian followed him downstairs as somebody's phone rang, causing them all to look at theirs.

Cyd was the one who answered. "Hey, hon, I thought you and Chase were at the matinee. . . . Oh, really, why?"

Treva continued wrapping dinner plates.

"Yeah, I think so, too." Cyd said. "Romans is the go-to verse for that. Why, what are you doing? With Jordyn?"

Stephanie turned to look at Cyd.

"Where are you?" Cyd said. "Okay . . . Okay . . . Love you, too."

Stephanie kept staring at Cyd as Cyd returned to packing.

"So what's the deal?" Stephanie said.

"Jordyn's filming a Christian-themed video, and I guess she got the idea from Cedric." Cyd stuffed the bottom of a box. "So she asked for help with making sure she was saying the right things."

Stephanie looked at her a moment more then turned back to what she was doing.

"They're at the church," Cyd said.

Treva rubbed Wes's back, looking between them both. "Do I even want to ask"—she shook her head—"no, I don't think I want to ask."

"On another note," Cyd said, looking at Treva, "I'd love to talk next week to get some legal insight. Based on comments after the debate, there may be complaints filed against me, at least within the university system. Have you ever handled anything like that?"

"I would need to look into their particular policies and regulations," Treva said. "But I can definitely do that."

"Girl, sometimes I forget you're an attorney," Stephanie said. "Do you ever want to go back to practicing law?"

"It's weird that I can actually say I don't," Treva said, "at least not in the way I used to. But once in a while I'm compelled to take up an issue. If anything is filed against Cyd, I'll help however I can."

"Mom, Reggie and I just decided . . ." Faith walked into the kitchen. "We're doing a big wedding. I mean, not *big*, but bigger than we thought."

"Wow," Treva said. "I thought your top choices were eloping or Lance marrying you at home."

"I know," Faith said. "But after being here with my cousins and spending time with Reggie's family . . . I just think it'll be nice to celebrate with people we love."

Treva bounced a little with Wes as he began to fidget. "Part of the reason you liked those other options was because you said it would be hard to walk down the aisle without your dad. You're sure?"

"It'll be hard without Dad regardless," Faith said. "But being surrounded by family . . . that'll be special." She paused. "But will it be weird for Lance to walk me down the aisle then jump to the other side and do the vows?"

Treva looked at her. "You want Lance to walk you down the aisle?"

"I asked him just now, out by the moving truck," Faith said. "He said I picked a fine time since he didn't need to be all emotional, carrying a sofa."

"All of it is making me emotional," Treva said. "I remember asking Hezekiah why he was setting up a wedding fund for you girls, on top of the other funds you had." She sat down to feed Wes. "He said he'd been praying for your future husbands from the time you were born, and he wanted to be prepared to celebrate when God answered." She reached out to hug Faith. "This was your dad's vision for you."

Faith lingered in the hug. "Okay, I better get back to helping David and Trevor with their room. I thought Joy and Hope were messy."

"Thanks for helping them, Faith." Jillian passed her as she returned to the kitchen. "They'd be here till next week trying to tackle that mountain of stuff."

Treva checked her watch as Wes snuggled against her. "So what's the plan exactly? I know the goal is to have the truck loaded by sundown, then it's got to be unloaded at the storage facility. But we need to get on the road before too late. We're driving through the night so Lance can get back for church. Will you have enough help?"

"Definitely," Jillian said. "More people from church are heading over this afternoon. It's a huge blessing."

"So everything will be stored by evening," Treva said, "the kids leave with Mother tonight—"

"Then cleaning the house top to bottom—got help with that too," Jillian said. "And wow, I guess I'm on the road to St. Louis tomorrow. Faith said she'd ride with me."

Treva reached for her hand. "You're my favorite sister in the whole world."

"Why are you saying that?" Jillian said.

"Because you are," Treva said, "and because I love you, and because I'm praising God for the strength He's giving you."

Jillian's grip tightened in Treva's hand. "Don't make me cry and set myself back."

"Crying is not a setback," Treva said. "You'll continue to cry. But let it be on God's shoulders."

$\mathcal{C}$edric navigated his car toward home, feeling an unsettling awareness that too much of the day had been spent with Jordyn.

"Chase is knocked out already," Jordyn said, glancing at the back seat. "After being amped for two hours straight."

"Dave and Buster's is an amusement park for him," Cedric said. "He could've stayed on those arcade machines another two hours."

Cedric had promised Chase they would go while Cyd was out of town. After Jordyn's video shoot, he'd reminded Cedric, saying they could also eat there. And Chase wouldn't rest until Jordyn said she was coming too.

"Thank you, again," Jordyn said, "for all your help with the video. You basically wrote the script."

"Nah, I just gave an outline," Cedric said. "You thought up the questions, which was key. It was an awesome idea."

"Well, you're the one who got me thinking about doing a Christian video," Jordyn said, "even if you weren't entirely serious when you said it. And I have so many questions about Christianity and the Bible myself that it was a way for me to learn more." She looked at him. "Seems like you learned a lot fast. How did you do that?"

"I don't know if I would call it fast," Cedric said. "It's been a number of years, just studying the Bible bit by bit."

"And you could tell the difference it was making?" Jordyn said. "Because clearly you've come a long way—you said you were a handful."

Cedric glanced at her. "I said I *may* have been a handful. And yes, I could tell I was growing."

Jordyn shifted toward him. "So, assuming you were a handful —what did that look like? I can't even picture it."

"There's no point in going there," Cedric said. "I'm just thankful I'm in a different place."

"Can I ask a question, though?" Jordyn said.

Cedric gave her a look, waiting.

"You're such a devoted husband and father," Jordyn said. "Were you always sort of like that—a one woman guy? Because if you were the type with lots of women, that's an amazing change."

"Let's just say I know about amazing grace," Cedric said.

"Wow."

"What's the wow?"

"So you were a player, huh?"

"I plead the fifth," Cedric said.

Jordyn folded her arms, looking at him. "I can kind of see it. You were probably fine back in the day."

Cedric couldn't help but show amusement. "Thank you . . . for making me feel like I'm sixty."

"Okay, I'm kidding," Jordyn said. "You're still fine. Just didn't think I should tell you."

Cedric stared at the road, taking the last couple of turns toward home. He passed Jordyn's car at the front curb and pulled into the driveway.

Jordyn unhooked her seatbelt. "I was right, I shouldn't have said that, sorry. Didn't mean to make things awkward."

Cedric turned off the engine. "Everything's cool, Jordyn. Let me get your equipment."

Cedric got the video lights from his trunk and transferred them to Jordyn's.

Jordyn closed her trunk and looked at him. "Thank you again."

Cedric nodded. "No problem. Drive home safely."

Cedric woke Chase and walked with him into the house, his heart rate uneven as he closed the door.

CHAPTER 20

*J*illian woke in time to see a mile marker whizzing by —147 miles to St. Louis. "We're only two hours away?"

Tommy looked over at her. "Hour and a half at most."

She yawned. "I must've been knocked out for more than three hours."

"Drool coming out your mouth and everything," Tommy said. "It wasn't pretty."

"As long as I wasn't snoring."

"Some of that too."

Jillian reached into the cooler in the back and got two bottles of water, putting Tommy's in a cup holder. "I can take the wheel whenever you want," she said, uncapping hers, "now that I'm rested. I feel bad. You've done all the driving, and it's my car." She took a drink.

"I'm in a zone," Tommy said. "And you know I'm good as long as I've got my music."

"Thank you," Jillian said, "for everything yesterday with the moving, for changing your plans last minute to ride with me . . ."

Tommy leaned in as if he couldn't hear. "To do what?"

114

"Okay, to drive me."

"Ah . . ." He smiled a little. "You know I got you."

"And thank you for snapping me out of that dark haze." Jillian sighed. "It's still hard and it still hurts, but you were right—going through it *with* God makes all the difference. I might be curled up in bed still, trying to figure out how I'm moving all that stuff, and where to."

"I was shocked you decided to come to St. Louis," Tommy said.

"Me too," Jillian said. "I really do feel it's God, but it'll be quite an adjustment, especially this period without the kids." She got her phone and checked it. "I left all three of them messages before I nodded off, and not one reply." She dialed Sophia.

"Mom, can I call you back?" Sophia said.

"What are you guys doing?" Jillian said. "Did you get my message?"

We're at Grandma Darlene and Grandpa Russell's house," Sophia said. "David and Trev are helping Grandpa Russell with something in the garage. I'm talking to Devin."

"Please tell Devin thank you again for helping at the storage facility last evening," Jillian said.

"I will," Sophia said. "But did you want something?"

"Just calling to check on you all," Jillian said, "to know how you're doing."

"Okay, so . . . Can I call you back?" Sophia said.

"Call me back, Soph," Jillian said. "I love you."

"Love you too, Mom."

Jillian hung up with a sigh. "I literally feel like I'm in a twilight zone. Like I'll wake up and the entire past week didn't happen." She stared out the window. "This can't be my life."

"You should write down everything you're feeling," Tommy said. "The good, the bad, and the ugly. I remember that used to help you."

"Cecil and I just talked about my journals," Jillian said. "Whole stack in a closet we were cleaning out last weekend." She could see him, on a step stool, taking the stack from a high shelf. "I said it had been a while since I'd journaled, and he said . . ." She shuddered at the memory. "He said, 'You always get back to it, usually when you're dealing with something.'"

Tommy looked at her, his eyes wearing a sadness.

"But it's what I need." Jillian took a tissue from her purse and dabbed her eyes. "A prayer journal. The last couple days I've been really real with God in prayer, but something about getting those thoughts on paper . . ."

Tommy nodded soberly. "And you'll have a record of where you've been and how God's kept you."

Jillian looked at him. "You sound like you know something about that."

"I keep a mental record," Tommy said.

Jillian watched more signs whiz by. "I remember Momma was so upset with me when I decided to stay home with the kids. She said I was wasting my education and talents. And I know she was a very different person then, but maybe there was some wisdom in that." She stared into the night. "Because I wouldn't feel so stuck right now, no clue as to what kind of job to look for. If I had any talents, who knows where they went. I feel completely inadequate."

Tommy looked at her. "So you're going back, what, almost twenty years and second-guessing yourself? I wasn't even around and I *know* you and Cecil had to have prayed and felt you heard from God in that."

"We did," Jillian said softly.

"So, stop," Tommy said. "God was leading you then, and He's leading you now. He'll show you what to do."

Jillian sighed. "I know." She gave him a look. "But can you get more of an empathetic side? You won't let me get away with feeling sorry for myself *at all*."

Tommy sat quiet a moment. "Maybe that's something I need to work on."

"Um, I was kidding actually," Jillian said. "I'm glad you won't let me get away with that, pointing me back to God instead."

"Still . . . I've been praying for God to show me areas I need to work on," Tommy said. "Showing empathy might be one." He glanced at her. "But since it helps, I'll make sure I'm still hard on you."

"Well, back in the day you were hard on me *without* pointing me to God," Jillian said. "So this is an improvement."

"Did you just go there?" Tommy said. "You said *I* was"—he glanced at her—"give me one example."

"I don't even have to think hard." Jillian had her head against the headrest. "Remember I was so into that guy Steven—even though we didn't do anything but grab something to eat now and then in the Union. But I wanted it to be more, and he wasn't vibing like that. And I asked you what I should do." She rolled her eyes over to Tommy. "You were like, *get over it and move on.* Classic Tommy . . . I don't even know why I called you my best friend, as cantankerous as you were."

"Don't even try it," Tommy said. "When I was dating Regina—"

"Not the Regina story," Jillian said.

"*When I was dating Regina,*" Tommy said, chuckling slightly, "and heard talk that she was seeing somebody else, I said, 'Jill, I don't know if I should ask her about it straight out because things are real cool between us, maybe ignorance is bliss'"—he looked over at her. "What did you say?"

"I said you were a fool because you'd heard more than 'talk'— one of your boys had seen her hugged up with some guy." Jillian remembered it all, as if it were yesterday. "*Then* when you finally asked and she said it was nothing, you believed her. Took you months to finally see what she was about." She shook her head. "Telling me, *get over it and move on,* but couldn't do it yourself."

"Calling *me* cantankerous." Tommy gave her the side eye. "I remember when I humbly asked for help with my papers, and you gave me a hard time."

KIM CASH TATE

"Oh, man, you're back to first semester freshman year?" Jillian said. "That's how we met, in that English class."

"As if I could ever forget." Tommy stared at the highway. "I said who is this girl getting these A's while I'm over here struggling with C's—and I thought I was a decent writer." He glanced at her. "Asked if you could help me out, look at my papers . . ."

Jillian smiled a little. "I said you should go to the writing center where there were people who actually wanted to help with that sort of thing."

"Just mean," Tommy said.

"Then I felt bad," Jillian said, "when you said you'd gotten help from over there on your last paper, and still got a C."

"Which was a lie."

Jillian's eyes widened. "I totally bought it. I can't believe you."

Tommy shrugged. "Hey, I wasn't always saved. And I was confident I could benefit from your help." He looked at her. "All that red pen you used to mark up my papers and tell me how to improve? To this day, seriously, it stuck with me. I hear those tips in my head when I'm writing reviews and such—'never use five words when one will do . . .'"

"You hated those red marks, though."

"With a passion," he said.

"And you never paid me for my tutoring services."

"Here's your payment right here," Tommy said, pointing at the odometer. "Seven hundred miles and counting. And I'm *sure* I bought you at least a dozen Roy Rogers burgers over the course of those tutoring sessions."

"Ohh," Jillian said. "Remember your little girlfriend tried to get an attitude when she saw us in a Roy Rogers booth that day? Sat down in the booth beside you. Made sure I knew you'd been dating since high school. I was thinking, girl, I know you see this red pen in my hand—we are *working*."

"Candice was so jealous of you," Tommy said. "Just could not believe that nothing more was going on."

"A lot of people thought that," Jillian said. "'You mean there's *nothing* going on with you and Tommy?'" She drank more water. "In hindsight that was a blessing, being strictly friends. Our lives are so connected now—family, friends, about to be in the same city and church. Can you imagine if we'd been in a relationship? I'd be cutting my eyes at you during the sermon, still mad about how you did me wrong."

"It's crazy," Tommy said. "First time we've lived in the same city in two decades." He shook his head. "But we're a long way from those carefree college days."

"A mighty long way," Jillian said as her phone rang. Treva's name flashed on the screen. "Hey, we're only about an hour out."

"Girl, all this time I thought Faith was riding with you," Treva said. "Just talked to her and she's with Reggie."

"Yep, the lovebirds decided they couldn't be apart for several hours on the road," Jillian said. "So Reggie's driving Tommy's car, and Tommy's driving mine."

"Well, we've got your room all ready and lots of food," Treva said. "See you soon."

Jillian hung up as Tommy took an exit to get gas.

"So have you talked to Allison?" she said.

Tommy stared ahead. "I don't want to talk about it." He made a right off of the exit and continued to the gas station.

Jillian looked at him. "I can tell you're hurting."

He pulled up to a pump and cut the engine. "You could always tell. I hated that."

She watched him get out and unscrew the gas cap. "Here you go," she said, handing him a credit card through the window.

"I got you," Tommy said, swiping his. "You can get the next one."

"You said that last time," Jillian said, "and there won't be a next one."

As the car filled up, Tommy walked into the convenient store and returned with a bag of goods. He put the pump back, screwed on the gas cap, and got in.

Jillian peered over. "What'd you get?"

He started pulling them out.

"Funyuns?" Jillian said. "And Starbursts?" She grabbed them. "I can't remember the last time I had either one of those."

"And of course . . ." He lifted two bottles of Mountain Dew from the bag.

"Of course." Jillian took hers. "Late night study material. Get hyped up on sugar and crash and burn later."

Tommy opened his Mountain Dew. "Sometimes you just need some of that throwback carefree."

Jillian opened her bottle and clinked it with his.

CHAPTER 21

"*H*eyyy, this is so cool." Cinda checked a link she'd gotten as she and Alonzo drove to dinner. "Kelsey made a few of those 'celebrity sighting' blogs."

"From the birthday party the other night?" Alonzo glanced at it when he came to a red light. "Dope look with the black on black." He nudged her. "Why you let her wear all black but always insisting on color with me?"

Cinda checked another link Kelsey sent. "What's the difference between people's comments about your style now versus before?"

Alonzo thought a moment. "They didn't really talk about my style before."

"Exactly," Cinda said. "Color looks *so* good on you." She pulled him closer and kissed him before the light changed. "But I admit —so would black on black. One day I'll let you."

Alonzo turned, bringing them closer to the West Hollywood restaurant. "I hope you know things were a lot different with my former stylist. She didn't have this much say in what I wore."

"Things better be different," Cinda said. "If she was dressing and undressing you like I do . . ."

Alonzo smiled as he drove. "Yeah, I don't mind you being 'extra' with that."

"Ha," Cinda said, looking at another text from Kelsey. "She said, 'You know you're on the right track when people start pinning you to Pinterest style boards.'" She looked at Alonzo. "I knew it would be good for her to go and do a trial run. Thanks for letting me take her."

He shrugged. "I didn't feel like doing the nightclub thing, but I knew it would be a nice event. I'm glad you could make it work professionally."

Alonzo's phone sounded, and he glanced at it on the console. "Is that Shane?"

Cinda nodded, looking at the text. "Says he's there, got a booth."

"I'm wondering what this project is that he wants to talk about," Alonzo said. "All he would say is it's an opportunity for us to work together again."

"That would be awesome," Cinda said.

"Depending on the project," he said. "Everybody's telling me what I need to do next. I just really want to hear from God."

Alonzo pulled his Range Rover behind a Porsche at the front curb of one of the newer trendy hotspots. The valet opened Cinda's car door, and she stepped out as Alonzo came around to her side, looking rugged casual in jeans and a red plaid shirt, unbuttoned to show his gray tee underneath. He took her hand and led her toward the entrance, pausing briefly for photographers snapping pictures of celebs as they arrived on a Saturday night.

A bouncer stood in the doorway, which had surprised Cinda the first time they came. She'd learned there was no open seating, and they were selective even about reservations. The big guy nodded and moved aside as they reached the doorway, and inside, one of the restaurant owners shook Alonzo's hand.

"Alonzo, where've you been, man?" the owner said. "Haven't

had a chance to congratulate you on the Oscar win. That was incredible."

"Appreciate that, man," Alonzo said, smiling. He gestured toward Cinda. "And you remember my wife, Cinda?"

"Of course." The owner kissed her hand. "Wonderful to have you with us again."

"It's good to be here," Cinda said.

A hostess escorted them up the elevator to the rooftop, where a bar and pulsating music greeted them. As they made their way past, a woman moved from the bar area toward Alonzo, breasts spilling from a lingerie top.

"Hey, handsome," she said, hugging him. "I saw Shane come in and wondered if you'd be here too. Where've you been hiding?"

"Just chilling," Alonzo said, tugging Cinda closer. "Let me introduce you—"

Before he could say it, another woman hugged him.

"I was looking for you at Riley's birthday party," the second woman said, smiling up at him. "Been missing that pretty face of yours." She turned as someone called her then turned back to Alonzo. "Let's catch up soon." She kissed his cheek before walking away.

The hostess continued leading them, and seconds later, Cinda felt a tug on her free hand.

She turned, the one hand dropping from Alonzo's. "Oh. Donnie, hey," she said.

Donnie moved from two women with whom he'd been talking at the bar. "Good to see you again, Cinda." He hugged her then backed up a little, eyeing her. "Definitely looking hot this evening."

She felt herself blush, glancing down at her cropped leather jacket over a shift dress with high heels. "Thank you," she said, reaching for Alonzo. "You've met Alonzo, right?"

"I haven't, actually." Donnie shook his hand. "Good to meet you, man. Love your work."

"Likewise," Alonzo said. "Good to meet you as well."

Donnie smiled at Cinda. "I'm guessing no Pineapple Train-wrecks tonight?"

She smiled. "No, I'm good," she said, continuing on.

The hostess led them to a quieter area with lush plants and funky lighting, to the booth where Shane was waiting. He got up and hugged them.

Alonzo moved into the booth, looking at Cinda. "Donnie? I didn't even know he went by that. Since when do you know him?"

"Who are you talking about?" Shane said.

"The R&B singer," Cinda said, moving in beside Alonzo. "Donovan Shores." She looked at Alonzo. "We met at that birthday party."

"So what's up with the Pineapple Trainwreck—he bought you a drink?" Alonzo said.

"He didn't *buy* it," Cinda said. "The server was making rounds and he got one for me."

"Why would he get you one?" Alonzo said. "You don't even drink."

"Which was what he found out," Cinda said.

"So you're both great this evening?" Shane said. "I'm doing well also."

"Two women hugged you on the way over here," Cinda said, "and I didn't say a word. One guy approaches me, and you have a problem?"

"You couldn't tell he was flirting with you?" Alonzo said. "I heard what he said—'looking hot this evening.'"

"That could have simply been a statement of fact," Shane said. "Cinda actually does look hot tonight."

Alonzo gave Shane the eye.

"So I'm supposed to do what, Zee?" Cinda said. "Women flirt with you all the time. You just keep it moving, like I did."

"So now it's nothing to you when a man flirts," Alonzo said. "When I met you and told you you looked good, you blasted me.

Maybe I should've bought you a Pineapple Trainwreck for starters."

Cinda shook her head. "This is so ridiculous."

"It actually is." Shane looked at Alonzo. "Dude, if anybody knows, I know that women come at you all the time. And I'm amazed how well *Cinda* keeps it moving when they come at you."

"Well, not with Simone," Cinda said.

Shane tossed Cinda a look. "Yeah, she's special," he said. "But I never hear you say to Alonzo, 'Who was that? Did you date her? What about *her?*'" Shane leaned in, his eyes on Alonzo. "And nobody could blame her for going there."

Alonzo's jaw tightened as he listened.

"So Cinda's in the business now," Shane continued. "She's going to meet lots of people, and guess what, bruh? She's fine. Brothers are gonna flirt. You think she can't handle herself?" He looked at Cinda. "What did you say when he said you looked hot?"

"I said, 'thank you' and introduced Alonzo," Cinda said.

Shane gave him a look. "Man, stop tripping. You're just mad 'cause you feel like he disrespected you—just like a lot of women disrespect Cinda."

Alonzo was quiet a moment then looked at Cinda. "You do put up with a lot, and I hadn't really thought about it because none of that stuff means anything to me." He shook his head. "Then the first time I have to deal with something, I snap." He added, "But it *was* disrespectful."

Cinda gave him a smirk.

Alonzo put an arm around her and brought her closer, kissing her lightly. "I'm sorry, baby."

"Now that Alonzo's no longer tripping," Shane said, "we can get to the actual reason—"

"Good evening, I see your full party is here," the server said. "Can I start you off with something to drink? A cocktail, perhaps?"

Shane smiled. "The lady will have a Pineapple Trainwreck."

Cinda and Alonzo laughed then placed their real order.

"All right, Shane," Alonzo said, "the floor is yours. Ready to hear this news."

Shane leaned in again. "I just signed on to direct a project that's perfect for you as the lead."

"Tell me about it," Alonzo said.

"About a preacher's family—and before you say it's been done, it hasn't been done on this level. Canyon Features financed development of the script, and Weiss and Goldman are exec producing."

"Why the big money behind this particular one?" Alonzo said.

"Vince Burnett wrote the screenplay."

"He's really hot right now," Cinda said.

Shane nodded. "Best Original Screenplay Oscar last year. And he's got another movie out later this year. Top gospel artists are already clamoring to be part of the project."

"So what's the story arc?" Alonzo said. "And please don't say— preacher dreams of son following in his footsteps and taking over the church; son gets the courage to find his own path outside of the church."

"The opposite," Shane said. "Son works in the world of finance. Discovers his preacher father has been living a double life— cheating on mom, corruption in the mega church. Son has a true heart for God. He finds the courage to call out his father, step into the ministry he's always known God was calling him to, and lead the congregation on a right path toward God."

"Wow," Alonzo said. "Wasn't expecting that. I'm surprised they'd put that kind of money behind a Christian film."

"You know they had to see the potential revenue," Shane said. "There've been a couple of movies lately that have drawn heavily from a cross section of black moviegoers and churchgoers—and took the industry by surprise with the results."

"True," Alonzo said. "One hit number one opening weekend, and everybody was shocked."

"And this one has huge potential at the box office," Shane said. "With Vince writing and you starring? You're not only an 'Academy Award Winning Best Actor'—you're the one with all the talk swirling right now about your faith. Church folk are already rising up and speaking out on your behalf—how proud they are that you're representing. They'll come out to support. You're perfect for this role."

Cinda looked at Alonzo. "This really is perfect for you. Sounds like God is answering your prayers."

"I'm trying to get Kelsey on this project too," Shane said. "She'd play your younger sister. Since she's open about her faith as well, grass roots support could be crazy."

"That would be awesome for Kelsey," Cinda said. "A breakthrough opportunity."

"When can I read the script?" Alonzo said.

"Early next week," Shane said. "Everyone's excited about you coming on board, and you know where I'm at. Working with my dude again?" He nodded. "Epic."

Alonzo nodded also. "You in the director's chair gets me praying it'll work." He smiled. "And hey, maybe this'll give you a reason to go to church. Research and what not."

"Funny you say that," Shane said. "Kelsey's been trying to get me to visit her church."

"Oh, so you've got *other* reasons for including Kelsey on this project," Alonzo said.

"All I said was she invited me to church," Shane said. "Stop jumping twenty steps ahead."

Cinda smiled. "She invited us too, actually—I forgot to tell you, Zee." She looked from one to the other. "Tomorrow?"

∼

Cinda took the steps quickly with Alonzo to the front entrance of the church. "How are we late? This is so embarrassing."

"How are we late?" Alonzo cut her a look. "You were taking out your twists when we should've been leaving the house."

"It was a rhetorical question," Cinda said. "And it wouldn't be so bad if it weren't a smallish church."

"I told you I wasn't excited about coming anyway," Alonzo said. "When people know you're looking for a church home, and they invite you to *their* church, and it doesn't work out—it's awkward."

"Oh, it'll be fine—hi, how are you?" Cinda smiled at an usher holding the door as they approached.

"Welcome to Christ Tabernacle Church." The young man shook Cinda's hand, then Alonzo's. "This is crazy," he said. "You're like, really walking into my church." He took his phone from the pocket of his black trousers. "Can we get a quick pic?"

"Could we do that after service?" Alonzo said. "It's our fault, already running late."

"Oh, sure, sure," the guy said.

They moved inside, another woman arriving right behind them. "You cannot tell me God is not an on-time God," she said. "Alonzo Coles?"

He turned to look at the woman, probably late thirties, hair in long, pretty dreads. "How are you?" he said, shaking her hand.

"I was mad at myself for running late, but look at God." She shook her head, eyes focused on him. "Anybody who knows me *knows* I love some Alonzo Coles. I have seen every one of your movies a dozen times"—she paused, shaking her head again—"and my God, you are every bit as good looking up close, and so well built. Can I just hug you?"

She pulled him in as Alonzo looked to Cinda with eyes that said, *help.*

Phone in her hand, the woman lifted it for a selfie of the two of them. "My best friend is inside," she said. "She's going to *lose it* when she finds out you're here." She snapped the picture and checked it.

"We'd better get a seat," Cinda said, taking Alonzo's hand. She smiled at the woman. "It was nice meeting you."

"Nice to meet you too," the woman said. "You're beautiful yourself, sis. The two of you—equally yoked."

An usher stood just inside the closed sanctuary doors. Cinda adjusted Alonzo's yellow striped tie as they waited. Seconds later, the door opened as a woman walked to the podium.

"We'll be fine right here in the back," Alonzo whispered to the usher, pointing to an empty pew.

The usher nodded, starting in that direction as the woman up front began sharing the announcements. When the usher stopped mid stride, Cinda looked up, then looked at Alonzo. Someone was waving them forward.

"The pastor wants you to come up front," the usher said.

"But we're late," Alonzo said. "I really don't want to interrupt the service. I'm thinking we'll just—"

"Oh, don't be shy." The pastor, a middle-aged man with graying hair and a healthy midsection, had taken the microphone. "We like to give our esteemed guests a place of honor," he said. "And church, is it not an honor to have Oscar winner Alonzo Coles and his lovely wife in the house today? Give God a praise."

Members of the church clapped as the two of them moved up the aisle. Cinda spotted Kelsey near the front smiling, Shane beside her.

The pastor shook their hands as they approached, and they moved into the front row as the service continued.

Alonzo leaned his head close to Cinda's. "Do I have to say it?"

"No," she whispered back.

"I need to hear you say it then."

"Shh," Cinda said.

"Nope. I need an acknowledgement."

She glanced over at Kelsey then back to Alonzo. "Super awkward."

CHAPTER 22

ordyn held her breath as she looked over Faith's shoulder in the rear of the sanctuary. "I know it's really basic," she said. "I just thought, for people like me who don't know much. Well, who don't know hardly anything . . ."

"Jordyn, why are you making excuses?" Faith watched the video on her phone, listening through earbuds. "I'm loving this."

Jordyn hesitated as if she'd heard wrong. "Seriously? I mean, what do you love? Because it's so basic—you probably knew this stuff in third grade."

"It's not about age or grade level," Faith said. "Somebody could be sixty years old watching this, learning about Jesus for the first time."

"I just thought of all the questions I still have," Jordyn said, "or things a lot of you just *know*, that I had no clue about. I figured somebody out there might have the same questions."

"And might not want to ask anybody, thinking it's 'too basic,'" Faith said. "This way they can pull up your video and get a simple and clear explanation of really important stuff. That's what I love about it—Zoe, where are you going?"

"I'll get her," Jordyn said, heading after Zoe as she toddled out of the sanctuary and into the lobby area. Jordyn picked her up and brought her back.

Faith took out the earbuds. "So you're planning to do more of these, right?"

"I want to." Jordyn had Zoe on her hip. "The problem is I don't know much, obviously. Cedric helped with this one."

"I'll definitely help if you want," Faith said. "You could also do one telling your testimony."

"Another word that gets thrown around," Jordyn said. "I'm embarrassed to say I'm not sure what it means."

"Oh, girl, you're right, great example," Faith said. "So think of a courtroom where a witness testifies about what she's seen and heard." She paused, hugging someone goodbye. "As believers we're witnesses to Jesus' power to save and transform lives. So when we give a 'testimony,' we share how we used to be, what we used to do—doesn't have to be in detail, depending who you're talking to. And then we share how we've been changed through faith in Christ. I like to share the gospel as part of it too. Does that make sense?"

Jordyn nodded. "That would be an awesome video, giving the basics of what a testimony is, then sharing a testimony." She let Zoe get back down. "I don't actually have one myself, though. But the weird thing is, I'm thinking more and more about Jesus, faith, and Christianity now that I've started these videos."

"I'm thinking you'll have a testimony soon enough"—Faith turned suddenly as Zoe darted away again—"little girl, you're everywhere at once today."

"She was coming for her daddy." Jesse walked up with Zoe in his arms. He hugged her tight. "Daddy'll see you tomorrow, princess. I love you."

Zoe squeezed his neck.

Faith turned to Jordyn. "You should do Jesse."

"Do what with Jesse?" Jesse said.

Jordyn hardly looked at him. She'd avoided him last Sunday at church and thus far today. And near as she could tell, he'd done the same.

"Jordyn's doing Christian videos," Faith said, "and she wants to do one on sharing testimony. I'm saying she should do you—where you share your story on video."

Jesse looked bothered. "And why would I do that?"

"Because you're a new believer," Faith said. "I think your testimony would be fresh and relatable, and on Jordyn's channel you could impact a lot of people."

Jordyn looked away. *Unless he doesn't really have that 'changed' part down.*

"Hey, you ready?" Reggie walked up to Faith. "Lance is meeting with us in thirty at the house."

"Ooh," Jordyn said, "wedding stuff?"

Faith nodded. "Putting everything on the calendar. Pre-marital counseling sessions and, of course, we need to pick a date."

"I love that you're doing an actual wedding," Jordyn said, "so people can celebrate with you. You two are just . . . special."

"You gonna give Daddy another hug before you go?" Jesse said.

They squeezed one another and Zoe kissed him.

"Aww, she's such a sweetheart," Jordyn said.

Faith took Zoe into her arms and started off with Reggie. "We'll see you guys," she said.

Jordyn cleared her throat. "Um, the video thing Faith was talking about—you don't have to give it another thought. I know it's complicated, with you and Jade and all."

"What do you mean, me and Jade?" Jesse said.

Jordyn looked at him. "Spending the night in our apartment?"

Jesse shook his head. "I don't know why I didn't leave right away. She was so mad at me."

"Mad at you?"

"I'm sure she told you," he said. "Because I wouldn't sleep with her."

Jordyn tried to hide her surprise. "Well, why were you there then?"

Jesse frowned a little. "So you're low key grilling me?"

"You're right, none of my business." Jordyn shouldered her bag. "Have a great week, Jesse."

"You don't have to swing all the way to an attitude." Jesse took a couple of steps in her direction. "Look, if you want to do a video with me sharing my story . . ." He seemed to think a moment. "I'm down."

~

Jordyn set up her equipment in Jesse's duplex apartment later that afternoon. "So you're not writing down notes or anything?"

"I thought about it." Jesse sat in an armchair, clad in jeans and a black polo shirt. "But I don't want to be tied to a script. I looked up some verses while I was waiting for you, though."

"Don't worry if you need to stop and start over or whatever." Jordyn set up the second camera angle. "I'll make it seamless when I edit."

"I thought you were into hair and makeup videos," Jesse said. "You're switching it up?"

"A little," Jordyn said, checking her camera settings. "Wait, can you get up a minute?"

She pushed his armchair closer to the window then checked the camera's exposure. "That's better," she said, moving now to adjust her lights.

Jesse sat back down, his dog Lancelot sprawled at his feet. "So how much of my story am I supposed to tell?"

Jordyn looked over at him. "I think that's up to you," she said. "You don't have to go into detail. Share a little about your past, how Jesus has changed you, share the gospel . . . That's what Faith was telling me at church."

"The irony," Jesse said.

"What do you mean?" Jordyn said.

Jesse shook his head. "Nothing."

"Okay, we're just about ready." Jordyn approached him with a makeup bag. "I just need to powder your face a bit."

"Why?" Jesse said, clearly unenthused.

"Lighting."

Jordyn took his hand and tested a couple different shades on his almond brown colored skin, then applied the powder to his face. He stared ahead as she stood over him, taking in his thick brows and long lashes.

"I think we're good to go," she said.

"We should probably pray," Jesse said.

"Oh," Jordyn said. "Hadn't thought about that."

Jesse shrugged. "I wouldn't have either. It's just, all the time I've spent around Lance these past few months."

"So you're gonna pray?" Jordyn said.

"I haven't actually prayed out loud myself . . ." Jesse seemed to think a moment. "I guess, let's just hold hands or something." He took her hands in his and bowed his head, letting several seconds lapse. "Lord, I don't know what to say, in the prayer or the video. I just pray you lead us. That you would use it." He paused another few seconds. "I'm not even sure what my story is—I'm still in the middle of it. So if You would give me words, in Jesus' name."

"Amen," Jordyn said. She turned on the lights, pushed the record button on the second camera, the one aimed at his profile, then moved to the one positioned in front of him. "Whenever you're ready," she said.

Jesse leaned in a little. "I'm here to share my story about committing my life to Jesus—which is funny because I've never been big on commitment." He paused several seconds. "I was the guy parents warned their daughters about. Nice guy, did well in school, girls said I had a cute baby face—so they were drawn to me." He stared off for several seconds before turning back to the camera. "It was nothing for me to have sex with them. It didn't mean anything to me. But depending on the girl and how long I wanted her around, I would lie. Say it meant something. Even say I was committed, if that's what it took."

Jordyn focused on him through the camera, drawn to his every word.

"My father never committed to my mother, never committed to me or my brother either. So you could say it runs in the family. Except, not anymore." Jesse's eyes brightened somewhat. "I have a little girl, just over a year old. In my senior year of college I started seeing her mom—not exclusively, of course. And when she got pregnant with my daughter, I told her . . . I told her to have an abortion." He blew out a breath, pausing again. "Because I didn't want to be committed, to either one of them."

Jordyn blinked back tears. Something in Jesse's voice. He sounded so real.

"But when my daughter was born, God did something in my heart," Jesse said. "I could feel it, being drawn to Him, but I wasn't ready to commit. My mom raised me in the church, and I knew enough to know that Jesus would change my life—and I wanted to hang onto it the way it was." He took his time, exploring his own life. "I could feel myself being drawn to the mother of my baby too, but I wasn't ready to commit to her either . . . until it was too late. I had broken her heart one too many times, and in the end I got what I deserved—a broken heart."

Jesse paused as if thinking about what he'd said, then got up. "Stop the camera."

Jordyn watched him disappear inside a bedroom. She blew out a sigh, then another, trying to stem the emotion. It wasn't just his story but the fact that too much of it touched on her own. She needed a moment to gather herself as well.

Jesse returned a few minutes later. "So, I don't know where that came from, the broken heart and all that—"

"It's okay, Jesse," Jordyn said. "I'll edit it out."

Jesse stared into the distance. "I didn't even realize that's what

I was dealing with—a broken heart." He glanced upward. "Thanks, Jesus, for enlightening me right in the middle of the video." He walked back to the chair. "Don't edit it out. Hopefully somebody besides me will need all this."

~

Jordyn wrapped up the cord on the lighting stand and set it by the door, then packed up her camera lenses.

"I don't know about you, but I'm starving." Jesse's head was in the fridge. "But then, I'm the one who had everything drained out of me today."

"I had no idea it would be that powerful, Jesse." Jordyn set her camera equipment by the door as well. "I was doing everything I could to hold back tears. I feel drained myself."

"Hold back tears?" He peered around the fridge. "It wasn't that emotional, was it?"

"Are you kidding?" Jordyn said. "The way you spoke from the heart—just raw. And the things you said about finally making that commitment to Jesus. How you thought you'd have to give up so much, but instead He *gave* so much. Oh, man . . ." She waved a hand before her face. "I'm feeling it again. You don't have to worry about somebody else needing this. *I* needed it. And yes, I'm starving." She walked toward the kitchen. "But why am I thinking that thing is empty?"

"Mostly," Jesse said. "But I've got some leftover pizza in here."

"From where?"

"Pi."

"What's on it?" Jordyn said.

"It's deep dish," he said. "Roasted chicken, peppers, barbecue sauce . . ."

Jordyn smiled. "My stomach just rumbled, hearing that."

"Cool," Jesse said, pulling it out. "Takes a little longer but it's tastier warmed in the oven instead of the microwave."

136

"Sounds good to me," Jordyn said, taking a seat at the oval kitchen table.

Jesse turned on the oven and joined her, settling into his seat with a sigh. "It's weird, knowing you know all this about me now."

"Well, it'll be more than just me," Jordyn said, "once I upload it. And I didn't even have to grill you to get it out of you."

"Yeah, about that," Jesse said. "I hated everything about the way I handled that night and didn't want to talk about it. That was a low point, seeing you when I was walking out."

"How could it be a low point?" Jordyn said. "After hearing your story, I would think you felt good about the fact that you didn't sleep with Jade."

"But like you said—why was I even there?" Jesse shook his head. "Now that my broken heart is out there, I'll just say—I was hurting for real that night. Then Jade said she needed a ride and invited me in. I knew what was up, and for a minute I just wanted to go back to the old Jesse and numb the pain."

Jordyn listened, remembering that had been the evening he found out Faith was engaged.

"But when we kissed," Jesse said, "it was all wrong. I just knew it was all wrong." He paused, his brow bunched. "I'm trying to figure out how you got me *totally* oversharing today." He sighed. "Anyway, I got up to leave, like five minutes after I got there. And she kept saying, 'just stay' and she just wanted to talk. So we talked, and I fell asleep. When I woke up, she'd taken her clothes off and . . ." He sighed again. "You know the rest—she got mad when I wouldn't sleep with her. Then I walk out and somebody from *church* sees me, and I know how it looks. It was a low point."

"I actually didn't know any of that," Jordyn said. "Jade led me to believe the two of you slept together."

"Why would she do that?" Jesse said.

Jordyn clicked an ink pen absentmindedly. "Well. I may have burst into her room and told her I didn't appreciate her going to

Cyd's house, running her mouth, then sleeping with a brother from church. It kind of got uglier from there."

"So whatever thought I had about twins being joyful BFF's twenty-four-seven—"

"Yeah, no," Jordyn said. "Long, complicated history between us. And it's only gotten worse since I started attending Living Hope. We're very different."

The bell sounded to signal the oven had fully warmed. Jesse put the deep-dish slices on a tray and into the oven. "So let me guess," he said, returning to his seat, "Jade's the wild child and you're the little angel. While I was out here acting a fool, you could probably do no wrong."

Jordyn sat quiet a moment. "No," she said. "Most of our differences have to do with personality, temperament, that sort of thing. In other areas, it's fair to say I've been wilder than Jade." She stared at the table. "That's why your testimony hit so hard today."

Jesse cocked his head a little, looking at her. "Nice try, thinking you're gonna clam up after that. Not after all my oversharing."

"I *really* don't think you want me to share," Jordyn said.

"No, I think I do," Jesse said, nodding. "We're pretty lopsided right now. Might as well even it out."

CHAPTER 23

"*T*hus far I know of three students who are filing a grievance against you."

Cyd listened as Alice, head of her academic department, brought the update she'd been awaiting.

"I talked to them personally," Alice said, seated across from Cyd's desk. "They were offended by your statements regarding your religion—and frankly, so was I."

Cyd nodded. She and Alice had had a good relationship as colleagues long before Alice had been promoted to department head. And Alice had always known that Cyd was a Christian. But based on several conversations Cyd had had since the debate, it was clear that many were surprised that she actually believed the truths of Christianity.

"But given the setting in which the statements were made," Alice said, "these grievances won't go anywhere. There's no basis to allege discrimination. Your record as a professor is exemplary, course evaluations always high, and students love you." She paused. "Well, at least, till now. You'll experience blowback on a personal level, and you'll have to respond to these grievances. But from a faculty governance standpoint, you can breathe easy."

"Well, as you know," Cyd said, "blowback has already begun." She glanced at the campus newspaper on her desk, where two articles had already been written, both unfavorable toward her. And then there was the social media barrage. "But we move forward from here." She stood to shake Alice's hand.

Alice paused before leaving. "You know my daughter and son-in-law are in Michigan now," she said. "Both Christians. We've had our own little debates around the table at Thanksgiving. Anyway, somehow she got wind of your debate and watched it on YouTube. Sparked another rousing discussion when she called to talk about it."

Cyd smiled a little. "Tell Susan I said hello. Maybe we could chat sometime."

"Oh, I bet you two would love that," Alice said as she walked out.

Cyd sighed as she sat back down, relieved she wouldn't have to endure lengthy legal procedures. Treva had looked into it and told her as much, but it was good to hear it confirmed. She picked up her phone to call Cedric and let him know—as Micah Daniels walked into her office. She watched him take the seat Alice had just vacated.

"Is there something I can help you with?" Cyd's tone reflected her irritation.

"You issued a challenge," Micah said, "and I thought I would take it up, given that you followed through with the debate."

Cyd looked at him, waiting.

"The challenge was to read the entire gospel of John in its original language," Micah said. "So that was my plan. One evening several nights ago I picked up the text, intending to read steadily through and be done. But I have yet to get past the first few verses." He paused. "It's more accurate to say I can't get past one word."

"Logos," Cyd said.

"Which I've read before." Micah leaned in. "That's what's

strange. I've read this part of John, and of course I'm familiar with the word 'logos' in Greek thought. But reading it this time—I got stuck. It's actually bothering me."

"So why are you here?" Cyd said.

Micah stared vaguely for a moment at the papers on her desk. "For the past few days I've seen your door open and, with all of this swimming in my mind . . . I thought maybe we could talk it out."

"Talk what out?" Cyd said.

"The whole concept of 'logos'—the word—and what John envisioned when he wrote it," Micah said. "He had to have chosen that word carefully, knowing its implications in a Greek-influenced world."

Cyd sat back. *Lord, I don't feel like talking to him about anything. I'm dealing with daily blowback because of him while he's moving along just fine. I really don't* like *him.*

She sighed inside, hearing words in her head to respond to Micah. She knew how God was leading her.

"Certainly John used the word purposefully," Cyd said. "To Greek philosophers, even to Jewish philosophers, 'logos' was related to reason. It was this force at work in the universe, but it was abstract, impersonal." Her voice held little feeling. "John said, let me give you the true understanding. The 'logos'—the Word—is not abstract or impersonal. The Word is a person, Jesus Christ."

Micah moved forward in the chair. "And John's first use of it, in fact he starts the gospel with it—Ἐν ἀρχῇ ἦν ὁ Λόγος—"

Cyd nodded. "In the beginning was the Word . . ."

"For some reason that's troubling me," Micah said.

"I don't understand," Cyd said.

"Again, I've read it before," Micah said. "I know what Christians claim. But I've been focused on the fact that Jesus didn't exist as a person who walked the earth. That those narratives were made-up." He paused, as if processing his thoughts. "And something about those words . . . It's like they're mocking me.

Almost as if, whether Jesus existed as a human or not, He still existed."

Cyd looked at him. She'd suspected he had some angle and it would only take a matter of minutes to figure it out. But was he sincerely grappling with this?

It seemed obvious, but Cyd guessed she should say it. "That's what John is saying," she said. "Before Jesus walked the earth as a man—and, yes, even if He had never walked the earth as a man—He always existed, from the beginning. John's words are tied to the first words in Genesis—'In the beginning'." She sat up a little now. "And John leads you to his next points, that the Word was not only in the beginning—the Word was with God and the Word *was* God. And then the Word put on flesh—became human."

"Okay, I want to get to each of those points," Micah said, "but first I want to talk about the Greek construction of 'the Word was God,' because that was troublesome too . . ."

Cyd took a breath as he went on, one ear to Micah, the other to God. *Lord, if You're working in his heart, please give me the words. Open his eyes to the truth. Help him to put aside his reasoning and theories—and simply believe.*

∼

"For two hours he asked questions?"

"Can you believe it?" Cyd passed the rice to her husband at the dinner table. "At one point went to his office to get some books and came back."

"It's crazy when you're praying for something"—Cedric spooned more rice onto his plate—"and you actually see God move."

"This is the professor you debated?" Jordyn said. She'd stayed for dinner at Cyd's invitation.

Cyd nodded. "And he was still very much a skeptic when he left my office," she said, "but he asked if we could have an ongoing dialogue. It got to be really interesting, actually. Exploring nuances in the grammar, debating use of the article 'the' in key phrases, looking at the history and philosophy of the times . . .''

"Wow, you're really into this stuff," Jordyn said.

"Definitely her passion," Cedric said.

"And you get to make a living of it," Jordyn said. "That's awesome. By the way, can I get seconds? This stir-fry is really good."

"The spicy turkey part is good," Chase said. "Not the green bean part."

"You're doing a good job eating, though," Cyd said. "And Jordyn, of course you can have more. And you're pretty passionate about these videos. I think that's awesome too."

"I'm actually behind on the makeup videos I'm supposed to do." Jordyn added more of the stir-fry to her plate. "But whenever I get a new idea for one of these Christian videos, I want to jump on it."

Cyd looked at Cedric. "Have you seen the one she did with Jesse? Uploaded, what, yesterday?"

Jordyn nodded. "We filmed it Sunday, and it took me two days to edit because I wanted it to be just right."

"It was powerful," Cyd said. "Drew me in, and I already knew much of the story. Oh, and I loved the title—*When I'm Broken*."

"I not only saw it," Cedric said, "I called Jesse to tell him how moved I was by his vulnerability. Not too often a man will cop to a broken heart. But Jesus sure got the glory."

"You don't know how much it means to get this feedback," Jordyn said. "My sister and I had another blowup when she saw it. Got so bad we ended up in a fist fight, and that's never happened."

Chase's eyes widened. "Who won?"

"Neither of us," Jordyn said. "The whole thing is stupid."

Cyd looked at her. "Maybe a healthy separation would be good for the two of you."

"Trust me, I thought about getting my own apartment," Jordyn said. "But we signed a one year lease, and I wouldn't leave her hanging like that." She shrugged. "It'll blow over."

"Well, next time things are about to blow up," Cyd said, "just come over. Consider the guest bedroom yours when you need time away."

"Thank you, Cyd," Jordyn said.

"Meanwhile," Cedric said, "we need to be praying for Jade just like we're praying for Micah Daniels."

"Can you put my mom on that list?" Jordyn said. "And um, don't forget to keep me on there too."

"I'm fascinated," Cyd said, "all these Christian videos you're doing while reminding us that you're not actually a Christian." She smiled at her. "I see God all over it."

"You really think so?" Jordyn said. "So what should I do?"

Cyd looked at her. "Exactly what you're doing."

∽

Cyd turned out the light and climbed into bed, nestling next to Cedric.

He put his arms around her. "Sweetheart, we need to talk about that open door you gave Jordyn."

"About coming over here when she needs to get away?" Cyd looked up at him. "I wanted to help."

"But we have to be wise." Cedric was quiet a moment. "I don't think I ever told you, but a little after we got married, I had a sit-down with Lance. I wanted to talk accountability and safeguards I should put in place."

Cyd nodded slightly. "Because of your history with women."

"I told Jesse my own story when I talked to him," Cedric said. "Told him I saw myself in his testimony, except I lived like that till I was *forty*. You know, babe—I was Jesse on steroids. High-end condo, sports car, more money than I could spend, and lots of women." He rubbed her back. "As much as I love you, I would've been a fool to think my flesh would never be tempted."

"So at work," Cyd said, "you keep your door open when you meet with a woman."

"And my assistant's desk sits where she can see inside my office," Cedric said. "And you know I try to avoid one-on-one situations with women, whether face-to-face, texting. Last week with Jordyn—should've never happened."

"But you weren't even alone with her," Cyd said. "You agreed to do the video at church, since activities were going on up there at the same time. And Chase was with you the whole time. I could just hear him begging her to go to Dave & Buster's."

"Still too many one-on-one moments, when Chase was off playing or whatever," Cedric said. "And I told you, the convo on the way home . . ." He shook his head. "I don't ever want to be in a situation with a woman where the vibe is like that."

"But if Jordyn needs to stay over, that's not one-on-one," Cyd said. "I'd be here, like tonight."

"Baby, she could show up one night when you're away. And even if you're home . . ." Cedric came up on an elbow. "It's not even that I'm worried something would happen. What if I see her in the upstairs hallway, wearing who knows what? I don't want my flesh or the enemy to be able to take hold of the slightest thing. I don't want her in my *thoughts*."

"I hadn't told you," Cyd said, "but Steph had similar concerns. I told her she was just suspicious by nature."

Cedric looked into her eyes. "Cyd, you have to remember that Steph and I have both lived a little differently than you. We've been *out there*. We're like this," he said, nodding vigorously, "when the apostle Paul says, 'nothing good dwells . . . in my flesh'. I ain't mad at all about Steph voicing her concerns. My sis was looking out."

"So what now?" Cyd said. "I can't say, on second thought, Jordyn, if things blow up? You're on your own."

"Steph's home is her work, so she's almost always there," Cedric said. "Set it up so Jordyn's got an open door at the B and B."

"Wow," Cyd said. "You're really not playing."

Cedric brought her close and kissed her. "Not when it comes to our marriage."

CHAPTER 24

On Thursday morning Lance drove onto the Living Word complex and parked near the main entrance. A good number of cars had beat him there, people who worked full-time on the administrative staff, in one of the church ministries, or for the worldwide ministry that consisted of books, Bible studies, and an ever growing online presence. Gone were the days when he knew everyone at Living Word. The church had grown exponentially since he'd first stepped through its doors nearly twenty years ago. But many of the people on staff were like family.

Lance got out, spotting Reggie's car as he walked, and headed toward the two-story glassed entrance. Up the cascade of steps and into an atrium flooded with sunlight, he couldn't shake the gnawing in his gut as to why he was here. He could already hear Pastor Lyles's words—"I'm retiring." He just didn't know what he would do with them.

"Hey, Lance, look what I've got." Kara, on the women's ministry staff, approached with an iPad.

"Hey, Kara," Lance said. "What you got?"

Kara pulled it up on the iPad and showed him. "Isn't it beautiful?" she said, swiping pages.

"Treva's Promises of God study." He took in the page design, chapter titles—*If I Dwell, If I Trust*—Treva's name as author. "This is amazing. Has she seen it?"

"I got it in my inbox right before I saw you," Kara said. "I'm about to send it to Treva and Cyd to see what they think." She looked at him. "And you should know the whole team was in tears reading your foreword to the study."

"I was in tears writing it," Lance said. "Thinking about how God used Treva to minister to me through that promise while she was unconscious, fighting for her life . . ."

"Can I tell you a secret?" Kara moved closer. "When Treva films the teaching for the study, we're planning to have you talk about it with her, during the *If I Believe* segment." She smiled as she started off. "But only if you're willing."

Lance started toward the elevator. "You know I couldn't say no to that."

He rode to the third floor and made his way past several offices, walking into Pastor Lyles's outer office.

"Good morning, Lance," Ruth said. "Pastor said to tell you to go right in."

Lance smiled at the woman who'd served as the pastor's executive assistant for over a decade. "Good morning, Ruth, I see you brought donut holes just for me."

The older woman gave him a wry smile. "You're one of the few around here who doesn't eat donuts and such."

"Yeah," he said, "but I'm thinking it's just the kind of treat I'll need this morning."

Lance popped one into his mouth and walked into the pastor's office—and stopped short.

"Good morning," Pastor Lyles said, seated behind his desk.

"Good morning." Lance moved closer. "I've been dreading this, thinking you were going to announce your retirement. But it's . . . it's not that." He gathered himself as he walked around his desk, facing him. "You're sick."

"How can you know that?" Pastor Lyles said.

"I see it in your eyes." Lance had tears in his own now. "Used to see it day in and day out, taking care of Kendra. What's the diagnosis?"

"An aggressive form of prostate cancer. They gave me seven months, four months ago."

Lance felt himself wobble a little. "Oh, God . . ." He put his arms around the pastor's neck and allowed the tears to fall on his suit jacket. "When I saw you three weeks ago, I didn't see it . . ."

"It's progressing rapidly," Pastor Lyles said. "Plus all the treatments they keep pumping into me. Make anybody's eyes go bad."

Lance leaned against his desk, wiping his eyes. "So you've known since, late last year?"

"November," he said. "God's been gracious, giving me strength to take care of matters, so that the transition can hopefully go well."

"You seem resigned to this," Lance said.

"We've done the radical chemo and all of that," Pastor Lyles said. "My life is in God's hands, so that part I'm not worried about. What I'm feeling is an urgency to do what He moves me to do, while I've got strength to do it." He clasped his hands. "That's why you're here."

Lance nodded. "I know you wanted an update on Living Hope, where we are with replacing Randall as elder, and—"

"None of that is pressing," Pastor Lyles said. "Have a seat."

Lance took the chair opposite him and waited.

"I know you, son." Pastor Lyles looked into his eyes. "I know your fears, your insecurities, and your perceived weaknesses. You recounted them when I said you should step into the youth pastor position, and again when I asked you to lead the new church plant."

Lance frowned a little, wondering where this was going.

"So I already know what you're going to say," Pastor Lyles said.

"But here it is—I'm recommending that you replace me as pastor of Living Word church."

Lance looked at the pastor as if he'd lost his mind, then shook his head. "Pastor, I can't even believe you're saying that, but I'm sorry, it's an automatic no. It's not so much the insecurities and all that. God is blessing us at Living Hope. I thank God that you talked me past—and prayed me past—my fears about being the pastor there. I love the community we have. Love the spiritual growth God is bringing about. And I love that we're still small, just under three hundred. But this . . ." He spread his hands. "I couldn't even *think* about being pastor here." He looked at him. "What are *you* thinking?"

"I'm thinking that I want to obey God," Pastor Lyles said. "There's nothing I've prayed about more from the time of my diagnosis. None of this is optimal—clearly. If it were up to me, I'd know at least three years in advance when I would step down and put a long-range transition plan in motion. As it is, I have to trust that God will give us what we need since He *did* know in advance." He paused. "There's only one person He keeps spotlighting in my heart and mind as my replacement. You."

"I could name four pastors on staff here who would jump at this opportunity," Lance said. "Truly gifted men of God."

"So I should take your recommendation over God's?"

"So I should abandon the church plant you asked me to take?" Lance's voice was soft. "I should abandon the people who joined?"

"Lance, I would be concerned if you weren't concerned about the members of Living Hope." Pastor Lyles had his fatherly tone. "You have a shepherd's heart. That's one of the reasons people left here to join you—and by the way, they'd likely return with you. But in any case, you wouldn't be abandoning them. God would raise up someone to take your place." He leaned in a little. "Son, it's not your church—it's Jesus' church. We're all replaceable. I have no doubt that God would work all of that out."

"Why the urgency, though?" Lance said. "You could choose an interim pastor and Living Word could do a pastor search."

"That's not the direction God is giving," Pastor Lyles said. "And frankly I'm thankful for the opportunity to seek Him in this. I remember seeking Him long ago, when He put the thought in my mind to start this church. And I remember when He moved in my heart to start the prison ministry. Still remember the day I met Lance Alexander." Emotion filled his voice. "If you could only know how full my heart is, seeing it all go full circle . . ." He nodded to himself, looking down.

"Pastor, I—"

"And we could meet more regularly, every few days as far as I'm concerned, to prepare you." The pastor checked a calendar on his desk, as if ready to schedule him in. "You should begin preaching regularly here as well, so members can see you, since they'll have to vote. But I guess I'm getting ahead of myself. I'm asking that you pray earnestly about this. Pray about moving forward in this process."

Lance got up and paced the office, thinking through everything the pastor had said, then turned. "Respectfully, pastor," he said, "and you know I love you and my heart is breaking for what you're going through . . . I have to give the same answer. No."

∽

"This is such devastating news." Treva lifted the baby from the bassinet as he woke from a nap. "The thought of Pastor Lyles retiring was sad. This is heartbreaking. When will he tell the congregation?"

"He's calling a meeting for next week," Lance said.

"We need to be praying for Sister Gloria as well," Treva said. "I can't even imagine what she's going through."

"I'm praying he lives way past the doctors' predictions," Lance said. "I'm praying he gets to see what he'd always hoped for—a lengthy transition process for the next pastor of Living Word."

"Oh, so you *do* still pray." Treva laid Wes on a changing pad on the bed. "Because that was awesome, man of God. Didn't utter a single prayer about the pastor's request. Just—no."

Lance sat next to her on the bed. "Some things you just know, based on what God has already called you to do."

"And what has God called you to do?" Treva leaned into the baby and smiled as he laughed and kicked. "I see you, you little cutie . . ."

"He's called me to pastor Living Hope Church," Lance said.

"I thought he called you to the youth pastor position at Living Word."

"He did," Lance said, "for a season."

"Interesting." Treva put the baby's pants back on. "So the specifics can change season to season, while the primary calling remains the same—teaching, preaching, shepherding."

Lance gave her a look. "The season hasn't changed."

Treva laid the baby between them on the bed. "If I knew you were absolutely sure of that, I wouldn't say another word. I'm just wondering why you won't do what you always do—pray."

"Picture me as lead pastor of Living Word," Lance said. He waited only a beat. "If you're honest, you can't—because it's ridiculous."

"Wow," Treva said. "And why is that?"

"The thought of me as lead pastor of *any* church was ridiculous," Lance said. "Let's just acknowledge *that*. No seminary training. No college degree. *Dropped out of high school.*" He stood and started pacing. "So the high school dropout replaces the seminary-trained pastor who built a world-renowned ministry? 'Ridiculous' is the absolute first word to come to mind."

Treva stared at him. "Thank you."

"For what?"

"Admitting why you wouldn't pray about it." Treva played with

Wes's legs as he kicked. "It's what Pastor Lyles said—fear, insecurities, perceived weaknesses."

"It's actually not," Lance said. "God gives us wisdom to assess situations. Everything points toward continuing to serve as pastor at Living Hope. And I'm beyond joyful about it."

"So that's it then?" Treva said. "You won't pray about it?"

"Babe," Lance said, "how many ways can I say I already know the answer?"

"But you agree this is a dire situation," Treva said. "Pastor Lyles has a terminal diagnosis and wants to begin the process for selecting the next pastor. He believes God is pointing to you. You're saying no."

"It's absolutely dire," Lance said. "This church is close to his heart. He wants to be hands-on with the transition in the time he has remaining."

Treva nodded, picking up her phone.

"What are you doing?" Lance said.

"Calling for reinforcement."

Lance sat with Treva in their living room that evening, waiting as Cyd and Cedric took in the news about Pastor Lyles.

"I didn't see it," Cyd said, her head on Cedric's shoulder. "He told me he was stepping down, and I assumed it was retirement." She wiped tears. "Why did he wait so long to say something?"

"I don't know," Lance said. "And I feel bad because I'm sure he wanted to be the one to tell you." He looked over at Treva.

"I really wish I didn't have to call you two"—Treva returned Lance's look—"but Pastor Lyles's illness raises a pressing situation. And you're two of Lance's most trusted friends. Plus you've been part of Living Hope since before it started."

Cedric nodded. "We were doing weekly Bible studies right here in this living room. It grew from there."

"And Cyd," Treva said, "the fact that you've known Pastor Lyles and been part of Living Word for more than thirty years gives you unique insight—"

"Okay, what in the world is going on," Cyd said, "beyond the news you just shared?"

Treva looked at Lance.

Lance gave a sigh. "Pastor Lyles said he's been praying about who should replace him, and God keeps showing him me."

Both Cyd and Cedric's eyes widened.

"And Lance rejected it out of hand," Treva said. "Won't even pray about getting into the process."

"Because God has called me to Living Hope," Lance said.

Treva bumped his arm. "Admit to the rest, babe."

Lance gave her a look. "I said it would be ridiculous for a high school dropout to replace someone like Pastor Lyles—which is fact."

"So it's the same thing," Cedric said. "You said you couldn't do the Living Hope church plant because of your 'bio.'"

"How is it the same thing?" Lance said. "Filling Pastor Lyles's shoes takes it to an infinitely higher level." His eyes skimmed the three of them. "I want to know which of you is willing to be real with me. Admit it—Pastor Lyles's educational background made him uniquely qualified to do what he's done at Living Word."

"Wow," Cedric said. "That's practically blasphemous." He looked at Cyd. "Doesn't that sound blasphemous?"

"Totally," Cyd said.

"Please," Treva said, "speak on it."

Lance gave her the eye.

"Truth in love, babe." Treva kissed him.

"Lance," Cyd said, leaning forward, "Living Word isn't what it is today because Pastor Lyles went to seminary. Are you kidding? You and I both know lots of seminary grads—and a seminary degree doesn't equal giftedness." Her voice was earnest. "Living Word is what it is because God's hand has been on Pastor Lyles.

You know he'd tell you the same—it's nothing but the power of God, the blessing of God, and the grace of God."

"I don't know why you can't see how heavily God's hand rests on you, bro." Cedric focused on him. "And you act like you haven't put in the level of study equal to a *few* seminary degrees. When I look at your life and ministry, all I see is how *faithful* you've been to your calling. What did Jesus say? 'Well done, good and faithful servant. You were faithful with a few things—'"

"'I will put you in charge of many things,'" Treva added.

"But honestly," Lance said, "I'm content with the 'few'. I love what God is doing at Living Hope. I'm wrong if I want to stay there?"

"Might be nice if you ask God what He thinks you should do with *His* church," Cedric said.

"Can I just say what I think about all this, from the heart?" Cyd said.

Lance nodded. "I'd like to hear it."

"Growing up, Pastor Lyles made me fall in love with the word of God." Cyd's eyes seemed alive with the memory. "I could tell *he* loved it. And more than that, I could tell he loved the Lord. Just this deep love where he wasn't enamored with the growth of the church or the ministry, could not have cared less about the spot-light—they never could get him on social media. He just wanted to please God and shepherd the flock."

"So true," Lance said, nodding.

"I don't know if I've ever told you, Lance," Cyd said, "but you remind me so much of Pastor Lyles. Your deep love of the word and faithful preaching. Your deep love of Jesus and love for people. I can't even describe how blessed I've been to sit under you as my pastor for nearly three years. And the thought of you potentially taking Pastor Lyles's place . . ." She leaned in. "I'm asking you—pray with everything in you to know what God is saying." She paused. "And we're not leaving till we pray *with* you, to be sure some praying's going on."

Lance sat back, staring downward. "I'm overwhelmed by that."

Cedric stood and took Cyd's hand, bringing her up with him. Treva stood and took Cyd's hand, and reached for Lance's.

Lance took Treva's hand, rising, and kissed her. "I love you so much," he whispered.

"I love you more," Treva said.

Lance bowed his head as Cedric started them off in prayer.

CHAPTER 25

reva checked her phone as Lance lingered near the door with Cedric and Cyd went downstairs to get Chase. A few notifications appeared, but only one stood out—a missed call from Allison. Treva had sent text messages and left voicemails, but Allison hadn't responded, till now. She walked upstairs, dialing back—and was glad when Allison picked up.

"Treva, thanks for returning my call," Allison said.

"Thanks for returning mine," Treva said. "It's good to hear your voice, Allison. I've been worried about you."

"I wanted to call," Allison said, "because Lance left a couple of messages too, about my obligations as a church member and the need for marital counseling and restoration"—she sighed—"basically, I'm leaving Living Hope. I'll submit a letter, but I wanted to let you all know that you don't have to do the church thing and check up on me."

"Allison, I wasn't doing a church thing," Treva said. "I thought we were friends. I was reaching out to see what was going on and whether I could help. And I don't understand—you're leaving Living Hope?"

"I just can't with the oversight," Allison said. "I'm a grown woman."

Treva sat on her bed. "Allison, what happened? You don't seem like yourself. I remember you said you and Tommy were having a lot of conflicts and marriage wasn't what you'd anticipated—"

"Honestly? I made a mistake." Allison's voice seemed to soften. "I've thought about it and thought about it, and I know it sounds awful, but it's the truth. I shouldn't have gotten married. And in my mind it'd be worse to drag this out. I even looked into annulment to see if I could make a case."

"Where are you with God in all this, Allison?" Treva said. "Are you seeking Him, are you praying? I was in that Bible study with you. I heard your heart for God. We should sit down and talk, and pray together. Somehow the enemy's gotten hold—"

"I know you mean well, Treva," Allison said. "And I did enjoy those Bible studies—to a point. But the more we talked about the promises of God, the more I realized I wasn't seeing them unfold in my life. You wouldn't understand because you and Lance are the fairytale—everything is peaches and cream."

"Allison, I almost died a few months ago," Treva said. "And I was honest during that study about my struggles."

"You were struggling with being pregnant at forty-six," Allison said. "You weren't struggling with your marriage. You have no idea what this feels like. It got to the point where I'd wake up and all I could think was how much I missed the life I had before. The freedom to go and do and be. I'm an entrepreneur—I have an entrepreneur's spirit. I thrive on setting my own course."

"Allison, please listen to yourself," Treva said. "You said you'd wake up and 'all I could think was'—that's the enemy in your head, wanting you to be discontent, focus on self, dismiss the marriage vows you made before God. You know this isn't God's will for you." She felt a sadness inside. "And I had very real struggles in my first marriage—we could talk about that and how God showed up. But whether you talk to me isn't nearly as important as talking to Tommy—and to the Lord. I'm praying for you and Tommy, Allison. I truly believe you can get past this."

Several seconds passed. "I know I need to talk to Tommy," Allison said finally. "Despite my issues with him and our marriage, he has a really good heart. And I just . . . I don't want to hurt him."

"He's already hurt, Allison. Talking to him will at least put you on the road to healing."

"But if we talk, I'll feel like I need to tell him . . ." Allison let another few seconds elapse. "I've been with another man."

Treva hesitated. "You're saying in these last few months, since you got married?"

"Just recently," Allison said. "The guy I dated before Tommy. I didn't intend to. I needed a place to stay because I sold my condo before I got married, and he and I were still friends. It just . . . happened."

"Wow . . ." It took a moment for Treva to take that in. "Wait," she said, "I thought you've been out of town all this time. You've been here in St. Louis, with your ex?"

"For the past three weeks," Allison said. "I'm in the boutique at least a few hours a day, thankful for a very competent manager."

"I'm surprised you're telling me all this," Treva said.

"I guess I wanted to express how complicated this is," Allison said.

"But all things are possible with God, Allison—"

"Treva, I'm sorry, the promises are so cliché to me right now."

"And yet, they're true," Treva said. "Allison, there's hope. We can work through this. You know you have to leave this situation with your ex. Then just tell Tommy the truth. It'll be hard, but as the two of you look to God for grace and healing—"

"Treva, I'm not going back to Tommy," Allison said. "That's the conversation I've been avoiding."

Treva stared vaguely, feeling the weight of her words. "You

have to tell him, Allison. He's your husband. He deserves to know the truth."

Allison sighed. "You're right. I just have to do it. I'll drive over there tonight."

Treva walked downstairs, the conversation turning in her head, sadness grabbing hold as she pictured Allison and Tommy at their wedding last May. Could the enemy really wreak destruction so quickly? Bible verses went through her mind—about the devil's lies and schemes, how he prowls about like a roaring lion, seeking someone to devour, that he comes only to steal, kill, and destroy. But to see it happening in real time before her eyes . . .

She paused before she reached the kitchen, a sudden urge to pray. God was more powerful. Despite what Allison said, it wasn't over yet.

~

"So I've got a job possibility."

Treva looked as Jillian came into the kitchen the next morning. Her heart heavy still, she'd been praying as she cooked breakfast, wondering if Allison had followed through. She suspected she had, since Lance had taken a call before dawn, but it could've been from anyone in the congregation.

"That's awesome news," Treva said. "Doing what?"

Jillian sat on a bar stool. "I talked to Cyd when she was here last night. She said they need a copy editor on staff for the new women's ministry, for everything from books to online content." She checked a notification on her phone and replied. "Said she thought of me because of a conversation we had about the English coursework I do with the kids."

"Okay, that's *really* awesome," Treva said, "because you'd love the content itself."

"Exactly," Jillian said. "And it would be amazing to work for Living Word Ministries after years of doing the Bible studies. I don't know what it pays; I may need a second job. But she's going to set up an interview for me to meet with people on the team, and they're sending sample content to edit, sort of as a test."

Treva flipped french toast on the griddle. "You'll blow that away. I used to be mad whenever you'd look at something I wrote, because I'd think it was good and you'd mark it up—and make it better."

"Nobody likes that red pen," Jillian said, "or these days, track changes. The kids complain every time."

"Have you FaceTimed them this morning?"

"You know I did." Jillian showed her phone. "And texting back and forth right now." She paused. "This weekend is two weeks already, and I'm still torn about the arrangement. I miss things like dinnertime, catching up on the day, hearing their heart before bed—which is especially important now. I want to stay on top of how they're handling their grief and where they are emotionally."

"What's the sense you're getting as you talk to them?" Treva said.

"They're all handling it so differently," Jillian said. "Sophie doesn't always want to talk about her grief, but she'll text a sad face or a face with a single tear, and I'll just stop and pray."

"That's making me so sad right now," Treva said.

"And almost every night Trevor will say, 'Mom, remember when . . .' And it's a story about Cecil, and I love that he's so comforted by the memories, though I'm always in tears and hoping my voice doesn't show it." Jillian took a breath even now. "And David's never been one to really share how he's feeling, but he sent me his argumentative essay yesterday. It was supposed to be about time spent on smartphones—that's the prompt he'd chosen a little over two weeks ago. But he'd changed it to whether buying and accumulating more stuff makes you happier." She paused again, her fingers stemming the tears. "Whole essay was basically about his dad taking a lower paying job in ministry, knowing he'd have to downsize and live off of less—and David said it was one of the happiest times in his dad's life."

Treva cut off the griddle and went to sit beside her.

"And then Courtenay . . ." Jillian looked at Treva. "She told me the other day she felt bad because she hadn't talked to her dad as much these past few months. I told her she's away at school, of course Cecil understood. But she was upset and kept saying she should've stayed in better touch." She paused, looking at a new text message. "And then there's this"—Jillian wiped her face as she showed Treva—"David taking a selfie in front of the flat screen in his room, saying he's never leaving Grandma Patsy's."

"And loving that he's in that room by himself," Treva said.

"Oh, he and Trevor both," Jillian said. "First time they've had their own rooms. I'll have to pry them away."

Treva looked at her sister. "So how are *you* doing?"

Jillian stared downward. "I wake up in the night and reach for him." She let several seconds lapse. "And having one toothbrush in the bathroom and one set of towels . . ."

Treva stood and brought Jillian close as she wept.

"In some ways," Jillian said, "I'm glad to be out of the house. I can't imagine having to face the same routines . . . expecting him to walk into the kitchen . . ."

Treva nodded, remembering what that was like. The pain had seemed unbearable.

"I got a journal, though." Jillian took her time, wiping her face with a napkin. "This morning was one of those times I woke up feeling angry, and I just wrote it all down . . . asking God, *why?*" She looked at Treva. "I know God loves us and cares about us—I know that. But there are moments when it doesn't *feel* like it."

"I know," Treva said. "I had a lot of those—"

"Mom, is breakfast ready?" Hope came into the kitchen. "I was waiting for you to call us."

"Sorry, sweetie," Treva said. "It's ready. And we're still good on time. You and Joy can eat then I'll take you to school."

"Joy, come eat," Hope called. She got her plate. "Mom, don't forget I'm going to Anna's after school."

"Is the sleepover still on at Haley's tomorrow?" Treva poured the girls some juice.

Hope glanced at her as she buttered her french toast. "Why wouldn't it be?"

"Because two weeks ago when you were supposed to go over there," Treva said, "something happened and suddenly she wasn't your friend anymore."

"Mom, we got over that by the next day," Hope said.

"We need to leave in ten minutes," Joy said, breezing into the kitchen. "I'm meeting up with Lindsey before school."

"Let me put my shoes on," Treva said, "and see if Lance needs me to take Wes." She paused on her way out of the kitchen, looking at Jillian. "Something with one of the kids?"

Jillian looked up from her phone, brow furrowed. "It's Tommy." She showed Treva the text.

No South Hill in STL...maybe Forest Park will do.

"I don't understand," Treva said.

"South Hill was where we went on campus when things got hard," Jillian said. "He hasn't wanted to talk about his situation thus far. Something must've happened."

CHAPTER 26

*J*illian walked with Tommy across a mini-bridge in Forest Park, then along a path that wound around a water basin filled with spraying fountains. Spring had newly arrived and with it, budding trees, fragrant flowers, and a slight chill. Glad she'd brought a jacket, Jillian put it on now, glancing over at Tommy. He'd hardly said a word, and she was resolved not to ask. If he only needed her presence, that's what she'd give.

Tommy stopped by the water, watching a paddleboat move up stream. "We haven't really been friends as adults," he said.

Jillian looked at him. "We weren't adults in college?"

"Technically, at some point," Tommy said, "but I'm not counting that. I'm saying after college, with you dating and marrying Cecil and me moving away . . . the friendship faded. Which was cool," he added. "It fit the season we were in, then it no longer fit."

"Then *twenty years* go by"—Jillian shook her head at that—"and I come to St. Louis for a women's conference. We fell right back in the flow." She looked at him. "I thought the friendship was back on."

"I did too." Tommy began walking again. "But when you had that marriage issue and Cecil wasn't happy about us being confidantes—I could totally feel him on that—I knew we had to back off the friendship."

"Still, I couldn't believe you cut it off," Jillian said. "It made me cling to Jesus, which you knew I needed. But we had just reconnected—I had my brother again—and you were like, *I'm out*. I shed some tears."

"That's because of everything you were dealing with," Tommy said. "It probably felt like a double blow."

"It *was* a double blow," Jillian said. "You left me hanging, in my hour of great need."

Tommy gave her a look. "You always had a flair for the dramatic." He focused on the pathway. "Anyway, I was thinking about all this around seven this morning. In a season filled with chaos, maybe the friendship finally fits once again."

Jillian thought about that. "And it would be so much more," she said. "We weren't praying for one another back then or speaking real truth to one another." She paused. "But wait, it still doesn't fit. Before, we had to cut it off because of Cecil. Now there's Allison."

Tommy paused again, under a clump of trees. "Allison said she's not coming back."

Jillian looked at him. "When did she tell you this?"

"Last night. She's living with her ex."

"Oh, Tommy . . ."

He walked again. "I did all the crying late last night. And all the crying out to God. Talked to Lance at five, Cedric at six. More tears over breakfast, telling Reggie. So I'm not going there right now with the emotion. I just—"

Jillian tugged his jacket, moving him to a stop. Her eyes filled as she hugged him. "I'm so sorry you're going through this. I know it's incredibly painful. It's a very real grief."

"Something's wrong with me, Jill." Tommy's chest heaved. "That's two marriages. Total fail. I can't get it right."

"That's where you're not going." Jillian looked at him. "You're the one who's been home, praying and waiting, asking God to move in your marriage."

"But she wouldn't have left in the first place," Tommy said, "if she hadn't been dissatisfied. I want to be angry with her, but I still love her. I still want my marriage." He gave a hard sigh. "So many things I wish I could do over."

"You could do everything over and she could still leave—because of *her* issues. So stop beating yourself up." Jillian looked into his eyes. "The productive thing to do is to fight for your marriage in prayer."

"What do you think I've been doing?" Tommy said. "Now she's living with *another man*." He threw up his hands. "Seriously, am I a punk? Is this the Regina thing all over again?"

"Oh, goodness, stop it," Jillian said. "This is *marriage*. Sacred. Vows. Being one before God. Praise God you have a heart to fight for your marriage, Tommy. *Keep fighting*. God can still do miracles." She started walking with him again. "And this is where our renewed friendship kicks in. I'll fight in prayer with you—for your marriage and against the self-pity—I'll even add a kick in the pants for the latter one."

Tommy walked in silence for a while, then looked at her. "Man, Jill . . . We would've never thought we'd be here. Both of us grieving."

"We wouldn't have thought we'd be *here* either—both of us loving Jesus, both of us believing in the power of prayer, both of us standing on His promises."

"Look at you," Tommy said, "trying to operate in some strength."

"It's moment to moment for me," Jillian said. "This morning was really hard. Well, some part of every day has been really hard. But my old cantankerous best friend reminded me I could get through the mourning and everything else . . . with God."

Tommy sighed. "Amen."

∾

"You're seriously saying yes, Aunt Jillian? You'll be my wedding coordinator?"

"As long as you understand I'm only an amateur." Jillian spoke above the chatter in the Mexican restaurant. "But I love helping with events, and you said it won't be too big. So hopefully I won't be over my head. It should be fun."

"Well, cool," Reggie said. "Wedding coordinator and best man checked off in the space of ten minutes."

"I might be a little emotional about you giving me that honor," Tommy said. "Standing up for my baby brother. I remember changing your diapers."

"And I remember changing Faith's," Jillian said.

"Okay, really?" Faith said, eyeing them both.

"Sorry," Jillian said. "We've been in reminisce mode all day. Helps to escape from all the . . . you know."

"Hey, if it helps, *please* reminisce," Reggie said. "With everything you've both been dealing with? You can pull out our baby pictures, embarrassing video—"

"What about your old poetry notebook?" Tommy said.

"That's going a little too far," Reggie said.

Faith smiled at Reggie. "You told me about that. I'd love to see it."

"Sounds like someone might be writing his own vows," Jillian said.

"We haven't talked about that," Reggie said, turning to Faith. "But a chance to speak from the heart about my commitment to *this* woman? I already know my answer."

Faith leaned over and kissed him. "I actually, completely love you."

"You putting that in your vows?" Reggie said.

"It's not a vow," Faith said. "It's a statement."

"You could vow to actually, completely love me for all of our days, even when I act a fool."

"I don't know if I'm promising all that," Faith said.

Reggie nudged her.

The server stopped on her way to another table. "Just checking—you all are still okay?"

"We're good, thanks," Jillian said. They'd finished dinner and lingered with the remaining chips. She looked at Faith as the server walked away. "So you've got graduation in two months, wedding in September, you're looking for a job, soon looking for a place to live . . ."

"I need a life coordinator," Faith said. "At least I know I'm staying in St. Louis."

"You guys can take your time looking for a place to live," Tommy said, "and save money while you're at it. Just move into the house, Faith. There's plenty of room."

"That's what I told her," Reggie said. "You know I'm all about saving a buck."

"You have no idea what you're saying, Tommy." Faith took some chips from the basket. "You're not ready for toddler life."

"I'll take Zoe and two more if you got 'em," Tommy said. "The more distraction the better."

Jillian knew he meant it. After the park they'd gone to lunch, a matinee to see a superhero movie, and Home Depot, because he suddenly needed all the fix-it items he'd put off getting for the past year. Then, unwilling to go home just yet, he'd called Reggie and set up dinner.

"So Faith and I were talking earlier," Reggie said, "and we've got a question for you two."

Faith hit his arm. "We do not have a question for them. That was between us."

"You have to say it now," Tommy said. "What's up?"

"We were wondering," Reggie said, "why the two of you never dated. At least, you *say* you never dated."

"It's true," Jillian said. "Never."

"It's just kind of odd," Faith said. "You obviously click. Aunt Jillian is beautiful. And Tommy, all I'll say is you're Reggie's brother, you favor each other, and my fiancé is dreamy. So . . . what's the deal?"

Jillian and Tommy looked at one another.

"I'm not even sure how to answer that," Jillian said. "You want to take the first stab at it, Tommy?"

"So we ended up in the same English class," Tommy said, "two young freshmen. And of course I'm like, 'who is that?' because she really was pretty—especially when she cleaned up and combed her hair."

"Whatever," Jillian said.

"But I was dating this girl I'd been with since high school," Tommy continued. "So I wasn't trying to get with Jill, at least not like that. I hit her up for help with my papers."

"And when Tommy and his girlfriend broke up," Jillian said, "I was seeing someone. By then Tommy and I had this rhythm where we hung out and could talk about *any*thing, so we became each other's go-to for advice."

"What about Mom?" Faith said. "Wasn't she on campus?"

"She was two years ahead," Jillian said, "and still dealing with junk from the past. Treva was laser focused on excelling in school, needing to prove herself. Until she met your dad—then she was laser focused on school and Hezekiah. Tommy was my day-to-day buddy."

"So you've got this day-to-day rhythm," Reggie said, "you can talk about anything . . ." He made a face at Tommy. "Bruh, you weren't ever like, let me see where *else* this can go?"

"Seemed like one or both of us was always in a relationship,"

Tommy said, "and always some kind of drama in the relationship. Our friendship was an oasis from the drama. That's not to say we didn't go at it sometimes—but Jilli-Jill was my homie. We could kick it and know things would be simple and uncomplicated." He shook his head. "I *knew* where else it could go—someplace that would mess all of that up."

"Plus at one point I dated one of your boys," Jillian said. "Dating Tommy after that—not happening. But I do have this one memory."

Faith leaned in with a smile. "What?"

"Finals week," Jillian said. "Up late studying, loopy from no sleep—"

"Which time?" Tommy said.

"I think fall semester senior year," Jillian said. "We got to laughing about something silly, and I remember this thought sliding into my mind—*what if?* But that thing was gone a second later."

Faith and Reggie gave one another the eye.

"Riight," Reggie said, "a second later."

"You two are funny," Jillian said. "I know you'd love to find some deep, underlying current of *something*, but that's our story."

"And you're sticking with it," Reggie said. "Hey, mad props to your dedication."

Jillian shook her head, looking at Tommy. "Your brother is crazy."

Tommy signed the bill. "Glad you're finally getting to know the young fellow."

They walked out of the downtown Clayton restaurant to a parking garage, where they hopped into separate cars.

Tommy pulled out of the space. "Dessert?"

Jillian checked notifications on her phone. "You're dropping me off, then you're going home."

"Everything closes in on me at home," Tommy said. "When I think about the fact that my wife is somewhere in this city, living with another man . . ." He looked at her. "My *wife*. I've never felt anything like this."

She looked at him, the pain in his eyes. "Turn on this next street and park."

"What for?"

Jillian nodded, resolved. "We need to do some fighting."

CHAPTER 27

APRIL

*C*inda leafed through two racks of clothing in her lower level studio, trying to find the tailored jacket she had in mind for a pair of distressed jeans. "Where is it?" she muttered, flipping faster now through a range of colors and fabrics. Then she spotted it—the garment bag hanging on a third rack across the room. How could she forget she'd already packed her preferred pieces?

She groaned, wondering how she would get a handle on all the elements that needed to come together by five in the morning. When she'd agreed to handle Kelsey's magazine shoot, she'd had an idea what it would entail, having styled Alonzo for two during awards season. But he didn't need hair accessories and glittery bracelets and an assortment of pumps, booties, and stilettos. Today alone she'd been to several showrooms, searching for drop earrings to set off a Miu Miu dress, a choker she'd envisioned for a street look, and sunglasses to fit not only Kelsey's face but the mood they were after.

Cinda moved to her table of accessories, fifteen pairs of shades staring back at her, when she heard Kelsey's ring tone.

"You're on your way?" Cinda had her on speaker as she lifted one of the necklaces.

"I got held up," Kelsey said, "and you won't believe the reason. Just left my management team. I'm actually the first choice to play Alonzo's sister in *Greater Glory*. Girl, my first movie role."

Cinda beamed. She hadn't told her it was a possibility in case it didn't work out. "Is this magazine shoot timely or what?" she said. "Soon you won't be 'breaking through'—you'll *be* there. I'm too excited for you. And not bad, when your first movie's got Shane directing."

"*Yes*," Kelsey said. "I love Shane's work. *And* I get to be in a movie with Alonzo? I feel silly fan-girling around you, but girl, I'm sorry—it's Alonzo Coles." She chuckled. "This is my own personal dream team."

"Alonzo's a fan of your work as well," Cinda said. "Shane too. So they benefit from having *you* on the project." She held the choker to the tailored jacket. "But first things first. I need to see some things on you before the shoot, and time is winding down."

"Okay, be there in about an hour," Kelsey said.

Cinda opened two suitcases and began packing shoes and accessories that Kelsey wouldn't need to try on. Wasn't hard to see why stylists needed assistants. Cinda had thought she'd have to have several clients before that kicked in, but—

"Hey, baby."

Cinda turned. "I didn't know you were home." She walked over to Alonzo. "See, I remembered what's first." She put her arms around him and kissed him, then stepped back, searching his downcast eyes. "What's wrong?"

Alonzo came further into the studio. "Had a difficult meeting with Shane."

Cinda waited, looking at him.

"Remember I said we needed to be praying about this *Greater*

Glory project?" At her nod Alonzo continued. "I had some concerns when I read through the screenplay and talked to Shane about a week ago, to see if we could work through them and move on."

"What concerned you?" Cinda said.

Alonzo rested on the leather love seat. "Okay, so my character is supposed to be devoted to the Lord," he said. "He's reluctant to take up the call to ministry but in the midst of all that's going on, he's the beacon of light."

"Right," Cinda said, sitting next to him. "That's what Shane said the night he told us about it."

"So we see him confronting issues in the church," Alonzo continued. "We see him confronting his pastor father for cheating on his mother—because adultery is the *big* sin." He paused. "And at night we see him and his girlfriend in bed—repeatedly." He looked at Cinda. "Like, no big deal. No grappling with it. No acknowledgement that this is contrary to how he should be living. Basically, no different than other movies I've been in."

"And that's what you talked to Shane about a week ago?" Cinda said.

Alonzo nodded. "He said they're keeping it real about what happens in the church. And yeah, of course it happens—but you can't make dude the devoted beacon of light while he's single and hopping in and out of bed. So I said, how about this?" His voice got animated. "Show him living like that to begin with, and while he's confronting everyone else, he's forced to take a close look at himself. Somebody speaks truth into his situation. He's convicted. He turns from it. Now you're really 'keeping it real' by showing our weakness as humans and the power of God to change a life."

"So they're considering that change?" Cinda said.

"They rejected that change," Alonzo said. "That's what Shane told me today. The producers want to play up the romance between my character and his girlfriend. They said to suggest that sex is somehow wrong for two single people—they're not willing to go there." He shook his head. "We keep telling the same Christian caricature stories."

Cinda frowned a little. "I'm not sure what you mean."

"Christian life is all about Sunday at church—choir on point, clothes on point, lingo on point—'bless the Lord' and 'God is good all the time'—but no real power at work in people's lives."

"Well, when this movie does well," Cinda said, "you'll show Hollywood once again that people will pay to see a movie with Christian themes. Then you can do another one with a deeper message."

Alonzo looked at her. "That's basically what Shane said."

"It's a valid point, Zee," Cinda said. "Sometimes change is incremental. You've got a project on the table that at least deals with exposing corruption in the church and the pastor's ways—"

"Then the son becomes the new pastor, living with his girlfriend."

"My point is," Cinda said, "there are good things in the movie, and the movie's got a green light. I think you should finalize the deal and—"

"Cinda, I turned it down." Alonzo looked at her. "They want to bill it as a 'Christian' movie so they can get churchgoers into the theater, and this is the message? I'd rather do another action movie than be part of something like this."

Cinda stared at him. "I can't believe you actually turned it down. Everybody assumes you're doing it, especially after one site ran the story about you being the top pick—and the perfect pick—for the role. And your management team said this was what you needed right now."

"I know," Alonzo said. "But remember when you prayed with me about whether to accept the other movie? I felt God was telling me to turn it down, and you encouraged me, told me to trust that He'd make my path straight." He shifted more toward her. "In the meeting with Shane today, I heard so clearly—turn it down, trust God. I knew that's what I had to do."

Cinda got up with a sigh. "I have to be honest . . . I'm disappointed. Kelsey called a little bit ago, excited about the project. And it was exciting to think about the two of you starring in this together, with all the fun of styling photo shoots and what not. Plus you know Shane was trying to get me on the costume design team." She looked at him. "Are you sure you're hearing right? Because what if—just what if you're being a little over the top with this?"

Alonzo looked at her. "Are you serious? That's what you think?"

"I'm just saying," Cinda said. "Kelsey's a Christian and she's on board. Gospel artists are coming on board. Two nationally known pastors are serving as advisors to the movie." She paused. "You're the only one who has a problem with it."

Alonzo stood, nodding to himself. "So my wife is in the 'Alonzo's too Christian' camp. By the way, Shane said the same thing— I'm over the top. 'Lighten up. It's just a movie.'"

"That's not fair," Cinda said. "You know I'm not in that camp."

"Do I? Not based on what you just said." Alonzo looked at her. "Did you even hear me when I said I heard clearly from God to turn it down? Or were you just focused on what it would mean for you?"

Alonzo left the studio and headed for the stairs.

"Zee," Cinda said, going after him. "Don't leave upset like that." She reached for his hand. "What's first?"

He stared into her eyes for several seconds, then turned and headed up the stairs. "This is the week we were supposed to be in St. Louis," he said. "I'm going with that plan B you suggested— booking a flight out tonight."

CHAPTER 28

*J*ordyn sat on a stool before her brightly lit vanity table, dabbing an eyelid with the pad of a finger. "As always you want to start off by priming your eyes, which helps your eye shadows last throughout the day." Her finger moved to the other lid. "My favorite is this Mac smudge proof primer"—she held it up—"I'll have the link in the description box. But I love this one because—"

"Wow, a makeup vid." Jade walked into her room. "You're still doing those?"

Jordyn clicked off her camera. "I don't have a lot of time, so . . ."

"You must be happy about that video you did with Jesse." Jade sat on her bed. "With all the views, looks like people find it really touching."

Jordyn shook her head. "I can't believe you'd even bring up his name."

"You're the one who can't seem to talk about him without getting upset," Jade said.

Jordyn swiveled around. "It's not talking about him that gets me upset," she said. "It's talking about how you lied about sleeping with him."

"I actually did sleep with him."

"You know what I—" Jordyn sighed, swiveling back around. "Can you just go so I can finish this?"

"I'm assuming all the Christian video stuff is out of your system," Jade said. "I know it was payback for the two I did, so we're even."

Jordyn turned back. "You inspired me, that's for sure. But I'm not doing it as payback. It's helping me personally, and I'm hoping it's helping others."

"It's also helping to dilute our brand," Jade said.

"Did you think about that when you were so bent on doing that Alonzo video?" Jordyn said.

"That's actually within our brand," Jade said. "We've been doing entertainment videos for over a year. It's the Christian stuff that's way off."

"I see it as a natural flow," Jordyn said. "You did a video attacking Alonzo's faith, then another that piled on. I followed up with videos that explain that faith." She shrugged. "It's actually expanding the brand. We've got new subscribers who appreciate the Christian content."

Jade looked at her. "All I'm saying is—you need to be done."

"That's interesting," Jordyn said, "since I'm just getting started." She sighed. "I'm not trying to get into another fight, but I won't let you bully me either. The fact is—I'd start my own channel if we didn't have so much tied to this one. As it is, I'm moved to do a whole series based on the response Jesse's video has gotten."

Jade rolled her eyes. "You're 'moved' to do it? You've been around these church folk too long. Or you've morphed into dad."

Jordyn turned her words over, savoring them. If she was becoming more like Randall, she just might be on the right track.

~

"I had no idea that's why you wanted me to come by." Jordyn sat in the B and B's sitting room with Stephanie and Faith. "And Cyd set this up?"

Stephanie nodded. "She really wanted you to have some place to go, even if just for peace of mind. I'm pretty much always here, and Cinda's old room is just sitting there."

Jordyn couldn't help but remember that Cyd had offered their guest bedroom first. She wondered if Cedric had had something to do with the switch. He'd been extra reserved since her comment in the car. She still couldn't believe she'd told him he was fine. But truth was, she'd been thinking it. And in hindsight, it scared her. She was glad he'd shut down the conversation.

"As long as you don't expect me to clean like Cinda did," Jordyn said.

"Girl, I wish," Stephanie said. "Been using a cleaning service, but this place hasn't been the same since she left."

"And Cinda was supposed to be here this week," Faith said. "I told her I'm still bummed she had to work."

"Alonzo decided to come still," Stephanie said.

"Really?" Faith said.

"Called a little while ago," Stephanie said, "making sure the room was still available. His flight gets in late tonight. Lindell's picking him up."

"I remember the first time I came over here," Jordyn said, "when Jade and I took Cinda's picture to 'expose' her as a maid." She shook her head at herself. "We had to be your least favorite people. And here you are now, opening your home." She focused on Stephanie. "I don't expect to be here much at all, but I really appreciate it."

"This place gets kind of addicting, though," Faith said. "I'm trying to figure out why Steph hasn't given me a room, much as I'm here."

"Girl, you're not here nearly as much as you used to be," Stephanie said. "I'm surprised you're not with Reggie right now."

"He had to work late," Faith said.

"Ha," Stephanie said.

"Faith, I hadn't had a chance to ask you . . ." Jordyn hesitated. "I don't know if you've seen the video with Jesse yet. I hope it didn't make you uncomfortable."

"I appreciated the heads-up after the filming," Faith said. "I don't know if it made me uncomfortable. Just . . . a little sad."

"About the broken heart?" Stephanie said.

Faith nodded. "Which is crazy because he definitely broke mine. But I don't revel in the fact that he got hurt too. You know? Ugghhh. Life."

"Watching that video, you just know Jesus is real," Stephanie said. "Just flat out change-your-life *real*. I had to give Jesse a hug at church on Sunday."

"I'm glad you did the video," Faith said. "It's not about me and my comfort level. I read some of the comments, and it's making an impact."

Jordyn pondered whether to ask the other thing on her mind. "Faith, I have another question, or comment—not sure what to call it, but it's really awkward."

Faith looked at her. "I'm the last person you need to be awkward with. What is it?"

"It's just . . . I guess I could say I have a crush on Jesse," Jordyn said. "And I didn't want to and he doesn't know and totally doesn't feel the same, but it's weird and probably wrong given that the two of you—"

"How could it be wrong?" Faith said. "I'm engaged to Reggie."

"But your heart was tied to Jesse for a while," Jordyn said, "and of course, you've got Zoe. And we're part of the same circle, and it just seems like something you don't do—not that there's anything to *do*. Like I said, there's nothing to it. I just felt like I needed to clear my conscience or something."

"Jordyn, seriously," Faith said, "don't give it another—"

"And look at that," Stephanie said as the front door opened and closed. "The man himself."

"Who, Jesse?" Jordyn whispered.

"He's dropping Zoe off here," Faith said.

Zoe beat him to the sitting room, motoring around the corner with a big smile. "Mama-mama . . ."

Faith picked her up. "There's my sweet girl." She hugged her tight and kissed her. "Did you have a good time—"

"Juice, mama," Zoe said. "Juice."

"Zoe, you know we're not drinking a lot of—"

"I may have promised her," Jesse said, coming into the room.

Jordyn gave him a glance then focused on Zoe.

"You know how it is when she wants something and gives you that look," Jesse said.

Faith raised a brow at him. "I know she's got her daddy wrapped around her little finger."

"Mama, juice. *Juice.*"

"I can take her to the kitchen to get some," Jordyn said, moving toward Faith.

"Thanks," Faith said, "but it's fine, I'll take her."

"I'll go with y'all"—Stephanie gave Jordyn a knowing glance —"to show you the *milk* that's in there too."

"*Juice,*" Zoe said.

"Little girl, don't be getting fresh with Aunt Stephy." Stephanie reached over and tickled her as they left.

"So you're back to avoiding me, Jordyn?" Jesse said.

She looked at him. "I don't know what you mean."

"After you saw me in your apartment, you steered clear of me at church." Jesse shrugged. "I get that. But you avoided me this past Sunday, after all the sharing. And just now you wanted out of the room. Something I said?"

Jordyn looked away as she gathered her thoughts. "No." Her eyes found their way back to his. "It was just, something about the filming opened up all of that, and afterward, when I thought about all I'd told you . . ."

Jesse looked at her. "What?"

"Clearly you had to have a low opinion of me," Jordyn said.

"You're saying that, given all the stuff you know about me?" Jesse said. "And we went beyond what I shared in the video."

"It's not the same," Jordyn said. "And you weren't involved with someone who's married."

"So we're comparing who's more messed up?" Jesse said. "Let's just call it a tie."

"See, you can joke about it," Jordyn said, "but I couldn't sleep .. . thinking what you must think of me."

"I wasn't joking," Jesse said. "And why would you care what I think? But if you wanted to know, you could have asked."

Jordyn's heart rate ticked up. "As blunt as you are? No, thanks."

Jesse looked at her. "You really think I have a low opinion of you?"

"I don't even know how we got on this," Jordyn said, "but I have to go." She got her bag from the sofa. "If you could tell Stephanie—"

Jesse caught her arm as she passed. "Despite all the sharing we did, there's something you're not saying. You want to go somewhere and talk?"

~

Jordyn sat with Jesse at a table for two in the student union, after going with him to the campus library to pick up some books. With steaming cups of coffee, they lingered mostly in silence amid the chatter of nearby students.

"I thought you wanted to talk," Jordyn said.

"I said there was something you weren't saying." Jesse blew steam from his coffee and took a sip. "So I'm waiting for you. Unless . . . was I wrong?"

"Why do you think there's something I'm not saying?" Jordyn said.

"Because after sharing as much as we did, we should be really cool," Jesse said. "Might even say, friends. Instead, you're avoiding me and can't sleep because of what I supposedly think of you? What's the deal, Jordyn?"

Her heart beat out of her chest. Should she just *say* it? "So you know most of my relationships have been . . . not too deep. As in, mostly physical. Not a lot of talk about 'feelings' because it's understood that's not what it's about."

Jesse nodded. "I know exactly how that is."

"And it's not often that I feel anything, and when I do, it's wrong, like . . . with that guy who was married." Jordyn sighed. "So I don't say this with anything attached to it, definitely zero expectation. But since you asked and the worst that can happen is I'll just keep avoiding you—"

"Jordyn. Please try it. Be blunt."

She took a breath. "It's just . . ." She took another breath. "I like you. Okay."

"You made that as gray as possible," Jesse said. "I like you too, Jordyn. I like my dog Lancelot. I like this student union, with all the food choices. I really like our church—"

"I *like* you," Jordyn said. "Crush type of like."

"I thought that's what it might be," Jesse said.

"Then why'd you make me spell it out?"

"I wasn't *certain* that's what it was," Jesse said.

"So that's all you have to say—I thought so?"

Jesse sipped some coffee. "I *like* you too, Jordyn. Semi-crush type of like."

"Why do I feel like you're patting me on the head like Lancelot?" Jordyn said.

"You know this is new for me," Jesse said. "I want to respect you by being up front from the get-go."

"So what does 'semi-crush' mean?" Jordyn said.

"It means my head isn't in a space where I can even think about a potential relationship," Jesse said. "Otherwise, it would be a 'crush'—although, I've never used that word. I'd just be working some angle to get you in bed." He paused. "You know what I'm saying—in the past, that's the angle I'd be working."

Jordyn pondered his words for a moment. "I'm actually surprised. I wouldn't have thought 'semi' even. You hardly pay me any attention."

"Again, it's my current head space," Jesse said. "And we know the heart I'm dealing with. So it was nothing personal. I wasn't paying anybody any attention."

"Until Jade."

"Don't even go there," Jesse said. "But at my apartment with the filming and the way we talked after . . . Whole new experience for me, in terms of connection. And hearing your story . . ."

Jordyn braced herself for the rest.

"You were in tears as you shared that," Jesse said. "How could I have a low opinion of you? You were clearly broken and talked about how you'd asked God for forgiveness and wanted a different kind of future." He paused. "So after all that, yeah, you were on my mind."

"That's pretty gray," Jordyn said. "I bet your classes are on your mind, Lancelot's on your mind—gotta go home and walk him, your to-do list—"

"You were on my mind in a Jordyn is really cute, tender heart, dope body—sorry, I still notice—*why am I feeling her?* type of way."

Jordyn was sure her face turned red. "Well, thanks for returning to blunt."

"But like I said—"

"You can't think about a potential relationship," Jordyn said. "Which makes all the sense in the world anyway. You'll be gone in less than two months."

Jesse focused on her. "It's on you, Jordyn. Are we avoiding each other till the end of May . . . or do two messed up people see about cultivating a friendship?"

CHAPTER 29

"*I* actually do know what it's about, but I can't really say." Cyd moved around her office, packing books and papers to take home. "But the meeting's in a matter of hours, Dana. Everybody will know soon enough."

"Remember the last time we had an all-member alert like this?" Dana said. "The pastor was starting that series on sexual sin, after he learned of Scott's affair."

"Girl, how could I ever forget?" Cyd said. "It seems like yesterday." She'd been with Dana when Dana caught her husband in bed with another woman. As co-leaders of the marriage ministry, Dana and Scott's ordeal played out publicly. "We had one service that Sunday, and it was *packed*. I loved the way the pastor handled it. So much grace and love."

Dana sighed. "I've been thinking about so many memories over the years, all the impact he's made. We've been part of Pastor Lyles's ministry since we were what, thirteen? And now all this talk that he's stepping down."

Cyd felt the sadness, wishing that's all it was. "Think about the impact he made on us as young people especially," she said. "The church was too small for separate youth group services. We just

185

sat under him, and actually loved it. Were we weird?" She chuckled.

"It just speaks to the kind of pastor he's been," Dana said, "which is why I'm worried what will happen if he steps down. I'm hearing this other rumor . . ."

"What's that?" Cyd said.

"A few people on staff are whispering that Pastor Lyles will recommend Lance to take his place," Dana said. "I'm sorry, but if that's true, I don't agree with that choice at all. Even you'd have to admit he's not a good fit for lead pastor at Living Word."

Cyd paused in the middle of her office. "Even *I'd* have to admit?"

"I know you and Cedric are good friends with Lance," Dana said, "and you left to join him at Living Hope. But honestly, Living Hope is where he should stay. The two churches have a totally different vibe."

Cyd blew out a silent breath. "Let me guess your first point —dress."

"It's not a factor?" Dana said. "Lance has that casual aesthetic, along with all the mostly young people who go there. Pastor Lyles is always suited, which to me, shows respect for the service."

"So Lance is disrespectful."

Dana sighed. "Every time we talk about the two churches, you get an attitude. If you want to know the truth, I don't think our friendship has been the same since you left to join Living Hope."

"I don't think it has anything to do with my leaving," Cyd said. "It's the comments you've made about Lance and our church. Yet, you've never once visited. Have you even heard him preach?"

"At the women's conference," Dana said, "and you know I think he's gifted. No doubt about that. But that's a far cry from replacing Pastor Lyles. I just hope it's a false rumor."

Cyd felt a sudden dread about the meeting tonight. How many others felt like Dana? "You do realize that at some point, someone has to take pastor's place."

"I don't think we'd have to look any further than Wayman Johnston," Dana said. "Been on the pastoral staff six years, he's got his MDiv—wife went to seminary as well—plus he's written three books that hit the Christian bestseller lists. It'd be hard to have an issue with him as Pastor Lyles's replacement."

"Bottom line," Cyd said, "Pastor Lyles's recommendation is just that—a recommendation. The congregation has to vote. Whenever the time comes, I just hope we're all prayerful about that decision."

"Amen," Dana said.

"But as far as the meeting tonight—" She looked as Micah Daniels walked into her office.

"Do you have a minute?" Micah said.

"Not really," Cyd said. "Hey, Dana, we'll talk later this evening." She turned back to Micah. "I'm actually on my way out."

"I'm supposed to tell you that you have a fan," Micah said. "My mother."

Cyd walked around to the front of her desk. "How did I get that honor?"

"She watched the debate on YouTube." Micah approached her desk in khakis and a button down shirt. "Said you had her clapping and praising."

A brow raised as she straightened her desk. "Your mother's a believer?"

"And a committed one," Micah said. "Despite my father leaving her for another woman. He's a pastor, by the way."

Cyd looked at him. "You grew up in church?"

"That's the focus of the book I'm writing," Micah said. "My story of being raised in the church. Raised to believe there was a right and a wrong. And seeing my mother's heart torn out as this charlatan of a pastor—my father—flaunted his affair in front of her." His tone showed it still hurt. "The book chronicles my evolution from preacher's kid to full-on skeptic."

Cyd felt moved to sit. "So tell me about your mother."

Micah sat across from her. "My mother," he said. "It's complicated. I was upset with her for a while. I felt she should have left my father early on. Instead she looked foolish—people knew—and the marriage ended when *he* left *her*." He angled one leg over the other. "Through it all, she kept saying she was praying and didn't think God wanted her to leave—as if she couldn't think for herself." He seemed irritated even now. "In the years since—going on two decades—I've never seen her faith waiver. That woman acts like Jesus is her best friend."

"What does she think of your 'evolution'?" Cyd said.

Micah looked aside a moment. "It's fair to say I've broken her heart as well. I've heard, 'I'm praying for you' a thousand times. She said to tell you that you're an answer to prayer. And I quote —'I been praying for someone to get in your face about that junk you spout.'"

"Have you told her about your study of John?" They'd met a second time, diving into the Scriptures and history.

"She'd get too happy," Micah said. "Texting everyday, wondering if I've been 'delivered' yet. Anyway, I wouldn't say I'm studying John. I'm responding to a challenge."

"So what's the latest?" Cyd said.

"The challenge is still a challenge," Micah said.

"Meaning?"

"It's disturbing. Whatever I'm reading—it haunts me. Might be one word or phrase. Right now, it's all the Ἐγώ εἰμι.'"

Cyd nodded. "Jesus' 'I am' statements."

"I feel like *Jesus* is in my face. 'You want to tell the world I don't exist? Let Me tell you who I am.'" Micah paused. "I especially can't shake the one you quoted during the debate—'I am the way, and the truth, and the life.'"

"Can I be plain with you," Cyd said, "especially now that I know you grew up in church and have a praying momma?"

Micah only looked at her.

"This is disturbing to you because what you say you believe is crumbling." Cyd was matter-of-fact. "And that's frightening because you can't handle what it would mean for your career, your book, your platform." Her eyes stayed with his. "But your very soul is at stake, Micah. Despite your railing against God, He loves you and He's drawing you. Talk to Him. Tell Him you're angry and hurt over what happened with your father—He can handle it. *Ask* Him if He's real. Seems to me He's already showing you. But you know what you need to do ultimately, Professor Daniels? Bend the knee."

Micah's jaw tightened as he looked away. He rose and walked toward the opened door, turning as he reached it. "I almost wish I hadn't challenged you to a debate."

"Interesting," Cyd said. "I'm only now beginning to appreciate the fact that you did."

~

Cyd and Cedric arrived early for the meeting at Living Word. Pastor Lyles had "strongly advised" members of both churches to attend, and the parking lot was filling already. They took Chase to the children's ministry building then made their way to the main building, with several stops in-between as they hugged long-time friends they no longer saw on Sunday mornings.

A range of emotions hit as Cyd entered the sanctuary. She came to Living Word all the time, but primarily the building that housed the ministry. Being here tonight raised a lot of feel-good from the past—and an unsettling about the future.

Cyd spotted her parents Bruce and Claudia waving them forward. "I wonder where they'll be with all this," Cyd said, as she and Cedric walked toward them. "Mom and Dana are close. Both stayed at Living Word. I bet they've got their heads together."

"That talk with Dana got you worked up," Cedric said. "Let's just see how it plays out tonight. And anyway, your parents have always been supportive of Lance and Living Hope."

"Dana's supportive of Lance at Living Hope too," Cyd said. "It's the other scenario—hey, Mom, Dad." She hugged them both, moving into the pew. "Steph said to save her and Lindell a seat."

"She needs to do the unusual then," Claudia said, "and get here on time. Look at all these people coming out tonight." Her eyes skimmed the sanctuary.

Cyd spied Lance and Treva one section over, near the front, and felt a swirl of butterflies. She and Cedric had fasted and prayed with them about his decision. But his decision was only the beginning—the congregation would need to make theirs.

Claudia leaned to Cyd's ear. "Your dad said Mason's feeling pretty good today," she whispered. "He had us praying that his health would cooperate for this meeting."

"I'm really glad to hear that," Cyd said. She'd learned her parents had known of the pastor's diagnosis early on, though they weren't privy to his succession plan. "I went to see him earlier this week and his mind was certainly on this meeting."

"He's kept his intentions close to the vest," Claudia said, "but if I had to guess . . ."

Cyd followed her mother's gaze to the front row, where Wayman Johnston sat, along with other pastors on staff.

"You think Wayman?" Cyd said. "Why?"

"Well, who else?" Claudia said. "Makes perfect sense."

Cyd's phone buzzed with a text message from Stephanie.

Where u sittin? Girl, why is EVERYbody out here on tonight?

Cyd texted their location, then added—**Start praying NOW for God to move in this place. It's about to be an interesting night.**

CHAPTER 30

"*I* can't believe I let you talk me into coming to a members meeting of a church I don't belong to." Alonzo stood by Reggie's car in the Living Word parking lot. "And I'm hungry too? It better be what you said—no more than an hour."

"Man, stop whining." Reggie leaned against the door. "You were the one shouting out your pastor and church fam in St. Louis during your awards speech—so do your member duty."

They moved toward Faith as she came from the children's ministry building where she'd dropped off Zoe.

"So explain this to me," Alonzo said. "Lance is pastor of Living Hope, but this is Living *Word*. They're separate churches, right?"

"Living Word's been around for a little over thirty years." Faith walked with them toward the main entrance. "Almost three years ago, Living Word planted another church in the city—Living Hope—to reach a different demographic. But they're very much connected, like one big family."

Reggie looked at Alonzo. "So how we doing this, bruh? You're walking in like, whatever? I saw you take off your hat in the car."

"We're going to the balcony, right?" Alonzo shrugged. "I'll be good between here and there."

"Just the matter of getting mobbed *in* the balcony area," Reggie said, "but okay, cool."

"We're late," Faith said, "and that's a good thing because everybody's seated. Hopefully we can ease into a spot in the back."

Alonzo kept his head angled downward as they headed inside. Other latecomers seemed focused on getting a seat, so they moved unnoticed, taking the stairs to the upper level. An usher stopped them at one of the entrances to the balcony.

"We're all full," she said. "You'll have to head to the overflow room in the children's ministry building."

Faith looked beyond her. "I see seats in the back, though. Can we take those?"

The usher shook her head, barely looking at them. "I need you to proceed to overflow."

Another usher walked out to tell the first usher something— and her eyes fell on Alonzo.

"Is that Alonzo Coles?" The second usher spoke to the first as if he couldn't hear.

The first usher looked more closely at him. "Girl, I think it is," she said.

Alonzo extended his hand, eyeing their badges. "Really nice to meet you, Alicia and Sandy."

"Oh my gosh," Sandy muttered. "I am such a fan. What are you even doing here?"

"Would you mind if we took a picture with you?" the other said.

"Not at all," Alonzo said.

"I'll get that," Reggie said, taking her phone. He snapped three pictures at least.

"I know we're late," Alonzo said. "You think we can grab those seats back there?"

"Oh, no problem." The first usher moved aside. "So good meeting you."

Faith snickered at Alonzo once they were out of ear range. "I guess I'm not as charming as you."

"It's all in the tone," Alonzo said.

They quieted as they moved into the back pew, realizing the pastor had already begun speaking. It didn't take long to sense the mood around them. Faith looked at Reggie. Reggie looked at Alonzo. Were people crying?

Faith whispered to a woman in front of them then passed Reggie and Alonzo the news—Pastor Lyles had terminal cancer.

"My wife and I and the rest of our family thank you in advance for all of your prayers," Pastor Lyles was saying. He sat in a chair positioned front and center in the pulpit area. "It's a difficult time, to be sure. I'm told the disease is spreading, but my days were already numbered by the God of heaven. Amen?"

"Amen" sounded softly around them.

"What, you don't believe it?" Pastor Lyles said. "I need somebody in here to believe that our times are in *God's* hands."

"Amen," sounded with more force.

"So there's a question on everybody's mind," Pastor Lyles said. "You all think I don't hear the whispers. People want to know who will replace me as lead pastor of Living Word. Which is to say, what is God's plan for this church going forward?" He paused. "That's the question I care about. I hope that's the one you care about. What is *God's* plan?"

Alonzo glanced around, thinking the pastor had to be right about this being on people's minds. Every face focused on Pastor Lyles.

"So I've been praying," the pastor said. "And I praise God for His faithfulness in answering so clearly. I come tonight to announce that the person I am putting forward as my recommendation for the next pastor of Living Word is Pastor Lance Alexander."

Alonzo looked at Reggie. Reggie looked at Faith. And their faces seemed to match the rest of the sanctuary, all of whom appeared shell-shocked.

"Lance Alexander, as many of you know," the pastor said, "is the current pastor of our church plant of nearly three years, Living Hope."

Applause and a few cheers sounded below in the main sanctuary, no doubt from Living Hope members.

"Living Hope has seen robust growth particularly among a younger demographic," Pastor Lyles said, "including college students, given its proximity to a number of campuses. Prior to Living Hope, Lance served faithfully here at Living Word as our youth pastor. Participation in our youth church multiplied during that time under Pastor Lance's leadership, and more importantly, so did decisions for Christ and baptisms among the youth. Lance served as a faithful member of Living Word for almost two decades."

Pastor Lyles lifted himself slowly from his seat and walked closer to the congregation. "Lance, please stand," he said.

Alonzo raised up a little to see Lance below. He'd seen him earlier today, and Alonzo now knew why he seemed somewhat preoccupied.

"Pastor Lance Alexander is a man after God's heart," the pastor was saying. "I say that as one who has walked alongside this man through many a season, outside of the spotlight. He is a gifted and faithful preacher of the word of God. He shepherds people well. And he leads his church well. I wholeheartedly believe that by the grace of God, Lance is ready to step into this new role and lead this church forward, to the glory of God."

Applause sounded again, and Alonzo saw Cyd and Stephanie rise, then others he recognized from Living Hope. Before he knew it, he was on his feet himself, along with Reggie, Faith, and a smattering of others in the balcony.

"Pastor Lyles, I'm assuming the meeting is open for questions and comments."

The sanctuary quieted and everyone sat as people looked to see where the voice was coming from. A man stood in the center aisle at a microphone.

"Absolutely, that's what's intended," Pastor Lyles said, returning to his seat.

"First, I am so sorry to hear of your diagnosis, and my wife and I will be earnestly praying for you," he said. "Who will replace you as lead pastor is an important question indeed. I appreciate your endorsement of Pastor Lance, and I'm thankful for the ways in which the Lord has used him. But I'm concerned that you did not highlight his full background, as there are many here who may not be familiar."

Faith looked at Reggie. Reggie looked at Alonzo. Alonzo blew out a breath.

"I just think this decision is too monumental," the man said. "Everything needs to be on the table. And an important fact that needs to be heard is that Lance Alexander has a criminal past, for which he spent time in prison. Moreover, he dropped out of high school. With apologies, Pastor Lyles, and meaning no disrespect to Lance—I have a hard time believing he's the best man to replace you as lead pastor."

Chatter erupted in the balcony and below.

"Did you two know this was going down tonight?" Alonzo said.

Reggie shook his head. "Not at all."

Faith leaned in. "Mom didn't even tell me. And I'm not sure how I feel about it, if this is any indication of the attitude over here."

"I'd like to address Carson's comment."

The three of them looked, recognizing Cyd's voice.

"The implication seemed to be—and maybe it was just me," Cyd said, "that these facts were somehow hidden in an effort to boost the recommendation. If I may, by a show of hands, who in here did *not* know these facts about Pastor Lance?"

Alonzo saw very few hands go up in the large crowd.

Cyd continued. "Pastor Lance has been featured in viral videos and national interviews because of the way he loved and shepherded his first wife through terminal cancer. His past was highlighted in each one. His story is well known." She turned slightly, looking at another section of the congregation. "Again, I may be wrong, but I think the real implication in Carson's comment was that Lance's past somehow disqualifies him." She looked directly at Carson. "You would raise as 'important' what Lance did over twenty years ago, before he was saved by the blood of Christ? You would hold up his high school record, as if he hasn't been sought after nationally as a Bible teacher? *I'm* having a hard time—"

"Cyd, I have to co-sign what Carson said."

Faith's eyes widened as she looked below. She leaned over to Reggie and Alonzo. "That's Dana, Cyd's best friend, on the other mic."

"It's not that Pastor Lance's past disqualifies him in a biblical sense," Dana said. "Carson was simply saying, given the entire picture, is he the best man to replace Pastor Lyles? I think it's a valid question worthy of serious consideration. I'm sorry but we can all see the headline—'Ex-Con Replaces World-Renowned Pastor'. And let's be honest about the schooling—"

"Well, first, I'd love to go back to your headline, Dana," Cyd said. "Yes, I can see that as an attention grabber. But what would the story say? It would have to tell how the power of Jesus transformed a man who couldn't see a future beyond drugs. It would have to tell how God chooses the foolish things of the world to shame the wise, and the weak things to shame the strong. God couldn't do anything but get the glory from that headline—just as I believe He'd get the glory with Lance as lead pastor here."

"But Cyd," Dana said, "there are certain realities we need to face . . ."

Reggie turned to Alonzo as more people lined up at the mic. "Man, I've heard enough. I can't sit and watch person after person come at Lance. You ready to go get something to eat?"

Alonzo turned to him. "I can't leave," he said. "I need to hear every minute of this."

~

Alonzo sat amongst a group at Lance and Treva's house. They'd headed there after the meeting, needing to gather and debrief, though Lance and Treva were nowhere in sight. After three long hours at Living Word, discussion had run as heated at the end as it had been when it began.

"I was ready to go to that mic a *few* times," Stephanie said, "and Cyd wouldn't let me. Totally pulled the big sister 'no' like I was two."

Cyd looked at her. "If I was ready to go off, I knew you were. Cedric had to tell me not to go back up there."

"Enough people had said what needed to be said." Cedric had an arm around Cyd. "It got to the point where we just needed to pray. I couldn't believe some of the stuff people were saying. It felt like a spiritual attack against Lance."

"I was as shocked as most people when he said Lance's name, though," Stephanie said. "I feel like we're hitting our stride at Living Hope. And I love Lance *at Living Hope*." She paused. "But none of this is ideal, certainly not for Pastor Lyles. I have to keep telling myself the main question—What is *God's* plan?"

"I'm new to all this," Jillian said, "but I'm trying to understand the dynamic. I thought you all were one big happy family."

"Till the top spot is up for grabs," Tommy said. "Power and politics. You notice how Wayman got up and touted his credentials, like he was reminding Pastor Lyles? Living Word is a world-wide ministry. Pastor Lyles never felt led to do radio or television, or to develop a huge online presence for himself. He didn't even write as many books as he could've, because he was focused on developing Bible studies. Whoever takes his place can step into all of that."

"That's part of what's going on," Cyd said. "Then there's the dynamic where some people just think if you don't have certain 'credentials,' you're not qualified for certain positions in ministry."

Reggie nodded. "There was *a lot* of that going on."

"But there were people who supported Lance too," Faith said, "even from Living Word. I was encouraged by that, especially the people who got up to share how he'd changed their lives as teens —and they're now adults living for the Lord."

The door to the lower level opened and they all looked as Lance and Treva descended the stairs with baby Wes.

Faith got up and went to Lance, hugging him. "I just want you to know I love you and I'm so thankful God gave me you as a second dad."

Reggie followed, hugging him. "I don't care if you're at Living Hope, Living Word, Living Truth—doesn't matter. I'm there. Love you, man."

Each went to Lance, who looked weary and beaten. Alonzo got up last, hugging both Lance and Treva. All night he'd been heavy in thought. Now he felt moved to share those thoughts.

"Can I just say something that's been on my mind tonight?" Alonzo said.

Lance led Treva and the baby to a spot on the sectional. Everyone waited.

"I'll keep it brief," Alonzo said, taking a seat himself, "because it's all fresh and I'm still pondering it." He paused, wondering where to begin. "I left LA yesterday because I needed some time away. I turned down a project that everybody expected me to do. Who knows—my management team might be ready to drop me. But I kept feeling like God was saying *trust Me*, that He would lead me to what I needed to do. And I think He showed me tonight."

Curious eyes stayed with Alonzo.

Alonzo looked at Lance. "I want to tell your story," he said. "I want to do a movie about your life."

"What?" Lance said. "Why?"

"Cyd sparked it, with that comment about the headline," Alonzo said. "She asked what would the story say—and what she shared was just the tip of the iceberg. I think it would be compelling, showing your life growing up, how you cared for your drug-addicted mom, your hopes for making it out of the neighborhood and going to college—hopes that were crushed when you were expelled from high school and ended up serving time."

"I'm getting goose bumps," Faith said, "and you haven't even gotten to the good part."

"Exactly," Alonzo said. "I'm seeing the scene where Pastor Lyles shares the gospel with you in prison, then you're grappling with it, ultimately falling on your knees in repentance—that's how it happened, isn't it?"

Lance nodded soberly.

"And people think, 'Oh that's the end of the story, he gave his life to Christ, roll credits.' No," Alonzo said. "It's compelling still to watch you overcome obstacle after obstacle, including your own doubts and fears. And dealing with people who want to hold that past against you. All the while, seeing how God keeps raising you up despite *all of that*. And how He *keeps* getting the glory through you." He felt it deeper in his gut as he talked. "It would be a powerful story."

"Oh, totally," Stephanie said. "But how does that work? You can just make a movie like that?"

"I've got a production company," Alonzo said. "Financial backing already in place. And I've been trying to figure out what our first film will be. Wasn't thinking 'Christian' film, but this is burning in me right now. I have to believe it's God."

"I could see a whole lot of people inspired by Lance's story," Reggie said.

"And I hope you'd take it up to present day," Cedric said. "Imagine *that* scene, where the guy who fell on his knees in a jail cell and gave his life to Jesus—replaces the pastor who mentored him."

"It's not gonna happen," Lance said.

All eyes turned to him.

"I appreciate the thought, Alonzo, I really do," Lance said, looking at him. "But your movie would have a pretty boring ending." He glanced around the room. "We came down here to tell you—and Treva and I are in full agreement. I have no interest in being pastor at Living Word. I'm pulling out of the process."

CHAPTER 31

"*Y*ou're not saying anything I haven't already said." Treva nursed Wes, joined by the other women at the kitchen table. "I encouraged Lance to pursue this process. I believed it was God's will—that Pastor Lyles had truly heard from Him. *And* I could actually see Lance in that position. I *know* he's gifted. I know God's hand is on him. But my heart broke in that meeting tonight." She felt she might cry even now. "I wanted to take Lance out of there after the first few minutes. We shed *tears* in the car afterward."

"We were all heartbroken," Jillian said. "We love Lance, and we knew he was hearing some hurtful things. But Cedric said something that resonated—this was a spiritual attack. It took all that prayer and fasting just to get Lance into the process, and the enemy came straight for him, to take him back out. There's so much at stake. I'd hate to see Lance give up."

"It's not about giving up," Treva said. "We talked a long time, and he genuinely doesn't want the position. I can't say I blame him."

"But is tonight the night to make that decision, with emotions running high?" Jillian said. "Lance said yes to the process only because he thought it was God's will. Did that change?"

Treva stared downward at the baby.

"I'll be honest, I'm glad Lance is out of the process," Stephanie said. "We can keep doing what we do at Living Hope and"—she threw up two fingers— "deuces to our Living Word fam." She looked at Treva. "But did Lance really feel this was God's will before the meeting?"

"He said no the moment Pastor Lyles asked him, and for a good while after that." Treva's eyes remained on the baby as she cuddled him. "Cyd and Cedric talked to him, then we set a time to pray and fast—Jillian was part of that. And last night he said he believed God was telling him to go through the process, through to the vote. And to entrust the outcome to God."

"Oh, wow," Stephanie said.

"Exactly," Jillian said.

"So what's the process?" Faith said.

"Well, first the pastor asked if he wanted to preach certain Sundays at Living Word," Treva said. "I guess that's what's typically done, so the congregation can get a feel for the potential replacement. But Lance felt strongly about his responsibilities at Living Hope. He didn't want to give up any Sunday mornings. So Pastor Lyles suggested he do a Wednesday night Bible study for four weeks."

"That hasn't been done in years," Cyd said. "We moved to an entirely different model, with people doing studies in small groups in homes. With a lot of grumbling, I might add. People had wanted to get back to this kind of format."

"And after the study," Treva said, "members would meet and vote. And based on what we saw tonight, I think we've got a pretty good idea how that would turn out."

"But Mom," Faith said, "you said you believed it was God's will for Lance to pursue the process. How did the meeting change that?"

"Faith, it's just . . . complex," Treva said. "Lance was crushed. Every negative thing he's ever thought about himself was magnified a hundred times, by his own church family. If you're saying I should encourage him to continue in something that would only get uglier . . ."

"Mom," Faith said, "I'm simply asking what Aunt Jillian asked —do you think God changed His mind?"

Treva looked into the women's faces as they waited for an answer. "No. I don't think God changed His mind."

Silence engulfed the table.

Treva sighed. "And only God knows what I'm supposed to do with that."

∾

Treva leaned on Lance's shoulder as their plane touched down in Tallahassee, Florida. "I'm glad you took some time to get away," she said.

Lance held the baby to his chest. "It's not exactly a vacation."

"I know." Visiting his mom was a mix of joy and sadness, heartache and praise. "But Pamela finally gets to meet her grandson. And you needed this."

Lance nodded vaguely. "I definitely miss my mom." He kissed Treva. "You always know what I need."

Treva hadn't been able to sleep last night after the church meeting and then the gathering at their house. She'd fallen asleep muttering in her heart, *Lord, show me what to do.* Before dawn, she woke up with Pamela on her mind, and she knew. She was thankful her attorney savings had come in handy once again.

"I needed this too," Treva said. "I love your mom. I think about our visits with her long after we've left."

They deplaned and, with no checked bags, proceeded to the car rental desk. The minimum-security federal prison was a short distance away. In no time, they'd entered the world of barbed wire and armed guards. The line moved slowly as prison staff processed only a few visitors at a time, but at least it was short. Within thirty minutes, they'd cleared the metal detector and sat waiting for Pamela to enter the room.

"Eleven years she's been in this place," Lance said, his eyes roaming their surroundings.

Treva had the baby in her arms. "It pains me to think about," she said. "How many get a fraction of that time for *violent* offenses? Even with time off for good behavior, she's still got years to go."

"I'll never forget hearing the judge give her twenty years—just matter-of-fact," Lance said, "then watching the guard haul my mother off in handcuffs. One of the most painful days of my life."

"I know she praises God for saving her in here," Treva said, "and she's impacting so many. But you'd think she was a drug lord, all this time she's serving."

"You've heard her yourself, though," Lance said. "She doesn't make excuses. She let her boyfriend deal drugs from her home, and she enjoyed the fruits of it as a user. But man, she got no mercy from the system."

Treva shook her head. "No mercy at all." The dealer boyfriend got minimum time, because he gave up another dealer. Pamela had no one to roll over on and got the full sentence.

Treva stood with Wes, smiling as Pamela walked toward them. Petite in her prison-issue khakis and shirt, she was beaming, eyes on the baby.

"Oh, my Lord, he's absolutely beautiful." Pamela took the baby straightway and cuddled him. "Thank You, Jesus," she whispered, looking into Wes's eyes. "I'm so thankful to see my grandson."

"I see that." Lance was smiling. "Your son used to be first to get a hug."

Lance leaned over and embraced her, and she put a single arm around him, keeping a tight hold on Wes.

Treva hugged her next. "It's so good to see you, Pamela. And so good to see *this*. I wish they allowed phones in here so we could take a picture of you and Wes."

They walked into a courtyard and settled at a table, the baby nestled still in Pamela's arms.

"From the pictures you two send, I was seeing a lot of Treva in him," Pamela said. "But now I can see my own baby boy in there too. Lance was a cute little thing."

"No surprise there," Treva said.

Pamela looked at Treva. "All you went through to bring this little boy into the world . . ." She shook her head. "I'm *still* thanking God for how He brought you through and blessed you." Her eyes scanned Treva more closely. "And got the nerve to be looking good too? Where's the baby weight?"

"Oh, trust me, it's there," Treva said.

"Maybe she'll believe me now." Lance put an arm around Treva's waist and squeezed her. "I keep telling my wife she looks *good*."

"And you better keep telling her," Pamela said. "That's a special woman you got there. Treva, if he steps out of line, *please* let me know."

"Without hesitation," Treva said.

"Hold up," Lance said. "I'm the one who's known you the longest, and my wife and son get all the special treatment?" He chuckled. "So Mom, how's the situation you mentioned in one of your last emails, the woman whose kid was in critical condition after a car accident. You asked us to pray."

"Oh," Pamela said, leaning to a whisper. "That was Raylene, one of the guards. Didn't put it in the email 'cause whoever reads those don't need to know who I'm close to. Next thing I know, Raylene'll be reassigned—they can be funny like that. Anyway, her daughter's recovering well, praise God."

"So, wait a minute," Lance said. "You're telling me you're friends with the guards, and they tell you what's happening in their lives?"

"Been that way a long time," Pamela said. "Pray for Raylene's salvation too," she whispered. "I've been talking to her about the Lord almost two years. Since the accident, she's been open to me sharing more Scripture."

Treva shook her head. "Literally every time we come here, we find out some new way the Lord is using you."

"Look around," Pamela said, glancing here and there, "ain't nothing to do *but* serve Him."

"Well, I don't know about that," Lance said. "I think you're just pretty special. It's amazing how God's plans exceed our own imagination."

"Amen to that." Pamela rocked with the baby, smiling into his eyes. "I said the same thing about you and that pastor position at Living Word."

Lance looked at Treva then back to his mom. "So you heard about that."

Pamela nodded. "All the way through to yesterday's meeting and you backing out of the process."

He looked at Treva again.

"I told you I emailed Pamela this morning," Treva said.

"To tell her we were coming," Lance said.

Treva shrugged lightly. "I didn't say that was *all* I told her."

"Lance, I need to say something to you," Pamela said. "The junk you dealt with at that meeting is because of me—"

"Mom, what are you talking about?"

"Please, Lance. Just listen." Pamela focused on her son. "People have to go back twenty years to say anything negative about you —high school dropout, ex-con. That was fallout from *me*, your drug-addicted momma. You might as well have been the parent, the way you took care of me as a boy. And you saw what it did to me. Lance, you *hated* drugs. Said you couldn't wait to move us away from all that, and you pinned your hopes on being bussed to Clayton for high school. From there you'd go to college. You could see it."

Treva moved closer to Lance, slipped her hand in his.

"Then you show up at school one day and your friend starts taunting you," Pamela said. "Saying your mother slept with him, as payment for drugs. Calling me names I deserved. Hurt you so bad you swung at him—and broke the teacher's nose who'd stepped in." Her eyes were glassy. "That was *my* fault. *I'm* the reason you got expelled and your dreams got crushed. When you started selling drugs and got locked up—"

"Mom, those were *my* choices." Lance wiped tears that streaked his face. "I could've finished at the neighborhood school, but I gave up. Could've made an honest living—I went after fast money. I could've—"

"Lance, if it weren't for me, you would've graduated from Clayton and gone on to college." Pamela's tears fell. "I know you would've. You were doing well there. But after they put you out, I saw the hope drain completely out of you. And for you to turn to something you'd once hated . . . I knew I had brought you down low, with me."

Lance got up and walked a ways, staring into the distance.

"It's hard for him to go back to that time," Treva said.

"I know," Pamela said. "We rarely talk about it. Believe me, it's hard for me too." Her eyes stayed on Lance. "But that email you sent tore me up. I said, *Lord, whatever I can say to my son . . .*"

"I don't get why you're saying all this." Lance was back, standing over the table. "I don't get why you think it's helpful to take the blame. It's in the past—"

"It's apparently *not* in the past," Pamela said, "not if you're letting the enemy use it here in the present. He knows it's your sore spot. Whenever the Lord wants to use you, here comes the past—right back in your face. So, fine. Let's look at the past—all of it." She finger-stabbed the table. "Go on and sit back down. They don't give me but so much time."

Lance sighed, joining Treva once again.

"I just want us to be real about where we were," Pamela said, "and what it was like to be slaves to sin. Giving the enemy victory after victory. Watching our home, our plans, our very lives go under. And the enemy thought he had you." Her eyes lingered on Lance. "But then I saw a *new* hope in you."

Pamela wiped her eyes as Treva's filled, thinking of the goodness of God.

"And I couldn't understand it," Pamela was saying, "'cause you were locked up. And you started telling me about Jesus—*all the time*." Her eyes smiled. "And when you got out, you practically lived up at Living Word. Always talking about Pastor Lyles and what he was teaching you. The father you never had."

Lance's gaze was fixed on the table, but Treva knew he was listening to every word.

"It wasn't till I came to know the Lord myself that I saw it," Pamela said, "the gifts He'd put in you. You not only led me to Jesus; you helped me *grow* in Jesus. Remember those long emails where you'd be laying out Scripture? I'd ask questions, you'd explain . . . and I remember thinking, *he's not just sitting at the feet of Pastor Lyles; he's sitting at the feet of Jesus.*" She shook her head, as if thinking on that still. "I prayed Jesus would keep teaching you and using you. And I said, 'Lord, all I did to mess up my son's life . . . please don't let it get in the way of the plans You have for him.'"

"You actually prayed that?" Treva said.

"Years ago," Pamela said. "And Lance, I watched you become youth pastor. And I watched you become pastor of Living Hope. And I praised God because He's more powerful than your past. Sitting at His feet is more powerful than sitting in somebody's class." She paused until he looked at her. "And I praise Him now for showing Pastor Lyles that you're the one to replace him."

Lance sighed. "Mom, even if I wanted that position, I'd have to go through a process and a vote. But I'm not going through a process for a position I don't want. I love what God is doing at Living Hope."

"Oh, now it's about you and what you want?" Pamela said. "What did you hear from God when you prayed and fasted?"

Lance looked aside.

"How is it the only time you think it's okay *not* to obey God is when He wants to elevate you?" Pamela lifted Wes a little. "Tell your son you're okay with giving the enemy a victory. Say it out loud. So you can understand where you're at."

"Ooh, that's good, Pamela," Treva said.

Lance looked at Treva. "I thought you were on my side in this."

"That meeting got me upset," Treva said. "But the women talked to me last night. Then I got Pamela's reply when our plane landed. She said she knows it's hard because I love you. But whenever your past rises up and you're tempted to not follow God, I can't be standing with you in"—she looked at Pamela—"how did you put it?"

"Foolishness," Pamela said.

"So this is what happens," Lance said, "when my wife and mom get close—and they're both tight with Jesus."

Treva leaned over and kissed him. "And both mad about you."

Pamela held up the baby again. "So what you gonna tell Lance Wesley Alexander, Jr.?"

Lance stared at his son, then got up and took him into his arms. "Your daddy's got a lot of growing to do, Wes." He looked into his eyes. "Whole lot more to learn. But I'm sure of this—God is powerful to save and able to keep us in His will." He kissed Wes's cheek. "And in this family, we're only interested in *Him* getting the victory."

CHAPTER 32

"So what do we learn about God in this chapter?" Jillian sat at the kitchen table, her Bible and phone before her, FaceTiming her kids.

"He doesn't like complaining, that's for sure," Trevor said.

"And we saw this before when we studied Exodus, didn't we?" Jillian said.

"Was just about to say that," David said. He gathered with Trevor and Sophia around their grandmother's table. "It's in my notes—Exodus 16, where they complained about hunger. That's when God sent the manna. Now they're complaining because they want meat."

Jillian nodded. "And like Trevor said, God's not happy about it—"

"Three times it says His anger was kindled," Sophia said.

"Which tells us to really take note," Jillian said. "Does it tell us why God is angry?" She watched as the three of them searched the chapter.

"Verse 11:20," David said. "It says, 'because you have rejected the LORD who is among you and wept before Him, saying, "Why did we ever leave Egypt?"'"

"Wow," Jillian said. "Why do you think God calls this rejection? They're just wanting something different, right? What if you had to eat the same thing, day after day?"

"You mean like David telling Grandma he was tired of oatmeal for breakfast?" Sophia said.

"I did not," David said. "I just said Mom cooks eggs and pancakes and stuff like that."

"And to answer your question, Mom," Sophia said. "The problem was that the people weren't thankful for what God had given them." She shot David a look.

"And they're longing for Egypt," Trevor said, "after everything God did to deliver them."

"You all are on point today. This is really . . ." Jillian paused, feeling a rise of emotion.

"What is it, Mom?" Sophia said.

"You all know I love this," Jillian said, "starting our days this way. And I hadn't felt like doing it, because mornings are probably the hardest for me. So I told myself it wouldn't work anyway, given the distance. But since starting back up a few days ago . . ." She got a tissue from the counter. "It's just a blessing, the way you're engaged and prepared—which isn't always the case."

"That's because we've got so much other work," David said. "But I don't know, I just got it done this week."

"And here's the other thing," Jillian said. "I don't know how much longer we'll be able to start our mornings like this, once I start working. So I think God is encouraging me that you do know how to study your Bible—and I'm trusting that He'll meet you Himself."

"But speaking of that other work," Sophia said. "Pre-Calc is definitely calling me."

"Okay, we'll finish up with Numbers 11 on Monday," Jillian said. "David and Sophie, we've got lit discussion this afternoon, which means I'd better finish the reading myself. Trev, I'm still waiting on your paper."

"Um, about to get to it right now," Trevor said.

"And you guys," Jillian said, "we shared prayer requests and prayed at the beginning, but please—reach out during the day when things get hard." She looked as Faith walked through the front door. "And not just to me but to each other. I'm praying this will be a time when you really start praying for one another."

"Hey, before you hang up," Faith said, walking up. "Sophie, check your email. I've got bridesmaid questions."

"Oh yeah, sorry," Sophia said. "I'll get on it. But wait—Joy said Alonzo Coles is in the wedding. Is that really true?"

"It's true," Faith said.

"His wife is your matron of honor," Sophia said, "so he'll need someone to walk down the aisle with. I need you to make sure that's me."

"I'm pretty sure I won't be in charge of that," Faith said.

"Do you know how huge this is, though?" Sophia said. "In the same wedding as Alonzo Coles? Which means he'll be at the rehearsal and the rehearsal dinner and—"

"I thought Pre-Calc was calling you," Jillian said. "And by the way, Alonzo was here at the house last night."

"He was *not*," Sophia said. "Why are we in Maryland?"

Jillian shook her head. "Be ready for lit this afternoon, girlie," she said, clicking off. "Hey, Faith, you convinced me—I think I'll go with you all to the Kirk Franklin concert this evening."

"Oh, cool," Faith said. "Reggie and I both thought it would be good for you and Tommy. I mean, it's work for Tommy, but still . . . should be uplifting."

"I figured I might as well," Jillian said, "with Treva out of town and Hope and Joy doing sleepovers tonight." She got up to take care of the breakfast dishes. "You dropped off Zoe?"

"Yeah, she's with Jesse," Faith said, "and I've got class. Forgot my book, though." She headed upstairs.

Jillian sent Tommy a text—**Still got a 4th ticket for Kirk? Decided to go**—and started cleaning.

A few minutes later she got Tommy's reply—**I got u. And appreciate ur prayer. Saying amen. But do u know any vocab besides 'wait' and 'endure'? ijs**

Jillian had prayed for Tommy earlier this morning then texted him the prayer. She re-read it now, seeing both words three times. **That's what you need...grace to wait...grace to endure.**

Tommy's reply came—**So answer is no?**

Boy, hush.

"See you later, Aunt Jillian," Faith said, rushing out.

"Have a good day, Faith," Jillian said. She looked at Tommy's next text.

Wrote a prayer too. One min.

Jillian washed the skillet in which she'd made eggs for the girls this morning. When she was done, the text was waiting.

Father, You are the King of glory, strong and mighty...I pray Jill and each of her four children see Your glory in their lives and feel Your strength. You are the Good Shepherd...I pray You make them lie down in green pastures, lead them beside quiet waters, restore their soul. Lord, You are their help, their comfort, their peace, and their refuge...I pray You would be those things and more to them daily. May their lives overflow with Your love and faithfulness. In the mighty name of Jesus...

Jillian read the prayer twice, tears in her eyes, receiving it into her heart for her and her children. *Thank You, Lord. Thank You that You are all we need.*

Another text came as she held her phone.

Almost put 'weeping may endure for a night...' but didn't want to take ur word.

Jillian shook her head through tears, typing back. **You are dumb.**

She typed again. **Thank you, bff.**

～

"I can't believe you actually kept this. And what is this *pose*?" Jillian leaned against Tommy's kitchen counter, a Polaroid picture in hand.

"That ol' tryna-be-cool DC look." Tommy struck the pose. "Then you had to look serious and stare off into the distance."

"And this asymmetric bob thing I had going." Jillian shook her head. "Concerts at the Capital Centre—so many memories. I'm trying to recall which one this was."

"Michael Jackson," Tommy said. "His first solo concert tour, off the *Bad* album."

"How do you remember stuff like that?" Jillian said. "Forever into music. You've got the perfect job." She put the Polaroid back into the shoebox. "You got the tickets?"

"I put them in the mail pile so I wouldn't forget," Tommy said, heading there, "then I forgot."

"And I'm trying to figure out why you didn't check to see if you had the tickets *before* you picked me up," Jillian said. They'd found out an hour ago that Reggie and Faith had to cancel and would be attending the concert tomorrow. "If I hadn't asked on the way to the venue, we'd be there right now, getting turned away at the door. As it is, we're about to be late."

"No, we're about to be late," Tommy said, "because you wanted to see if I really had that picture. Then I had to find the shoebox. But you know Kirk Franklin is here for two nights so we can always . . ."

Jillian looked as he lifted an envelope. "What? You found them?"

"Reggie must've signed for this." Tommy stared at the envelope a moment then opened it and pulled out the contents. His eyes scanned one page then another then another, then he flung them across the kitchen.

"Tommy, what is it?" Jillian said.

"Divorce papers," Tommy said. "She filed." He sighed as he moved into the family room. "Wonder if her boyfriend tagged

214

along to the courthouse. Probably went for drinks afterward to celebrate. But then, why go out? They could just head back home, since they've set up house—"

"This is just an initial step," Jillian said, following him. "Don't be thrown by it. You've been fighting through prayer, and you have to believe God is working. A lot can happen between now and the time a divorce becomes final."

Tommy took one of their wedding pictures from the fireplace mantel. "The morning of our wedding I woke up and had my coffee out there on the deck. I knew I was set in my ways, so I said, 'Lord, make me the husband I need to be, just mold and shape me, knock me upside the head, do whatever it takes.' I really wanted to do this right." He paused several seconds, staring at it. "And less than a year later, here we are."

He hurled the picture frame across the room and it hit a wall, the glass shattering. He got another from the end table—and Jillian took it from him and set it back down.

"Tommy, this is not the end." Jillian looked at him. "And nothing has changed as far as your part. You know this is spiritual. Now is when you pray *more*. Believe *more*. In fact let's pray right now—"

Tommy moved past her, to the sliding glass door, staring into dusk. "If she wants me out of her life—I'm out. She needs to come get the rest of her stuff, and we can dispense with the lengthy court procedure. Just tell me which one of those papers to sign and let me get my life—"

"Tommy, stop," Jillian said. "I know this hurts—"

"She ripped my heart out and stomps on it every time she goes home to him." Heartache colored his tone. "And while she's got her 'freedom', I'm out here trying to manage the pain." He turned. "I don't have any more fight in me, Jill. I'm done."

Tommy walked around her and she pulled him back.

"You're not alone in this," Jillian said. "I'm fighting with you. Like you always tell me . . . I got you."

Tommy looked at her, his eyes smoldering with emotion. He brought her closer and held her, tighter by the second as the pain found its release.

"I'm sorry, Tommy," Jillian said. "I'm so sorry this—"

She felt his lips brush hers. Her heart beat faster as she looked into his eyes . . . and their lips touched again. And again. More deeply. Then more.

Her hands searched him in ways they never had, pressing against his back, engaging his muscles—even as his arms hemmed her against him, his lips finding her neck.

"Tommy, what are we doing?" Jillian asked as she kissed him again, breathless, skin tingling from his touch.

He shortened the kiss and took a step back. "I don't know, Jill, I . . . I'm sorry." He sighed, dragging a hand across the back of his neck. "Let's just . . . I'm taking you home."

Their eyes lingered on one another, and Jillian couldn't tell who moved first, but it wasn't toward the door. She was back in Tommy's arms, the kiss more passionate than before. Their touch more provocative. Intention more sure.

For a second she thought it was Cecil, the stirring as they slept, the leg against hers. Jillian came fully awake, her heart pounding. *Oh, God* . . .

She could feel herself shaking as she got out of bed. Groping in the dark, she found her clothes and escaped into the bathroom, closing the door. But when she turned on the light, it was no escape. Allison was everywhere—the shampoo bottle, the lilac colored rugs, the vanilla scented candle, lipstick and perfume on the marble sink top.

Jillian's stomach heaved and she knelt by the toilet, emptying the dinner she'd had before leaving home. Knees on the rug, her mind replayed the evening, then the replay shifted—to Tommy and Allison standing at the altar, exchanging vows. Jillian looking on. Cecil beside her.

Cecil.

How could she have been in another man's bed—a *married* man's bed?

Oh, God . . . Please forgive me.

Jillian heaved again, spitting into the toilet, and stayed there, her head by the bowl, tears streaming from her eyes. *How could I have done that? Lord, please . . . Please forgive me.*

She got up and checked the time on a clock in a nook in the wall—one-twenty-two. And the replay from the evening started again. And the shaking. She held herself. She just needed to get out of there and get home.

Jillian got dressed then opened the door and walked out. Tommy sat on the edge of the bed in sweatpants.

She looked away, headed for the bedroom door.

"Jill."

She paused but couldn't turn.

"Did you forget I have to drive you?"

She sighed softly. She'd forgotten.

Tommy headed to the bathroom. "I'll be right out."

They left the first floor bedroom together, moving toward the door, the television playing in the family room.

"Aye, Tommy," Reggie called, "Faith'll be here early tomorrow and we'll be gone for the day, so I need the tick—"

Reggie walked up on them and Jillian kept moving toward the door, unable to look at him.

Tommy pointed him to the tickets and they left.

They rode in silence most of the way, Jillian gazing out the passenger side window.

"Can we just say the obvious?" Tommy said finally. "We know tonight shouldn't have happened . . . and we'll be dealing with it before God, painfully so."

"He's already dealing with me." Jillian glanced at him only briefly. "We need to cut this off again."

"I know." Tommy turned, nearing the neighborhood. "I thought this was our season to finally be friends again. I didn't know . . ." He sighed. "I'm sorry, Jill. I'm really sorry."

"What are you apologizing for?" Jillian said. "I was as much a part of it as you were."

"I started it," Tommy said. "If I could relive that moment and take back that initial kiss."

"And if I could relive the next moment and not kiss you back." It went through her head again, for the hundredth time. "It's both of ours to own, and it's already painful."

They lapsed into silence again the rest of the way. Tommy pulled into the driveway, the engine idling.

"Jill," Tommy said, "I hear what you're saying, but I know it's on me, and I'm truly sorry." He looked at her, tears in his eyes. "Lance gets back later this morning. I plan to meet with him and confess."

Jillian nodded soberly. She already knew she'd be talking to Treva. She put her hand to the door and opened it, looking back at Tommy only a moment, then got out and walked inside. Downstairs she showered then lay in bed, staring into the darkness.

Lord, it was wrong. I know it was. And I hate that it happened. Jillian felt herself trembling even under the covers. *And at the same time, Lord, I have to confess—I can't even repent right because it's still turning over in my mind, in all the wrong ways. Help me, Lord. Help me to see it as You see it . . . as sin.*

∿

A knock sounded on the door. "Jill, everything okay?" Treva said.

Jillian turned over. "You can come in."

Treva opened the door and peeked in. "You're usually up and

about early so just checking on you. I know mornings can be especially hard."

Jillian glanced at the clock—ten-fifty-three. "When did you get back?"

"About an hour ago," Treva said. "But I don't want to disturb you. Get your rest—"

"No, stay." Jillian sat up a little. "I um . . . I need to talk to you."

Treva came in and sat on the bed, waiting.

Jillian closed her eyes, nausea threatening to overtake her. "I was at Tommy's last night." Saying it out loud made the sick feeling worse. She glanced at Treva then stared at the comforter. "We slept together."

Treva stared at her a few seconds. "So you're saying . . ." Her brow knit. "I don't even know what to say, I'm genuinely . . . Jillian, he's *married*."

Jillian only looked at her.

"And his wife and I are friends," Treva said. "I've talked to her during all this and I'm praying for them—and my *sister* . . ." She put a hand to her head. "Oh, my Lord . . ."

"You know what?" Jillian got out of bed. "My heart was burdened to confide in my sister because I *know* Tommy is married and I feel *horrible* and even if he *wasn't* married I'd feel horrible because we had sex and *we're* not married. And how about I feel horrible because I'm grieving my *husband* and feel like I betrayed *him*. And oh yeah, I feel horrible because Reggie saw us leaving late at night, surely guessed what was up, and probably told *Faith*. But you obviously don't care—"

"Jill, come here." Treva stretched out her arm.

Jillian nestled next to her on the bed. The tears came easily.

"I'm sorry," Treva said. "I know you. I know you feel horrible." She looked at her. "How did it happen?"

"We stopped by his house to get tickets for the concert," Jillian said, "and he saw divorce papers from Allison."

"She actually filed?" Treva said.

Jillian nodded. "So Tommy's emotional, I'm trying to console him . . ." Her tears wet Treva's shoulder. "And he just . . . kissed me. Very lightly. But it was like . . . it unlocked something, in both of us." She paused as it turned over in her head. "I don't know, I can't explain it and I need to stop thinking about it." She shook her head. "What's crazy is I've been praying for him and Allison too. Now the enemy's used *me* to get in their marriage."

"He's crafty," Treva said, "and he loves to tempt us when we're weak."

"But I didn't have to enter into it." Jillian stared downward. "I could *feel* God helping me out of a deep pit these past few weeks— and I just plunged myself a hundred yards deeper."

Treva put an arm around her. "His mercies are still new every morning."

Jillian closed her eyes. "Can you just . . . pray for me?"

CHAPTER 33

*C*inda walked up the familiar flight of steps, knocked softly on the door, and covered the peephole.

Footsteps approached. "Who is it?" Alonzo said.

"Your biggest fan."

The door came open, and Alonzo stood looking at her.

"You gonna let me in?" Cinda said.

"I remember when I showed up here unannounced and got a door slammed in my face," Alonzo said. "Maybe I owe you one."

"Still upset with me, I see."

Alonzo pulled her inside, shut the door, and put his arms around her. "You know I'm not upset. But I do owe you this." He kissed her, long and slow, the way she liked.

"I went two days without that." Cinda put her head to his chest, inhaling him. "And you know I'm addicted to kissing you."

He twirled one of her curls in his finger. "So you're just using me for kisses?"

She put her lips to his, taking another one. "You got a problem with that?"

He looked upward as if thinking about it. And she pinched his side.

"See, I was about to serve your addiction the rest of the day," Alonzo said. "Now no more kisses till tonight."

"I'm not worried." Cinda kicked off her shoes and made herself comfortable on the bed. "You're as addicted as I am."

"Probably more," he said. "So why didn't you tell me you were coming?"

"I wanted to surprise you," Cinda said. "And say I'm sorry."

"You already said that."

"Not like I can in person." She pulled him onto the bed with her, stealing another kiss. "I had another reason for coming, though. Same one you had—to get away."

"Why, something happen?"

"Well, first, the thing with us," Cinda said. "I felt so bad after you left. Like, what? How could I encourage you to compromise? My perspective had gotten skewed." She sighed. "Then Kelsey had this great cover shoot, the clothes looked *gorgeous* on her, she was excited about everything I pulled together—"

"But what?" Alonzo said.

"Afterward, she started talking about the *Greater Glory* movie and working with you and Shane. I had to tell her you turned it down." Cinda looked at him. "She said, 'So now Alonzo is too Christian for a Christian movie?' I told her why the role was problematic, and she said, 'When was the last time you met a Christian who was single and not having sex?'"

"She said that?" Alonzo said.

"So I told her *we* didn't have sex before we got married, and she *actually* said, 'There's no way Alonzo Coles would buy a car without test driving it.'"

"Why would she say that to you?" Alonzo said. "Never mind that she doesn't know me. But I thought you two had a really cool working relationship. She basically called you a liar."

"She was upset about the movie," Cinda said, "wondering what'll happen now that you're not on board. Anyway, after all that, I was ready to get away myself." She spotted the laptop on the desk and smiled, walking over to it. "You're working on it? The Lance screenplay?"

"He gave me the go ahead last night," Alonzo said, "after visiting his mom. Had him on the phone for three hours filling in details about his life, with much more to go. But I woke up at five this morning and started writing."

"Wow." Cinda looked at him. "I don't think I've ever seen you up that early, without a scheduled appearance or flight to catch."

"Baby, it's coming alive," Alonzo said. "Scenes in my head. Dialogue in my sleep. I've only written two screenplays, and they weren't serious efforts, so I was nervous about attempting this. But God is giving me the words, walking me step by step." His eyes sparkled. "And every time Lance gives me more, I'm like, come on, dude—really? This is made for movie stuff."

"Everybody was so sure what your next project needed to be," Cinda said, "including me. But God knew. Zee, I'm so excited—" She heard her phone and went to check it. "Oh, hey, Jordyn."

"Girl, you're here?" Jordyn said. "And didn't tell anybody?"

"It was last minute," Cinda said. "Only got here a little bit ago. How'd you know?"

"Stephanie told me," Jordyn said. "I'm downstairs."

"What are you doing at the B and B?" Cinda said. "I thought you were headed to Chicago for your mom's wedding."

"I'm leaving later today," Jordyn said. "But come down. Can't wait to show you what I'm doing."

Cinda hung up, looking at Alonzo. "Come with me downstairs to see Jordyn."

Alonzo gave her a look. "Nah, I'm good. I'll just keep working."

"Zee, stop."

"What?" Alonzo said.

"You've still got a little something against the twins for how they treated me," Cinda said. "And you should've gotten past it long ago with Jordyn."

223

"I'm cool with Jordyn," Alonzo said. "Saw her Thursday night at the end of that Living Word meeting I told you about."

"Did you speak?" Cinda said.

"I spoke," Alonzo said.

"More than two words?"

He shrugged. "Three, maybe four?"

Cinda shook her head and took his hand. "You're coming."

They walked down and heard voices coming from the library. When they entered, Stephanie and Jordyn were shifting furniture around.

"Heyyy, stranger," Jordyn said, giving her a big hug. "Missed you, girl."

"That's the same thing I said." Stephanie finished moving the piece. "And the same name I called her."

"The missing goes both ways," Cinda said. "I didn't realize how much till I got here."

"Alonzo, good to see you again," Jordyn said.

He went to hug her. "Good to see you too, Jordyn."

"So what's going on down here?" Cinda said.

"Ooh, let me tell," Stephanie said, smiling. "So you saw the video Jordyn did with Jesse? Tell me you both saw it."

Alonzo nodded. "Cinda showed me. I loved it." He looked at Jordyn. "And I appreciated the one you did before that. Cinda said it was a response to the one Jade did about me. But the way you spoke to simple questions about the Christian faith—dope."

"That means a lot, Alonzo, thanks, "Jordyn said.

"So Jordyn stopped by yesterday," Stephanie said, "and said she's turning Jesse's video into a series and needed decorating ideas for the video background."

"You know how everything in the B and B is so specially appointed," Jordyn said. "I wondered where Stephanie got all the beautiful knick-knacks with Bible verses and what not, because I want the background to be inspiring."

"Then we got to looking room to room," Stephanie said, "to see if she could film the videos here."

"Which was beyond awesome," Jordyn said, "because filming in my apartment is *blah*. We lost all the ambiance and pretty decor for our videos when we moved out of the house."

Stephanie spread her hands. "And this is where we landed. We're setting up this alcove over here for Jordyn to be able to come in and shoot."

Cinda moved closer. "And you've gathered knick-knacks from all over the B and B. I recognize this framed verse from the Ever After room."

Jordyn surveyed the scene. "Everything about it, so beautiful." She happy-sighed. "I got my ambiance back. Stephanie is the bomb."

"That she is," Alonzo said.

"So what's the series about?" Cinda said. "Testimonies, like Jesse's?"

"Not exactly," Jordyn said. "I want to capture the vulnerability of what he did. I called it *When I'm Broken* because it was so *in the moment*." Her tone was thoughtful. "I want to do a series with *now* moments—what Christians are dealing with and how they're dealing with it. People feel the rawness. And it helps people who are dealing with the same thing."

"It's an awesome idea," Cinda said. "I just wonder how many people you'll get to be that raw on camera. I was surprised where Jesse went with that."

"He was surprised too," Jordyn said. "So you do have a point." She hesitated. "I actually thought about you, Alonzo." She looked tentatively at him.

"Why me?" Alonzo said.

"Well," Jordyn said, "now that this latest news hit, there'll be a new round of comments—but no one's heard from you on any of this."

"What latest news?" Cinda said.

"About Alonzo refusing the lead in *Greater Glory*," Jordyn said. "Now they're saying—'Alonzo Coles is too Christian for a Christian movie.'"

Cinda looked at Alonzo. "Sound familiar?" She turned back to Jordyn. "Who was interviewed for the piece?"

"An anonymous source," Jordyn said. "Said Alonzo took issue with the lead character's sex life, and that he has an unrealistic view of how Christians should live. Also said Alonzo's a hypocrite given his own love life that's been tabloid fodder."

"I'm calling Kelsey right now," Cinda said, whipping out her phone.

"I wouldn't bother," Alonzo said. "She'll only deny being the source. But at least you know what she's about." He sighed. "People love throwing the old stuff around—and I realize it's not *that* old—but it's as if people can't change. And it's not like I'm sitting around saying, let me be supercritical of every script that comes my way. I *wanted* to do *Greater Glory*. Sat down excited to read the screenplay. *I* was surprised by how I started feeling. But I knew it was God. Maybe I should've told *Him* His expectations are unrealistic."

Jordyn was looking at him. "You're in the moment." She nodded toward the video setup. "I've got time before I leave for Chicago this evening. You want to talk about it?"

"Jordyn, that's the last thing Alonzo needs to do—talk about something 'in the moment.'" Cinda shook her head. "His PR team preps him for every interview. And for something as hot-button as this, they wouldn't want him to comment at all. I know it would be good for views, but—"

"I'll do it," Alonzo said.

The women looked at him.

"Cinda's right," Alonzo said. "My team would say no, and typically, so would I. But I'm feeling what you're doing, Jordyn. It's a God thing." He shrugged. "I'm just getting this nudge like, *do it.*"

"Don't you want to take some time to pray about it?" Cinda said.

Alonzo nodded. "I'm going up to pray for the words."

~

Cinda stood in the shadows with Stephanie as Jordyn finalized her setup with Alonzo.

"I still think you should change," Cinda said. "Why would you wear that boring old gray shirt?"

"Because that's what I had on, and Jordyn said to be authentic." Alonzo pointed at the shirt. "This is authentic me."

Cinda frowned slightly. "But I just think—"

"Girl, if you don't relax and let that man get his mind right," Stephanie said. "You're getting on *my* nerves, talking about that shirt."

Cinda leaned closer to her. "You know he'd look better in a different shirt."

"And this B and B would look better if you cleaned it," Stephanie said. "You need something to do?"

"Appreciate you, Steph," Alonzo called out.

"You weren't supposed to hear all that," Cinda said.

Jordyn moved one of the studio lights to a different spot. "I think we're ready," she said. "Stephanie, can you pray?"

"I'm not the one who's usually picked, but okay," Stephanie said.

Stephanie and Cinda moved closer to Alonzo and Jordyn, the four of them holding hands.

"Lord, only You could do something like this," Stephanie said, her head bowed. "Jordyn reminded me of when she first came to this B and B. And it's safe to say we weren't crazy about each other. But you've got us here together, love flowing, united with a common purpose—to glorify You. Thank You, Lord.

"And Lord, Alonzo just keeps going against the grain—turning down movies and probably lots of money, now doing a video he's got no business doing . . . except it's motivated by You. Bless him, Lord. Give him courage, and powerful words. And bless Jordyn, Lord, to grow closer to You throughout this series. In Jesus' name."

"Amen," they all said, as spontaneous hugs followed.

Alonzo perched himself on the stool, and Cinda and Stephanie moved back to the shadows.

"Ready when you are," Jordyn said. "And I know you know—take your time, start and stop, whatever. Editing magic happens later."

Alonzo looked downward a few seconds then brought his eyes to the camera. "I don't really get to talk to you like this," he began, "just straight, me to you. I deal in scripts and talking points, interviews where everything is measured. And when talk is swirling about me the way it is now, I don't say anything at all."

Cinda watched him stare downward again. This was harder than he'd thought.

"And I probably would've stayed quiet still," Alonzo said. "But today I saw where somebody called me a hypocrite for having an issue with sex scenes in a movie, when my own life has been so . . . active." He looked aside a moment then gave a vague nod. "I get that. I get why people might be confused about what's going on with me. Because you don't know me for real—it's all rumor and gossip. So I figured I'd change that, get personal for once. Let's talk about it—about my sex life."

Jordyn looked over at Cinda, brow raised. Cinda looked at Alonzo, stunned.

"I didn't have much of a sex life for a long time," Alonzo said. "You've probably seen my old pics—skinny, thick glasses, crooked teeth. I mean, come on. Nobody was trying to get with me." He spoke naturally, as if to a friend. "Then I started getting work in Hollywood. Put some money toward braces, laser surgery for my eyes, gym membership. And after all that, I remember showing up on set for my first movie role. A small part. People hardly recognized me. And I was getting all this extra attention." He paused. "Everything started to change."

Cinda saw Faith and Reggie slip in and waved them over. She'd texted Faith to let her know she was in town as they set up the shoot. Cinda hugged Reggie then grabbed a tight hold of Faith.

"It's so good to see you," Cinda whispered, hugging her still.

"Been waaaayyy too long," Faith whispered, rocking with her in the hug.

Jordyn looked over at them.

"Sorry," Cinda mouthed.

"Got my first big break after that," Alonzo continued, "plus the women are suddenly showing me love." He paused. "Funny—never saw a headline that said, 'Is Alonzo Coles Becoming Too Wild?' But that's what was up. More parties. More drinking. More women. And here's the *really* wild part—I had just become a Christian. An assistant director had led me to Jesus, but I had no clue what it meant for my life, other than heaven one day. My life was about working hard and playing hard. And playing hard meant a banging sex life."

Faith turned surprised eyes on Cinda.

"Girl, I know," Cinda whispered.

Alonzo continued with a shrug. "I didn't see a problem, since I never lied to women about where I was—no ties, no commitment." His eyes engaged the camera. "Then about a year ago, I'm doing a photo shoot for *Bonds of Time* and end up talking with Randall Rogers about God. He gets me reading my Bible. Next thing I know, I'm talking to his pastor and other brothers from his church. *More* about God and the Bible. *And this stuff is rocking me.* I start noticing—*I'm turning down sex.* And this one woman I had had a crush on and would've definitely . . ." He shook his head. "I'm literally looking at my life like, *what is going on?*" He paused.

"But what really let me know my life had become unrecognizable . . ." He glanced over at her. "Cinda."

Cinda focused on her husband, thinking about all that God had done.

"We met at the *Bonds of Time* St. Louis premiere—you might've seen that," Alonzo said. "What you don't know is at the end of the night, this woman refused to give me her number. I had to fly *back* to St. Louis just to talk to her. You've seen her—she's beautiful. But that's not what moved me. It was her heart that was seeking the Lord. And as I got to know her and started falling for her, I wanted to be committed—that's never happened. And as we dated I committed to something else—no sex." He gave the camera a look. "You *know* that had never happened. I thank God we kept that commitment until we became husband and wife."

Cinda watched Stephanie slip out, preparing for guests to arrive.

"Bottom line," Alonzo said, "there's a lot of talk about what I'm becoming. God is doing so much in my head and heart that *I'm* trying to figure out the new Alonzo. But this 'too Christian' label . . . I couldn't touch that if I wanted to. I hope I'm growing to be more like Jesus, but come on, y'all . . . I'm just a flawed man, thankful for grace." He paused. "And for any woman who ever had anything to do with me relationship wise, I apologize. For real."

Cinda hoped people could feel the sincerity. She'd heard Alonzo express regret more than once for the causal way he'd viewed relationships.

"Let me end with this," Alonzo said. "I love what I do. I'm humbled to be able to do this work and mad humbled by all your support. But I love Jesus more than all of this. And at the end of the day, I need to feel good about the work—as a reflection of who I am in Him." He added, "That being said, I'm not going anywhere. Are y'all still rocking with me?—because I'm excited about what's ahead. And you know, I kind of like this me-to-you approach." He smiled a little. "Maybe I'll do more of these."

Alonzo signaled he was done, and Jordyn turned the cameras off. Cinda walked over, pulled him from the stool, and kissed him.

"You're not upset with me for saying all that?" Alonzo said.

"It was nothing I didn't already know," Cinda said, "except that woman you had a crush on, whoever it was. And you actually could've said more—like, 'God gave me an even better banging sex life—with my wife.'"

"Ohh, dope," Reggie said. "I guess I should pretend I didn't hear that. But for us engaged folk . . ." He chuckled.

"Seriously," Faith said. "It needs to be said. Married people *should* be the ones with a good love life. But Cinda, girl, how did you—we need to talk."

"Why am I just a little embarrassed about this convo?" Alonzo said.

Cinda gave him a look. "After everything you just said?"

"I can't wait to edit this, Alonzo," Jordyn said. "I love how you took a part of your life—the part people love to talk about—and showed how God transformed it."

"Do you know what you might call this one?" Cinda said.

"It came to me while Alonzo was talking," Jordyn said. "*When I'm Changed.*" She looked as Jesse walked in. "Hey," she said.

Jesse came closer, looking at Jordyn. "Hey. We're still going?"

Jordyn nodded. "Soon as I pack all of this up."

Cinda gave Jesse a hug, and when he moved to talk to Alonzo, she turned to Jordyn. "I don't think I got this update," Cinda said.

"What update?" Jordyn said.

"You and Jesse," Cinda whispered.

"There's no update," Jordyn said. "We're friends."

"And he's going with you to your mom's wedding?" Cinda said.

"Helping me stay awake on the road," Jordyn said.

Cinda moved closer. "You like him, though?"

"We'll talk," Jordyn said, moving to take her camera from the tripod.

"It's a simple question," Cinda said.

"Whether you admitted it or not," Jordyn said, "you liked Alonzo from the beginning. But was anything about it simple?"

Cinda glanced over at him. "No. But you just answered my question." She eyed her. "Maybe you'll have even more to tell me when you get back."

CHAPTER 34

"*J*didn't know Faith would be at the B and B when I suggested we meet there." Jordyn glanced at Jesse as she moved onto the highway heading north. "Sorry."

"I see Faith all the time because of Zoe," Jesse said. "It's not some traumatic thing."

"But does it still hurt?" Jordyn said. "Especially when she's with Reggie?"

Jesse gave a bare shrug.

"I don't see how you didn't recognize what you had," Jordyn said. "I think Faith is amazing—"

"Really, Jordyn?" Jesse said. "If I'd known this was what we'd be talking about . . ."

"Well, it's just interesting—okay, sorry." Jordyn moved into the outer lane. "And thank you again for riding with me."

"You said it would help, so no problem." Jesse looked over at her. "Although, you could've just asked, without an excuse."

"It wasn't an excuse," Jordyn said. "I do have trouble staying awake on road trips." She glanced at him. "And I wouldn't have just asked because I know how busy you are with school. I felt bad asking as it was."

"I thought we were cultivating a friendship," Jesse said. "So you shouldn't feel bad asking whatever, just like I won't feel bad saying no if I can't do it."

"You're always blunt and crabby," Jordyn said. "But I'm learning to listen to what you're saying. Sounds like you actually want a friendship."

"Just generally?" Jesse said.

"With me."

"Obviously. Or I wouldn't be here." He reclined his seat. "And I'm not crabby."

"You *are* crabby."

Jesse looked at her. "Did you ask your mom if there's room at her house for me to stay?"

"I told her you were riding with me," Jordyn said, "and yes, she said there's room. She was so glad I decided to come, she would've done what she could to make room."

"You thought about not going?" Jesse said.

"I still have mixed feelings," Jordyn said. "She's marrying the man she was seeing when my dad was alive."

"I didn't know," Jesse said. "What's your relationship like with your mom?"

"We used to be close," Jordyn said. "But finding out about her affair, and that dad knew and stayed with her . . . That was hard to deal with. *Then* she had the man in their bed a couple weeks after Dad's death. Who *does* that?"

Jesse looked over at her.

"What?" Jordyn said.

"Just a different kind of messy, Jordyn."

"Meaning what?"

"Did you ever think—she's broken too?" Jesse said.

"She doesn't look broken to me," Jordyn said. "She's mighty happy about this wedding."

"And you look mighty happy smiling at the camera, putting on your makeup," Jesse said. "No one would guess what's underneath."

Jordyn glanced at him. "You checked out my makeup vids?"

"That was a side matter," Jesse said.

She smiled at him. "I can't believe you watched."

"One video, three minutes at most." Jesse shifted to get more comfortable. "But now I know how you 'achieve your brow'."

Jordyn chuckled. "All my beauty secrets uploaded for the world to see."

"You ever go without makeup?" Jesse said.

"If I'm home all day."

"What if you're running errands?"

"I wear an everyday natural look."

"Would you go to church without makeup?" Jesse said.

"Nope."

"Interesting."

"Go ahead," Jordyn said. "Tell me I'm hiding. Don't want the world to see what I'm really about."

"Which is probably true," Jesse said. "I only asked because I'm curious what you look like without it."

"Why?" Jordyn said. "Because you were used to Faith not wearing makeup?"

Jesse focused on her. "So what's the deal, Jordyn? First it was, 'Faith is amazing.' Now you think I'm comparing you to Faith."

"How could you not?" Jordyn said. "She's the one person who truly captured your heart—and it's no wonder. She *is* amazing on many levels. And hey, let's not forget she was a virgin when you met her. It's hard for anyone to measure up to that."

"I'm confused," Jesse said. "Why would you need to measure up to that?"

"I'm just saying," Jordyn said. "That's what you fell in love with, and obviously you and I are just friends, but I can't help but think that even if you got to the point where you were ready to be in a relationship, it wouldn't be with *me* because I'm so far from . . . from *that*."

"Jordyn," Jesse said, "I'm not even worth all this angst you've got going. Who knows what I'd be like in a relationship these days. I could be the same jerk I've always been. You're already calling me crabby." He turned more toward her. "But I'm thinking Faith and the makeup go hand in hand. It's not about me and how I see you. It's about how you see yourself. And maybe you need to find out how God sees you."

Jordyn stared at the road a couple miles at least, feeling the sting in his words. She glanced at him finally. "I don't know what I did to deserve a blunt, crabby friend."

Jesse looked over at her. "But you're grateful?"

"I didn't say that."

"You might as well," Jesse said.

"Blunt, crabby, and cocky."

∾

Jordyn pulled up to her mother's home in the north suburbs of Chicago close to eleven-thirty Saturday night, eyeing her sister's car in the driveway. "Jade's here?" she said.

"Well, this'll be interesting," Jesse said.

They walked to the door with their overnight bags, and Jordyn rang the doorbell. To her surprise, it was Warren who opened the door and welcomed them inside.

"It's wonderful to see you, Jordyn." Warren hugged her. "Glad you made it safely."

"Warren, this is my friend, Jesse," Jordyn said.

Warren shook Jesse's hand. "Welcome to our home," he said. "I'll let Janice know you two are here." He went upstairs.

"It's been a while," Jade said, walking up. "Lovely to see you, Jesse."

Jesse gave her a nod. "Likewise."

Jordyn looked at her sister. "I asked you the other day if you wanted to ride together. You said you weren't coming."

"I wasn't," Jade said, "till Mom told me about your guest. Didn't want to miss the party." She moved in closer. "Did you know Warren was living here?"

"Had no idea," Jordyn said.

"Hey, you made it," Janice said, coming down the stairs. She hugged Jordyn. "It's so good to see you, sweetheart. And who's this?" she said, smiling.

"Jesse Edmonds," Jordyn said. "Jesse, this is my mom, Janice Rogers."

"For only a few more hours," Janice said. "Then I'll be Janice Dempsey." She hugged Jesse. "Very nice to meet you, and please make yourself at home."

"I appreciate that, Mrs. Rogers," Jesse said. "Thanks for having me."

"Mom, can you show us which rooms we're staying in," Jordyn said, "so we can take our bags up?"

"Of course," Janice said. "Follow me."

They walked up the stairs to a spacious second level. Janice stopped at the second bedroom on the right.

"I've got you in here," Janice said, flicking on the light.

"You've got who in here?" Jordyn said. "Me or Jesse?"

"I assumed he was staying in the room with you," Janice said.

"We're not like that, Mom," Jordyn said. "We need separate rooms."

"That might be a problem," Janice said. "We've got five bedrooms, but Jade's got one. Warren's daughter and son are arriving in the next two hours, and they've each got one. And his niece has the pullout sofa downstairs."

"Jesse will take Jade's room," Jordyn said, "and Jade will come in here with me."

"You'd better clear it with her first," Janice said. "You know how she is."

Jordyn took a step toward the stairs. "Jade, can you come here?" she called, explaining the situation once she'd come.

Jade put a hand to her hip. "Jesse drove me across town and slept in my bed. You two drove five hours, and he won't sleep in yours?"

Janice looked between them, confused. Jesse was clearly biting his tongue.

"Jade, just go get your stuff and bring it in here," Jordyn said.

They settled their things in their rooms and gathered in the kitchen for food Janice had set out.

"I miss having my girls under the same roof." Janice sat with them at the kitchen table. "It means so much that you both came. I'm actually still hoping you'll consider moving in here with us."

Jade looked up from the piece of chicken she was eating. "Mom, I'm sorry, but you're in fantasy land. That would never happen."

"Why would you say that?" Janice said.

"If Jordyn and I can agree on anything these days," Jade said, "it's that we have no desire to live with you and Warren. Do you not get how hurt we were when we found out about him?"

Jordyn glanced around, making sure Warren hadn't wandered in.

"It's been nearly a year," Janice said. "How long are you planning to hold onto that?"

"How long did you hold onto your issues with Dad?" Jade said. "You acted like he betrayed you just because he joined a church."

Janice glanced at Jesse. "No need to air any of this right now," she said. "And Jade, your attitude has been ugly of late. If this is how you intend to behave, I would've preferred you stay in St. Louis than ruin my wedding weekend."

"Fine, I'll head back right now," Jade said, standing.

"This is crazy," Jordyn said. "We've been here twenty minutes, and we're going at it already? So much has changed since Dad's been gone." She looked at her mother. "Jade is right. You did act like it was the worst thing when Dad became a Christian. But Dad's love of Jesus was the only reason our house didn't crumble long before it did. It's the only reason we had a measure of *peace*."

"I really miss Dad." Jade stood by the table still, staring downward. "I miss everything about him."

"So do I." Jordyn stood and hugged her sister.

Jade tightened her grip. "I was so hurt that our biological father didn't want a relationship with us, that I didn't appreciate the father we had." Sadness coated her words. "Dad *loved* us. He's the *only* man who's ever loved me. I just *hate* that I never told him how much . . ."

Emotion choked her words, and Jordyn held her as she cried.

Jordyn saw Warren walk in, then turn and walk back out.

"So the night before I marry Warren," Janice said, "you two choose to reminisce about Randall and his great love for us, because of course, Randall was a saint."

Jade wiped her eyes and moved closer to her mom. "I can't believe I'm just seeing it," she said. "I used to be so glad you said we didn't have to go to church with Dad. We didn't have to believe what he believed. Well, thanks for this awesome alternative. We're all doing really well being *miserable* in life."

"Speak for yourself," Janice said. "I'm far from miserable. In fact, never been happier."

Jade stared at her in disbelief. "You know what—I can't. I'm getting my things and heading back. I want no part of this."

Jordyn watched Jade walk out of the kitchen. "I'm leaving too," she said. "I thought I could do this, but—"

"Jordyn," Jesse said. "Can we talk a minute?"

Jordyn and Jesse went to the room in which he was staying, since Jade was packing up in the other.

Jordyn looked at him, shaking her head. "Welcome to my life." She paced a little. "My family is *so* messed up. I hate that you had to see this, but this is *exactly* who we are." She turned to him. "Did you hear her? Like we're supposed to be celebrating her and Warren? I'm so sick"—she groaned—"let's just go."

"I don't think you should leave," Jesse said. "Did you see the tears in your mom's eyes when Jade walked out?"

"After the 'never been happier' comment?" Jordyn said. "No, I missed that."

"Jordyn, this is bigger than this weekend," Jesse said. "God can use you in your mother's life. Who knows, might be years from now. But she'll remember that you were here. Let her know your relationship means something to you."

"Seeing her in this house with him . . ." Jordyn shook her head again. "I just keep thinking about Dad, and it makes me sad. I don't want to *celebrate* with her, especially after her funky attitude. She couldn't even acknowledge our hurt. She's *never* acknowledged our hurt. Always saying Dad wasn't perfect and Dad wasn't a saint, as if that justifies her—"

"Jordyn." Jesse looked at her. "Maybe this is why I'm here, to help you through this. But you need to stay."

∼

Eleven o'clock the next morning, Jordyn's eyes roamed the white and red roses that filled the living room. Twelve others stood with her—all Warren's family, save for Jesse—as her mom and Warren recited their vows before an officiant, a candlelit fireplace their backdrop.

". . . for better for worse, for richer, for poorer . . ."

Jordyn glanced at Warren's daughter who moved to snap a picture of the bride and groom. The daughter was smiling. They all were. And Jordyn was trying to find something to focus on, something to lift her just a bit, so she could at least pretend—

". . . to love and to cherish, till death do us part . . ."

Jordyn's eyes went to her mother as she spoke the words . . . and all she could see was Randall. She blinked back tears, surprised as Jesse put his hand in hers. They'd prayed together last night for her mom and Jade, for Warren, and for Jordyn to have the right heart for them all. Still, she'd been wishing all over that she'd left.

"I now pronounce you husband and wife . . ."

Jordyn looked on, a lone tear coursing her cheek as her mom and Warren embraced and kissed, his family members applauding. She hugged her mom, then Warren, then she and Jesse made their way downstairs, where a champagne brunch would be served.

Jordyn exhaled. "I'm not staying much longer, and you can't make me."

"We can leave right now if you want," Jesse said. "You did what you needed to do."

"Can we go somewhere and celebrate?" Jordyn said. "Downtown. Deep dish pizza."

"Oh, so we're celebrating the fact that you toughed it out and stayed," Jesse said, "instead of celebrating their union with the champagne brunch."

"Exactly," Jordyn said.

Jesse smiled a little. "I'm down with that."

They headed upstairs to get their bags, and Jordyn paused outside her room.

"Can I hug you?" she said.

"That's a weird request," Jesse said. "You could've just . . . hugged me."

"But we've never *hug* hugged, outside of the quick church hugs, and I don't know what our boundaries are since—"

Jesse pulled her into his arms. "Is this a *hug* hug?"

Being this close to him made the butterflies swirl. "It is."

"So why'd you want to hug me?" Jesse said.

"To say thank you," Jordyn said, "for coming, for helping me get through this."

"You could've just said thank you."

"I tell the grocery clerk thank you, the mail guy, YouTube subscribers I've never met . . ." Jordyn had goose bumps now. "A thank-you *hug* is a little more. Thank you, Jesse, for everything."

"You're most welcome," Jesse said.

He moved toward the room and she moved inside hers, her heart palpitating. She wanted to live differently. Wanted to see the very changes Alonzo talked about in his video.

But right now, all she wanted to do was walk across that hall and into Jesse's room—and be with him.

CHAPTER 35

MAY

*C*yd cut the ribbon at the entrance to the beautiful addition to Living Word's ministry complex. "It's official," she said. "Construction is complete. We've moved in. And our newest ministry—Living Water—is launched!"

Applause and cheers sounded.

"Speech! Speech!" a few of the women said.

"I definitely don't have a speech," Cyd said, smiling. She looked among the people gathered for the Monday evening reception to kickoff the women's ministry, then zeroed in on one in particular. "But I have to acknowledge Pastor Lyles—so thankful you could be here, pastor. He's the one who had the vision for this. We've had a women's ministry at our local church almost since the beginning. But after our women's conference two years ago, Pastor Lyles envisioned a national scope, taking what Living Word Ministries has been doing for decades—and targeting women in particular." She moved closer to the pastor, whom they'd given a seat. "Thank you, pastor, for getting behind that vision in every way and seeing it through."

Applause sounded again as he stood.

"Pastor, you don't have to stand," Cyd said. "Conserve your energy."

"Cydney, I'm fine." Pastor Lyles waited for quiet. "Cyd didn't have a speech, but I do."

Chuckles sounded.

"When we first talked about this two years ago, I didn't know I'd soon be battling a disease," Pastor Lyles said. "But I thank the Lord I could see this day." He glanced around. "So many of you have served at this church in one capacity or another for years. And not only served, but dedicated yourself to growing in the Lord. You have a heart for God's people. And as long as there's breath in this body, I'll be praying for the Lord to use each of you and this ministry mightily, for His glory."

"Amen" sounded around them.

Pastor Lyles turned to Cyd. "Cyd, you've led our women's ministry and the young adult ministry, and of course, for a number of years, the singles ministry. I'm thankful Cedric rescued you from that."

Cyd smiled, looking over at Cedric and Chase. "I'm thankful too, pastor."

"We've already laid hands and prayed for you, Cyd," the pastor continued. "So I'll simply say this as Living Water launches—may you lead faithfully, not turning aside to the right or the left, eyes fixed on Jesus. May the Lord's power rest upon you. And may His faithfulness surround you as a shield."

Pastor Lyles hugged Cyd to more applause, and people moved to partake of refreshments.

"I'm so excited about what God will do with this ministry." Cyd's mom Claudia hugged her. "And this space turned out beautifully. That fountain at the entrance sets it off," she said, pointing to it.

Her dad hugged her next. "I was having a moment over there," Bruce said, "thinking about our early days at Living Word, meeting in the school auditorium, praying my daughters would have a heart for God." He pulled Stephanie over. "I thank God for both of you and the grace He's shown in your lives. He has truly answered my prayers."

Stephanie put an arm around her dad. "Sorry you had to pray extra hard for me," she said. "Then had to do a lot of waiting on God to answer."

"Your mom and I prayed extra hard for you both," Bruce said. "Still do. For your families too."

"Praying extra hard for this church situation now," Claudia said, glancing over at Lance. "I just wasn't expecting the pastor to name Lance—and you know I love Lance . . ."

"Mom," Stephanie said, "I've heard you say several times now that you weren't expecting that. And actually, neither was I. But you always have this tone that says you can't get behind him."

"Well, I don't like to say much," Claudia said, "because I'm already seeing what's happening with Dana and both of you."

"That's all you needed to say," Stephanie said. "If you're thinking like Dana—"

"And here she comes," Cyd said, giving Stephanie a heads-up.

Dana hugged Cyd. "This is beyond amazing," she said. "I've been praying about all this since you first shared the vision. Shoot, I've been praying for *you* in ministry for who knows how long. I saw gifts in you when we were teens."

"You've prayed me through more seasons than I could count." Cyd hugged her again. "You know I'm thankful for our friendship."

"Dana, you going to the Bible study Wednesday night?" Stephanie said. "I thought you, Jillian, and I could grab a bite beforehand then go, since we've been trying to get the Praying Wives together—or whatever we're calling it now."

"You know I want us to get together," Dana said. "But I'll have to let you know if Wednesday night works. I think Scott and I are checking out Lance's study together."

"You sure you're not avoiding us because Jillian and I are in the 'other' camp?"

"Stephanie . . ." Her mom looked at her.

"Mom, Dana's my girl," Stephanie said. "You know we keep it real."

"I'm actually hoping we can talk about that," Dana said. "I'd hate for any church stuff to come between us. We've seen God do too much with our prayers."

"I think we should add the church stuff to our prayers," Stephanie said. "No personal agendas. Just praying for God's will."

Dana gave her a nod and turned as Jillian walked up.

"We were just talking about a Praying Wives get together," Dana said. She paused. "You're probably upset with me, after the meeting last Thursday. Cyd sure was."

"No need to rehash it," Cyd said. "We talked it out over the weekend."

"This is all new for me," Jillian said, "as far as the churches. But it goes without saying—I love my brother-in-law. I felt some of the comments overall got too personal and even mean-spirited. But that said, you know we're sisters, Dana." Jillian hugged her. We've come too far to let this fall apart. And I *know* I need prayer right about now."

"You all need to congratulate Jillian," Cyd said. "She got hired *and* started her new job today."

"What?" Stephanie said. "Where?"

"Here at Living Water," Jillian said. "I'm a copy editor."

"Another answered prayer," Dana said. "We were praying you'd get a job, and that's an awesome one."

"It really is," Jillian said. "I'm so thankful."

Cyd saw Cedric waving her over, then smiled when she saw who was with him—his sister Kelli and her husband Brian.

Cyd walked over to them, giving them both big hugs. "I didn't know you were in town," she said. "Probably only for a minute."

"Got back from Brazil last night," Kelli said. "But only weekend dates for the next few weeks. Lance just asked if I'd lead praise and worship for his Bible study, and I said yes."

"So you know I'm good to go," Lance said, "knowing Kelli will be ushering in the praise."

"Kelli, I listen to your music all the time during workouts," Treva said. "Girl, you are anointed."

"Thank you, Treva," Kelli said. "That means a lot."

Cedric hugged his little sister. "God completely passed over Lindell and me with the singing gift and dropped it all in Kelli. But I ain't mad. She's amazing." He looked at Cyd. "We're talking about getting a group for dinner. We need to grab Steph and Lindell too."

"Sounds good." Cyd looked at Treva. "And we can talk about your big day tomorrow—filming the Promises of God study. You ready, girl?"

"More ready than I was yesterday," Treva said. "Cinda went shopping with me today. It's kinda nice having a stylist in your life."

"You got the breakdown of tomorrow's itinerary, right?" Cyd said. "Because if not, I can get—one second." She checked her phone then looked closer at the text.

I need to know...how does one 'bend the knee'? If you're on or near campus, would help to discuss. -Micah

Cyd showed Cedric the message. "I think I need to go."

～

Cyd entered her building and went to Micah's office, surprised to see his door closed. She knocked.

"Come in," Micah said. "And close the door back."

Cyd opened to see him staring out of a window, into the

lighted quad. She closed the door and moved inside. "I'm actually on my way to meet my husband and friends for dinner," she said. "But your message seemed important, so I thought I'd stop by. How'd you get my mobile number, by the way?"

"Kristina," he said.

Cyd nodded. The office assistant.

"I went beyond your challenge," Micah said, facing the window still. "Completed all of John. Twice. Matthew, Mark, and Luke. Paul's letters. And John's, including Revelation."

"Almost all of the New Testament," Cyd said.

"The annual conference is in August," Micah said, "and I'm supposed to give a lecture as well as participate in a panel discussion, all in advance of the book I'm working on."

"I did see that on the conference schedule," Cyd said. She'd be presenting a paper there herself.

"And I stand here," he said, "with my mind going against everything I'm to write and lecture about."

Cyd moved further into the office. "Explain what you mean."

Micah threw up his hands. "He not only lived. Jesus *lives*. I can hardly think of anything else. I've lost sleep for days. I'm stressed and tired and sick—my stomach is upset constantly—and I keep hearing those three words you used—'bend the knee.'" He turned. "What did you mean by that? I take it, it wasn't literal."

"Humbling yourself, from the heart," Cyd said. "Repenting of your sin, acknowledging that Jesus is Lord and Savior, confessing Him as *your* Lord and Savior. That is, if you believe."

Micah turned back to the window. "It's inescapable. I've tried, and I just . . . *can't* escape it."

"That's God's mercy," Cyd said. "He won't let you escape the truth, because He loves you."

"After everything I've done?" Micah said. "Everything I've said?"

"We've all done and said all kinds of things," Cyd said. "You read Romans 3:23—'All have sinned and fall short of the glory of

God.' And Ephesians 2:4—'But God, being rich in mercy, because of His great love with which He loved us' . . . He saved us."

"I don't know what to do with all of it." Micah's voice seemed to break. "I don't know what'll happen, I don't know—"

"Micah," Cyd said, "you don't have to figure it out. God will do that for you. Just pray."

"How do I do *that?*" Micah said.

"Just talk to God," Cyd said.

He turned again. "Will you pray for me?"

"I think God wants to hear *your* words from your heart," Cyd said. "But I'll stand here with you, if it helps."

"Can we just, get on our knees?" he said. "I know it wasn't literal, but . . ."

Cyd watched him move to his knees in his beige khakis and joined him.

She closed her eyes. *Give him grace, Lord. Draw him to Your throne. Save him, dear God.*

Micah bowed his head and stayed quiet so long that Cyd assumed he'd started praying silently. She wished she'd left him to pray alone. Seemed awkward leaving now, yet awkward kneeling beside him too. She eased onto one foot, ready to tip out, and saw him swiping tears.

What am I supposed to do now, Lord?

"I can't," he said finally. He swiped more tears. "I can't do it. I can't talk to Him."

"Yes, you can," Cyd said. "Just speak from your heart."

He knelt in silence a few moments more. Then, "God, I don't know what to say and I don't know if You hear me or why You would hear me. I've run from You for so long. I've actively opposed You. You sent Your Son to die for me, and I called You a liar." His voice broke and he waited a few moments. "I've got no right to ask Your forgiveness, but I kept seeing it over and over— that You forgive. And so I ask, Lord . . . please forgive me. Please . . . *forgive me.*" On his knees still, he was near prostrate, emotion clogging his voice. "I believe," he said. "I believe that Jesus came and died to save me. I believe He rose again." He breathed a heavy sigh. "Jesus, please forgive me. You are Lord and Savior, I know that now. Please . . . be *my* Lord and Savior."

He slumped with his back against the desk, head in his arms.

Cyd sat against the desk chair, trying to grasp what had just happened. *Lord, You are full of goodness and mercy. You are worthy to be praised. Help Micah to walk this out. It won't be easy, but You are gracious.*

"So what's your story, Cyd?" Micah looked at her, his face streaked with tears. "How did you come to Jesus? Were you ever hostile toward Him, like me?"

"I was in middle school," Cyd said. "My parents had talked about Jesus for as long as I could remember, and I just had a heart for Him. It was only God's grace that I received Jesus the way I did."

He stared at her a few seconds. "I apologize, Cyd, for mocking you for your faith. For my arrogance. I don't know why you didn't blow up at me."

"I thought I did at one point," Cyd said. "I certainly wanted to. But no need to apologize. We're all blind until we see." She stood. "I really need to go. My family's waiting for me."

Micah stood as well. "You knew this would happen, didn't you, when you issued that challenge?"

"I challenged you at the end of that debate," Cyd said, "when I was completely vexed. I can't say I had anything good in mind. But afterward I did start praying for you." She moved toward the door. "Oh, and you should check out our church. It's called Living Hope." She gave him the address. "It would be awesome for you to meet other believers, especially brothers who are good at helping one another walk this walk."

Micah nodded. "I just might," he said. "And I'm hoping you'll help me too, Cyd. No one understands what I'm dealing with career wise like you do. And I don't know who else I could sit with and geek out on Greek language and ancient history."

Cyd nodded as she opened the door. "Definitely willing to help and geek out. And you need to learn biblical Hebrew too," she called over her shoulder.

"Ah, another challenge," Micah said. "So we're diving into the Old Testament as well."

Cyd continued down the hall. "Or you could always enroll in seminary instead."

"So everything I've said is fair game."

"Pretty much."

"The Bible says forgive and forget," Micah said.

"That's not Bible, Professor Daniels." Cyd opened the outer door. "It's a cliche."

"No harm in adopting it, nonetheless," he called after her.

CHAPTER 36

*T*reva looked over the producer's shoulder at some of the footage they'd gotten on the second day of filming. "Oh, Katie, those hills look gorgeous in the background," she said.

"Exactly what we were after when we scouted this location," Katie said. "That rolling green effect." She looked at Treva. "And you look gorgeous yourself in this footage."

"Thanks to the hair and makeup people," Treva said, "and my wonderful wardrobe assistant and nanny." She turned to Cinda who held Wes. "I can't thank you enough for helping me both days. You've been amazing."

"It was either this or watch Alonzo work on his script." Cinda cuddled the sleeping baby. "Seriously, I'm the one who benefitted. I got to hear the promises study again, in a fresh way. I really needed that."

"Hey, Treva," Katie said, turning from the big camera, "that last take was perfect. You are done, my dear. Awesome job."

The film team applauded, grateful. Despite the rain delay earlier that morning, they'd been able to accomplish everything scheduled. Later in the week, they'd do the portion with Treva and Lance in the Living Word studio.

Treva thanked everyone and walked back with Cinda and Wes to the big country house that served as their base for the day.

"So when do you and Alonzo head back to LA?" Treva said.

"We thought this past Monday," Cinda said. "Then we found out Lance's study was kicking off tonight and we wanted to be there, so we rearranged some things. Of course Alonzo's calling it research." She looked at Treva. "I don't know if you know how excited he is that Lance agreed to do this movie."

"I'm biased, but I think the story is compelling too," Treva said, "especially when you get his mom's perspective. I hear Alonzo's planning to go to the prison to interview her."

Cinda nodded. "He's already on it, doing twenty things at once." She held the baby close as he woke, whimpering a little. "It's his first time handling all this pre-production stuff, and he just might drive himself crazy."

"I know it's early yet," Treva said, "but I wonder who'll play Lance."

"*Alonzo* will," Cinda said.

"Are you serious?" Treva said. "I can't even get my mind around Alonzo on screen, playing Lance."

Cinda smiled. "He said he's not as good looking as Lance, but he'll have to make do."

"Ha." Treva opened the side door to the house and held it for them. "It's amazing when I think how God connected them. Who knew all this would come about?"

They went into an office Treva used as a changing area. She slipped out of a deep purple embroidered tunic and black slacks, and into comfortable jeans and a linen jersey top.

"Cinda, do you see my flats over there?" Treva said.

Cinda glanced around. "I think you left them in that bedroom where you got your makeup done."

"That's right," Treva said.

She went upstairs and found them beside the bed—

"The petition's got a couple hundred signatures already. I don't know how many it'll take to sway Pastor Lyles, but he needs to seriously consider Wayman Johnston as a candidate."

Treva recognized the voice from inside the bathroom. A woman on the film team, and member of Living Word.

"It doesn't make sense to have one candidate," another voice said. "What happens when Lance doesn't get the vote—and he won't—then we start all over with another process? Just put both names before the congregation."

"Are you going to the Bible study tonight?" the first one asked.

"I'm not really seeing the point," the other said.

Treva walked back to the dressing area, beginning to feel what she'd felt at the meeting.

She looked at Cinda. "Which *I Will Believe* resolution did you memorize?"

"A few of them," Cinda said.

"The one that's your favorite," Treva said.

"'I will believe that God is God, and there is no one like Him, who declares the end from the beginning, who plans and brings to pass all that He has purposed.'"

Treva exhaled. "I need that on a tattoo. By tonight."

Holding Wes, Treva moved into a pew near the front with Jillian, Joy, and Hope. She'd been with Lance moments ago in Pastor Lyles's office as the pastor prayed with him. Lance had seemed especially calm; Treva was the one on edge. She hadn't told him about the conversation she'd heard, but it had stuck with her. Were most members planning not to come? She glanced around the sanctuary. About ten minutes till the start and it was maybe a third full.

"Stop worrying," Jillian said. "Whether people come or not may have nothing to do with Lance. This is the first time they've had Wednesday night Bible study in years, right? It's not in people's weekly rhythm."

"If Wayman Johnston was teaching, they'd find the beat real quick," Treva said. "Maybe they want to send Pastor Lyles a message this way as well—by not showing up."

Treva turned as Faith and Reggie filed into the pew behind them, along with Cinda and Alonzo. Alonzo had his phone out, panning the sanctuary. Joy jumped up and into view of the video camera when he got to her.

Alonzo chuckled. "Joy, you want to be an extra in the Lance film? Maybe you can be in a church scene."

"Extra?" Joy leaned over the back of the pew. "Why can't I have an actual part? I can play myself—Lance's step daughter."

"Hmm," Alonzo said. "I'll have to think about that, maybe give you a line or two."

Joy's eyes got big. "Don't play. My mom's a lawyer. I'll have her put that in—ooh, that means I get to work with *you*." She lifted her phone. "Wait till I tell Lindsey."

Treva shook her head, looking back at him. "Thank you, Alonzo. We won't hear the end of it."

"Hey, let's get a group selfie real quick," Alonzo said. "I'll post it on IG."

Alonzo held up his phone and Joy and Hope moved to crowd in with Faith, Reggie, and Cinda.

"Wait." Alonzo looked behind them. "Jordyn, Jesse," he called, waving them over. When they joined in, Alonzo snapped.

"What's the caption?" Cinda said.

Alonzo was typing on his phone. "'In STL with church fam, 'bout to hear the word from my fave preacher.'"

"Don't put your exact location," Cinda said.

"I'm not crazy," Alonzo said.

The musicians started playing as the praise and worship team came out, inviting everyone to stand and praise.

Treva glanced around again. More had arrived, but nowhere near the number present at the meeting last Thursday night.

Lance walked out with Pastor Lyles and they joined other pastors on staff who sat in the front row. Treva had asked Lance if he'd planned to change up his attire for this crowd, maybe even let Cinda choose some things for him. But he said he'd be nothing but himself. He was the lone pastor in denim.

"Hey, Treva." Alonzo tapped her from behind. "St. Louis people are asking in the comments where they can come here the word tonight. Cinda says it might be a distraction, but to ask you."

"If they're coming just to see you," Treva said, "they'd have to wait till the end, which means they'd hear a message first." She shrugged. "As long as you don't mind taking pics afterward."

"Let's do it then," Alonzo said, typing on his phone.

Treva focused forward, closing her eyes as Kelli sang. *Lord, please calm my heart. Help me to not be anxious about who's here and not here or how Lance is received. Thank You that You bring to pass all that You have purposed. Be with my husband tonight, Lord. Strengthen him. May he bring You glory . . .*

Treva raised her hands in praise as Kelli sang one of her favorites. This was what she needed, her heart and mind lifted to Jesus. She sang softly with the chorus, "You are holy, You are Lord . . ."

Hearing muted sobs, Treva opened her eyes. Jillian was seated, head in her lap, shoulders heaving. Treva sat next to her and rubbed her back, praying for her sister. The same had happened during worship on Sunday. That evening Jillian had confessed in tears to Lance, though she knew Tommy had already told him. She said she needed her pastor's prayers, and he and Treva had prayed with her.

A few minutes later, praise and worship ended and the sanctuary quieted as Lance got up.

"It's good to be here tonight," Lance said as he walked to the podium, "with my Living Word and Living Hope family, and everyone else who came out." He looked among the crowd. "My name is Lance Alexander, I'm senior pastor of Living Hope Church, and I'll be here at Living Word on Wednesday nights for four weeks. And in that four weeks, we'll be looking at what I believe to be a timely message contained in three books—Ezra, Haggai, and Nehemiah."

Treva's brow raised a little. Lance hadn't shared where he'd be going in the Bible study. She wondered what his focus would be in those books.

"But before I get into the message," Lance said, "I need to say something so you'll know where I'm coming from."

Lance looked behind him as a door opened. Wayman walked out, taking a seat on the front row.

"Most of us know why we're here," Lance continued. "Pastor Lyles put my name forward as his replacement, and this process is in place—these four weeks of Bible study—so members can determine whether I'm someone you can endorse as the next senior pastor of Living Word. But I need you to understand . . ."

Lance moved out from the podium, closer to the pews. "Because I'm hearing about people who don't want me here, signing petitions and what not." He shrugged lightly. "This is not a job interview for me. I have a job, one that I love. You can vote for me, not vote for me. I don't care." He took his time, looking into faces.

Treva's phone buzzed with a text from Stephanie. **Girl, your man is not playing tonight. He came with the holy swag lol.**

Treva typed back, **And I'm over here like, Lance, what??**

"I'm only here to be obedient to God," Lance was saying, "and bring the message He put on my heart. What happens from there is up to Him. And I promise you I'll be good either way."

He moved back to the podium. "But let me say this—this message is burning in my heart. Because it's not so much about who's standing up here in the coming months. It's about recognizing the moment we're in and the forces coming against us as

God's people—and how to stand in the face of that. Open your Bibles or your Bible apps to the book of Ezra."

Treva opened her Bible and smiled a little as Joy and Hope went to Ezra on their phones. She turned, noticing the church was over half full now, and wondered how many might've come because of Alonzo's post.

"While you're finding Ezra—a few books before Psalms," Lance said, "let's talk about where we're at in history. And for those of you who don't like history—wait, let's see your hands." Lance looked out. "See, my daughter's got hers up"—he pointed at Joy—"so don't be shy."

Hope nudged Joy. "You're embarrassing."

"You don't like history either," Joy said, lifting her hand for her.

"Will you stop?" Hope snatched it back down.

Treva leaned over. "Did you two just regress to toddler years?"

"Okay . . . okay . . ." Lance walked along the front, acknowledging hands. "Man, lots of y'all can do without history," he said, smiling. "But I'm hoping history comes alive for you tonight. Because when God is in *anything*, it comes alive, amen? And God is all in history. Not the kind you're used to, boring facts in a textbook. I'm talking about God *making* history, God *prophesying* what's to come. Who's familiar with King Cyrus?"

A smattering of hands went up.

"Okay, I see you," Lance said, nodding. "What territory was he king over?"

"Persia," a couple of people called out.

"Who else lived in Persia?" Lance said.

"Esther," several voices called out.

"I knew y'all would know that." Lance stopped and looked at them. "Why do y'all love Esther so much? 'For such a time as this.'"

People chuckled at the way his voice went up.

"By the way, I see some of the same ones who didn't like history—are all over Esther," Lance said. "She's a figure *in history* but I'm just gonna leave that right there."

Lance got his Bible from the podium. "So Ezra opens like this —'Now in the first year of Cyrus king of Persia . . .'" He paused, looking confused. "Why in the world would a book of the Bible in the Old Testament open with the king of Persia? Why isn't the scene in Israel? Why isn't the focus on a king within the territory of Israel?"

"God's people were in captivity," someone said.

"Stand up, young man." Lance walked forward. "What's your name? And how old are you?"

"Brett," he said. "I'm fifteen."

"So, Brett, why were God's people in captivity?" Lance said.

"They were disobedient to God," Brett said, "and that was God's judgment."

Lance moved closer. "Okay, and we're specifically talking about the people of Israel who lived in the Southern Kingdom of Judah—that was for everyone else, Brett. I know you know." Lance smiled. "But here's a bonus question—where did God send them in their captivity?"

"They were sent to Babylon," Brett said.

Lance gave him a look. "So you read your Bible?"

"Yes, Pastor Lance. I do."

"Please affirm this young man." Lance walked up the aisle and shook his hand as people applauded.

"So that's right," Lance said, coming back down. "God's people were taken to Babylon by King Nebuchadnezzar who was *the* king in power at the time. God told the people through Jeremiah that they would be in captivity for seventy years—then they would go home. God also said through the prophet Isaiah that a king named Cyrus would be the one to send His people back—He said this over a century before Cyrus was born." Lance paused. "Don't ever forget—God is sovereign over history. So as Ezra opens, *it's time.* Cyrus is now *the* king in power. And seventy years is up. It's time for God's people to go home."

Lance moved forward again. "Can I get somebody to come to

the mic at the front of this aisle and read the first three verses of Ezra?"

A young woman made it there first. She read from her phone:

"'Now in the first year of Cyrus king of Persia, in order to fulfill the word of the LORD by the mouth of Jeremiah, the LORD stirred up the spirit of Cyrus king of Persia, so that he sent a proclamation throughout all his kingdom, and also put it in writing, saying:

"Thus says Cyrus king of Persia, 'The LORD, the God of heaven, has given me all the kingdoms of the earth and He has appointed me to build Him a house in Jerusalem, which is in Judah.

"Whoever there is among you of all His people, may His God be with him! Let him go up to Jerusalem which is in Judah and rebuild the house of the LORD, the God of Israel; He is the God who is in Jerusalem.'"

"Thank you," Lance said as the woman returned to her seat. "Before we go on, let's pause and take this in, because this is the focus of the message tonight." He walked a few paces in silence. "Notice who's acting. It says King Cyrus. He issues the proclamation. But we know it's God. Even Cyrus acknowledges it's God. And in the proclamation he doesn't just say, 'Hey, you can go home now.' There's a mission. What's the mission?"

"Rebuild God's house," a couple of people said.

"The Babylonians had destroyed the temple when they raided Jerusalem and took the people captive," Lance said. "So God tells them their mission is to rebuild His house." He stopped near the middle section and looked out. "Here's a spoiler . . . Some of the people head back, they get to work—and the enemy comes to stop it. And because the enemy discouraged and frustrated the people, the work that God had planned and set in motion literally stopped—for sixteen years."

Treva skimmed notes she'd written in the margin of this

portion of Ezra. She was already looking forward to digging deeper into this passage later with Lance.

"I said this is a timely message for this church because this is what we're seeing before our eyes—the enemy aiming at us, ready to frustrate the work. The enemy would have God's people in strife, divided, tearing one another down—with the goal of tearing down what the Lord planned and set in motion here at Living Word decades ago."

Treva was surprised to see a few heads nodding around the sanctuary.

"That's one thing we're looking at tonight and in the weeks to come," Lance said. "But here's another . . . Tell me again—what was the mission?"

"Rebuild God's house," more people said this time.

"That's the *first* thing He called them to do when they returned," Lance said. "What did God's house—or God's *temple* —symbolize?"

"His presence," someone said.

"It just got really interesting." Lance paced a moment in silence. "So in God's mind, God's people should be about the business of dwelling in His presence. It's His priority for us." He paused. "I wonder if it's our priority."

Lance let his gaze fall on the people, and their eyes focused on him as well.

"And we don't need a hammer and nails to do it," Lance said. "We don't have to spend months building a structure like these people had to do—just to dwell in His presence. If you're a believer in Christ Jesus, you're indwelled by the Spirit of God. God's presence is *in you. You* are the temple." He walked, Bible in hand. "But are you dwelling richly with Him? Or have you let the enemy—including your own sin nature within—frustrate the work of God?"

Lance went back to the podium. "Let's dig into the study . . ."

CHAPTER 37

*T*ommy sat alone in the balcony, listening and watching. He'd known he needed to be up here. Church on Sunday had been too difficult. Seeing Jillian. Watching her dissolve into tears. He'd felt the reflex—to be there for her. But he'd been the one who'd caused her pain. And that caused him pain.

He needed to stay out of her way. Out of her life. He'd already decided—he'd be attending Sunday service at Living Word from now on. He was no longer serving as a deacon at Living Hope anyway. He'd stepped down when he confessed to Lance.

He'd come to the balcony so she wouldn't have to see him. But he could still see her. Even now she wiped her eyes as Lance talked about dwelling in God's presence. Tommy had wiped a few tears of his own tonight, thankful for the solitude up here.

Tommy looked at his Bible, trying to follow along with the Ezra passage, but his mind was all over the place. It'd been that way for days. Well, months really. But the ordeal with Allison was different. These past few days had been about Jillian—which was scary and perplexing and heart wrenching. He'd ruined their friendship. He couldn't count the number of times he'd replayed the moment he kissed her. He could chalk it up to impulse and emotion—both played a part. But it was deeper than that. All at once it seemed, he'd discovered what his heart had somehow hidden, and he'd acted foolishly. It lit a fire—and left them both burned.

Lord, it's painful on so many levels. Tommy stared into the rafters as Lance spoke below. *I sinned against You, Lord. I grieved Your Spirit. I feel like I've asked forgiveness a thousand times—and I feel like I've needed it a thousand times. I can't erase that night, Lord. I start thinking about it and everything rises back up. Every moment. Every word. I need Your help, Lord. Help me to let it go. Help me not to feel what I'm feeling. I know it's not right.*

Tommy looked down, his eyes on Jillian, his heart a tangled mess. And he wondered when exactly had he fallen in love with her.

～

Tommy sat at his kitchen table after Bible study trying to knock out an overdue movie review. He'd told himself to just write —*anything*—and once he got going it would flow. But even with his notes in front of him, he could barely remember the film.

He sighed, moving to the refrigerator. Or maybe it was coffee he needed. He emptied the grounds from this morning and refilled the pot with water, hearing Reggie's key in the door. No way he'd be able to work now. They'd watch some of the NBA playoffs, *then* he'd get back to his column.

He placed coffee beans in the grinder—and froze when he heard the sound of heels. Seconds later, Allison appeared in the kitchen.

Tommy pushed the button to grind, the sound filling the kitchen, then added the grounds to the coffee pot. He pushed *brew*, grabbed his laptop from the table, and started toward his office.

"You're not going to say anything?" Allison said.

Tommy looked at her. "The attorney I was forced to hire is working on my response to your divorce filing," he said. "Don't worry, we'll move this along quickly." He continued on.

Allison followed. "I don't know . . . I don't know if I want that."

Tommy went into the office and put his laptop on the desk, taking a breath before he turned to speak. "You've been gone three months." He could hardly look at her. "You kept saying how much thinking you had to do. Then I found out you were 'thinking' while living with your ex. Then you file for divorce." He focused on her a moment. "Now you show up saying you don't know what you want? It couldn't be clearer to me, Allison."

"It's just . . . some things happened that forced me to re-evaluate." Allison moved closer to him. "I was focusing on the things that made me discontent and lost sight of the things that stole my heart. Like the way you care for me, consistently. And your temperament. Always so even. So good natured. And you are *the* most dependable person I've ever known, and the most loyal—"

"You'd better re-evaluate that too," Tommy said. "There was another woman in our bed last week."

Allison hesitated as if she hadn't heard right. "In our . . . You're seeing someone else?"

"Not that it makes any difference to you," Tommy said. "You've had another relationship going for months."

"I'm just shocked," Allison said. "I was about to say you're the most God-fearing man I know."

"Like I said. Re-evaluate. On your way out." Tommy sat at his desk.

"Tommy, you don't even sound like yourself." Allison moved beside him, leaning against the desk. "And I know it's my fault. I know I hurt you—"

"So what happened, Allison?" Tommy rolled the chair back. "You and your boyfriend had a disagreement? You found out he hadn't changed since the last time, and you figured good ol' reliable Tommy would be here for you?"

"We had a falling out, yes, and I'm glad we did," Allison said. "It opened my eyes to a lot of things."

"Why are you here, though?" Tommy said. "Your 'freedom' is what you cherish most. Why aren't you off somewhere being free?"

"It shouldn't be strange that I'm here," Allison said. "I missed you. You're my husband."

"Wow. You actually remembered."

"I know I've hurt you deeply, Tommy, and I'm sorry," Allison said. "And I know it'll take time for you to forgive me, and trust me. I know things won't get back to where they were overnight." She looked at him. "But don't our vows mean something to you still?"

Tommy looked at her a moment. "So you thought you could waltz in here, throw an 'I'm sorry' at me, and what? I'd say, 'Cool, no problem'?" He gave an empty laugh. "And the funny part is you said you *still* don't know what you want."

"I want to try again," Allison said. "I want to lean into all the good that we had." She looked downward a moment. "I've drifted so far from God, but I want to lean into that relationship again too." She took hold of his hand. "I love you, Tommy. I still love you."

Tommy rose from the chair. "I need time, Allison. To think." He left the office, headed toward the front door. "I'm sure you can appreciate that. For now, I just . . . need you to go." He opened the door.

Allison stared into his eyes. "Where would I go?"

"I can name a dozen hotels off the top of my head," Tommy said. "Better yet—call Steph. She'll hook you up."

"Tommy . . ." Allison took his hand again, moving closer to him. "I want to stay here. I want to come home."

CHAPTER 38

"So it's not as much space as we had before, clearly." Jillian walked through the duplex, FaceTiming her kids. "But it's functional, and it's what we can afford right now."

"So with three bedrooms," Sophia said, "that means Courtenay and I have to share when she's home from college?"

"Yes, ma'am, that's what it means," Jillian said.

"Which is what we've had to do for forever," David said. "You'll live, Soph."

"And it's within walking distance of Aunt Treva," Jillian said, "so you'll be close to your cousins."

"Ooh, let's do it then," Sophia said. "That means I could go to school with Joy. We've been talking about that."

"Since when?" Jillian said. "You're the one who had all these plans for homeschooling senior year."

"Yeah, *in Maryland*," Sophia said. "Life is different now, Mom. Might as well do something different."

"We'll have plenty of time to talk about it when you're here in three weeks," Jillian said. "And I can't wait because I miss you guys." She walked downstairs.

"So you're headed to work, Mom?" Sophia said.

"As soon as I get back to the house and get my things." Jillian found the woman renting the property. "Thank you so much, I'll be in touch," she said.

"It's so weird, you going to work," David said. "You have an office and everything?"

"I have a cubicle." Jillian started the short walk back to Treva's. "And I'm looking forward to decorating it with pictures of all of you when our belongings get here."

"Did you got a coffee thermos?" Sophia said.

"Haven't done that yet," Jillian said, smiling a little. Cecil never left for work without his trusty thermos.

"Mom, remember that April Fools' joke?" Trevor said. "When David and I poured out Dad's coffee and replaced it with Koolaid?"

"And Dad doesn't even like Koolaid," David said. "I mean, didn't . . ."

"And I was the one who answered when he called on his way to work," Sophia said. "He tried to take it in stride, but he wasn't feeling that joke *at all*. He wanted his coffee." She chuckled a little.

"Then Mom told him she'd filled another thermos with coffee," David said, "and put it in the car."

"Dad had fun with that for days," Sophia said. "'You kids better recognize—my wife and I are a team. She was gonna make *sure* I had my coffee.'"

Jillian could hear Cecil's voice, see the smile in his eyes, could almost feel his arm around her when he got home that evening, thanking her for that coffee.

"Mom, we said we need to get to co-op," David said.

"Oh," Jillian said. "Okay, I'll talk to you all later today. I love you." The sidewalk blurred the rest of the way.

~

Jillian found herself thanking God throughout the day for her job

—and for His lovingkindness. It was hard to fathom, how He could be so merciful. She felt sadness still for what she'd done. Yet, He'd blessed her with a job where she was reminded all day of His goodness, His love, and His truth, through the projects she edited.

She'd even gotten to do the final edit of Treva's study today before it went to the printer, though she could barely get through *If I Dwell*. Between that and Lance's message on dwelling in God's presence, she'd felt the sorrow of straying from Him, and yet— renewed awe that He would welcome her return. She didn't know when that night would be fully behind her. But knowing God was with her, helping her . . . that's what she was clinging to.

Most of her coworkers gone already, Jillian decided to pack it in as well. She didn't mind working late. Preferred it even, since the kids weren't here yet. She planned to take home her current projects and work into the night.

Jillian made her way out of the Living Water wing of the complex and headed toward the main exit—and saw Allison coming in.

Her heart pounded. There was no way to avoid her. And given that they'd been around one another, no way she could ignore her. None of which mattered, since Allison had spotted her as well— and was coming directly to her.

"Allison, how are you?" Jillian said.

"Real good," Allison said, "not that you care."

"I'm not . . . sure what you mean," Jillian said.

Allison stepped closer. "You thought you could steal my husband, you little whore." Her words were a hiss. "All that talk about you and Tommy being such good friends. You couldn't wait to get in my bed."

Jillian stared at her, every ounce of air sucked out.

"Well, guess what," Allison said. "We're back together. Here for counseling this evening. And all I have to say to you is—stay away from my husband."

The outer door opened and Tommy walked in.

Jillian moved around him and out another door, and felt herself shaking as she walked to her car. Once inside, she started the engine and drove off, just to get out of there. But the tears flowed so hard she couldn't see.

Lord, I hate this. I hate what I've done. She back-handed tears then hit the brakes as a car pulled in front of her. *I was praying for them, fighting for them. Now I'm just . . . the other woman.* The sobs shook her chest. *How do I even show my face around here? Forgive me, Lord. I'll just keep asking—please . . . forgive me.*

She took a tissue from her purse and blew her nose at a red light, then stared at the sky through her windshield. It wouldn't end. That night would keep haunting her. Her phone rang as the light turned, but Jillian barely heard it, continuing home in a fog. When she pulled up to the house and got out of the car, Treva opened the front door.

"Why aren't you answering your phone?" Treva said.

"Not exactly in a talky mood." Jillian walked past her, thankful no one was in the kitchen, and headed downstairs.

Treva came behind. "Jill, I know you're upset, that's why I was trying to call."

Jillian sat on the sectional, looking at her. "How'd you know I was upset?"

"Tommy texted Lance." Treva sat next to her. "He said I should check on you."

"So he told Lance what happened?"

"Tommy said he saw you and Allison talking," Treva said, "and he asked what happened. Allison said she let you know that she knows about you and Tommy, and told you to stay away from him."

Jillian looked away. No point telling Treva the other things Allison said. Treva would only get upset. "I'm glad Tommy told her," Jillian said, "so there'd be no secrets between them."

"I hadn't realized they were back together," Treva said. "Lots of prayers have gone up for that." She looked at her sister. "How are you feeling? That had to be hard."

Jillian gave a light shrug, staring ahead.

"I know you're hungry," Treva said. "Let's go up, and I'll warm up a plate for you."

"No, thanks," Jillian said. "I just, need to sit and pray a while."

~

Jillian felt herself shaking again as she looked into the camera. She held herself and took a few breaths as tears slid from her eyes.

"Jill, I'm asking again," Treva said. "Are you sure you want to do this? Jordyn knows I love what she's doing, but maybe it's a millennial generation thing, sharing publicly like this. Definitely not for everybody."

Jillian nodded softly. "It's what came to me as I prayed. I just have to . . . it's all coming up . . ."

"I don't know where you're going with this," Stephanie said, "but I'm feeling it already. I'm over here praying for your strength."

"One second, Jordyn." Faith walked in front of the camera and crouched before the stool. "Aunt Jillian, I think you are so brave—"

Jillian let out a sob. "No, I'm not, Faith. I haven't had the courage to come talk to you. I figured you knew."

"I only found out a few minutes ago," Faith said. "And why would you need courage to talk to *me*, the queen of mess-ups?" She looked into her eyes. "All my life I've admired you, and I *still* admire you. I just want you to know I wish I'd had a video like this to turn to when I was going through." She hugged her. "You can do this. I love you."

"I love you, too," Jillian said. She took another moment before starting back up. "So even though you know that sin is sin in God's eyes," she said, "somehow certain sins become bigger in your own eyes. And you could never . . ." She felt the ache inside. "You could never see yourself doing *that* sin, whatever it is. And that was me. I thought I could never . . ." She took a stuttered breath. "Then I did."

Cinda wandered into the room. "I just got back and"— she glanced around—"this looks really private." She turned on her heels. "Sorry."

"Cinda, stay." Jillian flicked a tear. "Really. It's okay. Hey, it'll be on YouTube anyway."

Cinda moved beside Faith and looked on.

"And if we're honest," Jillian continued, "when you're engaged in it, it feels good. Or else, we probably wouldn't have been tempted in the first place. So now you're dealing with the fact that you're *enjoying* the thing you said you'd never do—and you *know* God is not pleased." She closed her eyes a moment, praying for strength. "And if you love God and *want* to please Him, oh, He'll be faithful to convict you. And then comes the grief."

Faith nodded. "And that grief hits hard." She looked at Jordyn. "Oops. You can edit me out, right?"

Jordyn looked back. "Yep."

"And what I'm realizing—and what makes me sadder," Jillian said, "is that the grief I'm feeling is probably nothing compared to the grief *God* is feeling. After all He's done for me, after sending His Son to die for me, after delivering me from darkness to light —*He watched me reveling* . . ." She paused, blowing her nose. "And *that* thought brings *more* grief."

"Oh, man, I can*not*." Stephanie walked closer to Jillian. "You did not just say, 'He watched me reveling' . . . I don't even know what you're dealing with specifically, but that just got really real. *Somebody* is about to get set free." She went back to where she was, shaking her head.

Jillian gathered herself to continue. "But I'm realizing something else," she said. "The conviction, the grief . . . they have a purpose. A good purpose. Because if I *didn't* feel grieved, maybe

I'd keep doing the thing that felt good, the thing I knew was sin. But I'd also be far from God." She pondered that a moment, thankful she didn't want to live that way. "Conviction and grief move me to repentance, so I can draw near to Him again. So I can cling to Him again. So I can have joy again."

Jillian took a Bible from the table beside her and flipped the pages. "Psalm 51:1-2 says, 'Be gracious to me, O God, according to Your lovingkindness; According to the greatness of Your compassion blot out my transgressions. Wash me thoroughly from my iniquity And cleanse me from my sin.'" She held the Bible in her lap. "As I sit here I can't tell you the grief is gone. I thought it was getting better earlier today, only to get hit with another wave. But as I've cried out to God, I can tell you He has absolutely been gracious. I've seen His lovingkindness and His compassion. The sin wasn't too big in His eyes." She stared into the camera. "His love covers that too."

～

Jillian pulled Faith aside once filming was done. "Thank you for what you said, Faith. Your words helped me get through it." She lowered her voice. "You have no idea how bad I felt when Reggie saw me leaving. And you said you just found out?"

"Reggie called right before you started," Faith said. "I told him I was with you, and you were doing a video. And I said you were pretty broken up about it." She spoke quietly. "He said, 'Yeah, Tommy was broken up about it too'—thinking I knew."

Jordyn walked up and hugged Jillian. "I know I don't know you all that well," Jordyn said. "So the fact that you would do this and be so transparent . . . It impacted me personally."

"I knew it had to be God moving me to do this," Jillian said, "because I'd never share something so personal. If you hadn't responded so quickly by doing it this evening, I might've lost my nerve. So thank you."

"I have a lot of grief," Jordyn said, "not just about one particular thing but about my *life*. It's overwhelming. And I've felt so alone because people don't usually talk this openly about feeling grief over what they've done."

"If you ever want to talk," Jillian said, "I'm here."

Jordyn hugged Jillian again and lingered there a moment. "Thank you. I just may take you up on that one day."

CHAPTER 39

"**W**hat do you mean they dumped you?" Cinda stared at Alonzo in the Ever After room Friday morning, the phone still in his hand.

"How did they put it?" Alonzo said. "I'm out of control and unmanageable. Turning down lucrative projects. Too zealous about my faith—Jordyn's video might've been the tipping point."

"That video went viral within twenty-four hours," Cinda said. "Over a million views in two days. They can't see that your message is resonating with people?"

"Well," Alonzo said, "*some* people. A lot of people out there hating on it too. And you know I got some cancellations for interviews and other appearances as a result."

"But what about the action movie you filmed in London?" Cinda said. "It's coming out later this summer, and some are saying it'll be a blockbuster. You'd think your management team would at least wait to see what happens with that."

"They made their decision," Alonzo said, "and honestly I'm fine with it. As I listened to them I kept thinking, why would I even want a team that's telling me to minimize my faith—especially when it seems like God is doing the exact opposite."

"What do you mean?" Cinda said.

"For whatever reason," Alonzo said, "He's putting my faith front and center." He walked a little, thinking. "It's no coincidence we're here right now. We both felt a need to get away, right when everything is happening with Lance—which inspired the movie idea. And the movie is all about faith in Christ. Even the fact that we're here as Jordyn kicks off this video series, which prompted the one I did—again, all about faith. And it's *crazy* . . ."

Cinda watched him processing it all. "What's crazy?"

"All this focus on faith—I'm convicted as to how much I'd been slacking." Alonzo looked at Cinda. "In LA we went months without going to church. Blaming a busy schedule, not wanting to get out and visit churches. And yeah, we'd listen to Lance's sermons online when we could, but it's not the same. We weren't getting the nourishment and fellowship we needed."

Cinda nodded. "I pretty much said that to Treva. I feel like I've been gorging myself this week—in a good way—because I was starving."

"So we could set our minds on finding a church home in LA when we get back," Alonzo said, "*or* . . ." He paused, looking out the window.

"Stop doing that," Cinda said. "Or what?"

Alonzo turned toward her. "I think God wants us here."

"What do you mean, *here*?" Cinda said. "Move to St. Louis? How is that even possible?"

"Not sell our house in LA," Alonzo said. "But buy something here and make it our base. Lots of actors live in other cities."

"But, Zee, what would that be like?" Cinda said. "I kind of like the Hollywood vibe. And what about my work as a stylist? I can't do that from here."

"I'm just throwing it out there as it comes to me," Alonzo said. "You would have to be one-hundred percent on board before we do anything. But again, we'd keep our LA house and go back and

forth for whatever business we need to do. We're also halfway to
New York for business out there."

Cinda nodded slowly. "And with you working on this movie
and filming it here . . ."

"Exactly," Alonzo said. "St. Louis will be a base regardless, for
a while."

Cinda thought a few moments then walked over and put her
arms around him and kissed him.

"Was there a reason for that," Alonzo said, "or was that an
addict kiss?"

Cinda kissed him again. "That was an addict kiss. I had a
reason for the first one." She looked into his eyes. "I love the man
of God I married. I can see it, the ways you're changing. Before
you would've flipped out over being dumped by your management team. Now you're focused on God and what He's doing, and
wanting to grow." She thought a moment. "I want to grow too. I
want to trust what God is doing. And what *I* see Him doing is
leading my husband, decision after decision. And I can get one-
hundred percent behind that."

Alonzo held her. "So what are you saying?"

"Let's pray about all this to be sure," Cinda said. "But I'm
thinking as long as I can keep the client I started with"—she
kissed him—"and dress and undress him as I see fit"—her fingers
started unbuttoning his shirt—"I'm good."

"We need to deal with 'as I see fit'." Alonzo watched her move
slowly down his shirt. "In St. Louis I should have full degrees of
freedom as to what I wear."

"So we're negotiating terms?" Cinda reached the last button.
"Do I need to hire Treva?"

"Go ahead," Alonzo said. "I got Steph. And you know she's part
gangster."

"But just so I'm clear," Cinda said. "I'm sure we can agree in
moments like this what you should be wearing." She slipped the
shirt off his shoulders.

Alonzo pulled her close and kissed her. "On that, Mrs. Coles, we are in full agreement."

~

"Is this really the look you want?" Cinda stood in the dressing room of the bridal boutique as Faith tried a selection of gowns. "All princess-y? As your matron of honor and bridal stylist, I have to tell you—I see you in something different. You kill sleek and sexy."

Faith tossed her a look. "When do I ever do sleek and sexy?"

"That dress you wore to the *Bonds of Time* premiere," Cinda said. "The one that changed the whole game with Reggie."

"But just look at this." Faith turned, the layers of sparkle tulle in the skirt shimmering. "Isn't it beautiful and romantic?"

"It's gorgeous," Cinda said. "It would be hard to find a gown that *isn't* gorgeous on you. But that's the only style you've tried so far. Is that your dream gown? What you've always envisioned for your wedding day? If so, I'll hush up."

"I can't say I've ever had a dream gown in mind," Faith said. "I'm just not the sleek and sexy type. Remember you had to talk me into trying on that dress for the premiere."

Cinda looked at her. "So when you say you're not that type, you'd do sexy just for Reggie, right? Say, on your wedding night?"

"Remember I said we needed to talk?" Faith lifted the dress as she stepped down from the podium. "I'm anxious about that —the whole 'wedding night, first time' thing." She added, "And obviously it's not my *first* time, but I had so many hang-ups with Jesse, like not wanting him to see me because I knew it was wrong and I've always been shy about my body anyway—so now I'm afraid I'll have all these hang-ups with Reggie. And honestly, just the thought of wearing lingerie or whatever makes me feel awkward." She gave a sigh. "I know all this sounds crazy."

"Nope," Cinda said. "I was anxious the whole plane ride to Antigua."

"Where you eloped?" Faith said. "I would've thought you'd be super excited."

"Excited, yeah," Cinda said, "but mostly out of my mind with nervousness. Think about it—you've got months to think about this and prepare. I went from engaged to married in *days*. And I was like you—not comfortable with my body *at all*. The whole flight, I'm thinking, we're headed to an island, which means he'll see me in a *swimsuit*. I'm gonna be his wife which means I guess we're having *sex*. What do I *do*? I was totally freaking out."

Faith moved closer. "So what *did* you do?"

"You won't believe it," Cinda said, "and to this day it's been our secret, but after the plane landed I snuck in a call to your mom."

"What?" Faith said. "You talked to my mom about all that?"

"I never had a relationship with my mom where we talked about anything that mattered really," Cinda said. "But I felt I could talk to Treva—caught her right before she landed in the hospital on bed rest. Anyway, I told her we were about to get married and I was scared I wouldn't know what to do and I wasn't comfortable with him seeing my body . . . all of that."

"This is so wild to me," Faith said. "What did Mom say?"

"Well, she shared personal things that helped—you'll have to ask her about that," Cinda said. "But she also said something I thought was funny—'Have you talked to God about it?' I said, 'Huh?'" She chuckled even now. "It was so crazy to me that I could ask God to help me not only be comfortable but *enjoy* intimacy with my husband." She looked at Faith. "And your mom's a trip. She said, 'Let's pray you blow his mind.'"

"My mom *did not* say that," Faith said.

Cinda gave her a look. "Girl, you thought you needed to talk to me. You need to talk to your mom. She's serious about the 'ministry of the bedroom' in marriage, as she calls it."

Faith shook her head. "That is completely awkward to even begin to think about."

Cinda stood and moved toward the door. "While you ponder it —awkward as it may be—I'll be right back."

"Where are you going?" Faith said.

"To pick out a few sleek and sexy gowns." Cinda smiled at her. "Just to see."

∼

Cinda got back to the B and B, ready to shower and change for dinner with Alonzo, Faith, and Reggie. She headed up the stairs, checking her phone. She'd left two messages for Kelsey and hadn't heard back. Did Kelsey still have an attitude—

"Cinda."

The voice surprised her. Cinda turned. "Jade? What are you doing here?"

"Stephanie said I could wait for you." Jade looked tentative. "Can we talk a minute?"

"I don't have much time, but . . ." Cinda walked back down. "We can go in the sitting room."

Cinda led the way, taking a spot on the sofa, already tensing up. Jade forever brought the drama. "What's up?" she said.

Jade looked at her as if she might speak, then looked away. "Last weekend," she began, "I went to Chicago for my mom's wedding but couldn't stay because I got so angry with her. She *still* doesn't get what she did to Dad or our family, and she expected us to *celebrate* as if we were actually happy for her."

Cinda nodded slightly. Jordyn had told her about the experience.

"So I got back on the road at one in the morning and drove through the night," Jade said, "off of adrenaline really because I was so upset. And about three hours in, I started having these thoughts . . . *You're no different, Jade. Except, you're actually worse.*

279

Selfish. Mean. Hateful." Her voice had none of its usual bite. "I'm not Jordyn. Never been warm and fuzzy or whatever. But the hurt from my biological father, you showing up, losing Dad, finding out about Mom . . . there's this ball of rage in me. I'm starting to scare *myself.*"

Cinda watched her check a notification, though she didn't seem focused on it.

Jade heaved a sigh. "Today for the first time I watched the video Alonzo did with Jordyn," she said. "And it sounds really stupid at this point, but I know you remember how obsessed I was with Alonzo." She gave Cinda a quick glance, staring away mostly. "Could not *wait* to meet him. Had all these fantasies in my head about him asking me out, getting to know him—like I said, I know it's stupid, but it's the truth. Then here *you* come, first stealing our dad's heart, then Alonzo's."

"I didn't steal Randall's heart," Cinda said. "He had more than enough love for us all."

"It's just how I saw it," Jade said. "So I watched the video and when he got to the part about meeting you and what your relationship was like, I got tears in my eyes—and I can count on one hand the number of times I've cried. And two of those have been in the past week." She seemed to tear up even now. "I kept thinking, that's what I want, something beautiful like that. Someone to see *me* like that and treat me like that. Yet I've *hated* the fact that you two *have* that."

Cinda moved the box of tissues closer to Jade.

"I haven't even talked to Jordyn yet," Jade said. "If it's possible, I've been meaner to her than I've been to you, so there's a lot to deal with there. And I won't lie, it's hard for me to swallow my pride. But I'm . . . I'm sorry. For every stinking thing I've said to you and thought about you and done to you from the moment I met you."

Cinda hadn't felt anything as Jade spoke—until that moment. Tears welled in her eyes, and she looked at Jade as she stared downward. She didn't know how Jade would respond, but Cinda stood and moved closer to her. Jade rose and brought her arms around Cinda, and they held one another.

"I'm sorry," Jade said again, emotion filling her voice.

"I accept your apology, Jade," Cinda said.

"And I guess I could say I was even more hateful toward Alonzo," Jade said. "I know he could never forgive me, but could you just tell him . . . tell him I do feel bad and I'm sorry."

Cinda looked at her. "Maybe you should tell him yourself."

Jade had a look in her eyes Cinda hadn't seen. "I couldn't. I couldn't even face him after that video I did."

"I think you need to," Cinda said. "I'll go get him."

Minutes later, Cinda walked with Alonzo into the sitting room.

Jade stood, keeping a distance. "Cinda probably told you why I'm here," she said. "I've apologized to her, and . . . I want to say I'm sorry for mocking you and your faith." She met his gaze only briefly. "Jordyn was right. I was basically mocking Dad and I . . . I don't know how I could . . ." Her words choked. "And I don't blame you if you can't forgive me—"

"Jade." Alonzo moved closer. "Cinda said you watched that video I did. So you know the regrets I have about things I've done, people I've hurt. How could I take Jesus' forgiveness, and not extend it to you?"

Jade brought her eyes to him. "That's something my father would say."

"I take that as a huge compliment," Alonzo said. "Your father was an amazing man."

"I'm seeing that more and more," Jade said. She started toward the door. "I'd better go."

"Jade," Alonzo said, "you should come to our church on Sunday."

Jade paused. "I don't think I'm ready for all that," she said, "plus I never went with Dad and now Jordyn goes, so it'd be weird."

"If you could come here and talk to us . . ." Alonzo shrugged a little. "Just think about it."

Jade nodded as they walked her to the door. They closed it behind her and looked at one another.

"I guess wonders never cease." Cinda headed for the stairs. "And did you hear how you said 'our' church?" She looked back at him. "I think you've already moved in your heart."

CHAPTER 40

*J*esse sat in the middle of his living room floor, legs spread in a V, tussling with Zoe.

"Go on, try it," Jesse said, smiling.

Zoe kept a wary eye on him as she moved to all fours then stood—and he pulled her back down and rolled her over, her laughter filling the air.

She crawled a few feet away, determined to get to a firm stand without interference.

"Oh, you're smart, huh?" Jesse said. "You think you got Daddy this time?"

Jesse let her get to her feet, barely, then wrestled her down again to high-pitched squeals.

Lancelot lumbered over, stopping between them.

"Really?" Jesse said. "How you gonna be Team Zoe? I'm the one who feeds you and walks you."

Zoe saw her opportunity and crawled further away, not only standing but taking off toward the kitchen.

"Ahhh," Jesse groaned. "You and Lancelot double team me every time."

He went after her, lifting her above his head as he walked back.

"Shpin, Daddy! Shpin!"

Jesse spun her around, laughing at her belly laughter.

Back on the floor, Zoe crawled on top of Lancelot as he lay on his side. Jesse watched, unable to take his eyes off of her. He wanted to soak in every minute, knowing he didn't have many more. And the more he watched, the more his eyes filled.

He rubbed her back. "Zoe, I pray you never meet a guy like me. At least, the guy I was when I met your mother."

Zoe lay her head on Lancelot now, rubbing his fur.

"I pray you're never hurt by someone who's not worthy of you," Jesse said. "Protect her, Lord."

Tears fell as he imagined prayers that Faith's father must have prayed.

"Zoe, Daddy loves you so much, and even though I won't see you as often—" The doorbell sounded and Lancelot barked. "That's your mommy," Jesse said.

Zoe popped up. "Momma!"

Jesse picked her up and took a breath as he walked to the door, wiping his eyes.

"Momma!" Zoe said again when the door opened. She lunged forward, into Faith's arms.

"How's my sweet girl?" Faith kissed her. "I missed you." She looked at Jesse. "How'd it go?"

"Everything's good," Jesse said. "Let me get her things."

Jesse got the diaper bag and inserted a sippy cup with milk from the refrigerator and her toys. He handed the bag to Faith, who threw it over her shoulder.

"Say bye-bye to Daddy," Faith said.

Zoe reached for a hug, and Jesse squeezed her.

"Um, Faith, you got a minute?" Jesse said.

"Reggie's waiting in the car," Faith said, "and we've got to drop Zoe home then head out—"

"I just wanted to tell you I'm leaving," Jesse said. "Moving back to DC."

"Oh," Faith said. "You got an offer out there?"

"I got one here too actually," Jesse said. "But that's the one I'm taking."

"Oh," Faith said again. "I thought you said you wanted to be near Zoe, to be part of her life. But, okay."

"That's definitely what I want," Jesse said, "but I'm trying to consider you." He paused. "I remember how upset you were when I transferred down here for school. I don't want to be presumptuous. I don't want to interfere with your life. It's just best that I go."

"Best for whom?" Faith said. "Do you know how much Zoe loves her daddy?" She looked as Zoe played with Jesse's hands even now. "I did get upset when you moved down here, and I was wrong. Watching the two of you, the bond you have—reminds me of my dad and me. I would feel awful if Zoe didn't have you in her life, and I was the reason."

"That's really . . . I appreciate that, Faith." Jesse nodded vaguely, trying to stuff too much emotion. "And Faith, I just want to . . ." He blew out a breath. "I just want to say I'm sorry, for the way I treated you."

Faith frowned a little. "I'm sure you've already apologized, Jesse."

"But I'm starting to understand things in a deeper way," Jesse said. "I didn't even care that you were a virgin, it just made it more of a challenge. And when I look at Zoe . . ." He no longer cared. He let the tears fall. "I'm just really sorry, Faith. You deserved so much more. And God has given you so much more."

Faith looked at him. "And God has given Zoe so much—in you." She started for the door then turned. "Don't stay in the past, Jesse, and you've got to stop taking all the blame. I made my own choices. Really, you've got so much ahead." She watched Zoe reach for him. "It's a blessing," Faith said, "seeing the man Zoe has for a father."

Jesse hugged his little girl again, and when they'd left, he picked up more toys, the ones that remained at his place. Staring at a stuffed dog, all he could think was that he'd actually be able to help raise his daughter. He was the one who'd been blessed.

~

Lancelot's bark let Jesse know the doorbell had rung. He came from the bedroom where he'd been studying and opened the door.

"Jordyn, hey," he said. "I didn't know you were coming by."

"Well, it's Friday night," Jordyn said. "You said you had nothing going but the usual—your studies. So, I figured you at least had to eat." She lifted a carryout bag from Maggiano's. "I got your favorite, to celebrate."

Jesse moved aside so she could enter. "What exactly are we celebrating?"

"Your two offers," Jordyn said. "And graduation coming up. It's an exciting time for you."

"If you say so," Jesse said, watching her take the food to the kitchen.

"I see you're your usual crabby self." Jordyn got plates and set them at the table.

"I'm actually feeling pretty good." Jesse got utensils and napkins. "I decided to take the St. Louis offer, so I can be near Zoe."

Jordyn turned to look at him. "Wow. That's pretty big news. You had all but accepted the DC one."

"True." Jesse sat at the table. "I talked to Faith today. Got a different perspective."

Jordyn opened the containers of Rigatoni D and chicken Parmesan. "So, St. Louis. You're actually settling here."

"I guess this is where I become a full-fledged adult," Jesse said. He took her hand, bowed his head, and prayed for the food, then looked at Jordyn. "Thank you," he said, digging in. "I didn't know what I was doing for dinner yet."

"I figured," Jordyn said. "And it's eight o'clock."

Jesse savored the penne pasta. "So you've been rolling with the videos. What's next?"

"Did one last night," Jordyn said, "with Jillian, Faith's aunt."

"Really?" Jesse said. "What's the theme?"

"The title was easy." Jordyn cut into the chicken Parmesan. *"When I'm Grieved."*

"Oh, makes sense," Jesse said. "I know she lost her husband."

"Actually she's talking about a different kind of grief," Jordyn said. "Grief from sin."

"Whoa." Jesse paused. "How are you getting people to talk about this stuff on camera?"

"It's like with you," Jordyn said. "I haven't planned a single one in advance. It just happens." She ate a forkful.

Jesse looked across the table at her. "When are you doing one?"

"Well, if they're all impromptu," Jordyn said, "I guess I'll know when I know."

Jesse heard the buzz of the dryer. "You know what, if I don't get that right now," he said, "I'll be ready to crash tonight and mad that no sheets are on the bed."

He went to get them from the dryer and headed to his room.

"I can help," Jordyn said, following.

"I can actually handle it," Jesse said. "It's not that hard."

Jordyn came anyway, helping fit the bottom sheet, then tucking the top one. She spread his blanket overtop then sat down.

Jesse looked at her, poised to return to the kitchen.

She extended her hand. "Come here a second."

"Jordyn, let's just go back—"

"I won't bite, Jesse. Just come here."

He moved closer and she stood, putting her arms around his waist. "I've been really curious about this . . ."

Jordyn put her lips to his, and Jesse responded easily, holding her, taking the kiss deeper.

Jordyn backed onto the bed, pulling him with her. Jesse could feel his heart beating, not a beat of anticipation, but one he'd never felt—one of warning.

He lifted himself a little, and Jordyn enclosed him tighter, kissing him still.

"Jordyn," Jesse said, "we need to stop."

"You really want to?" Jordyn's hands moved under his shirt.

Jesse closed his eyes, wanting nothing more than to go where this was taking them. Yet, another part of him . . . *Lord, help me.*

He kissed her a little more then felt another tug. He sat up. "We have to. We have to stop."

Jordyn entwined her fingers with his, pulling him back down. "I want to stay with you tonight." She raised up a little, took off her shirt.

"Jordyn." Jesse blew out a sigh, getting out of bed. "Put your clothes on. You have to go."

She looked at him. "Why?"

"Why?" Jesse stared at her, perplexed. "You know I'm trying to move past all this. You said *you* were trying to move past all this. Why are you in my bed?"

"I just . . ." Jordyn pulled her shirt over her head. "Being around you . . . stirs things in me."

"Then you don't need to be around me."

Jesse walked to the kitchen and packed up the food. "You can take this home," he said.

Jordyn had tears in her eyes. "I got it for you. Just keep it." She looked at him. "Why do I have to go? We'll just stay out here."

Jesse hesitated. Maybe he was being too harsh. But he wanted to use the strength he had—while he still had it.

He walked to the door and opened it. Jordyn walked past without looking at him. And Jesse closed it.

And exhaled.

He got his phone and dialed a number in his favorites.

"Jess, what's up, my dude?" Lance said.

Jesse could still feel his heart beating. "You know how you said the power of God could help me resist temptation?"

"I do," Lance said.

"I just found out for myself."

"Wow," Lance said. "You want to come to the house and talk? Faith's out for the evening, and your princess is right here."

"It's Friday night," Jesse said. "I don't need to bother you."

"I'm here," Lance said. "Let's celebrate the victory."

CHAPTER 41

*J*ordyn hoped to slip quietly into the room Stephanie had given her at the B and B. She hadn't yet used it, but if ever she needed a night away from it all, this was it.

From the entryway, she could hear voices. Sounded as if they were coming from the dining room. Jordyn moved toward the stairs and started up.

"No, I've got it in my bedroom, I'll go get it."

Stephanie. Jordyn heard her heels clicking on the marble tile.

"Hey, Jordyn, I didn't know you were here." Stephanie stood at the bottom of the stairs. "You should join us. We've got some good food in there."

"Oh, thanks, Steph, I'm fine—"

"Jordyn's here?" Jillian appeared next. "Yes, come down. It's just three of us, our prayer group."

"Seriously, I'm fine, thank you, though," Jordyn said. "I just need to . . . be alone."

Jillian moved closer. "You look sad. Is everything okay?"

Put your clothes on. You have to go.

Why are you in my bed?

The words bore through her for the fiftieth time, causing her to tremble slightly. Jordyn took hold of the rail. "I'm okay," she said.

Jillian said something to Stephanie and took to the stairs. She hugged Jordyn when she got to her. "How about we go have that talk?"

Jordyn gave a nod.

They went to the third floor bedroom and sat next to one another on the king bed.

"You said it the other night," Jillian said. "We don't know each other well. But you also said the grief is overwhelming and you feel alone." She turned more toward her. "I don't know what you're going through, and you certainly don't have to tell me. But when I look at you, I think of my two daughters, seventeen and nineteen. And my momma's heart just wants to hug you."

Jillian took her into her arms, and the dam broke.

The way she'd tried to seduce Jesse.

Her extended affair with a married man.

The other men with whom she'd shared a bed.

Every experience assaulted her, racking her with guilt. She'd never sobbed like this.

"I'm . . . sorry . . . for breaking . . . down . . . like . . . this."

"Shh," Jillian said, rubbing her back. "Don't you apologize. Cry it out. Just cry it out."

"I can't . . . believe . . . I tried to get him . . ." Jordyn couldn't stop shaking. " . . . to have sex with me . . . tonight. I can't *believe* . . . I did that."

Jillian went to find tissues in the bathroom, and brought the box over, handing Jordyn a few.

"Do you want to talk about tonight?" Jillian said.

Jordyn wiped her eyes even as more tears came. "It was Jesse," she said, giving Jillian a tentative glance.

"Okay," Jillian said.

"And I've had a crush on him, but he only wanted to be friends and I knew that . . ." Jordyn blew her nose. "And I knew he was praying to change his life and meeting with Lance and all that—and I wanted to change *my* life . . . But I actually tried to get him to sleep with me."

"And what happened?" Jillian said.

"He told me to leave." Jordyn dissolved into tears again. "I don't know what's wrong with me. I *do* want to change, but maybe sex has been part of my life for too long . . . I just *go there*. It's like, a default for me—and I know that sounds *awful*. Here I am going to church and wanting a different life, and at the same time, totally wanting Jesse."

"So let me ask you," Jillian said. "Where are you spiritually? Would you say you're saved? Born again?"

"I think I'm in a weird place," Jordyn said. "I've asked God's forgiveness for different things, but haven't quite made a commitment to Him. I'm sort of still in the seeking and learning phase."

Jillian nodded. "So everything you're saying makes sense. You have no power."

"What do you mean?" Jordyn said.

"You're trying to do better and make changes on your own, but it's not possible." Jillian's eyes were soft. "I know you've heard the gospel many times at Living Hope. How we're born in sin, and the wages of sin is death . . . but Jesus paid that penalty for our sins on the cross."

Jordyn nodded. "And if we repent and believe in Him, we're saved."

"But before we're saved," Jillian said, "we're slaves of the enemy. Slaves to sin. We literally can't break free of that pattern on our own." She got up and looked for a Bible, finding one in the drawer of a nightstand, then flipped somewhere toward the back. "I want you to read this out loud—Ephesians 2:1-3."

Jordyn took the Bible. "'And you were dead in your trespasses and sins, in which you formerly walked according to the course of this world, according to the prince of the power of the air—'"

"That's the enemy," Jillian said. "The devil. We all did *his* will."

Jordyn shuddered inside. "'. . . of the spirit that is now working in the sons of disobedience. Among them we too all formerly lived in the lusts of our flesh, indulging the desires of the flesh and of the mind, and were by nature children of wrath, even as the rest.'"

Jordyn felt her heart rate speed up. "This right here," she said, pointing, "about lusts and indulging desires . . ." She looked at Jillian. "How is this so completely my life?"

"It's so completely *all* of our lives in one way or another," Jillian said. "That's why Jesus came, to rescue us. Being saved isn't just about heaven. Salvation means freedom and new life *now*. Keep reading."

Jordyn looked back down. "'But God, being rich in mercy, because of His great love with which He loved us, even when we were dead in our transgressions, made us alive together with Christ (by grace you have been saved), and raised us up with Him, and seated us with Him in the heavenly places in Christ Jesus . . .'"

Jillian stood. "So this is where you are now." She put one hand low to the ground. "Captive to the enemy. Indulging your lusts. It's dark down here, no hope, horrible." She lifted the other hand high. "This is where God wants you to be—in the light, alive, new creation, new heart, seated in heavenly places. And guess what? You don't have to get there on your own. His mercy, grace, and love get you there." She moved closer. "And guess what else? When you're saved, you're given God's Spirit. God's Spirit gives you *power* to do His will. Not perfectly—you heard my video. I messed up big time. But His grace helps us grow."

Why are you in my bed?

Jordyn closed her eyes as the words assaulted her again. "How can I just *receive* this? I'd literally be in Jesse's bed right now if he hadn't told me to go. What must God think when He looks at me?"

Jillian sat back down. "So you know Living Water just launched, the women's ministry?"

Jordyn nodded.

"The name comes from the story of the woman at the well in the gospel of John," Jillian said. "She could've very well just come from a man's bed—not her husband—when Jesus offered her the greatest gift imaginable. Let's look at it . . ."

∽

Jordyn stared into the camera she'd set up on the tripod, removing the makeup from her forehead, nose, cheeks, and eyes. On her third wipe now, she took her time, erasing the layers, dropping them into a wastebasket beside the stool.

"I've done makeup tutorials on this channel for years now," Jordyn said. "And though you've seen me bare-faced many times, somehow that didn't bother me. A few seconds in, I'd start adding on and adding on, until I achieved my perfect face." She blew out a soft breath. "Doing it in the reverse is terrifying."

Jordyn glanced over at Jillian, Stephanie, and Cinda, who'd gotten back close to midnight. It was one in the morning now, and Jordyn was spent. But she needed to do this.

"I don't want you to see me," Jordyn continued. "I don't want you to see what I really look like or who I really am. Because I know the ugly that's there." Her breath caught and she closed her eyes.

Cinda walked over. "You can do this," she said. "The night started one way and Jesus got hold of it and flipped it. He's got you."

Jordyn nodded. She'd told Cinda everything, thankful she could confide in her sister.

"I saw the ugly tonight, and not just this face with the splotches over here and uneven tone over here." Jordyn pointed them out. "I saw the ugly inside of me. I saw the things I delight in, things that don't please God. I saw myself take something good —a friendship—and push it toward evil." Her mind went to Jesse opening the door for her to go, and her eyes closed again.

Jordyn took a breath. "And I guess I knew this, but it became super clear about two hours ago—as much as I don't want people to see me, *God* sees me. The real me. He sees *all* the ugly, things I haven't done that I want to do. And I don't know why, but . . . He still loves me. He still *wants* me . . . to be *His*."

Jordyn wiped her tears and saw Jillian wiping as well.

"Tonight, I asked God to forgive every ugly thing I've done, and I placed my faith in Jesus Christ for my salvation." Jordyn took a moment. She hadn't yet grasped it. "I don't know if He's going to do anything about these splotches on my face." Her eyes smiled a little. "But from what I saw in the Bible tonight, He took everything that's ugly in me—and He cleansed it. He made it new." She picked up the Bible. "I just want to share a couple things that rocked me . . ."

～

Jordyn didn't know what had gotten into her, but as tired as she was, she wanted to get her video edited and uploaded tonight. Well, this morning, since it was already past three.

Her bedroom door opened and Jade walked in.

Jordyn looked over her shoulder. "I thought you prided yourself on knocking."

"I think I became a Christian tonight," Jade said.

Jordyn turned in her chair, staring.

"Say *something*," Jade said.

Jordyn stared a few seconds more. "So did I," she said. "I'm editing a video about it. *When I'm Made New.*"

"All this time and you weren't a Christian already?" Jade said. "Isn't this eerie, though? Born on the same day, then born *again* on the same day?"

It slowly sank in, what Jade had said. "You became a *Christian* tonight?"

Jade nodded.

"And how do you know about being 'born again'? What in the world happened?" Jordyn stood and hugged her sister tight. "I need to hear every bit of this."

CHAPTER 42

"*I* have to say, I didn't think you would move this quickly." Cyd talked with Micah at a lunch spot on campus. "You actually returned the advance to the publisher?"

"First I wondered if I could finesse it," Micah said, "make the book more about me and my evolution, leading to present day. But I re-read my proposal and book outline. The focus was clearly supposed to be on my beliefs about Jesus. The old beliefs. I had to back out."

"What about your upcoming talk and panel discussion at the conference?" Cyd finished the last of her salad.

"Surprisingly, the conference committee thought the evolution was intriguing. They want me to talk about it." Micah picked up what remained of his sandwich. "But this blog I need to do, telling people who follow me? I might just be stoned." He took a bite.

"You'll be in good company," Cyd said. "Stephen in—"

"The book of Acts." Micah nodded. "But he never spewed false rhetoric about Jesus."

"Saul did," Cyd said. "Jesus was with him after that road to Damascus. He's with you too."

Micah looked at her. "You've been doing this a long time, you and Jesus. Do you worry about anything?"

"Lots of things," Cyd said. "For one, I was beside myself about that debate, worried what the repercussions on campus would be."

"But there weren't any, were there?" Micah said.

"I had student complaints to contend with," Cyd said. "Another student, a young woman I adored, no longer wanted me as her advisor. A couple of long time colleagues don't have much to say to me. To name a few."

Micah looked at her. "I'm sorry, Cyd. If I hadn't promoted it the way I did . . . If I hadn't asked you to begin with . . ."

"Don't be ridiculous," Cyd said. "God clearly used the debate. Although, He could've used it without all that crass promotion."

"Crass?"

"I could've killed you that night you had that tweet storm going," Cyd said.

"Nice," Micah said. "The mature Christian woman, with murder on her mind."

"And you *knew* I didn't agree to all that," Cyd said. "I thought you were the most pompous, self-seeking, arrogant—"

"Arrogant and pompous are synonyms."

"I needed the double emphasis," Cyd said.

"At least you said *were*," Micah said. "Hopefully your opinion has changed."

Cyd drank some of her water. "Remains to be seen."

"You know what I thought you were?" Micah said. "Intimidating."

"Why?" Cyd said.

"I would see you at conferences and then when I got here on campus, and you have this presence about you." Micah seemed to think a moment. "Not arrogance, but an assurance. And you listen more than you talk, so it's hard to know what you're thinking, which holds its own power. And when you do talk, you don't mince words." He nodded. "But now I know your secret."

"What's my secret, Micah?"

"As you live and breathe—Jesus."

"Hard to know what to say to that." Cyd got up and threw away her trash.

They started the short walk back to their building.

"I thought you might come to church on Sunday," Cyd said.

"I flew to Phoenix," Micah said. "My son had a school program Saturday night."

Cyd looked at him. "I didn't know you had a son. You don't have a single picture in your office."

"I have to do better about that." Micah took out his phone and scrolled to a picture. "Brandon. He's twelve."

Cyd smiled. "Handsome young guy. He's your only?"

"He's my only," Micah said. "His mom and I split six years ago." He looked at Cyd. "And I know you've got a son too."

"Because I've got framed pictures."

"Oh, we're bragging?"

"Stating facts."

"You could always help a brother out," Micah said, "if you've got extra frames lying around."

"Then you'd have to print the pictures," Cyd said, "in the right size. No need to stress yourself out."

"I think you just called me an idiot."

"No," Cyd said, "that was the night of the debate."

"Ohh"—Micah nodded—"okay. The gloves came off."

Cyd stifled a smile. "Idiot's not worse than pompous, is it?"

"Of course it is," Micah said. "One goes to intellect, the other to attitude."

"That's unfortunate," Cyd said.

Micah let out a chuckle. "I take back my 'live and breathe Jesus'. You're actually brutal."

"All I said was I had framed pictures." Cyd opened the door to their building. "You took it from there."

"I need to see some καρπὸς τοῦ Πνεύματός," Micah said, walking in with her. "That's all I'm saying."

Cyd chuckled this time. "So you're throwing Greek phrases at me? And I've shown lots of fruit of the Spirit. Self-control kept me from throttling you."

"Did I really make you that mad?" Micah said. "As cool, calm, and collected as you are?"

"You pushed more buttons than I knew I had," Cyd said. "You and your little Twitter army."

Micah paused, taking out his phone again, typing.

Seconds later, Cyd heard her phone buzzing with a notification. She looked at it. Micah had tweeted: "Had a lovely lunch with my colleague & sister in Christ @CydLondon. Yes. God still does miracles. I now believe. In Jesus."

Cyd looked at him. "You've rendered me speechless."

Micah continued to his office. "I like speechless Cyd better than brutal Cyd."

~

"Chase, did you finish your homework?" Cyd called after her son, who had zoomed out of the kitchen to play a video game.

Chase came back in. "Mom, Jordyn makes sure I do it when I get home from school."

Cyd rinsed a dish and put it in the dishwasher. "How much screen time have you had today?"

"Um . . ." His eyes rolled upward as if he couldn't remember.

"That means too much," Cyd said. "It's time to go read, sweetie."

"Mom," Chase said, "just like, twenty minutes."

"When I hear you bargaining for extra reading time," Cyd said, "then you might get extra screen time."

"Well, there you go." Cedric cleaned the stovetop. "All you have to do is up your reading game, son."

"Come on, Reese," Chase said, trudging up the stairs as the dog bounded ahead of him.

"That's your son," Cyd said.

Cedric chuckled. "Oh, *my* son, when he's got to get checked."

"I wish I'd caught Jordyn before she left." Cyd rinsed another plate. "I'm still marveling over her video. Watched it again and still had me in tears."

"It's wild," Cedric said. "We could see God working in her heart, and we were praying. But you never know the moment it'll happen."

"And when she showed up at church with Jade . . ."

"I got a little misty myself," Cedric said, "thinking how moved Randall would've been."

Cyd started wiping the counter. "God has truly been showing *out*."

"Speaking of . . ." Cedric turned to her. "What's the latest with Micah?"

"He gave back the advance money," Cyd said.

"No way," Cedric said.

"I know." Cyd dropped crumbs into the sink. "And he's planning to talk about his conversion at the conference. Even tweeted today that he's a believer."

Cedric shook his head. "When God said nothing is too hard for Him, He meant *nothing* is too hard for Him."

Cyd heard her phone buzz and went to check it on the counter.

"Mom, can you come here?" Chase said. "How much of this do I have to read?"

"This boy's going to be a scholar," Cyd said, heading up. "He just doesn't know it yet."

Cyd negotiated with Chase how much he needed to finish and returned—to Cedric holding her phone in the kitchen.

"So Micah's your text buddy now?" Cedric said. "You've got your own secret language?"

"You're reading messages on my phone?" Cyd said.

"Is that a problem?" Cedric said. "Because I don't have a problem with you reading anything you want on my phone." He got it and handed it to her. "You know the password. Go for it. Didn't know yours was top secret."

"I just wouldn't pick up your phone and start scrolling through messages." Cyd put his phone back down. "And of course it's not a secret language. It's Greek. I told you he'll ask Bible study questions from time to time."

"Oh. Okay. So the Greek words together with the part about lunch and you being brutal . . . Bible study."

"We grabbed a bite on campus," Cyd said. "It was basic conversation. He was joking about the fruit of the Spirit because I told him what I thought of him around the time of the debate."

Cedric nodded, phone in hand. "And then there's the text chat on Friday—"

"Is this an inquisition?" Cyd took her phone. "You know he asked if I could help him think through career decisions he needed to make. That's what led to the updates today." She looked at him. "You actually have an attitude?"

"So you wouldn't care if you saw me having text chats with women?" Cedric said.

"You put that boundary in place for yourself," Cyd said, "because of your past. So, yes, I'd wonder what was up." She laid her phone on the counter. "Didn't know it was a household rule, though. Not to mention—I've filled you in on everything with Micah from the beginning."

"I think you skipped the lunches," Cedric said.

"Today was the first," Cyd said, "but I do lunch with colleagues all the time. And Cedric, you know what a unique situation this is. I should help lead Micah to the Lord—which you encouraged— then when he's a brother in Christ, cut him off?"

"I just think you need to put some boundaries in place yourself," Cedric said. "Dude is texting you in the evening when you're home with your family."

"I doubt he's even thinking about it like that," Cyd said.

"I don't care how he's thinking about it, Cyd," Cedric said. "I'm saying *you* need to think about it."

"Cedric . . ." Cyd took his hand and leaned against the counter, bringing him close. "I don't think I've ever seen you like this. You can't possibly be worried about a few messages with a colleague I could hardly stand just a few weeks ago."

Cedric put his arms around her with a sigh. "I know I'm probably overreacting." He fell quiet a moment. "We've got people in the church who are really hurting right now because of situations that got out of control."

"Situations I know about?" Cyd said.

"I don't think so, no."

Cyd nodded. Cedric always had more info as an elder.

"It happens too easily, babe," he said. "It's back to the conversation we had about Jordyn staying over here. We have to be vigilant."

Cyd looked into his eyes. "I just want you to understand that there is absolutely nothing with the Micah situation."

"And I want you to understand that that's not the point," Cedric said. "We set boundaries and stay vigilant so nothing doesn't become something."

"You mean like the day after we first met," Cyd said, "when I should've had a boundary about your being at my house at night?"

"And you best believe I was trying to get with your fine self that night." Cedric kissed her. "See, there you go—you didn't have sense enough to keep me out."

Cyd kissed him back. "You had me mesmerized, though."

"Not *that* mesmerized," Cedric said. "Didn't take long for you to give me the boot."

"Which made you want to come back."

"And back." Cedric kissed her. "And back." He kissed her again. "Until you had me dropping rose petals, asking you to marry me."

Cyd leaned into him, her head in his chest. "I love our love story."

"And I'm all about protecting our love." Cedric held her. "The direction God gave Lance for this Bible study is so on point. Babe, we can't let the enemy interfere with the work God is doing in our marriage. And look what He's doing with you at Living Water. You think you don't have a target on your back?"

Cyd nodded slowly. "I hear you, babe," she said. "And maybe we should take this as an opportunity to be proactive about our marriage. You should come with me to San Francisco for our classical studies conference in August, as a getaway for the two of us."

"I like that," Cedric said. "I need to check my work calendar, and we need to see if your parents are free that weekend to watch Chase." He nodded. "But if it works, yeah, let's do it."

Cyd's phone buzzed again on the counter.

Cedric went back to cleaning the stove, and Cyd returned to the sink.

"It's probably Steph," she said.

"I didn't say a word," Cedric said. "But you'd better check it. Steph might have a pressing Bible study question—in Greek."

CHAPTER 43

"So I won't see you till later tonight, at Living Word?" Treva slipped into a pair of jeans and looked for a shirt she didn't care about.

Lance changed the baby's diaper. "I've got back to back meetings," he said, "then final touches on the message. I doubt I'll have time for dinner beforehand." He looked up at her. "But you've got a full day yourself."

Treva pulled a graphic tee over her head. "Whole rest of the week is full," she said. "Headed to Jillian's to clean her duplex for her so she doesn't have to take off of work—thank God Cinda's helping. Moving truck arrives tomorrow morning, so full day helping Jillian and the kids settle in. Mother, Darlene, and Russell arrive tomorrow. And Faith's graduation on Friday."

"Jillian's really excited about her kids getting here." Lance put Wes's clothes back on.

"I'm excited for her," Treva said. "She can get some of her equilibrium back." She pulled her chin-length bob into a ponytail. "So tonight's your second week. You know I'm praying. How are you feeling about the process now?"

"I was serious, babe," Lance said. "I don't care about the vote, so I'm not stressing. I'm pumped actually."

"Why pumped? Hey, sweet boy," Treva said, smiling at the baby as she picked him up.

"Sometimes I'm praying about a message," Lance said, "and I have to believe by faith that I've heard from God. And other times it's so clear." He moved into the bathroom and washed his hands. "These last couple weeks of study time have been amazing. I've been in a groove, just me and God. And when it's like *that*?" He shook his head. "I can't worry about the outcome. God can do what He will. As long as I can keep grooving with Him."

"I'll add that to my prayers," Treva said. "That you stay in the groove. And I'm loving the overflow. That was so good the other night, looking at a part of Ezra you didn't have time to get to last Wednesday."

Lance grabbed his keys from the dresser. "And I loved getting *your* overflow. That was good stuff you had in your notes from when you studied Ezra." He moved closer, kissing Wes's cheek then kissing her. "I'll see you tonight, babe. Love you."

"Lance," Treva said, "just so you know, I don't care how the vote goes either. I'm just thankful that either way, my husband is my pastor. I love studying with you and growing with you." She kissed him. "Thank you for the ways you tend to my soul."

Lance looked into her eyes. "So I'm supposed to leave for work after that?"

"Go," Treva said softly. "I'll see you tonight at church."

"Can you have a talk with Wes?" Lance started off. "Tell him his parents love him, but we need him in bed at a decent hour tonight and to stay asleep, in his own room."

Treva smiled. *Lord, may it be so.*

∽

"Is it just me, or is it kind of crowded?" Treva entered Living

Word Wednesday night wearing baby Wes, with Joy, Hope, and Jillian. "I wonder if another event is scheduled here tonight."

"People are moving into the sanctuary," Jillian said. "Looks like they're here for Bible study."

Treva looked ahead and saw Cyd and Cedric chatting with Tommy and Allison. Jillian gave them all a wide berth and disappeared into the sanctuary.

Treva stopped to give quick hugs as her girls followed Jillian.

"How are you, Treva?" Allison said, hugging her.

"I'm good," Treva said. "How about yourself?" She lowered her tone. "I'm really glad to see this, you and Tommy together."

Allison pulled her aside. "I'm surprised to hear that, since your sister set her sights on Tommy."

"All I will say," Treva said, "is you know I've been praying for you and Tommy and encouraging you to look to God for help to make it work."

"That's true," Allison said.

"So I'm praising God for restoration," Treva said.

Treva moved on, joining the others in the sanctuary.

"Just got a text from Darlene and Russell," Jillian said. "They're on the road to St. Louis. Darlene said Russell hasn't driven this many miles in a decade, so pray for his strength." She tucked her phone back into her bag. "I still can't believe they volunteered to drive the moving truck out here. I really want to bless them."

"They love you like a daughter," Treva said. "And it worked out because they were headed this way anyway for Faith's graduation. They couldn't have loaded the moving truck, though. Thank God for the volunteers at your church."

"What is the deal with all the people?" Faith stood in the aisle with Reggie, Cinda, and Alonzo. "We would've gotten here earlier had we known. I guess we'll make our way to the back."

"We can make room." Jillian put her purse in her lap and scooted down.

The group squeezed in, except Alonzo who'd gotten commandeered in the aisle for pictures.

"Did Alonzo post something on Instagram about tonight?" Treva said. "I'm wondering why there are so many more people."

Cinda shook her head. "He hasn't posted today."

A woman in front of her turned. "You're Pastor Lance's wife, right? I saw your promo for the Bible study."

Treva nodded and shook her hand. "Treva Alexander. What's your name?"

"Helen Reedy," she said. "I overheard you, wondering why so many people tonight." She leaned closer. "I'll just say there was an effort last week to suppress turnout, so a lot of members stayed home. I'm embarrassed to say I was among them."

Treva wished she could say she was surprised.

"But our small group leader forwarded a link to watch the message afterward," Helen continued, "then we talked about it in our group. Many were convicted." Her voice was near whisper. "I have to be honest, I felt Wayman should've been the one recommended, and I still can't say I'd vote for Lance. But I believe God has given him a word in season for Living Word, and a dynamic word at that." She looked out at the sanctuary. "I think that's what you're seeing tonight. That link got passed among several small groups."

"Thank you for sharing that," Treva said. "And I appreciate your candor. It's not about the votes, as Lance said. He just wants God to be glorified."

"Amen," Helen said. "And I'm looking forward to your study. You two make an awesome team."

Worship started and Treva stood, thanking God for moving in such a strong way. Whether Lance pastored at Living Hope or Living Word wasn't nearly as important as everyone walking in love and in the unity of the Spirit. If they could get behind the message that God had given Lance—even if that was all they got behind—that was a praise.

～

"God says, 'Consider your ways!' two times through the prophet Haggai." Lance walked with his Bible along the front. "If God says, 'Consider your ways!' once, you stand at full attention. If He says it twice, you fall prostrate before Him . . . because He's saying He doesn't like what He sees. Amen? He's saying, 'You need to consider what I've already *fully* considered, and found lacking.'"

Jillian leaned over. "I need my brother-in-law to stop convicting me with each and every message." She shook her head and resumed her note-taking.

"And we see what the problem was," Lance said. "All work on the house of God had completely stopped. Remember last week? The people of God returned to the land. God gave them a specific mission. What was the mission?"

"Rebuild God's house," several voices said.

"And they got it going, right?" Lance said. "Built the altar, laid the foundation, even paused to celebrate. The priests got out their fresh robes, they started gigging with the trumpets and cymbals . . ." He paused. "But then what happened?"

"The enemy," echoed throughout.

"The enemy is *always* concerned with what God is doing," Lance said. "From a human standpoint, these were the people living in the land around them. The Bible calls them their 'enemies' or 'adversaries,' depending on your translation. But be clear about it—it was God's age-old enemy at work." He moved to another section of the congregation. "And remember those enemies tried to be slick? Acted like they wanted to build *with* God's people and seek God. Listen—there will always be people among the flock of God who don't truly belong to God."

Heads nodded soberly around Treva.

"But God's people were hip to it," Lance said. "They said, 'No, we got this; we'll build it ourselves.' So when that didn't work, of course—the enemy stepped up his game. Started discouraging the people, frightening the people." He looked out among the congregation. "How many of you know about attacks of fear and discouragement when you're doing what God called you to do?"

Almost all hands went into the air.

"This attack was successful," Lance said. "We saw that the work stopped—for sixteen years." He paused. "But guess what? They got their own houses built." He looked at his Bible. "God said through Haggai, 'Is it time for you yourselves to dwell in your paneled houses while this house lies desolate?' They lost complete sight of the mission of God. They had no hunger for the presence of God. So God had to get their attention once more by telling them through Haggai—'Consider your ways.'"

Lance walked a bit, his head down, then went and whispered something to Kelli who sat up front. He looked out again at the congregation. "I'm moved to pause right now and . . . let's just consider our ways."

As the band and worship singers moved into place, Lance continued. "Let's consider where we've put our own plans and pursuits ahead of God." He paced before them. "Let's consider where we've lost sight of what's even important to God, because we're not in His word, not seeking His face . . ."

Treva had her eyes closed, thinking on Lance's words. She glanced up as Kelli began singing softly, and saw people standing all around the sanctuary, many with eyes closed and hands lifted.

"Let's consider," Lance said, "where we've allowed fear and discouragement to stop the work of God—because we don't trust that *He's* our strength. He's our refuge and fortress. He's our *rock*. Lord, put a hunger in us . . . for *You*."

Lance paused a few seconds and Treva opened her eyes again. He had his head down, hand lifted in praise as worship music filled the sanctuary.

"This is how awesome our God is." Lance was moving again. "He told His people they'd put their own agendas ahead of His. Even told them He'd withheld blessings as a result." He stopped in place. "But when the people humbled themselves and obeyed His voice—*boom.* They were right back in the flow with God."

"He is faithful," a woman said behind Treva.

"See, God doesn't hold grudges." Lance moved toward the congregation. "He doesn't make us repent fifty times, do twenty laps, wait a hundred days till He gets with us again. The first thing He said was, '*I am with you.*'" His voice rose. "In fact, just as He said, 'Consider your ways' twice, He says, 'I am with you'. . . *twice.* He *wanted* to be in their presence."

"Thank You, Jesus," Jillian murmured, tears streaming her face. "Thank You, Jesus."

"Ask Him right now," Lance said, "to *show* you your ways. Let Him deal with you—it'll hurt, trust me, I know. But when you humble yourself and obey His voice, you're right there . . . in the sweetness of His presence . . ."

~

Almost everyone had left the sanctuary, except a handful in Treva's row and the remaining two who'd waited to talk to Lance.

Treva looked at Alonzo, who'd had several requests for pictures afterward. "Are you waiting for people to clear out of the lobby?"

It took Alonzo a moment to realize she was talking to him. "Oh," he said, turning to her. "No. I'm just sitting here thinking."

"We've both been in a weird mood today," Cinda said, "knowing we're flying back to LA tomorrow."

"But buying a house here—is that a definite?" Treva said.

Cinda nodded. "Already started looking. After we do promo stuff for Alonzo's summer film, we'll be back."

"They released the trailer this week," Reggie said. "*Crazy.*" He looked at Alonzo. "Man, I knew you were filming an action flick in London last year, but I didn't know you got your *007* on." He put an arm around Faith. "And uh, I think a dope wedding gift would be red carpet premiere action."

"Oh, you think that would be dope?" Alonzo said.

"Super dope," Reggie said. "Treva and Lance got to do the red carpet for the *Bonds of Time* premiere. Tommy was out there. Jordyn. Cinda got her moment at the LA premiere. What did Faith and I get? Back door to the theater."

Alonzo looked at Cinda.

"Yeah, you might as well tell them," Cinda said.

"Already in the works," Alonzo said. "LA premiere. All expenses paid."

"Are you serious?" Faith said, moving to get Zoe from the pew behind.

Reggie looked stunned. He held out his hand and slapped Alonzo's, then pulled him to a hug. "I don't even know what to say, man. You know I didn't really expect . . . wow."

Lance made his way over. "Everybody's still hanging here?"

"I couldn't leave," Alonzo said. "Been thinking through the screenplay, and my time with Pastor Lyles earlier."

"He wasn't even feeling well today," Lance said. "You see he wasn't here tonight. But he really wanted to give you the time you needed."

"He gave me three hours in his home, videotaped," Alonzo said. "It was incredible. I feel like I got so much insight." He looked at Lance. "I thought the movie ending would play off of how things turn out with the church vote. And I thought it'd be awesome to show you stepping into Pastor Lyles' shoes. But after talking to him today, then listening to you tonight, I realized—you already have."

Treva watched Lance take that in. He looked at Alonzo, but no words came.

Alonzo stood. "I love you, man," he said, hugging Lance. "I don't know if I'll ever be able to step into your shoes and be the man of God you are. But at least I can pretend on screen."

"I'm not . . ." Lance shook his head, his eyes filling. "It's all Christ. *All* Him."

"We know, Lance," Reggie said. "And we can still acknowledge our love for *you* and the man of God you are."

"I'm just saying," Lance said, looking at Alonzo, "please don't write a screenplay that makes me out to be something I'm not. I'm not even comfortable with the focus being put on me. Put Jesus front and center."

"*Jesus!*" Zoe shot her arm in the air, as if Jesus were her superhero.

"That's right, Zoe." Lance scooped her up. "Let's get out of here. They're trying to wreck my emotions." He shifted Zoe to one side and took Treva's hand, starting up the aisle.

Treva leaned into him. "I know you didn't expect to stay this late tonight," she said. "You must be so tired and hungry."

"I was definitely surprised by the number of people who came up afterward," Lance said. "And soon as you said 'tired and hungry,' they both hit me." He smiled at Wes who was babbling. "But you look like you're good to go for another couple hours, young man. We're supposed to have a deal tonight."

In the lobby area they saw Jillian sitting off to the side with Jordyn and Jade. She got up and came to them.

"That 'consider your ways' message hit both of them pretty hard," Jillian said. "Lance, Jordyn wanted to go talk to you in the sanctuary and ask for prayer, but she felt funny because she knows you meet with Jesse."

"How is that an issue?" Lance said.

"I told her she should've gone up there," Jillian said. "Is it too late to pray with her and Jade now?"

Treva looked at her husband, already knowing his answer.

"Zoe, go to your Aunt Jillian," Lance said, passing her, then walked over to the two young women.

Treva looked at her sister. "Jordyn seems to have really taken to you."

"It's mutual," Jillian said. "We met again yesterday." She looked over as Lance prayed with them. "You saw her video. I think she's comfortable talking to me because she knows I've got some 'ugly' in my life too."

Treva nodded. "We all do."

"Yeah," Jillian said. "But for some of us it's still fresh. We're still healing."

CHAPTER 44

*J*illian took five pizzas from the delivery man and stepped between boxes and out of place furniture to get them into the kitchen. "You guys should break and eat!" she called.

Reggie came from upstairs, headed back out. "When you're on a roll, you have to keep it moving," he said. "Soon as I eat that, I'll be knocked out on the sofa with Grandma Darlene."

Jillian smiled over at Darlene, with baby Wes asleep on her chest. "Thanks again for doing this, Reggie. I feel bad that you took time from work."

"Not a problem," Reggie said. "We're fam. I might as well start calling you 'Aunt Jillian' too."

He left out, and Jillian felt it again—the dull ache of losing her friend. With Reggie helping and Tommy nowhere in sight, couldn't be more clear how wrong things had gone.

Treva came downstairs now. "The kids' bedroom furniture is in place," she said. "I'm headed to the airport to pick them all up."

"Momma called me when they were boarding," Jillian said. "In the space of five minutes she lamented three times about all her grandchildren being halfway across the country. So get ready."

"I've already heard it," Treva said. "I told her she should move out here too."

"Ha," Jillian said. "She'd never leave Northwest, DC." She watched Treva head for the door. "Are you forgetting someone?" She pointed at Wes.

"Oh, my, I sure did," Treva said. "Darlene's had him all day, except when his stomach was growling." She moved closer. "How can I wake them up, though? That's too cute."

Treva lifted her baby boy, curled in a ball.

"You got him?" Darlene mumbled, fatigued still from traveling through the night.

"I've got him," Treva said. "Go back to sleep."

Treva left out and seconds later, Lance and Cedric walked in with boxes in tow, headed for the stairs.

"Master bedroom," Cedric said over his shoulder. "Way in the back of the truck."

"Oh, what a relief," Jillian said. "I was starting to wonder if they'd gotten lost somehow."

Jillian followed them up and, once they'd set the boxes down, looked to see which ones they were. Black sharpie said, "Master bedroom - Cecil."

She'd been waiting for this, waiting to surround herself once again with tangible reminders of her husband. Having to move so quickly and leave most of their belongings—on top of everything else—had seemed especially hard. Her life would never be the same, but she needed to get something of it back. She sat on the floor next to the boxes, drew a breath, and opened the first.

The scent of Cecil's cologne doubled her over. So palpable . . . as if he'd walked into the room. Jillian took steadying breaths, then looked inside the box, realizing its contents—items from Cecil's nightstand. She unwrapped the cologne from its tissue and opened the top—and a thousand memories tumbled forth. The date nights they'd finally gotten good at keeping. Cecil getting dressed, then watching her get dressed. The flirting. The kisses.

Wondering if they should just stay in and lock the door—until one of the kids beckoned and they made a quick escape.

Jillian pulled the next items out. Cecil's Bible. A couple books from his to-be-read pile. Reading glasses. Random papers from inside one of the drawers—she couldn't throw a single one away. And a wedding picture . . .

Jillian looked up as Lance and Cedric walked in with more boxes, put them down, and quietly walked back out.

She eyed the picture, a young Jillian and Cecil. Their entire lives ahead of them. *Till death do us part.* It was supposed to be fifty or sixty years at least—not twenty. And the parting wasn't supposed to be sudden. And they weren't supposed to have second honeymoon plans.

Tears fell on the glass as Jillian thought about what the past three months should have been—she and Cecil enjoying one another, deepening their love. *You're supposed to be here with me, Cecil.* She stared at the picture, longing to hear his voice, feel his touch. The way he held her at night. Or as they cooked, the way he'd ease up from behind and slip his arms around her. They'd linger that way as she sautéed something in the pan, maybe no more than thirty seconds, but a sweet thirty seconds. Thirty seconds she'd never have again.

Jillian brushed tears from her face as she reached into the box and unwrapped another picture. She and Cecil last Christmas. Cecil had said, "I don't think Jill and I have taken a nice picture—just the two of us—in years." So Lance had taken this one in the backyard with his camera, and Cecil had gotten it framed.

Somehow this picture was even more painful. Only five months ago. How was that even possible? How could her entire world have transformed in such a short amount of time? How could . . .?

The beat of her heart went askew as more tears fell, the picture trembling in her hands. How could she be feeling *this* right now?

Jillian closed her eyes. Why couldn't she shake it? With all the prayers she'd prayed, *asking* God to take it away. Even now, when all she wanted was to focus on Cecil—here it was again. The thought. The feeling.

It's not real, Lord. I know this. It belongs to a night that should've never been. And it's not good, right, or pure. He's married. Please . . . I don't want to feel this. And since all things are possible with You—Lord, I need You to take it away.

Jillian held the picture close, thankful she could bare her heart, with all its flaws and weaknesses, to God. She couldn't admit it to Treva. Could barely acknowledge it within herself. But try as she might, she couldn't deny it—she'd somehow fallen in love with Tommy.

~

"So the oldest grandbaby is graduating college tomorrow," Darlene said.

"And getting married soon," Patsy added. "I don't think either of us gave our permission for Faith to grow up so fast."

After a big family dinner, the grandmothers sat next to one another downstairs at Treva's, the entire family surrounding. An NBA playoff game filled the screen in front of them.

"And have we properly vetted Reggie?" Darlene said.

Reggie looked over from the game, a brow raised.

"What's the vetting process?" Faith said.

"Criminal background check," Patsy said, "credit check, random surveillance checks, we need school transcripts, tax records . . ."

"Nope, none of that's been done," Faith said. "Better move quickly. We've only got three months."

"I'll gladly submit to all that," Reggie said, looking at the grand-mothers. "But first you have to promise—if you find one thing that's problematic, you'll take her off my hands."

Darlene chuckled. "Why do I love this young man already?"

"So, Reggie," Sophia said, "any younger brothers in the family?"

"I'm the baby," Reggie said. "My brother and sister are a lot older."

"Cousins?" Sophia said.

Jillian looked at her daughter.

"What?" Sophia said. "I think we're all agreed that Reggie's a great catch. Trying to see what else is in the water."

"I thought you were so in love with Devin," David said.

Sophia waved a hand. "I'm so through with him."

Joy piped up. "Girl, there are some cute guys over at—" She glanced at Treva who was looking at her, then looked back at Sophia. "We'll talk."

"All the secrets and thick-as-thieves stuff was cute when you two were ten and eleven," Treva said. "At sixteen and seventeen . . ." She looked at Patsy. "These are the ones who need surveillance."

"We already have it," Joy said. "Her name is Hope."

"I'm thirteen," Hope said. "I don't tell stuff like I used to."

Jillian exchanged a knowing look with Treva. Hope had been known to shed light on some things—and neither Jillian or Treva had been mad about it.

"So Faith," Patsy said, "what about the job situation? You're not concerned?"

"Not really," Faith said. "I always thought I'd work for some kind of ministry, and Cyd told me about opportunities at Living Water that sound awesome. But for some reason I'm not sure yet. I'm still praying." She draped an arm around Reggie. "And this guy said there's no rush. I could focus on taking care of Zoe if I want."

Reggie shrugged. "My brother won't even let us pay rent. So as long as Faith is up for more of that just-scraping-by student life, we're good."

"How is your brother, Reggie?" Patsy said.

"He's doing well, Grandma Patsy," Reggie said. "I'll tell him you asked about him."

"I was wondering where he was earlier today," Patsy said. "He was so helpful moving everything to the storage facility in Maryland."

Jillian kept her focus on the television screen.

"That reminds me," Darlene said, "Reggie, did Adrienne tell you we know one another?"

"My sister?" Reggie said. "How do you know her?"

"Let me guess," Faith said. "You do her hair. Grandma knows everybody."

"That's exactly it," Darlene said. "Been doing Adrienne's hair for years. She doesn't come in as much now that she's natural, but she stopped by for a trim and mentioned that both her brothers had been in town recently. When she said 'Tommy and Reggie,' I almost fell out."

"It's amazing how far back the connection goes," Patsy said. "I remember when Jillian would talk about her best friend Tommy when she was in college. And clearly the bond is still there after all these years. I think that's special."

"I'm looking forward to all of us coming together at the wedding," Darlene said.

Jillian sighed inside. As happy as she'd be for Faith and Reggie, everyone coming together at the wedding was the last thing she was looking forward to. There'd be no way to avoid Tommy.

CHAPTER 45

JUNE

"*I* don't think your old girlfriend likes me." Cinda helped Alonzo into his black suit jacket as he prepared for another round of promo shots, this one with Savannah Silver.

"You know she wasn't my girlfriend." Alonzo looked up as Cinda adjusted the collar.

"Well, you had a thing with her," Cinda said, "and she told the world what a great kisser you are, and I totally agree, so"—she shrugged—"I thought we could be friends." She'd probably never forget the picture of Alonzo and Savannah kissing in London— the one that caused her to end things with him.

Alonzo gave Cinda a look as she tweezed a couple of hairs from his brows.

She stepped back to check him out. "Okay, I think we're good," she said, her voice tentative. "No, wait . . ." She folded her arms, eyeing him. "For these shots with Savannah, you need some swag." She smiled a little. "Well. *More* swag." She took off his tie and undid the first couple buttons of his white shirt, adjusting the collar. She stood back again, nodding. "That's it."

Alonzo grabbed his iPad as they walked through a massive LA warehouse, headed to the set. "Baby, can you look to see if I heard from the prison?" he said. "We've been going back and forth about permission to film Pamela Alexander's interview. And if they said I can do it—"

"Look at your calendar and nail down a date," Cinda said. "You saw the phone interviews I scheduled, right? With Kendra's brother Trey and her dad? The dad is overseas so I had to accommodate the time difference. He said he'd be happy to talk about Lance and his daughter."

"Cin, you've been doing so much, thank you—"

"Also, while I had Kendra's dad on the line," Cinda said, "I asked about Kendra's style, which'll be important for your wardrobe and props departments, especially showing the contrast between Kendra as an attorney and when she's battling the disease." She walked at a steady clip. "So I asked him to email a selection of pics. And oh—I don't know how you're planning to do the conversion scene, but I was thinking it would be amazing to film in the actual jail cell—and even have Lance tell part of his story there as promo—so I made some calls yesterday to see if it's even possible. They keep pushing me to someone higher up, but I'll keep—what?"

Alonzo was shaking his head, smiling. "We need to talk about what other roles you can take on with this movie because you are extra with *everything*. And I love it."

"What do you mean, 'other roles,'" Cinda said, "as if I currently have one?"

"I thought you were my stylist," Alonzo said.

"That's for promo, red carpet, and whatever else you'll do in conjunction with the movie," Cinda said.

"I'm saying I thought you were my stylist *for the movie*," Alonzo said.

"You never said that." Cinda looked at him. "Like, *the* person handling wardrobe? On *Greater Glory*, we were saying I might *assist*."

"Yes," Alonzo said, "*the* person who *gets* the look and feel needed for the Lance film and acquires the outfits for the actors, which I know is simplified in terms of what's required, but"—he looked at her—"I dare you to tell me God can't do this through you."

"I mean, I know this isn't some period piece set in 1940's England or something that involves extravagant costume designs, but still . . . it's pretty huge." Cinda exhaled slowly. "And it starts *now* in pre-production." Her pace slowed a little as she thought about it. "I'd need to break down the script scene by scene in terms of the characters involved and the clothing required—and I'd need to highlight each character's story arc using colors—"

"How do you know all that?" Alonzo said.

"One of those pre-Oscar luncheons," Cinda said. "While you were off interviewing with someone, I had a long talk with the costume designer for *Bonds of Time* about what her job entails. I'm going to see if I can meet with her."

"I guess I should ask if you *want* to do this," Alonzo said. "It's a lot of work beyond styling. And of course you'd have assistants."

"You know I want to," Cinda said. "But you're always pushing me to do stuff before I'm ready."

Alonzo pulled her to a stop and kissed her.

"What's that for?" Cinda said.

"Because I love you," Alonzo said. "And I'm your biggest fan. Also, addict kiss," he said, kissing her again.

Cinda looked up and caught Savannah's eye as she passed with her team. She wore a little black dress to complement Alonzo's suit, as the studio had directed, and she looked gorgeous in it.

They moved to the set, massive in itself, with equipment from floor to ceiling, every kind of lighting, and various backdrops.

Cinda took a seat and opened the iPad—and saw an endless scroll of notifications.

What in the world? The last wave like this had been the news that Alonzo's management team had let him go. The consensus had been that Alonzo was on a fast moving spiral—downward.

Cinda looked closer, trying to get a sense of what had started this one, and saw *Lance* and *movie* throughout. With wide eyes she looked over at Alonzo, who was too busy to notice. He hadn't wanted this public yet. Had the news come from someone in St. Louis? They hadn't exactly stressed the need for confidentiality. They hadn't thought they needed to.

She clicked a link and skimmed—and her eyes widened more. Nelson Slater from Alonzo's production company? Some outlet had apparently interviewed him, and he'd expressed excitement about working with Alonzo, so much excitement that he'd mentioned the current project. Probably meant well, but still . . . With him, Alonzo had definitely hammered home confidentiality.

She looked over at Alonzo again. Savannah stood against him, her head on his shoulder as the photographer clicked away.

Cinda checked more links to get a feel for reaction, and found herself somewhat surprised. She and Alonzo tended to talk about Lance's upbringing, his conversion behind bars, and transformation thereafter as highlights. But almost every comment focused on the love story with Kendra, marrying her despite a terminal diagnosis. Many had even attached a link to the viral video of their wedding. People couldn't wait to see the story played out on screen.

Cinda wondered if they realized that would only be part of the movie. But regardless—the overall feeling was one of excitement.

She dug out her phone to see if she'd heard from anyone. Faith and Jordyn had gotten wind of it and texted her. And a text from Kelsey?

This Lance movie sounds so exciting. Maybe I could play Kendra :)

Kelsey had never replied to the last text messages Cinda had sent. And Cinda had seen where Kelsey had had a handful of events for which she hadn't called. Cinda held her phone, thinking up a reply, then left it blank.

~

"Man, you know I wouldn't let something like that come between us," Alonzo said. "And I'd hope you wouldn't either."

Alonzo reached across the back patio table for more Governor's chicken, among the several cartons they'd brought home. Cinda slid it closer to him.

"Yeah, but I said some things I shouldn't have." Shane feasted on sweet and sour chicken. "I just knew you'd sign onto that *Greater Glory* project, and when you didn't, I reacted." He looked at Alonzo. "But to attack you personally for your faith wasn't cool at all. I apologize, man."

Alonzo shrugged lightly. "Hey, could've been worse. At least our convo didn't show up in some article with an 'anonymous' tag on it."

"You know I'd never do that," Shane said. "That was between me and you." He added fried rice to his plate. "So this news today," he said. "It's legit?"

Alonzo nodded. "It's not supposed to be out there, but yeah, it's legit."

"No lie," Shane said. "When that wedding story went viral, I was thinking that would be a dope movie."

"Seriously?" Alonzo said. "The funny thing is I don't remember hearing about it back then."

"Oh yeah," Shane said. "I could see the part with her fiancée walking out on her just before the wedding, all that. But sounds like this has a different focus. Lance's life more than the love story is front and center."

"Exactly," Alonzo said. "But I can see some good conversations about what to play up and what to cut back. I'm looking forward to your input." He looked over at Shane. "If you agree to sign on as director."

Shane looked at him.

"It's an indie project, though," Alonzo said. "No big studio bells and whistles. Definitely no big studio money. And no 'golden boy' script writer."

Cinda looked between them. "But you'd have the dream team."

"And we could probably get it made faster," Shane said.

"We?" Alonzo said, smiling.

"Man, I have to say, I'm feeling that," Shane said. "But let me not jump the gun." He gave a wry smile. "I need to see the screenplay first."

"You know I can't argue with that," Alonzo said. "But you need to know—our heart's desire is to make a movie that's impactful for Christ. I'm going into this ministry-minded, so if that's a problem . . ."

Shane focused on him a moment. "Let me read the script," he said. "If I connect with the story, I'm in."

"So while you and Shane talked after dinner, I put some ideas together for the website." Cinda lay across the bed with Alonzo, the iPad between them.

"What website?" Alonzo said.

"Now that news about the movie is out there," Cinda said, "we need to create a site for the production company and make it *the* news source for updates about the movie." She showed him her notes on the iPad. "And not just press release-type news, but you need to upload videos with personal updates and reflections—also posted to a YouTube channel we'll create for the movie. And here's the main thing I'm thinking—we can get people praying for the project."

Alonzo nodded. "I remember Lance said Randall had a team of people praying as *Bonds of Time* was being made. And Randall didn't just want the audience to be impacted—he wanted people who worked on the project to be impacted. I know their prayers for me made a huge difference."

"Can you imagine people around the world praying for this movie?" Cinda said. "We can share specific requests, like prayers for you as you complete the script, prayers for casting and crew selection, everything. Invite people to be part of the journey—and then let them know how God is moving."

"So maybe it's a blessing the news got leaked, huh?"

"You weren't too hard on Nelson, were you?" Cinda said.

"He had left about a dozen apology messages by the time I got to my phone," Alonzo said. "I couldn't be hard on him. But look at you—your mind is rolling a mile a minute with this film." He stared into her eyes. "You're invaluable to this project, way beyond wardrobe. Too bad you don't act."

"Have you thought about who will play Kendra?" Cinda said.

"Shane and I thought about a few possibilities tonight," Alonzo said, "actresses with amazing depth and range. But somebody we haven't thought about could show up and surprise us. On-screen chemistry will be key as well."

"Like you and Savannah," Cinda said.

Alonzo looked at her. "Did it feel funny, seeing Savannah and me in all those poses today?"

"I thought it would," Cinda said, "but I could tell just by looking at you that you were working. I kept thinking—that's not the way he looks at me. That's not the way he holds me."

Alonzo put an arm around her waist and drew her close. "You mean like this?"

"Exactly like this." Cinda nestled beside him. "Oh, and Zee, I bookmarked three more St. Louis houses for you to look at." She pulled up one of them on the iPad. "And I talked to Stephanie about contractors she used for the B and B, because whatever we choose, we'll probably have to do renovations, and I'm thinking as soon as we return—"

"Baby," Alonzo said, "what's first?"

"What's first?" Cinda said. "We've been together all day."

"I'm calling it anyway." Alonzo took the iPad and put it on the nightstand.

"So our work day is over?" Cinda said.

Alonzo turned out the lamp. "Over." He brought her close again and kissed her.

"But the night's not over." Cinda sat up. "I still have to twist my hair."

"I'll do it for you in the morning," Alonzo said.

"Which totally misses the point," Cinda said, "even *if* you knew how to do it."

"You're trying to say I can't twist two pieces of hair together?" Alonzo said. "Go get the coconut oil."

"I don't use coconut oil to twist," Cinda said. "That's for pre-poo."

"Whatever you use," Alonzo said, "go get it."

"I really should," Cinda said. "Just to call your bluff."

Alonzo eyed her with a faint smile. "So what you gon' do, Mrs. Coles?"

She cozied up to him again. "What's first. *Then* you can do my hair."

CHAPTER 46

$\mathcal{J}$ordyn walked into Cafe Napoli, an Italian restaurant in the heart of Clayton, looking for Faith and Stephanie. They'd thought it would be fun to dress up for a ladies evening out, and invited Jordyn along. She pulled a black maxi dress from the closet, put her hair in a sleek bun, and went light with the makeup, a different habit of late. Felt good to be out. As much as she recognized the new in her life, she was still reckoning with the old. "Baby steps," Jillian had said.

Jordyn stopped at the hostess stand. "Hi, I'm meeting friends here. I think the reservation's under 'Stephanie London.'"

"Yes, right this way, ma'am," the woman said, leading her through a crowded dining room and into another more quiet space.

Jordyn saw him rise from the table in a button down shirt and slacks. The beat of her heart went erratic.

The hostess left the menu at her seat and quietly moved away.

Jesse walked behind her chair, waited for her to sit, and moved her forward, then returned to his seat.

She still couldn't look at him.

"You look beautiful tonight," Jesse said.

Jordyn brought her eyes to him, barely. "You got Stephanie to do this?"

"Faith," he said. "She told me about your video, then I asked if she'd set this up."

"Why?" Jordyn said.

Jesse eyed her a moment. "First, to tell you how much it rocked me, seeing you that vulnerable. Second, to celebrate being 'made new'—that's a praise that rocked me." He paused. "When did you film that?"

She stared downward. "Later that night . . . after I left your place."

"So how did that happen?" Jesse said.

"I went to the B and B just to be alone," Jordyn said. "Ended up talking to Jillian for a couple hours, then praying with her." She mustered the courage. "Jesse, I'm sorry. I'm mortified that I did that, and I'm *glad* you told me to go. But it's hard to even face you now."

"I know," Jesse said. "You went back to avoiding at church."

"I would've switched churches," Jordyn said, "but I really wanted Jade to hear Lance and get to know the people at Living Hope."

"Yeah, that rocked me too—seeing Jade there," Jesse said. "God's been up to a lot lately." He looked up as the server approached and Jordyn ordered her beverage. "So," he said, once the server had left, "I wasn't finished with my list."

Jordyn waited, wishing her stomach would settle.

"Third reason I set this up," Jesse said. "To ask if you wanted to go out on an official date."

Jordyn looked at him. "So what's this?"

"An official date, potentially."

"Why are you calling it 'official'?" Jordyn said.

Jesse took a moment to respond. "Because I think—and you can tell me if I'm wrong. I think we're both ready . . ." He hesitated again. "Ready to see if . . . I don't even know what I'm trying to say, this is all new to me."

"Ready to date, God's way?" Jordyn said.

Jesse gave a nod.

Jordyn looked at him. "Why are you suddenly ready?"

"I wouldn't call it suddenly," Jesse said. "It's taken me months to get here, and I'm still treading slowly. But from what I can see, God is working in both of us. And we've both got that crush thing going, so . . ."

"You didn't say 'semi'."

"Because I'm ready," Jesse said.

"And you're not as crabby tonight," Jordyn said.

"I was never crabby."

Jordyn glanced down again. "When you told me to go, I wondered if it was partly because the 'semi' had dropped to zero and you weren't attracted to me."

"You had to go because I was *too* attracted to you," Jesse said. "And if you're ever at my spot and the dryer goes off, don't help me with nothing." He gave a wry smile as he reached a hand across, taking hers. "So, yes or no to our official date."

"I'm already here," Jordyn said.

"Under false pretenses," Jesse said. "If you say 'yes,' it becomes a date."

Jordyn felt the flutters. "Yes," she said. "But, Jesse, what if we date and I'm tempted to go there again and mess it all up again?"

"We know our weaknesses," Jesse said. "We need some for-real boundaries. And prayer. And accountability. And we have to be willing to be firm with each other. You could easily be the one putting me out next time."

Jordyn found her smile. "So we're really doing this?"

"I didn't ask you to marry me, Jordyn. It's a date."

"There he is—Mr. Crabby."

Jordyn walked into Living Word Wednesday night with Jesse and Jade.

"It's still hard to believe all these people come out in the middle of the week for Bible study," Jade said. "It's like an alternate universe."

Jordyn glanced around. "Looks like even more people than last week."

"Only one more to go after this," Jesse said. "Then the vote."

They made their way into the sanctuary, looking for a seat.

"Isn't that Cyd waving you over?" Jade said.

Jordyn spotted the hand, and they moved to a middle section, where the three of them sat with Cyd, Cedric, Stephanie, and Lindell.

"Hello again," Cyd said, smiling.

"I know," Jordyn said, smiling herself. She'd just left their house less than two hours before. She leaned closer. "I didn't get a chance to ask you earlier . . . and this is really awkward."

"What is it?" Cyd said.

"When I did that video," Jordyn said, "it was right after I basically"—she leaned even closer—"tried to sleep with Jesse," she whispered. "And I've been looking for a book or Bible study with real talk about temptation and how to deal with it. Does Living Water have anything like that?"

Cyd thought a moment. "We really don't. Pastor Lyles has studies on different books of the Bible, so wherever there's a verse related to temptation, he deals with it frankly. But an entire resource devoted to that—I'm not aware of one."

Jordyn nodded. "I just want to be proactive. You gave me a good place to start, though. I'll get a notebook and write down verses related to temptation."

The praise and worship team came out, Lance with them, and everyone stood.

Jesse leaned in from her other side. "So this works, right? Can't get into too much trouble with a date night at church."

"How is it a date with my sister tagging along," Jordyn said, "and with a crowd of people?"

"That's what I'm saying," Jesse said. "Dope boundaries. All our dates need to flow like this."

Jordyn gave him a look. "*All?*"

She caught a slight smile as he turned to worship.

Jordyn focused as well, after sneaking a side look at him. It was silly, but she was pinching herself still. They were dating. *She* was dating. In the weirdest most exhilarating way she could've imagined.

CHAPTER 47

*C*yd clutched her phone, her heart in her throat. She lowered herself into her desk chair. "When?"

"Only minutes ago," Claudia said. "Your dad and I stopped by the hospital to visit, not realizing . . . I wanted to call you right away."

"How was he?" Cyd said.

"Very peaceful," Claudia said. "Gloria said it was as if he'd drifted off to sleep."

"Should I come to the hospital?" Cyd said.

"There's no need," Claudia said. "But come to the house this evening. We're having people over just to gather and remember Mason together."

"I need to call Lance and tell him," Cyd said.

"He was already here when we got here," Claudia said. "I think he was one of the last people to talk to Mason." She paused as Cyd's father said something to her. "Okay, I'll see you a little later, Cyd. I've got to keep making calls."

Cyd hung up her phone and held it, her mind cycling through memories. Besides her parents, who had had a bigger impact on her life? On paths she had taken—and not taken. On the way she viewed God and His word. Snippets of long ago sermons had embedded themselves in her heart. Counsel he'd given had shored up her thoughts. From critical to everyday decisions, Pastor Lyles's influence had been felt—for decades. And his kindness and love had been a steady anchor.

Cyd got up and looked out her window, watching students headed to summer classes and programs. She'd visited Pastor Lyles last week, and he'd known his days were short. As much as she'd wanted to focus on him, he'd steered the conversation back to her.

"I've been praying for you, Cydney," Pastor Lyles had said.

"For me?" Cyd said. "Why?"

"Well, it's not unusual," the pastor said. "You've been on my prayer list since you were a girl. But you've been on my heart a little extra." He'd looked at her. "You've got a lot going—family, Living Water, the university. If it's too much . . ."

"Pastor, I appreciate your concern," Cyd had said, "but I'm honestly not feeling burdened. I've always had dual tracks going with ministry and academia. And Chase is six so family has been in the mix for a while now too. By God's grace, it works—plus there's an amazing team at Living Water."

"I'm praying for your strength nonetheless." Pastor Lyles had taken her hand. "You know I love you like a daughter."

She'd gotten tears in her eyes, even as they flowed now.

"I love you too, pastor," she'd said, "like a father."

Cyd closed her eyes as the news took a firmer hold. She'd never hear his voice again, or his wisdom—

"Hey, Cyd, here's the book you wanted."

Cyd sighed inside, wishing she'd closed her door. "Thanks, Micah, can you put it on the desk?"

Cyd could hear him set it down, but he hadn't walked back out.

"Are you okay?" he said.

She shook her head softly. "My pastor from childhood . . . just got news that he passed."

"From childhood?" Micah said. "And you were still pretty close?"

Cyd nodded, staring still out the window. "He was like a second father to me."

"I'm really sorry to hear that, Cyd." Micah came closer, sat on the edge of her desk. "What's your most cherished memory of him?"

Cyd didn't have to think long. "When Pastor Lyles married my husband and me." She turned. "I was single till I was forty, and the pastor knew I wanted a family, so he'd been praying for me. And praying." She smiled inside a little. "Having him lead us in our vows and pronounce us husband and wife was just one of those special moments."

"Preacher or teacher?" Micah said.

"Definitely teacher," Cyd said. "Pastor Lyles made sure you knew the who, what, when, where, and why of every passage. History and geography lesson in every sermon. He wanted you to feel how long it took Jesus to walk from Galilee to Jerusalem." More images filled her mind. "Close runner up for most cherished memory—traveling to Israel in my early twenties with Pastor Lyles, along with my parents and others."

"I'd love to hear about that one day," Micah said. "Life changing?"

"In so many ways," Cyd said. "Solidified my career path, for one. Also deepened my relationship with Jesus. Hearing Pastor Lyles teach about Jesus calming the sea while in a boat on the Sea of Galilee, or about His crucifixion while in the Garden of Geth-semane . . . I can't even describe the experience."

"So if Pastor Lyles had never lived—thinking *It's a Wonderful Life*—you'd probably be something radically different, like a scientist."

"Science and I were never great friends, so no," Cyd said.

"Interesting point, though . . . I do bet my life would've had an entirely different trajectory."

"I'm not sure what I thought about death until recently," Micah said. "Maybe I tried not to think about it at all. There was certainly no hope attached." His tone was thoughtful. "But when I first read Paul's words—'For to me, to live is Christ and to die is gain'—I thought, death is better? It's *gain*? That was a seismic shift in my mind."

Cyd looked at him. "That's what I want to focus on, not so much my loss, but his gain." She blew out a breath and looked away, emotion rising again nonetheless.

Micah moved to hug her. "I'll be praying for all of you."

"Thank you," Cyd said.

She gathered her things to leave as Micah walked out, then picked up her phone to call Cedric—and saw she'd missed a call from him. She dialed back.

"Babe, Lance just called," Cedric said. "Have you gotten the news?"

"Mom called a few minutes ago," she said. "I was just about to call you."

"I know this is hard," Cedric said. "Are you okay?"

"Lots of sadness," Cyd said, "but knowing he's with Jesus . . . I can't even imagine. Hey, Mom said some people are gathering at their house. I thought we could head over."

"Sounds good," Cedric said. "I'll get Chase and see you over there."

~

It didn't occur to Cyd that the dynamics at her parents' house would be interesting—until she walked through the door. She saw Wayman first, with a couple other pastors on staff, huddled in the living area.

Wayman approached when he saw her. In his early forties, he

was tall and dark like Cedric, but with a heftier frame. "Sad day," he said, hugging her. "Pastor Lyles was one of a kind."

"He really was," Cyd said. "The loss will be felt."

"Would you mind if we talked for a minute?" Wayman said.

"Sure," Cyd said. She could hear voices coming from the kitchen area. Wayman led her to a corner in the living room.

"I want to be as delicate as possible about this," Wayman said, "because I understand where your allegiance lies."

"'Allegiance' is an interesting word," Cyd said.

"I also want to be transparent about changes that have been made," Wayman said.

Cyd raised a brow. "Changes so soon?"

"The elders have designated me as the interim senior pastor," Wayman said, "which means I'll be preaching on Sundays. Also, when it comes time to vote, Lance won't be the only name before the congregation. Both of us will be up for consideration."

Immediate thoughts swirled. Pastor Lyles had brought Wayman on staff six years ago, and since then Wayman had clearly leveraged the Living Word platform to sell books and build a personal brand. It was telling that as the pastor's health declined, he'd never once tapped Wayman to preach. "So why are you telling me this?" Cyd said.

"You're an influential voice in this church," Wayman said. "And since we know how this is going to go, I'm hoping you can help forge unity even now, so the transition can proceed smoothly."

"We know how this is going to go?" Cyd said.

"If we're honest," Wayman said.

"Interesting," Cyd said. "And you want me to help forge unity . . . by doing what?"

"Lance only has one more Wednesday," Wayman said, "but he'll have to skip next week because of the funeral. If he graciously backs out, we can move quickly to a vote and get to the business of moving Living Word forward."

"Oh, you want me to somehow persuade Lance to back out,"

Cyd said. "Which would be odd because I was one of the ones persuading him to get *in*." She looked at him. "What's the rush? Why not simply be prayerful, let the process play out, and see how *God* says it's going to go."

"I admire your ideals, Cyd," Wayman said, "but the reality is, changes should have been made at Living Word long ago." He gave a shrug. "But you know, you're right. If we have to wait a couple weeks more, that's nothing in the final analysis." He added, "And by the way, you have my word—we'll continue to fully support you all at Living Hope."

~

"I'm just not sure what the elders were thinking." Claudia looked at the Living Word website from Cedric's phone. "This is in poor taste. Mason's body is still warm and they've changed the site already?"

"We know exactly what they were thinking," Cedric said. "Wednesday nights have gotten too crowded. They needed Wayman out front, to steer the ship where they want it to go."

"I don't even know if I want to see it," Stephanie said. "I need to keep my blood pressure in check." She took a plate from the microwave and joined Lindell at her parents' kitchen table.

Claudia passed the phone to Lindell, who took a look.

"They've clearly been waiting for this moment," Lindell said. "They had to have this change ready to go. And this picture of Wayman on the home page"—he showed it to Stephanie—"that's bigger than any picture of Pastor Lyles I've ever seen on the site."

"And you can't miss 'interim pastor,' big as the font is," Stephanie said. "But how they gonna put, 'Remembering Dr. Mason Lyles' in small font, way further down, with a link that says, 'click for more.'"

"They skipped right past mourning to politics." Cyd had her own phone in hand, perusing the site. "We were supposed to be gathering this evening to focus on Pastor Lyles, and Wayman was working the room the whole time."

"Bruce, you've been quiet," Lindell said. "What are you thinking?"

"As a former Living Word elder, I'm saddened by it," Bruce said. "You all know Claudia and I thought Wayman would be the strong choice to replace Mason. But I was staying prayerful because Mason clearly felt he'd heard from God." He paused. "I thought the elders had that same regard, that they were being prayerful about the process as it unfolded."

"Daddy, you didn't think they were behind the petition?" Stephanie said. "And that little attempt to get people not to come out that first Wednesday?"

"I don't think they're that calculating," Bruce said. "These are men of God I respect."

Stephanie stabbed some pasta salad with her fork. "Yeah, okay."

"All of this maneuvering could have the desired effect," Cyd said. "Many were already in Wayman's corner. Seeing him in the pulpit on Sundays will make his rise to senior pastor seem inevitable. It'll be hard not to vote for him."

"Well," Stephanie said, "Lance said he didn't care if he gets the job. And I *still* prefer the status quo we've got at Living Hope. So as much as I may not like the way things are going down, when the 'worst case' scenario is my best case? I'm good."

"I love the status quo too," Cedric said. "But when I first heard that Pastor Lyles felt Lance was the one to replace him—it just resonated. And seeing him teach at Living Word these past three —" His phone rang on the table. "There's Lance right there," Cedric said, answering.

Cyd looked as Cedric moved away, speaking in a low tone. She'd thought Lance might stop by this evening, but given what had transpired, she was glad he hadn't. Cedric was probably letting him know—

"So Lance just talked to Wayman a few minutes ago." Cedric looked at them all. "He's agreed to forego his final Wednesday night and have the vote pushed up to next Friday night."

"Why is Lance doing that?" Cyd said.

Cedric seemed to be pondering it himself. "He wouldn't give details, but he said it's based on his last conversation with Pastor Lyles."

CHAPTER 48

*A*n hour before the home-going service for Pastor Lyles was set to begin Wednesday morning, the Living Word parking lot had reached capacity. Lance looked out of a window on Living Word's top floor as a shuttle brought people from a remote lot to the front entrance. But he hardly saw them. His gaze went to the clouds as he prayed, asking God again for strength to get through this day.

In a dark suit and burgundy colored tie, Lance turned, his eyes on Pastor Lyles's desk and chair. He no longer had his spiritual father of twenty years to turn to. He'd shed many tears over the past few days as he thought about the pastor and what he'd meant to him. Today he was simply overwhelmed by the task before him.

He looked up at the knock on the door. "Come in," he said.

Ruth, Pastor Lyles's executive assistant, walked in, silver haired and dressed in a black skirt and jacket.

"Feeling the pressure?" Lance said.

"I'm not bothered by it," Ruth said. "The elders, deacons, and everyone else can ask every five minutes who's giving the eulogy, and I'll repeat every five minutes—'At Pastor Lyles's request, the program will be distributed immediately before the service.'"

"It's just like the pastor to do something like this." Lance had gotten to the church at five this morning and sequestered himself in the pastor's office as instructed. "He planned his funeral down to the smallest detail."

"He had contingencies," Ruth said, "depending on when he went to be with the Lord. If you were already installed as pastor, we could've of course dispensed with the secrecy about the eulogy."

"The pastor wasn't able to talk extensively when I was with him that last day," Lance said. "Did he tell you why he wanted secrecy?"

"Indeed," Ruth said. "The pastor had gotten wind of plans being made by the elders, many of which were contrary to decisions made in formal meetings with the pastor present."

"Did he confront them?" Lance said.

Ruth shook her head. "The pastor said it wouldn't matter, that he'd soon be gone and they'd do what they wanted. But you know the pastor. He didn't leave it at that—he prayed about it. And this was the result."

Ruth's phone rang in the pocket of her blazer, and she checked it. "It's the tech guy," she said, answering. "Okay . . . Okay . . ." She covered the phone. "Lance, he said to tell you there will be more cameras than usual, due to the live-stream, but to pretend they're not there."

"Got it," Lance said, checking text messages on his own phone.

"Oh, thank you for that," Ruth was saying into the phone. "Awesome. Okay." She hung up, looking at Lance. "He said the live-stream will be featured on the Living Word home page today, and the replay for the remainder of the week." She gave a faint smile. "Pastor Lyles didn't specify that. That's all the tech guy. He couldn't say no to Wayman's changes to the website, but he didn't like them. This puts the focus back on remembering the pastor, at least for a few days."

Ruth headed to her outer office. "I'd better get out here and keep fielding calls," she said, closing the door behind her.

Lance dialed Treva's phone.

"Hey, babe." Her voice was near whisper, with loud chatter in the background. "You ready?"

The question moved Lance. "When the pastor said he wanted to talk to me about the funeral, I thought he'd ask me to serve as a pall bearer, which would've been a real privilege. I figured a guest preacher—distinguished seminary professor, national ministry head—would give the eulogy." He exhaled. "I doubt I could ever feel ready for this. What's it like down there?"

"People everywhere," Treva said. "I expected to see well-known pastors and ministry figures," she said. "But there are more than a few Christian recording artists, and Reggie's pointing out pro athletes."

"Pastor Lyles ministered privately to a lot of people over the years," Lance said.

"Babe, members got the notice about the vote this Friday," Treva said, "and some have asked me why you're not teaching the last lesson. They were looking forward to it."

"What did you say?" Lance said.

"I said you would explain," Treva said. "But I'm still wondering myself."

Lance leaned against the desk. "So, I told you how God's been showing up strong during my study time. I had the final Bible study prepared two weeks ago. When I visited the pastor on Friday, he asked what the last message was, and I told him." Lance paused, still in awe. "The pastor closed his eyes and mumbled, 'I praise You, Jesus.' Then he looked at me and said, 'That's my eulogy.'"

"Are you serious?" Treva said. "You're doing your final lesson this morning, as the eulogy?"

"I had to tweak it for the occasion," Lance said. "But it blew me away. God knew. He *knew*."

"That just gave me chills," Treva said. "Oh, wait—thank you," she said. "Ushers are handing out programs, so I guess we're about to start. Let me look . . ." She grew quiet. "Yep, you're in here. 'Eulogy—Pastor Lance W. Alexander, Senior Pastor, Living Hope Church.'"

Ruth gave a knock and peeked in. "They're ready to escort you down. You've got about five minutes."

"I have escorts?" Lance spoke into the phone. "Babe, I have to go."

Cedric and Tommy walked in, and Ruth closed the door. They both stared at Lance.

"Really?" Cedric said. "Tommy and I got a call last night, saying Pastor Lyles wanted us to escort the speaker down. I'm thinking it's someone from out of town. And I'm wondering why he didn't designate somebody over at Living Word to serve as an escort." He shook his head. "Pastor Lyles wanted your brothers with you. So this was part of the 'details' you couldn't tell me."

"This was it," Lance said, nodding. He looked at Tommy. "I know we don't have time, but I've been wondering how you're doing. You haven't returned my last couple calls. Been praying for you, man."

"I got some special time with Pastor Lyles last week," Tommy said, "a few days before he passed. You know how he had moments near the end when he was really lucid—that's where I caught him. And I told him everything." He sighed. "The way he ministered to me in the state he was in . . ." He shook his head. "Just been deep in one-on-one time with God."

"Hey, that's better than talking to me." Lance hugged him. "I know God is bringing you through all this. His hand is on you, Tommy."

Cedric checked his watch. "We've got two minutes," he said. "Let's pray before we head down."

~

"If you went to see Pastor Lyles during his illness, you know—he made the visit about you and not him." Lance stood at the podium, looking out at the vast crowd of people who'd come to celebrate Pastor Lyles's life. "That's how he was. He'd put up with one or two questions about his well-being. He'd answer truthfully, assure you that the Lord had his life in His hands, then flip it to you. And that's exactly how he wanted his home-going service to go."

Cameras moved in Lance's peripheral vision, but he did as requested and ignored them.

"You've heard lots of worship music," Lance said, "because Pastor Lyles wants you to know—that's what he's doing. In the presence of Jesus, worshiping. He couldn't be in a better place and *he* couldn't be better. He wants you to be assured that death has no sting. Mason Lyles fought the good fight, and he has the victory through our Lord Jesus Christ."

Lance looked to the front row where the pastor's wife Gloria nodded, clutching a handkerchief.

"Pastor Lyles didn't want a eulogy devoted to him and his life. He wanted to flip the message to you." Lance smiled a little. "But just between you and me, I found a way to do both."

Lance held up his Bible. "Pastor Lyles was known first and foremost as a great Bible teacher. That man loved his Bible. Hardly went anywhere without it. Which I never understood because he'd be talking to you about Scripture and would never actually open the Bible—he just seemed to know it all by heart."

A few chuckles sounded as heads nodded in the sanctuary.

"So you know we couldn't celebrate his life without opening the word of God," Lance said. "If you've got your Bibles or Bible apps, head to the book of Nehemiah. Pastor Lyles reminds me a lot of this man, Nehemiah. He was the cupbearer to the king of Persia. So he wasn't a great warrior like Joshua or King David. We don't read about his exploits in battle, slaying enemies and what not. But understand—this man was a fierce soldier nonetheless.

Nehemiah did his fighting in prayer—then he watched *God* fight for him."

"You might as well go on and preach," a voice called out in the choir behind him.

A chorus of "Amen" followed.

"Nehemiah had this flow with God," Lance said. "No matter what happened, he was shooting up prayers. And God responded." He opened his Bible and turned the pages. "As the book opens, Nehemiah finds out his brothers in Judah are distressed and the wall of Jerusalem—their protection—is broken down. He weeps, fasts, and prays, and *he's* distressed because he's hundreds of miles away and can't go to help—without permission of the king. So he asks God, 'make Your servant successful today, and grant him compassion before this man.'"

Lance looked out among the people. "So what happens? God totally shows up. The king notices Nehemiah is sad and asks why. When Nehemiah tells him his city is in ruins, the king says, 'What would you request?'" Lance had a puzzled look. "Really? What would you request? The king should've said, 'Sorry to hear that, but where's my wine? But this is *God* orchestrating this whole scene."

"Won't He do it?" a woman's voice called out.

"And look what Nehemiah does next—'So I prayed to the God of heaven.'" Lance took his Bible and moved out from the podium. "Please understand this man's close walk with God. Nehemiah is standing before the king, needing to answer a question, and he looks to *his* King first and *prays*. He answers when God gives him one. And because God has given Nehemiah favor, next thing you know, Nehemiah is in Jerusalem."

Lance walked, turning pages in his Bible. "We see it repeatedly. The enemies of Judah mocked Nehemiah and the others as they tried to rebuild the wall. Nehemiah didn't say a word to the enemy. He talked to God—'Hear, O our God, how we are despised!'" His voice boomed with feeling. "'Then Nehemiah found out their enemies were coming to fight against them. Their response? 'But we prayed to our God . . .'"

Lance shook his head in awe. "How many of you know—this is Pastor Lyles?"

Hands went up throughout the sanctuary.

"No matter the situation," Lance said, "the first thing he did was talk to God. Pastor Lyles was a warrior—in prayer. And it was that warrior spirit that allowed him to see God move in a strong way again and again and again with the Living Word church and ministry."

"Amen" rang throughout the sanctuary.

"But look at this," Lance said, in his Bible again. "First the enemy mocked the wall builders, then they wanted to fight, now they're threatening to kill the people in order to stop the work. What did Nehemiah do?"

Lance looked out with a long pause. "I want you to really listen because this is Pastor Lyles's heart. This is the legacy he leaves. Nehemiah saw fear in the people, so first he told them not to be afraid. Some of you are fearful of what the future holds for Living Word. You're not sure if everything that's been built will continue to stand. Pastor Lyles would say to you as well—don't be afraid. Instead, do these two things . . ."

Lance was surprised to see a few people stand, waiting.

"We're flipping it now," Lance said, moving closer to the people. "As we press forward, these are two things we must do, same two things Nehemiah told the people to do: *remember* and *fight*. Remember what?—'the Lord who is great and awesome.'" He moved along the front, his pace quickened. "That's first, always. We remember *the Lord*, that *He's* in control. That He's sovereign. That He knows the end from the beginning. That there is no one like Him. That whatever He plans, He will bring to pass. That He is *great and awesome*. When we remember *Him*, how can we fear?"

More rose to their feet, shouting affirmation and praise.

"Second thing Nehemiah said to do—*fight*. He says, 'fight for your brothers, your sons, your daughters, your wives, and your houses.'" Lance looked up. "Nehemiah told his workers to build with a sword at their side, so they could be ready for any surprise attack. But he knows who'll do the actual fighting. He says look, if the enemy shows up, we'll blow the trumpet and rally together, but understand this—'Our God will fight for us.'" Lance paused. "But in that moment when Nehemiah sees their fear, and he says *fight*—you know what I think he's saying?"

A camera moved in on his left side.

"He's saying *don't give up*," Lance said. "Keep the fight in your spirit." His pace quickened again. "And that's what *we* do as we move on without our beloved pastor. This is the work of God. We keep fighting the good fight of faith. Keep fighting by trusting God, staying in His will, remaining steadfast. Keep fighting in prayer—for *everything. Always.* Keep fighting with that sword—the word of God—at your side. Keep fighting knowing that *God* is fighting for us. If you're a believer in Christ, we are more than conquerors. That's the legacy *Jesus* has given us. And if you don't know Jesus as your personal Savior, let's take a minute to talk about that . . ."

~

"Zoe, good job on the spaghetti, but I need you to eat some of those green beans." Lance sat beside her at the kitchen table, feeding Wes a bottle.

"No like green beans, Granddaddy." Zoe did a fierce shake of her head.

"I only gave you a few," Lance said. "Eat up."

Zoe pushed her plate aside. "Cookie, Granddaddy." She pointed at the pan he'd taken out of the oven.

"No cookies, Zoe, until you eat your green beans." Lance looked down at the baby. "You all done, little man?" He set the bottle on the table then lifted Wes against him, patting his back.

"Granddaddy, cookie, pwease."

Lance chuckled. "Oh, you think a 'please' will do it? I said you had to eat your green beans, sweetie." He brought the plate closer and started feeding her himself.

His phone rang and he reached for it on the table. "Hey, babe."

"What are you doing?" Treva said.

"Feeding Zoe and Wes," he said.

"You sound so calm."

"How should I sound?" Lance said.

"You know I'm calling to tell you how the vote turned out," Treva said. "I'm thinking you should sound at least a little anxious."

"I don't—"

"Care. Yes, I know." Treva paused. "Well, at least we don't have to sell the house and move to a different city. Or get to know an entirely new group of people or—"

"Babe, what are you talking about?"

"It wasn't even close," Treva said. "The members voted over-whelmingly for Lance Alexander to be the new senior pastor of Living Word."

Lance rose from his seat with the baby and walked a little, his insides churning. "So . . . So what happened?"

"The meeting opened with discussion," Treva said. "Lots of people going to the mic like before. But this time the negative comments were aimed at Wayman and the elders. People were livid that they made changes to the process and even the website within hours of the pastor's death."

"Is Wayman there?" Lance saw Zoe finish her green beans and got her a cookie.

"He's here," Treva said. "But there were a lot of positive comments too—about you. Lance, you should've heard them, people in tears, saying they'd judged you based on your record as a teen, but after hearing you and your heart, they felt you were the one to lead Living Word. Dana even stood and said unequivocally that you had her vote."

Lance could feel his eyes brimming. "I don't even know what to think right now. It's too much."

"You might need to put Wes and Zoe in the car and drive up here," Treva said. "A couple of people said the current elders need to resign immediately, which started another discussion."

"The meeting's still going on?" Lance said.

"And getting heated," Treva said. "I'm headed back inside."

Lance hung up and did the only thing he could think to do—modeled for two decades by Pastor Lyles.

He prayed to the God of heaven.

CHAPTER 49

JULY

*J*illian sat at the kitchen table with her second cup of coffee, enjoying a quiet Saturday morning in the word of God. Courtenay was sleeping late. Sophia had spent the night with Joy. David and Trevor left an hour ago with Reggie to play flag football with other guys from church. And sometime this afternoon, Jillian and Faith would meet to tackle several items for the wedding. But right now, Jillian was relishing this extended time with the Lord.

She'd been delving more deeply into the books Lance had covered in his study—Ezra, Nehemiah, and Haggai. And today she'd been drawn back to Haggai. She sipped her coffee, reading chapters one and two again. It blew her away still that despite the disobedience of God's people, when they repented and turned to Him, He was quick to assure them, "I am with you"—twice. She marked those words now—"I am with you"—with blue colored pencil, meditating on them.

Moments later her eyes fell on another promise in chapter two —"My Spirit is abiding in your midst; do not fear!"

Her eyes filled as she stared at those words, thinking about her own fears. How were the kids managing their grief? How well were they transitioning to life in St. Louis? And what would they do about school in the fall? Did Jillian need a second job? How would they all adjust season to season without Cecil? And those were just some of the questions on her heart this very morning.

Yet here was God reassuring her that she didn't have to fear— because His Spirit was with her.

Lord, You are so gracious. Thank You for meeting me in such a personal way, letting me know that I don't have to fear. Thank You for Your promise that You are with me. Thank You for letting me dwell in Your presence. I'm overwhelmed by Your goodness.

Jillian turned to the beginning of chapter one again, wanting to go through the book one more time this morning, to hear all that God—

"Mom?" Courtenay walked into the kitchen in yoga pants and a tee, visibly upset.

"Honey, what's wrong?" Jillian said.

"I just watched this." Courtenay passed Jillian her phone. The screen showed the video she'd done with Jordyn.

Jillian's heart went to her throat. She walked with Courtenay to the living area and sat next to her on the sofa. "Sweetheart, I know you're upset and wondering—"

"I was googling," Courtenay said, tears in her eyes, "and I searched 'Psalm 51' on YouTube and couldn't believe I saw *you.*" Emotion ramped up. "And all this time . . . I was so afraid to tell you, but now . . . I feel like . . . I feel like maybe you won't hate me . . ."

"Honey, why would you say such a thing?" Jillian put an arm around her and held her close. "Your dad and I told you from the time you were young how much we love you—unconditionally. There's nothing you could do or say to diminish that."

"Well, I know I hate myself, so . . ."

Jillian stroked her daughter's hair. *Lord, give me the words. Be with us in a strong way. Guide us by Your Spirit.*

"You just watched my video," Jillian said. "So you know I know what it's like to be grieved by sin—"

"I was stunned." Courtenay looked up at her. "You've always been so . . . perfect in my eyes."

"I don't even know how you could say that," Jillian said. "You've seen every ugly attitude I have, just from losing my patience in homeschooling."

"But everybody has a bad attitude at one time or another," Courtenay said. "I just couldn't imagine you could ever, you know . . . do something so deep that you'd be in tears, looking at Psalm 51. And we know why King David wrote that . . . and I know why I've been turning to it . . ."

"So tell me why Psalm 51 is on your heart," Jillian said. "What happened, sweetheart?"

Courtenay leaned into her, head buried, taking her time before she finally spoke. "My first semester . . ." Her chest heaved. "I drank a couple of times at parties . . . and . . ." She cried softly. "When I got back after break . . . I went to this one party and afterward . . . I ended up having sex . . . I actually lost my virginity . . . while I was *drunk* . . ."

Jillian closed her eyes and wept with her daughter, who was sobbing now.

"I went against *everything* you and Dad . . . taught me. You both told me . . . so many times . . . to *value* what I had as a precious gift and I *gave* it away . . . like . . . it was *nothing.*"

Jillian's heart hurt for her. *Help her, dear God. May she know the strength of your love and mercy.*

"I know what you're feeling," Jillian said softly. "I lost my virginity in college too."

Courtenay looked at her. "I didn't know."

"I didn't know the Lord," Jillian said, "so it was years before I grieved over it. But Courtenay, it's like I said in the video—it's a mercy that you feel sorrow over sin. That's God's grace, not allowing you to stray too far, even moving you to read Psalm 51."

"I asked God to forgive me," Courtenay said, "but it kept weighing on me. And He led me to Psalm 51, then I was moved to see what else was out there that could help. And He led me to you." She looked at her mother. "I watched that video three times. It spoke to so much that I've been feeling. I hadn't thought of it as grief, but that's what it is. And not just grief over sin, but losing something I can't get back. Then on top of *that* grief, I lost *Dad* . . ."

Jillian held her through the next wave of tears, shedding more of her own.

Then she closed her eyes and looked up in her heart. "Lord, we come before Your throne, my daughter and I, so aware of our desperate need of You . . ." Jillian held Courtenay as the tears continued. "Thank You that You are merciful and gracious. Thank You that You are faithful to forgive. I pray we both fully receive Your forgiveness. I pray Your continuing comfort as we grieve Cecil. I pray for Your healing in every area we have need. I pray we cling to You and walk in Your ways. Strengthen us both to follow You in this season and every season hereafter." She rubbed Courtenay's back. "Lord, I pray You draw Courtenay even closer. Let this experience become a testimony, let it propel Courtenay to worship You and love You more deeply. Thank You that this isn't the end of her story—it's just beginning. May Your goodness and grace be woven throughout. We love You, Lord . . ."

Courtenay got up to get tissues from the bathroom and gave Jillian a few.

"So you've been dealing with this for months," Jillian said. "Did you talk to anyone?"

"I almost talked to Faith," Courtenay said. "But I felt dumb, like I should've learned a lesson from what she went through, and I turned around and did the same thing."

"You should talk to her," Jillian said. "She's gained a lot of wisdom from walking this road."

Courtenay looked at her. "Who did you talk to, when you were going through whatever prompted the video?"

"Your Aunt Treva," Jillian said. "But mostly God."

"It's been more than two months from the date it was uploaded," Courtenay said. "How are you feeling now?"

Jillian thought a moment. "It's hard to say. I wanted it to be behind me completely by now, but . . . it's a process. What I can say is it's moved me to a closer walk with God, and I couldn't have imagined that as a result." She got up to get her Bible. "Let me show you what I was studying this morning. I know it'll bless you too . . ."

CHAPTER 50

"Zee, you've got to get it to work." Cinda walked through the theater room, removing tags from the leather chairs that had been delivered. "People will be here any minute."

Alonzo did a quick check of equipment and wires. "It was working a few minutes ago, but now it won't play."

"Maybe you didn't set up the system right," Cinda said. "I told you we should've called in a professional."

"Baby, I don't think it's the system," Alonzo said. "Let me try this one . . . " The screen came to life, picture and sound. "The problem is this particular video." He looked over at Jordyn. "Did you mess with the settings?"

Jordyn looked up from her laptop, ensconced in one of the leather chairs. "I made some changes a little bit ago, but it shouldn't have made a difference." She checked. "Oh, wait, the private link changed, sorry. Let me send you the new one."

"I hear the doorbell," Cinda said. "Are we ready?"

"We. Are . . ." Alonzo clicked a few buttons and the video they wanted came on screen. "Ready."

Cinda walked upstairs and through the spacious home they'd

moved into only a few days before. She opened the door and smiled at the faces on the doorstep.

"Welcome, welcome," Cinda said. "I'd call it a housewarming— if we were officially ready to receive guests."

"Then why are we here?" Stephanie walked in with Lindell and hugged her.

"Because you're no guest," Cinda said.

"Ooh, girl, even empty, it's beautiful." Stephanie turned, glancing around.

"You know we've got renovations we want to do," Cinda said. "But once that's all done, you'll help decorate, right?"

"I'll be all over it," Stephanie said.

"I'm certainly intrigued about tonight." Lance walked in, carrying the baby in his car seat. "I told Treva I had a conflict, and I'd see her when she got back. She told me I needed to reschedule it and come."

"So you know what it's about, Treva?" Stephanie looked at her.

Treva crossed the threshold with Joy, Hope, and Jillian. "I can only say—no comment."

Faith arrived behind her with Reggie.

"Hey, cool, everybody's getting here at the same time," Cinda said. "Come on in."

"Did your bedroom furniture come yet?" Faith said. "I want to see how the room looks now."

"Do a whole tour afterward," Stephanie said.

"Hey everybody," Jesse said, walking in. "Jordyn invited me. I hope that's okay."

"Jordyn invited you because Alonzo and I told her to." Cinda hugged him. "Of course you're welcome."

Chatter filled the entryway as Cyd and Cedric arrived, making the guest list complete.

"Okay, everybody," Cinda said, "let's head down."

Cinda led the way and Alonzo greeted everyone as they

entered the theater room, telling them to grab a seat and get comfortable.

"There's no popcorn," Alonzo said. "But we'll have refreshments after."

"So we're watching a movie?" Stephanie said. "Hey, is this a private premier of your latest?"

"I'll explain when everybody's settled," Alonzo said. He waited a few moments. "So you all know I've been working on the screenplay for the Lance movie, and I've been interviewing people from Lance's life. Three weeks ago I had the opportunity to visit Lance's mom, Pamela Alexander, at the federal prison in Tallahassee."

Cinda looked at Lance, who nodded. He knew Alonzo had met with his mom.

"At the time of my visit," Alonzo continued, "Pamela had recently gotten some news that had left her a bit devastated. And she talked about it on camera."

Lance looked concerned now and whispered to Treva.

"With her permission," Alonzo said, "we're using that segment of the interview for a video that's been uploaded to Jordyn's channel, as part of her ongoing series. The video hasn't been made public yet. We wanted you to see it first. The title is—*When I'm Defeated.*"

Cinda flicked the lights, and the room went dark. Alonzo pushed a button on a remote and Pamela came on screen, clothed in her prison-issue khakis and shirt, a grayish wall behind her.

"I've been locked up eleven years." Pamela dabbed her face with a tissue. "Serving a twenty-year sentence. For years I thought, with time off for good behavior, maybe I'll get to leave once I've done sixteen years—so five years to go. And I made myself okay with that."

Pamela stared off into the distance a moment. "Cocaine was my drug of choice," she said, looking back at the camera. "I knew I was addicted when my son came crying to me one night, saying he was hungry. He hadn't eaten in two days. I'm sure I was hungry too, but I didn't care about food. I was consumed with how I could get more drugs."

Cinda glanced around the room. Every eye was glued to the screen.

"That was my life, for years," Pamela said. "And I found out the best way to feed my habit was to get close to the dealers. Which wasn't hard. People always said I was cute, so I used it to my advantage. And I thought I hit the jackpot when I hooked up with a serious player. He stayed at my apartment, conducted his business there, gave me whatever I wanted—and I thought I was in heaven." Tears slid down her cheeks. "Lord, help me, I was so lost."

Cinda looked at Lance this time. He held Wes, his expression stoic.

"We both got busted," Pamela said. "My boyfriend gave the prosecutors what they wanted, someone higher up on the food chain. And he got minimum time. I was bitter about my twenty— until I came to know Jesus as my Lord and Savior. I was delivered and set free, right here behind bars." Pamela glanced upward, murmuring, "Thank you, Jesus."

Alonzo leaned into Cinda. "There's so much of Pamela's life we could include in this movie too. Some tough choices ahead."

"I know," Cinda whispered.

"So for *years*," Pamela continued, "I said, 'Okay, Lord, I'm here. For a really long time. Use me in this place.' And I had lots of moments where I'd get depressed, wishing I had done this thing or that thing differently. And I'm telling you, God's hand was so heavy on me, He wouldn't let me stay there long. He'd put somebody in my path who needed to know about Him, and that kept me energized. Kept me thinking I could get through all these years I got left to serve. But then, several months ago, my daughter-in-law Treva got this legal team together, and I got this hope that maybe I could get out earlier."

Everyone in the room turned to Treva, but no one looked more surprised than Lance.

Pamela continued, "Treva told me about this new federal program where inmates could petition to have their sentences reduced. Tailor-made for people like me—non-violent, low-level offenders who got long sentences under those mandatory drug guidelines. Treva said a clinic at her former law school had won a couple of these cases, and she'd gotten them to take up my case. *But,* she did warn me—'Pamela, it's a long shot. Most petitions are denied.'"

Pamela paused, as if she were fighting to get through it. "Still, I dared to *hope.* I said, 'Lord Jesus, I don't deserve it, but if You would have mercy, please give me favor. Please reduce my sentence so I can be with my family, love on my new grandson. Lord, to see my son *preach.*"

"Pause it," Lance said, standing.

Alonzo pushed a button on the remote.

"I can't watch this." Lance shook his head. "You told us the title. You said she was devastated. Clearly the petition was denied. Why would I want to see my mom like this? It's too painful."

Treva took his hand. "Babe, you should keep watching."

"Why?" Lance looked at her. "You know how I get when it comes to my mom."

"You should keep watching," Treva said.

Lance sighed and sat back down. Alonzo pushed the button to continue.

Pamela had tears streaming now. "So after months of hopes and prayers, I found out a week ago that the petition was denied. And for the first time since I've known Jesus, I felt like I had no hope. I felt like He had abandoned me. I felt *defeated.* Like I would never get out from under my failures. I'd have to keep paying and paying . . ." She covered her mouth and closed her eyes as emotion took hold.

Cinda could hear sniffles throughout the room as people watched.

"But then," Pamela said, "Treva sent me the notes from my son's message on Nehemiah. She thought it would comfort me, and oh, how it did. God's people were feeling defeated then too, but they had to *remember* Him and *fight*. *I* had to remember Him. I had to remember what I *knew* about Him, that He hadn't abandoned me. That He wasn't punishing me. For whatever reason, it was His will for me to remain here, and we still had work to do *here*." She nodded. "And I had to keep *fighting* the good fight. How could I ever be defeated when I'm more than a conqueror? The devil is a liar! Jesus has already given me the victory!"

Murmurs of "Amen" spread throughout the room.

Pamela focused on the camera. "My dear Lance, if you see this, you need to know that for the thousandth time, the Lord used you in my life. The Lord used you to *speak* life to my soul. I thank God for you, son. I love you."

The video went dark, and the room stayed quiet as people processed what they'd seen. Lance's head was down as he held the baby. Cinda took Alonzo's hand.

"I give all glory to God," Pamela said. "That wasn't the end of the story."

Everyone stood in disbelief as Pamela came on screen again, this time outdoors, in black pants and a rose colored top.

"What in the world?" Stephanie said.

Lance stood transfixed, staring at the screen.

"My daughter-in-law appealed the denial," Pamela said. "And let me tell you about *my* God." She had happy tears now. "Treva told them the support I would have if I'm released, and she attached a link to my son's eulogy of Pastor Mason Lyles—that same Nehemiah message that gave me life. Turns out, the appeals officer knew and loved Pastor Lyles's teaching. Talk about *favor*." She lifted her arms and face to the sky, taking a moment to praise. "For years I've known by faith that I'm free and I have the victory and I'm more than a conqueror. Now I've got a better taste of what that feels like. Thank You, *Jesus*. I'm no longer behind bars."

Cinda turned on the lights as the door opened and Pamela walked in. Lance couldn't move. He stared at his mom, his face covered in tears. Treva took the baby, hooked her arm in Lance's, and walked with him. Cinda could barely see as Lance and Pamela embraced. The whole room was in tears.

Mother nor son could let go as they hugged and wept.

Lance turned to Treva finally. "You did this?"

"God did this," Treva said.

Lance hugged Treva almost as long. "I've never been so overwhelmed," he said. "I love you so much. And I can't believe you didn't say a word."

"So let me say this," Treva said, looking out at everyone. "Pamela and I both said we wouldn't tell Lance because even though we were praying and believing, the odds were against us. We just didn't want Lance to get his hopes up and then be crushed." She looked at her husband. "But we did need affidavits from family, and one from you was crucial."

Lance nodded. "So you gave me that story about needing to have something on file for when her release came up for consideration."

"Which was true," Treva said. "You just didn't know how soon that would be."

Lance looked between his mom and Treva. "So you two have already seen one another since she's been out?"

"Of course we have," Pamela said. "I've seen my grandson too. Got here yesterday, thanks to help from Alonzo and Cinda."

Lance shook his head and put his arm around his mom. "I can't even think right now. I'm just . . . overwhelmed."

"Well, how about you introduce me to all these people in here," Pamela said. "And is that my Zoe?" She beamed as Faith came toward her. "And I finally get to hug *Faith*. And where's Joy and Hope?"

Cinda looked at Alonzo. "This is everything. And why does this movie keep getting better—Lance voted in as pastor, now his mom getting a surprise release."

"I only hope the movie can do all of this justice," Alonzo said. "This is incredible, what we're witnessing right here."

"And I was talking to Pamela earlier about the prayer team idea." Cinda looked at the circle gathered around her. "She definitely wants to take part. She's all about God getting the glory for this movie."

Alonzo nodded. "It's no small thing that Shane's on board. I'm praying God's got more in store for him besides directing." He turned to Cinda. "It's crazy, Cin. The way God's been moving already? I can't wait to see what He'll do."

CHAPTER 51

AUGUST

"*H*ow about this cabinet by the stove?" Jordyn held freshly washed plates. "I think it's good for everyday dishes."

Jesse turned from unpacking a box. "Works for me. You know I'm not picky about where stuff goes."

"Until you're ready to eat," Jordyn said, "and wondering why you have to walk across this big kitchen to get a plate from a corner cabinet."

"Yeah, true." Jesse surveyed what they'd unpacked so far. "Why does it seem like I don't have that much? Handful of plates and glasses, frying pan, couple of pots . . ."

"You haven't needed that much," Jordyn said. "You get carryout nine times out of ten."

"So if I want to start cooking more . . ." Jesse said.

"You need to buy more kitchen essentials," Jordyn said.

Jesse looked at her. "And you'll help? Go shopping with me?"

"Like when we went shopping for bathroom essentials and cleaning essentials and light decor essentials?"

"What can I say?" Jesse said. "You're the bomb. I don't know what I'd do without you."

Jordyn put the plates in the cabinet. "Whatever. Soon as you get this house where you want it, you'll stop calling."

"I just moved in," Jesse said. "Why was I calling before that?" He looked at her. "Why do you think someone only wants to be around you, to get something from you?"

"Because that's how it's always been," Jordyn said, "and it's usually sex."

"So since I'm not trying to sleep with you," Jesse said, "your mind has to come up with *something*. So I'm using you for . . . shopping?" He spread his hands in disbelief. "I have a mom, Jordyn. She'll be here next week, and she *loves* to shop for house stuff. I could simply wait for her to get here." He leaned against the counter, looking at her. "I said I don't know what I'd do without you because I enjoy being around you. If we do nothing but sit and talk, that's dope to me. Because *you're* dope to me."

Jordyn leaned against the counter opposite him, wanting his words to penetrate her heart. Could she really believe that? That Jesse thought that way about her?

He moved toward her and took her into his arms, something he hadn't done in the two months they'd been dating.

"You're special, Jordyn," Jesse said. "Not because of what you can give me, but because of who you are."

She nodded into his chest, unable to speak.

"And you know what else is dope?" Jesse said. "That you're focusing more and more on the inside"—he looked into her eyes —"look at you, over here with no makeup. Vulnerable. And beautiful as ever."

"You two are a little too close, aren't you?" Jade walked into the kitchen. "What happened to 'boundaries'?"

Jordyn moved out of Jesse's arms, looking at her sister. "Maintaining boundaries is the *only* reason you're here."

"Oh, I'm not here to help?" Jade said. "Why was I just unpacking books in Jesse's office?"

"And I'm thankful," Jesse said. "For the boundary help and the unpacking help."

"You might be a little over eager, though." Jordyn looked at Jade. "We were only hugging."

"Hey, I thought it was unrealistic to begin with," Jade said. "But you're the one who said you didn't want to kiss—and looked to me like it was coming." She turned to Jesse. "I can start shelving the books. I've got an idea how they can be organized, but if you want to do it . . ."

"You don't mind?" Jesse said.

"Might as well," Jade said. "Better than staring at the two of you."

"You know what, Jade?" Jesse said. "The more I get to know you, the more I appreciate you."

"That's because she's as blunt and crabby as you are," Jordyn said.

"I appreciate you too, Jesse." Jade started back toward the office. "Who knew? You're actually good for my sister."

Jesse looked at Jordyn. "Jade was right. I was about to kiss you."

"I wouldn't have had a problem with that," Jordyn said. "You're the one who wanted that boundary."

"I never told you why," Jesse said. "Cedric told me he put that boundary in place when he dated Cyd. He wanted God to change his desires, and he told me how it moved him closer to God, and to Cyd." He looked into Jordyn's eyes. "That's what I want. To be closer to God, and to you, in the right way. This is the best relationship I've had."

Jordyn wondered if she'd heard right. "What makes you say that?"

"Because it's the first relationship where I've wanted to honor

God," Jesse said. "And the first relationship where I'm willing to let the Lord lead, wherever He wants to take it."

"What kind of mood are you in today?" Jordyn said. "I'm about to lose it over here."

"I just want you to know where I am," Jesse said.

Jordyn looked at him. "Well, maybe it's a good time to go ahead and ask. Faith and Reggie's wedding next month . . . I wondered if you would go with me."

"Why would I go to their wedding, Jordyn?"

"Because I want you to be my plus one."

"Which means I didn't get a personal invitation," Jesse said. "Because we all know it wouldn't make sense for me to be there."

"They probably did think it would be weird to invite you," Jordyn said. "But that doesn't mean it would be weird for you to come with me. Faith is the one who set us up on that date. I think she expects me to bring you."

"I'm not going, Jordyn."

"So I have to go by myself?" Jordyn said.

"By yourself?" Jesse said. "You'll know just about everybody there. And I thought you were doing makeup."

Jordyn pouted. "I can't persuade you?"

"No," Jesse said. "But you'll have fun. And I know Zoe will be crazy cute, so take lots of pics and video to show me."

Jordyn smiled inside. "I love your love for Zoe."

"That's my heart," Jesse said.

"We need to shop for her room too," Jordyn said. "Zoe essentials." She looked at Jesse. "The wedding is a small thing. I'm just glad I can be with you. Like this. Definitely the best relationship I've had."

Jesse got back to unpacking. "I want you to meet my mom. I told her about you."

"Oh, just like that, casual," Jordyn said. "You're full of surprises this afternoon. And here I thought we were just unpacking."

"Well, I'll have Zoe next week while Faith is in LA," Jesse said, "so of course my mom can't wait to spend time with her. I thought we could all go out one night for dinner . . . my three favorite girls."

She looked at Jesse. "Is this real? Why are you blowing my mind today?"

"I didn't ask you to marry me, Jordyn. It's dinner."

"Aaand you just ruined it."

Jesse paused, looking at her. "I did, I'm sorry. Let me change my answer. It's real. And if I'm blowing your mind today, it's because you've been blowing mine."

Jordyn felt the goose bumps. "I don't know if I can handle this side of you, being all open and thoughtful. But I like it."

"So I need to remember that—showing more of this side of me?" Jesse said. "Is that a Jordyn essential?"

Jordyn took glasses from the dishwasher. "You need to remember that."

"I'm making a list—Jordyn essentials," Jesse said.

"Stop blowing my mind."

CHAPTER 52

*C*yd finger fluffed her hair and touched up her makeup in the hotel room mirror, then put on the name badge she'd gotten with her registration packet. Transferring a few items to a smaller handbag, she heard her phone ring on the desk and moved to get it.

"Hey, finally," Cyd said. "I left two messages since my plane landed. How's Chase?"

"We just got home from pediatric ER," Cedric said. "Temperature's one-hundred-three—"

"What? Oh, poor baby."

"I know," Cedric said, "but no vomiting or diarrhea, which is good, and they didn't find any other issues. So right now, just working to bring down this fever. You should've seen Chase when the doctor said, 'Give him as much fluid as he wants'—until he followed it with, 'but no fruit juice.'"

"You should get popsicles," Cyd said. "Those work well."

"We got some on the way home," Cedric said.

"So are you still coming on Friday?" Cyd said. "Chase should be feeling better in two days, but either way, my parents can handle it."

"If he's not feeling better, I don't know," Cedric said. "I don't want us both to be gone."

"Well as we pray for him to get better, let's also pray he's fully recovered by Friday morning," Cyd said. "I want you here with me, babe."

"And you know I want to be there," Cedric said. "You headed out?"

"We've got the welcome reception here in the hotel tonight," Cyd said. "Then I hit the ground running early tomorrow with the first conference session. Kiss my little man for me."

"Will do," Cedric said. "Love you, babe."

"Love you, too."

Cyd rode the elevator down and joined a lobby full of conference attendees, almost all professors in classical studies. She threaded her way through pockets of conversation, pausing every few feet to hug and gab, then wound her way down a hall and around a corner where the reception was being held.

A hand touched her shoulder. "When did you get here, Cyd?"

"Rosemarie, hey," Cyd said. "I landed about three-thirty," she said. "I thought we were supposed to be on the same flight."

"I re-booked and got here last night," Rosemarie said. "Wanted to make the most of the time out here, before fall semester kicks off in a couple weeks."

"So this is the Wash U hangout spot." Their department head Alice walked up, a glass of wine in hand. "Are we on for our department dinner tomorrow evening?"

"Reservation for six already made," Rosemarie said.

"I'm starving right now, though." Cyd eyed an appetizer tray as it passed. "And these light hors d'oeuvres won't be enough. Who's up for some fine dining in San Fran?"

"I won't be able to join you," Alice said. "I'm meeting a friend from UT-Austin for dinner."

"I've got plans as well," Rosemarie said. "I was only stopping at the reception for a minute—but hey, there's Micah," she said, waving him over.

Cyd looked as he walked up in slacks, a button down shirt with no tie, and jacket. This summer with no classes to teach, they'd both been hunkered down in their offices, focused on research and writing—with joint Bible study sessions about once a week. And Bible study had extended to conversations about life and family and whatever else popped up. She'd been stunned one day to see that three hours had passed. Somehow he'd become easy to talk to. And for some inexplicable reason right now, he'd never looked more handsome. Cyd let her eyes skitter across the crowd.

"Good evening," Micah said. "Nice to see everyone made it safely."

"Micah, have you made plans for tonight?" Rosemarie said. "Cyd's looking for dinner company."

"Oh, no, I'm fine, actually," Cyd said. "I think I'll just order up in my room."

"In San Francisco?" Micah said. "I've been looking forward to this food for weeks. And I hadn't made plans for tonight yet. Let's pick a place."

"Seriously," Cyd said. "It's just, all of a sudden, I'm tired or something. The long flight, I guess. I think I'll head up—"

"Cyd, it's not even seven-thirty." Micah was looking at his watch. "If we go now, you'll be back by ten, in time for a good night's rest."

Live jazz music and chatter surrounded her, but all Cyd could hear was the weird rhythm of the beat of her heart. She looked at him. "If we can make it quick."

~

"So you were right." Cyd walked with Micah back to the hotel.

"That's the best Chinese food I've had. I could eat that scallops and broccoli every day I'm here."

"I can't even believe you tried to debate where to go," Micah said. "You're the one who was fine with room service."

"But once I was headed somewhere," Cyd said, "I wanted seafood. Didn't know I'd get the seafood of my life in the Chinese spot."

"That's odd, because I said you would."

"Don't gloat," Cyd said.

"Hey, I'm just glad you enjoyed it. And see"—he checked the time—"only nine-thirty."

"Which is eleven-thirty our time," Cyd said. "I'm beat."

"Still coming to my talk tomorrow?" Micah said. "Should be fairly interesting."

"That's an understatement," Cyd said. "Your first time speaking openly about your faith, other than that tweet."

"And I got dragged for days over that." Micah shrugged. "I was vocal in my opposition. How can I not be vocal, now that I believe?"

"I'll be there," Cyd said. "I'll be praying."

"And thank you," Micah said, "for the Bible studies. They've been sharpening me. Invaluable in terms of preparation for this week."

"I'm glad it's been helpful," Cyd said.

They walked into the hotel and caught an elevator headed up. Micah pushed "9" and looked at Cyd.

"I'm on the same floor," she said.

They got off and turned down the same hall. It wasn't lost on Cyd that this was the same as at work—within doors of one another.

Cyd stopped at her room and inserted the key.

"Sleep well," Micah said.

Cyd glanced back and caught Micah's gaze. Then she went in, closed her door, and leaned against it.

Lord, what is this? Why is my heart beating like this? I've never felt anything like this when we're studying on campus. Now all of a sudden. . .

Cyd walked further into the room then paused again. It couldn't be. Could she actually be attracted to him? *Oh, God, what do I do?*

Treva popped into her head.

Lord, it's almost midnight in St. Louis. I know Treva's asleep.

Her name sailed through Cyd's mind again, and she took out her phone, holding it. What on earth would she say? She took a breath and dialed.

"Hey, I thought you left for San Fran today," Treva said.

"I did," Cyd said. "Sorry to be calling so late, did I wake you?"

"Girl, no," Treva said. "I'm downstairs watching this hilarious card game. Cedric couldn't be here, so Lance and his mom are partners against Jillian and her son David—both of whom are just learning—"

"Treva, I really need to talk to you." Cyd could feel herself shaking a little.

"What's wrong?" Treva's voice went low.

"Can you go somewhere private?" Cyd said. "I'm not even sure how to say this."

"Okay, I'm walking upstairs," Treva said. "Go on, I'm listening."

Cyd went and sat on the bed. "So, Micah Daniels, the professor in my department . . ."

"The one you debated," Treva said, "and now he's a believer."

"And you know we do these Bible studies—"

"Mm-hm," Treva said. "And I remember what I said about that."

"I know." Cyd's eyes folded to a close. Treva had told her the enemy was crafty, that he wouldn't bring just any scenario at Cyd. He would take something good, even a God-glorifying thing, and twist it. "I couldn't see it before," she said. "I'd never felt anything before. But tonight . . ."

"Cyd, what happened?" Treva said.

"We went to dinner," Cyd said. "It was spur of the moment, I tried to back out, but there we were, the two of us at dinner, then taking a stroll back to the hotel."

"Okay," Treva said. "Keep going."

"And I don't know," Cyd said, "out of nowhere I started seeing him a different way, even as I was trying *not* to. And we're on the same floor and I got back in my room five minutes ago, and my heart is *still* beating like I narrowly escaped some bad car accident."

"Cyd, I'm honestly not surprised," Treva said.

"How are you not surprised?" Cyd said. "I'm over here shocked."

"The enemy's been seducing you," Treva said. "Subtle, slow, suited to your sensibilities. For *months*. Come on, bonding over Bible study won't work on just anybody. But all that time you've been spending—it moved you emotionally. And now that you're together for a few days in San Francisco—the enemy's turning up the heat."

"How can you see it so clearly?" Cyd said.

"Because I'm not in it," Treva said. "If it were the other way around, you'd see it—and warn me of it."

"So what am I supposed to do?" Cyd said.

"Cedric's coming out there on Friday, right?"

"Chase got a fever," Cyd said, "so it's iffy. But at this point, I'll be praying extra that he comes. Then I only have to get through tomorrow without him, which shouldn't be hard."

"Stay on guard," Treva said. "Handle your business at the conference and steer clear of Micah."

"I'm supposed to be supporting him at this talk he's giving tomorrow," Cyd said. "He's sharing his faith publicly for the first time."

"Don't go, Cyd," Treva said. "Temptation is only temptation— until you enter into it. You have to guard your heart. I always think about how the Bible says Eve *saw* that the tree was good for food and desirable, *then* she took and ate. She probably wasn't thinking about that tree until the enemy put it on her mind." Treva's words were earnest. "The enemy is putting Micah on your mind—he's shooting his fiery darts. Don't even look Micah's way. Pray whenever the thoughts rise up, and I'll be praying too. God will give you strength."

"I'm so thankful I can talk to you," Cyd said. "You don't know how much I needed this."

"Don't hesitate to call me, Cyd," Treva said. "Whatever you need to talk through or pray through . . . I'm here."

Cyd hung up and dialed her husband.

"Hey, babe, you sleep?"

"Not really, just lying here," Cedric said.

Cyd smiled inside. He was knocked out. "Just wanted to hear your voice. I love you."

"I love you too, baby."

～

"Rosemarie, I've got a two-hour break tomorrow afternoon." Cyd walked off a delicious dinner with the rest of her department as they headed back to their rooms Thursday night. "I can go shopping with you."

"I need to check the schedule again." Rosemarie glanced back at Cyd on the sidewalk. "If I only have an hour break, I may wait to shop on Saturday."

"Well, let me know," Cyd said. "I can't do Saturday. Cedric will be here." She'd been elated to learn that Chase was better, and Cedric would arrive early evening tomorrow.

"I guess this is where we branch off," Alice said, heading to a different hotel.

Cyd took note of who was branching. "None of you are in the main conference hotel?"

"I never stay in the main hotel," Rosemarie said. "Too crowded. But wait, you're not walking by yourself, are you? It's dark now."

"I'm in the main hotel too," Micah said.

Cyd glanced briefly at him as the others said goodbyes and walked off. She'd skipped Micah's talk, attending another instead. And hadn't seen him at all until dinner. Not ten minutes before, she'd been thanking God that the day was over and uneventful.

"I was looking for you at the talk today," Micah said.

"I couldn't make it," Cyd said. "Something came up. But I did pray. How did it go?"

"I got interrupted a few times," Micah said. "Got called a few names. It was about what I'd expected."

"Wow," Cyd said. "How did you handle it?"

"I tried to stick to what was true," Micah said, "instead of taking the bait and going where they wanted me to go." He looked at her. "Something I learned from you during our debate."

"Were you able to sit and talk to any of them afterward?" Cyd said.

"I offered," Micah said. "No one took me up on it, at least not yet."

"Which is a good point," Cyd said. "Someone may come back to you later, as the Lord works on their heart."

"Like what happened with me," Micah said.

They veered left, through a mini park-like setting, nearing the hotel, a strange silence looming.

"Cyd," Micah said finally, "you've given a lot of insight and advice. But this is the hardest question I've had to ask."

Cyd looked at him, waiting.

"What do I do . . ." Micah paused near a cluster of trees. ". . . if I'm falling for you?"

Cyd was certain she could feel the working of every internal organ. Nothing was still within. "There's nothing you can do, Micah, I'm married. We can't act on every thought or feeling that may come."

"Understood," Micah said. "But what do I do with it?" He paused. "Have you ever thought or felt something you couldn't act on?"

The look in his eyes, the tone of his voice, the very question itself . . . Cyd couldn't find words. Not that she needed them. She didn't have to answer that. She just needed to—

"Cyd . . ."

Micah reached for her hand and pulled her closer. His face moved toward hers, and their lips came together. Cyd felt his arms enclosing her—

Her heart hammered and she backed away suddenly and turned, making quick steps toward the hotel. *What did I just do?* Tears filled her eyelids. *O God, I kissed him.*

Cyd tried to catch her breath as she entered the lobby, moving toward the elevators.

"Cyd!"

Her heart stopped. Her watery eyes closed.

Cedric.

"I'm glad I saw you, I've been waiting . . ." Cedric looked at her. "Babe, what's wrong?"

"What . . ." Cyd took a stuttered breath. "I thought you were getting here tomorrow."

"I wanted to surprise you," Cedric said. "So I changed my ticket . . ." He looked left as Micah passed. "Were you two just out together?"

"Our department dinner was tonight," Cyd said. "Six of us."

"So where's everybody else?"

"We're staying in different hotels," Cyd said. "Let's just, go up to the room."

Cyd could feel Cedric looking at her as the elevator rose, but she couldn't look at him. She opened the door to the room and held it as he rolled his bag inside. When the door closed, he stood in place.

"What's going on, Cyd?"

"There's nothing going—"

"Cyd, just say it." Cedric moved closer to her. "Just say it."

Tears spilled from her eyes. "I kissed him," she said. "I don't know, it just . . . *happened*, on our way back to the hotel. But it was only seconds—"

"So if I hadn't been here, *he'd* be in your room right now?"

"Cedric, no." Cyd took his hand, and he shook it free. "I walked away from him. I was headed to my room. Alone."

"What about yesterday?" Cedric said.

"What do you mean?" Cyd said. "Tonight was the first and only time it happened."

"Did you spend time with him yesterday?" Cedric said.

Cyd looked away a moment. "We went to dinner, but it was spontaneous, I was trying to go with Rosemarie—where are you going?"

Cedric headed for the door.

"Cedric, don't leave," Cyd said. "Talk to me. Please."

He turned. "So dinner last night, a stroll together tonight, and he just, kissed you?"

"He said . . . He said he was falling for me."

Cedric looked at her for only a second, then opened the door and let it shut behind him.

Cyd held herself, pacing the room as the tears fell. Moments later she grabbed her phone and dialed Treva.

"Please pray for us," Cyd said. "I kissed Micah tonight, and Cedric's here. He knows."

CHAPTER 53

*C*edric felt his phone vibrate as he walked a random San Francisco block. He ignored it. Cyd had called twice, but if he'd wanted to talk, he would've stayed in the room.

He watched passersby, many of them couples, picturing Cyd and Micah. How familiar with one another had they gotten? Did their arms brush as they walked? They'd certainly gotten close enough to kiss.

His phone vibrated again, and he looked this time—and wanted to ignore it. He sighed, answering. "Come on, man. I can't be mad ten minutes without you calling?"

"You're outside walking," Lance said.

"As a matter of fact, I am," Cedric said.

"Go back upstairs, man," Lance said. "Talk to Cyd."

"So you know what happened?"

"She told Treva," Lance said. "And she said Treva could tell me, so I could talk to you."

"I don't want to hear it right now," Cedric said. "Try me tomorrow."

"So what's the plan for tonight?" Lance said. "You're not going back to the room?"

"I don't have a plan," Cedric said. "It *just* happened. If you'd let me roam these streets and fume for a while, I'll come up with one."

"Cyd called Treva last night," Lance said. "She asked Treva to pray because she was feeling tempted around Micah for the first time."

Cedric's steps slowed as he listened.

"Cyd *wanted* you to get there," Lance said. "She wasn't playing games, trying to cheat on you. But temptation is real, man."

"I told Cyd something like this could happen," Cedric said. "I told her we needed to be vigilant, set up boundaries. And *this* happens?"

"She couldn't see it," Lance said. "You know how the enemy works—he's subtle."

"I bet you wouldn't be this calm and analytical if it were Treva," Cedric said.

"I'm sure I wouldn't," Lance said, "and you'd be in my face telling me to go talk to her."

An image of the two of them flashed through Cedric's mind. "I cannot believe she kissed him."

"And cut it short and walked away," Lance said. "Should I remind you of when you were tempted a few months ago?"

"I didn't say I was tempted," Cedric said.

"Oh. Right," Lance said. "That's why I was praying for another sitter arrangement for Chase."

"I said I felt some kind of way around Jordyn *one time*," Cedric said, "and that I didn't want it to become a temptation. But you'd expect that with me. Who'd expect to see Cyd kissing some man on the streets of San Fran?"

"Because Cyd is perfect?" Lance said. "She's immune to temptation? Newsflash, bro—she's human. And she asked for prayer as soon as she sensed what was happening. Go talk to her."

Cedric stared into the night for a few seconds then gave a long sigh. "I will. Just . . . pray for us."

"You don't even have to ask," Lance said.

Cedric walked another two blocks, praying before turning around and heading back. At the door to the hotel room he paused, unsure whether he wanted to go in. Finally he knocked.

Cyd opened and he walked in, glancing briefly at her reddened eyes.

"Cedric, I really want to—"

"I just want to know one thing," he said, looking at her. "Are you in love with him?"

"No, I'm not in love with him," Cyd said. "I only felt a fleeting attraction, and that just rose up yesterday." She looked into his eyes. "You're the only man I love. You're the only man I want. I don't even know what happened tonight, I keep going over it in my mind, I'm sorry. I'm so sorry for hurting you."

Cedric returned her gaze. "The thought of you with another man . . . I couldn't see straight."

"I know, baby." Fresh tears fell. "I'm still shaking. I don't want to experience anything like that ever again."

"You'll still see him almost every day."

"I've already been thinking about that," Cyd said. "My office at Living Water will be my base. I'll go on campus for classes, meetings, and student office hours. That's it."

Cedric looked away.

"Babe, I'm sorry," Cyd said, moving close to him.

Cedric walked around her. "You said that."

"But you're being so cold," Cyd said. "You won't even hug me."

Cedric gave her a look. "I got here early so we'd have an extra evening together, and found out you were hugged up with somebody else. So forgive me if I'm not feeling romantic."

"But we don't have to throw the night away." Cyd came close again. "Can't we work on generating the romance?"

"That's the last thing I want to do right now," Cedric said. "I can't get the picture out of my head—you in Micah's arms."

"Baby, I'm asking you to forgive me," Cyd said.

Cedric looked at her. "It's not a question of whether I forgive you—you know I do. But I'm hurt, babe. You can't expect me to jump to romance."

Cedric brushed his teeth and got ready for bed, pulling back the covers and getting in. Cyd came from the bathroom, turned off the lights, and got in beside him. A moment later she moved closer, then put her head on his shoulder.

Cedric closed his eyes, his arms at his side. Maybe he'd feel different in the morning, but right now he couldn't engage her.

And yet, he couldn't sleep either.

Thirty minutes later he felt Cyd move beside him. "Are you awake?" Cedric said.

Cyd nodded.

"Get up for a minute," Cedric said.

Cyd gave him a curious look but obliged.

Cedric went to his bag, took out a container he'd gotten on the way to the hotel, and dumped red, white, yellow, and lavender rose petals on the king-sized bed.

Cyd stared wide-eyed. "Are these all the colors?" she said. "Like the day you proposed?"

Cedric gave a nod.

"How did you find lavender?"

"I'm resourceful," he said.

"You went through all that, then you showed up and . . ." Cyd shook her head, moving closer to him. "I'll keep saying it, I'm sorry, baby."

"Well," Cedric said, "they're not cheap. So I figured no sense letting them go to waste."

He lay back down on top of the petals, poised to chase sleep once again.

"Seems to me you're still letting them go to waste," Cyd said. "We can do better than that." She lay beside him and kissed him.

"I'm telling you," Cedric said, "if I see that Daniels tomorrow—"

"Can we just focus on you and me, and this romantic mood?"

"I'm not in a romantic mood."

Cyd kissed him again, and Cedric responded slightly more this time.

He paused. "Just so you know, we're having a conversation tomorrow about boundaries and what not."

"Okay," Cyd said. "Can we resume?"

Cedric looked into her eyes. "I really wanted to stay mad at least through the night."

"I know."

"It's not cute, what you're doing."

Cyd drew him into another kiss, and Cedric let himself go, bringing her close. Where she belonged. In his arms.

CHAPTER 54

SEPTEMBER

"*O*h, I'm gonna cry, Faith, you look so beautiful."

Faith looked over as best she could, while Jordyn worked on her eyes. "Cinda, you just saw me minutes ago, when you helped me get dressed."

"But that was before Jordyn got her hands on you." Cinda walked across the Living Hope Sunday School classroom in her coral gown. "Oh my gosh, you need a mirror so you can see yourself. I cannot *wait* till Reggie sees you."

"At rehearsal last night, Reggie said we should do professional pictures before the wedding," Faith said, "so he could see the dress."

"Reggie will have the full effect of that moment he sees you coming down the aisle," Cinda said. "And I'll have the perfect spot to see his face, 'cause girl, you are smokin' in that sheath dress." She looked at Jordyn. "And you're in here working your magic on *everybody.*" She checked her phone. "Wait, this is Zee calling." She stepped outside the room.

"I need Jordyn to hook me up in the mornings before school." Sophia stepped into her navy blue dress.

"Girl, right?" Joy slipped on her strappy sandals. "Show up every day looking like a snack."

"What in the world does that mean?" Faith looked at her sister as Jordyn turned, doing something with a makeup brush.

"It's just a saying," Joy said.

"And who's doing the snacking?" Faith said.

"Anyway," Joy said, looking at her phone now. "Sophie, did you see the comments I'm getting on the pics I posted last night of Alonzo and me at rehearsal."

"I don't even want to see," Sophia said. "I'm still mad you get to walk down the aisle with him. How is that fair?"

"But this pic right here, though," Joy said. "Don't we look super cute? I just can't. He is *so. fine.*"

"We need to see his latest movie again," Sophia said. "Because *girl*, that scene where he's in that fight and takes off his shirt—"

"Really?" Faith's eyes closed as Jordyn worked on her brow. "Are you two forgetting this is Cinda's husband?"

"Umm. No," Joy said. "*But,* Cinda totally knows Alonzo is my man crush, and we're just teenagers, so it's harmless."

"It's rude," Faith said, "so cut it."

The door opened and Treva walked in. "How are we doing in here?" she said.

Faith looked over at her. "We just got sidetracked with—"

"Nothing important," Joy said. "Sophie, let's find Courtenay and Hope. They said there's food somewhere."

"We're starting on time," Treva said. "A little less than thirty minutes, so be ready."

"The guys have arrived." Stephanie breezed in wearing her navy blue. "They thought they were looking good, stepping out of the limo in their tuxes."

Faith smiled. "You saw my man?" She'd gotten a long text from Reggie this morning, telling her how much he loved her.

"Reggie was the first one through the door," Stephanie said. "I told him no need to rush. Ain't nothing getting started till the bride is ready."

"That's what I'm coming to see about," Jillian said, walking in. "I got the guys settled in their area, hostesses are in place, greeting the first guests, a little snafu with the music got fixed—I just need to know about our bride."

"She's just about ready," Jordyn said, dabbing Faith's forehead with some kind of sponge. "Stand up so we can see the full look."

Faith stood, slipped her feet into sparkly crystal shoes, and looked at all of them as Cinda slipped back in. "Well . . ." She exhaled. "What do you think?"

"First word that comes to mind—exquisite." Jillian hugged her. "And now that I know you're ready, I have to go wrangle these young bridesmaids." She dashed off.

"I already said." Cinda walked a circle around her. "Smokin'. You and this dress—*this dress*—everything about the look is stunning, if I may say so myself."

Stephanie chuckled. "Girl, you better, 'cause Faith looks amazing and you got every detail on point. What is this in her hair?" she said, lightly touching it.

"When the dress was altered, I asked them to give me the extra lace," Cinda said, "so we could weave it through her hair when it got pinned up."

"Sweetheart, you are . . ." Treva gave a bare nod, as if trying to hold it together. "You are absolutely gorgeous."

Faith reached for her mother's hand. "Dad?"

Treva swiped a tear before it could fall. "He's really been on my mind. He so looked forward to this day for his oldest baby girl."

"How are you feeling, Faith?" Stephanie said.

"I woke up kind of sad," Faith said, "and went down to the kitchen early, just to get some juice, and Lance was there. We ended up talking close to an hour, about Dad and my memories of him. Somehow it made me feel better."

"Lance didn't tell me that," Treva said.

Jillian walked in again. "Photographer wants pictures outside with the bridesmaids."

Stephanie and Cinda did a quick check of their hair and makeup before heading out.

"And Jordyn," Jillian said, "Darlene's trying to do Zoe's hair, but Zoe's crying and asking for 'Yordy'."

"Wow, really?" Jordyn said. "I do her hair when she's at Jesse's, and I use this homemade mixture that's good with detangling. So it's a breeze."

"Do you have it with you?" Faith said. "Zoe is so tender-headed, and Grandma Darlene isn't exactly easy with the comb. Plus it always looks good when you do it. That is, if you don't mind."

"I've got my hair stuff in this big ol' bag," Jordyn said, lifting it. "And of course I don't mind. I promise, she'll look crazy cute, as her dad likes to say." She left out with Jillian.

Treva turned to Faith. "So how are you feeling about the other thing we talked about?"

Faith felt the butterflies. "I keep thinking, tonight's the night, and I'm nervous and what if it's weird—and by the way, it's still a little weird talking to you about it." She sighed. "But since our prayer, I've also been feeling kind of . . . excited? Which is also weird."

"Did you try on the lingerie we bought," Treva said, "so you could feel comfortable in it?"

"Yes, I tried it on—this is so embarrassing." Faith gave her mom a tentative look. "But that's what kind of got me excited, to see how Reggie reacts."

Treva smiled a little. "You already know how he'll react."

"*Mom.*"

"I'm just saying," Treva said. "We're praying that you'll be ready for how he reacts. Right?"

"Yes, true," Faith said.

"And sweetheart, it's a blessing that we're even having this discussion," Treva said. "You and Reggie honored God and abstained from sex. The fact that you're nervous is a good thing in that respect."

"I still can't believe you were nervous on your wedding night with Lance."

"I don't know why that's hard to believe," Treva said. "Your dad and I had been together forever, it seemed. And suddenly there was Lance. And I loved him—but I had no idea what to expect. Just like you. I didn't know how we would mesh, whether we'd feel comfortable with one another. So I was praying."

"And God answered your prayers?" Faith said.

"Mightily."

"*Mom.*"

"I was told it's time to come get the bride," Lance said, walking in.

Faith smiled at him. Treva put her arms around him and kissed him.

"Okay," Lance said. "What did I just walk in on?"

"A mother/daughter pep talk," Treva said, smiling. "So we're ready to start?"

"Ten minutes," Lance said. "But Jillian wants Faith in place. And we'll pray over her with the bridal party."

"I'm glad we're having the ceremony here at Living Hope," Faith said, "because it's more intimate. But it's funny how I'm already used to being at Living Word. How does it feel for you, Lance, being here?"

"I miss it," Lance said. "But Living Word is where I grew up and spent a lot of years. I was surprised to feel like I'm back home over there."

"I've got your bouquet," Treva said, picking it up.

Lance moved closer to Treva, eyeing her. "Have I told you how fine you look in that blue silk?"

"You have," Treva said.

Lance shook his head. "You can't be taking my breath away." He put Faith's arm through his. "You know I'm on duty." He looked at Faith as they started walking. "You ready for this?"

Faith nodded. "I'm ready."

CHAPTER 55

*R*eggie stood in the church fellowship hall as Jillian fixed his boutonniere.

"You've got a good fifteen minutes of singlehood left." Alonzo sat nearby. "Any last words?"

Reggie looked over at him. "Same last words you had—let's do this. I was down with eloping months ago." He watched Jillian fight with the stickpin. "How does she look?"

Jillian smiled. "My word was exquisite."

"You take a pic?" Reggie said. "Can I see?"

"I took lots of pics," Jillian said. "And no." She tugged lightly on the boutonniere. "I think that'll work," she said, stepping back to see. "You and Faith look so good I can't stand it. I can't wait to see you two *together*." She stood among the men. "It's almost time to start. I'll be back shortly to tell the groom and best man it's time to go in, and the rest of you to line up. So be ready to move."

"Jillian," Alonzo said, "can you tell Cinda to check her phone?"

"Okay, I'll tell her," Jillian said, walking out.

Reggie looked at him. "Man, you called her from the limo, now you in here sending love notes? You can't be apart for five minutes?"

"That could've come from anybody in the room, but you," Alonzo said. "Who was supposed to be hanging with the guys last night after rehearsal—"

"How many times am I gonna hear this?" Reggie said. "I did hang with the guys."

"And left early," Alonzo said, "because you just had to see Faith before the night ended."

"And why is it so hard to believe that I had a reason for seeing her?" Reggie said.

Alonzo gave him the eye. "'I love you' for the thousandth time could've waited."

"Hey, Reg, I'm looking at a pic of your bride in her dress." Fitz, one of Reggie's college buddies, had his phone in hand.

"How do you have that?" Reggie said.

"Joy just sent some pics," Fitz said.

"You're texting *Joy*?" Reggie said. "She's sixteen, man."

Fitz's eyes got big. "I thought she was like, nineteen."

"What about Sophia?" another college buddy asked.

"Seventeen," Reggie said.

"Both of y'all about to go to jail," Tommy said. "Y'all better back up off these young girls."

"*Man*," Fitz said, "they're both fine, too."

"Let me see that picture of Faith, though." Reggie went to look.

"Don't show him," Tommy said. "You'll see Faith in five minutes."

Alonzo came and put an arm around Reggie, holding out his phone. "I'm posting this," he said. "Me and the groom, my little brother." He snapped.

"Appreciate you, man," Reggie said. "For everything. LA was supposed to be the wedding gift, and you and Cinda turn around and give us a honeymoon in Turks and Caicos? *And* the bridal suite tonight at the hotel? Much love. For real."

"The premiere was never the wedding gift in our minds," Alonzo said. "We were talking about that months ago. But we need to have you two out to LA for a longer stay next time. That was big fun."

"It's time," Jillian said, walking in. "Groomsmen, come with me to line up with the bridesmaids." She looked at the remaining two. "Reggie and Tommy, you know what to do."

They made their way through a hallway that would put them at the front of the sanctuary.

"Hey, Reg," Tommy said, pausing a moment. "I want to say something to you . . . You haven't exactly seen marriage done well in our family. Our parents divorced. And you know my situation. But I know you, and I know you're not looking to other people as your standard. You look to Christ. You look to the word. And I know you'll love Faith well." He hugged him. "I couldn't be happier for you. I thank God for you."

"I thank God for you, too," Reggie said, hugging him again. "Love you, man."

Reggie led the way as they continued to the sanctuary. He walked to the spot they'd rehearsed the night before, except now the area was decorated with flowers and candles. He glanced out at the guests, soft music playing in the background, and saw the grandmothers being escorted in—one on his side, his paternal grandmother; three on Faith's—Patsy, Darlene, and Lance's mom, Pamela.

The music changed, and Reggie felt his stomach tighten as the wedding party started down the aisle. Thankfully they only had six on each side, which passed pretty quickly, and they'd dispensed with a ring bearer. So after Cinda came the flower girl, the only one who could threaten to outshine Faith today—Zoe.

Cameras filled the air as Treva walked with Zoe down the aisle. Faith and Reggie knew the risk of putting her in the ceremony. At twenty months, she could throw a tantrum, refuse to walk the aisle, or any number of mishaps. But Reggie was beaming now as she seemed to relish the moment. Both Treva and Zoe had a basket of white petals, and Zoe mimicked her grandmother as she tossed them to the ground. Then, halfway through, Zoe turned her basket upside down, dumping the rest—and reached for Treva's. Treva switched baskets and let Zoe continue dropping petals, then picked her up and held her when they got to the end. The guests applauded the little girl.

Everyone stood now as the music changed once again. The sanctuary filled with "How He Loves," a version by Anthony Evans, and Reggie felt the weight of the moment all at once. Not a heavy weight, but the seriousness of it. He was about to pledge his love and his very life to this woman, and he wanted nothing more. But to love her well, as Tommy had said, he needed so much grace. *Lord, help me to cherish Faith as You cherish her.*

The doors opened, and Reggie couldn't see with all the bodies in the way. But seconds later she appeared—and he'd never seen anything more beautiful. Exquisite—that was a good word. Everything about her. And she was about to be *his*?

He closed his eyes for a second, overcome. When he looked again, Faith's eyes were on him. They stared at one another as Lance brought her to Reggie's side. Faith passed her bouquet to Cinda, and Reggie took her hand as Lance changed position.

"You look amazing," Reggie whispered.

"And you look super dreamy," Faith said.

"You look so good, I just forgot all my vows," Reggie said.

"You didn't write them down?" Faith whispered.

"Yeah," Reggie said, "and it's at home. I had it memorized."

Lance cleared his throat. "I think they started without me," he said.

The guests chuckled.

"Faith Nicole Langston and Reginald Darnell Porter," Lance began, "you stand before us aware of the covenant you are making before God . . ."

Reggie took both of Faith's hands and looked into her eyes. This was what he'd been waiting for. The songs, the readings, the candle lighting—all necessary, he guessed. But he wanted to get to the vows, so they could get to the part where they officially became husband and wife.

"So, open confession—I can't remember my vows," Reggie said. "Something about the moment, Faith and this dress . . . I can't even think. So I guess I'll just speak from the heart . . ."

He heard voices of affirmation among the guests.

"I've been called a hopeless romantic," Reggie said. "I was never into all the relationship games. I just wanted true love. And I found it—in Christ. Jesus showed me that there really was such a thing as unconditional, strong, intimate love. But then I said, I guess that's the only place I'll find it—in Him—'cause out here in these streets, it's nothing but heartbreak. Nothing but shallow commitments." He squeezed Faith's hands. "But in you, Faith . . ." He blew out a breath. "In you I found the true love I didn't think was possible."

Reggie paused, and Faith brushed a lone tear from his cheek with her finger.

He stared into her eyes. "You're my best friend. And sometimes we fuss over the dumbest things, but you better know I'd take a bullet for you, girl. That's my promise to you—to protect you, to cherish you, to love you beyond myself." He wiped her tears now. "Because you deserve more than I can give. I promise to love you with the love of Jesus. I promise to stay in His face, seeking Him, through every season of our lives. I love you, baby." He looked at Lance. "I can kiss her now?"

Lance smiled at him. "Hey, I get it, but not quite. She's got a turn."

Faith's eyes were filled still as she looked at Reggie. "When you came into my life, I was wondering what God's plan B would be for me. I had made wrong choices and I knew God had forgiven me. But I thought I had forfeited His good and perfect gifts. And

God said, no. He gave me *you*." She flicked tears from her eyelid. "Because of the Christ in you, Jesus is more real in my life. You love hard, Reg, and when I hurt you, you forgive. You lifted my shame with grace. You healed the pain with . . . your stupid jokes and stories." The tears were coming faster now. "And you love Zoe like your *own*."

Reggie glanced at Lance, whose eyes were tearing up, and wondered how long he could hold it together himself.

"Reggie, I promise," Faith said, "to actually, completely love you for all of our days, even when you act a fool."

Soft chuckles sounded and Reggie smiled, remembering the convo.

"I'm flawed," Faith continued, "and can't be the wife you need in myself, but I promise to cling to Jesus so He can give me what I need—for you. I promise to enjoy my good and perfect gift—you, our marriage—and treasure it through each season God gives us. I love you, Reg."

Reggie could feel the anticipation rising as they exchanged rings. He eyed Lance, waiting.

Lance smiled. "Yes, sir," he said. "By the authority vested in me as a minister of the gospel of Jesus Christ, I now pronounce Reggie and Faith as husband and wife . . ."

Reggie took Faith into his arms. "I love you so much, girl." His heart swelled as he kissed her, his mind echoing Lance's words —'husband and wife'.

~

Reggie snuggled alone with his wife in the limo. "Can we skip the reception and go straight to our room?" He kissed her, savoring it.

Faith entwined her fingers with his. "Are you nervous about that?"

"About going to our—oh, about . . ." Reggie looked at her. "You're nervous about us being together?"

"I asked you first," Faith said.

"I can't say I'm nervous, no." He kept his hand in hers. "Is that what you're feeling?"

Faith nodded, her head on his shoulder. "I talked to Mom about it, and I've been praying about it."

"Baby . . ." Reggie sat up a little, looking into her eyes. "I'm glad you told me. We've got a lifetime ahead of us, we don't have to rush anything. We'll move at your pace."

"I said I was nervous," Faith said. "I didn't say I wanted to put it off." She leaned in and kissed him. "I'm nervously ready. Mom and I even went shopping for lingerie."

Reggie gave her a look. "Seriously? Your mom did that?"

Faith nodded again. "It really helped to be able to talk openly about it with her and Cinda—"

"You talked to Cinda too?"

"That's how I found out I wasn't alone in the way I was feeling," Faith said. "If I hadn't talked to them, I'd probably be a mess thinking about tonight. But now I'm a little excited"—she kissed him—"about becoming one physically with my husband."

"So you just brought us back to my original question." Reggie kissed her again. "Can we skip this doggone reception?"

CHAPTER 56

*J*illian walked from the hotel ballroom to a conference room the wedding party had been given in which to gather and refresh. "Listen, everybody," she said, waiting for chatter to die down, "guests are almost all seated. In about ten minutes you'll line up and go in as introduced—grandparents and parents, bridesmaids and groomsmen—same pairing —and so on—"

"What about the flower girl?" Patsy had Zoe on her lap, fast asleep.

"Zoe's supposed to walk in with Treva and me," Lance said. "If she's still sleep, I'll carry her."

"Faith and Reggie," Jillian said, "after you're introduced, remember, you go straight to the floor for your first dance. And Alonzo"—she surveyed the room till she found him—"word has somehow spread that you're here and people are gathering near the ballroom to get a glimpse of you."

"Seriously?" Alonzo said.

"They're welcome to come to the reception," Reggie said. "Tell 'em they can get a picture and one dance with Brother Coles. Fifty dollars a head."

"There's that solution," Jillian said, "or the one the hotel offered. They said they'll rope off the area once we're inside, and they can station a security guard to turn people away. But they'd charge us."

"We'll take care of the cost," Alonzo said.

"Okay, I'll set that up," Jillian said.

She left out and headed for the front desk—and caught a glimpse of Allison entering the hotel lobby. Jillian had seen her from afar at the wedding, first time in months. Living Word had two services, and since she never saw Tommy, she figured he and Allison attended the later one. Jillian continued to the desk and set up security then headed to the ballroom. When she walked up, Allison was talking with one of the hostesses, a college friend of Faith's.

"I just went in and looked at my table," Allison was saying. "I don't know a single"—she paused, seeing Jillian.

Jillian paused as well, seeing what appeared to be a baby bump.

"Can I help with anything?" Jillian said.

Allison looked at her. "I should've guessed you'd put me at a table in a far corner with complete strangers."

"Actually, I didn't handle table assignments," Jillian said.

"That's the overflow table, ma'am," the hostess said. "I'm assuming you RSVP'd late?"

"I wasn't sure I was coming," Allison said.

Jillian looked at the hostess. "Let's see what we can do. There must be some no-shows. Check the Porter family tables. Allison is Reggie's sister-in-law."

"Oh, sorry," the hostess said. "Actually, there's a seat at the table with Reggie's mom and sister Adrienne. A great aunt fell ill and couldn't make it."

"Perfect." Jillian turned—

"What about Cyd and Cedric London's table?" Allison said. "Is there an open seat at that one?"

The hostess checked. "That table is full, ma'am."

"I'll just take the one assigned," Allison said, moving into the ballroom.

"Hey, Jillian, can you verify the order of introductions?" The mistress of ceremonies approached with papers in hand. "I would hate to put the wrong name to the person walking in."

"Sure," Jillian said, staring after Allison, wondering what just happened.

～

Cecil should've been there. The thought wove itself through Jillian's mind during the dinner, the toasts, the cake cutting, and now, as she sat and watched the dance floor. The two of them would've been out there laughing and acting silly with their kids. They would've been reminiscing with Faith, finishing each other's stories, because they'd all been there. Cecil was her life, the glue in countless seasons and memories—

"Finally taking a minute to rest, huh?" Treva took the chair beside her, Wes in her arms. "You should definitely be tired. You've had everything flowing beautifully all day."

"I'm so happy for Faith and Reggie," Jillian said. "And they are seriously the cutest. Look at them."

They watched Reggie and Faith at the front of a line dance, Reggie clearly leading, Faith trying to pick it up.

"I've never seen half of these line dances," Treva said. "How do Joy and Sophie know them all? Must be a young folk thing."

"Girl, Cyd and Cedric are out there hanging right with them," Jillian said. "I didn't know they could go like that."

Moments later the deejay changed the music, and the dance floor shifted from younger to older.

"Frankie Beverly & Maze will never get old," Jillian said. "This is my jam."

"Okay?" Treva said. "I'd be right out there if I wasn't holding this sweet boy. But I see Lance got a replacement for me." She smiled, watching him and Hope on the floor.

Jillian's gaze skittered over to Tommy. This used to be his jam too. But right now he stood talking with family members. Allison must've left early. Jillian couldn't recall seeing her for a while.

Faith and Reggie came over to their table.

"We're about to cut out," Faith said.

"Already?" Treva said. "It's not even ten o'clock. I thought you'd be partying till midnight."

"You want us to announce it," Jillian said, "so people can get final hugs? Or are you sneaking out?"

Reggie gave her a look. "You already know, Aunt Jill. That first option keeps us here till midnight."

"And I don't think people will mind," Faith said. "We've made the rounds a couple times at least, trying to spend time with everyone. The hardest part was saying goodbye to Zoe. Jordyn took her to Jesse's for me."

"So I won't see you before you take off tomorrow morning," Treva said. "Let me get *my* hug." She embraced them. "Love you both. Have an amazing time, Mr. And Mrs. Porter."

They hugged Jillian next.

"You went above and beyond," Faith said. "We can't thank you enough."

The newlyweds made their way out of the ballroom, more slowly than they'd hoped as people stopped them every few feet. Treva got up to roam and talk, and Jillian sat a few moments more, her mind drifting again—

Her phone lit up on the table. **Aunt Jill, Faith left her phone. Probably where we sat for dinner. She said can u bring it to her?**

Jillian went to look and found it, and made her way up to the bridal suite.

Faith let her in. "Thanks, Aunt Jillian," she said. "I knew it would be quicker if you brought it up, than me going back down."

"Wow, this is spacious," Jillian said, glancing around. "And you've got a view of the Arch?" She walked toward the window.

"I know, I couldn't believe it when I walked in," Faith said. "It's even got—"

A knock sounded on the door, and Reggie, in his tux pants and shirt, went to get it.

"Man, how you gonna leave your keys—" Tommy paused when he saw Jillian.

Jillian looked at Faith. "Okay, what's going on?"

Reggie moved beside Faith. "So we were talking," he said. "And we've got a question for you two."

Jillian and Tommy looked at them, waiting.

"What's the deal?" Reggie said. "Between the rehearsal and dinner last night and everything today, you've spent hours around one another and hardly said two words."

"We're just wondering," Faith said, "why you're not even friends at this point."

Several seconds elapsed.

Jillian cleared her throat. "You both know what happened. We had to cut off the friendship."

"Right," Reggie said. "Had to, *then*. Why now?"

"What do you mean, why now?" Jillian said.

"I'm just saying," Reggie said. "Tommy's been divorced almost three months. But y'all are gonna act like strangers forever?"

Jillian looked at Tommy then stared downward.

"You didn't know, Aunt Jillian?" Faith said.

Jillian hesitated. "Seeing Allison today, something seemed off, but—and isn't she pregnant?"

"The baby isn't mine," Tommy said.

Reggie took Faith's hand. "So we're gonna head around the corner to the bedroom. Just let yourself out when you're done talking. No need to say goodbye—in fact, it's strongly discouraged." He led Faith away then came back. "And in case you didn't know—we love you."

When the bedroom door closed, Tommy gave Jillian a glance. "They mean well, but we can just go on back down."

Jillian looked at him, and Tommy looked away.

"Okay, Tommy." She headed for the door. "We'll do strangers forever."

Tommy sighed. "Jill, wait—"

"Do you know," Jillian said, turning, "how hard it's been to live with what happened between us? To be part of some cheap one-night stand with a married man? Being unable to talk about it or process it with you, which was *fine*." Emotion was rising quickly. "That's how it had to be. And I was praying to be fine with never talking to you again, for the sake of your marriage. But I didn't have to pray, did I, Tommy? Because you didn't want to talk to me *anyway*. Thank you for making me feel even cheaper."

Jillian opened the door, and Tommy closed it back.

"Jill, come on, you know that's not—"

"And I knew what it was for you, an emotional fling." Jillian swiped tears. "And I was fine living with that too, because I had to be. There was nothing right about that night. And yet, I needed to hang onto *something* so I wouldn't completely *hate* myself so I told myself you at least cared about me—and how stupid is *that*? as if it *mattered*—but now I know how *delusional* even that was."

She yanked the door open again—

"Jill." Tommy spoke softly, tears in his eyes. "I stayed out of your life because I hate that I hurt you, and I wanted to give you space to heal, just like I was trying to heal. But I didn't know you could ever think I didn't care or you were just some . . ." He walked a ways and when he turned, tears lined his face. "Jill, I love you. I'm *in* love with you."

Jillian stared into his eyes as she wiped her own, the door moving to a close.

"I'm guessing it happened in college." Tommy went and sat on the sofa. "I know I loved you then, even if we never said it. You meant more to me than almost anyone. But maybe . . . maybe it went even deeper than I was willing to admit. And got buried in my heart and probably would've never surfaced." He looked over at her. "But the *way* it surfaced . . . You were grieving your husband and I brought you into *my* turmoil and spun us both out of control. I will always be deeply sorry for that."

Jillian stood there a moment, taking in everything he'd said, then walked over and sat on the sofa. "We did say it."

Tommy looked at her, confused.

"Right before graduation," Jillian said. "Might've been our last walk on South Hill. We knew things wouldn't be the same, and it felt awkward."

Tommy nodded slowly. "And we hugged."

"Which we rarely did," Jillian said. "And I said, 'I love you' and you said it back and there was this silence . . ." She stared vaguely. "And I've pondered it these past few weeks. I can't remember what I was feeling exactly, but I had to be feeling something or I wouldn't have said it. Then we just . . . moved on to something else."

Tommy looked at her. "Why were you pondering that?"

It took her a moment to meet his gaze. "I'm in love with you too, Tommy." Her gaze faltered. "And I've tried to push it away and pray it away because, for my life, it was way too soon and felt all wrong, and for yours it *was* all wrong."

"I know," Tommy said. "I prayed those prayers too."

Jillian looked at him. "What happened, Tommy, with Allison?"

A few seconds passed before he replied. "She came home—showed up out of the blue—saying she and the guy had had a falling out. She said it forced her to re-evaluate, and she wanted to work on our marriage." Tommy looked at Jillian. "So I made counseling a non-negotiable. If she was serious, that had to be part of it. And we went—once. She wasn't back a full two weeks before things blew up again."

Jillian kept her eyes on him, waiting for him to continue.

"I found pamphlets in her bag about what to expect during

pregnancy and asked her about it." Tommy shook his head, looking away. "Long story short she came home because her boyfriend didn't want the baby and told her it was time to go."

"And you know for a fact the baby isn't yours?"

"For a fact," Tommy said. "And the most painful part? Her admitting she still didn't really want our marriage."

"I had no idea," Jillian said. "Treva didn't say a word about the divorce."

"Most people didn't know for a good while," Tommy said. "We got a judge who processed it quickly because it wasn't complicated—no custody or property issues. And I only told a handful." He shrugged. "I don't know if or when Lance may have told Treva."

"So how was it, seeing Allison today?" Jillian said.

Tommy thought a moment. "Through all of this, I wouldn't have thought I'd end up feeling closer to God, but I'm thankful that's where I am. And I found out today that He's truly healing me. I was able to see Allison, have a two-minute convo, and sincerely wish her the best. That wasn't the case a few weeks ago."

Moments of silence lingered between them.

"I saw your video," Tommy said. "It was tough to get through. And I heard you when you said it's been hard to live with what happened." He looked at her. "How are you, Jill?"

Jillian took her time answering, wanting to assess it for herself. "It's been a really, really hard year. Grief on top of grief. And knowing I caused some of it added more grief." She lapsed into silence a moment. "But I know what you mean about growing closer to God. My prayer life, study life, everything deepened. And that's amazing to me."

Tommy nodded. "You ever think about how *gracious* God is?"

"All the time lately." Jillian got up and walked to the floor to ceiling window, taking in the view. "And merciful. And loving."

"And *kind*." Tommy joined her at the window. "I don't think I'd ever meditated on His kindness before." He seemed to dwell on it even now. "As much as I beat myself up over what happened between us, He keeps reminding me how complete His forgiveness is. That it's washed away. That's just incredibly kind."

Jillian nodded soberly, grateful, as those words filled her.

They both stared out, letting silence reign.

"I don't want to do strangers forever." Tommy focused still on the view. "But I'll do whatever you want, Jill, whatever you think is best."

Jillian's gaze rested on the city lights. "I don't see why we couldn't be friends at this point," she said. "Although, I don't know what that will look like with feelings in the mix." She turned to him. "But that's all it could be—friends."

"Absolutely," Tommy said. "I don't have the capacity for anything more. I doubt I ever will again."

Jillian looked at him. "It's been a really hard year for you too."

"I feel like you're about to say something with 'wait' and 'endure' in it," Tommy said. "Don't do it."

"I miss my cantankerous best friend."

"I miss you too," Tommy said. "And I would hug you, but I'm afraid of taking a single misstep."

"A quick one," Jillian said, moving into his arms. "Just don't you dare kiss me."

"You don't have to worry about that." Tommy was moving out of the hug already. "I'm entering this third friendship attempt with fear and trembling." He started toward the door. "We'd better get back to this reception."

Jillian followed. "I guess it's 'mission accomplished' for Faith and Reggie."

Tommy opened the door and held it for her. "They got all up in our business, didn't they? But I'm not mad." They headed for the elevator. "Because you were supposed to be looking over a few of my columns, to see where I can improve."

"We didn't talk payment, though," Jillian said.

"You said you weren't charging me." Tommy pushed the elevator button. "Since I'm your oldest, bestest friend."

"I never said that, and 'bestest' isn't a word." Jillian walked onto the elevator.

"See how much I need your help?" Tommy said, following.

"I know what—you could do some handyman stuff around our duplex," Jillian said.

"Don't you have a landlord?"

"They've been slow to respond when I call," Jillian said.

"How is that my issue?"

"Tit for tat," Jillian said, the elevator descending. "You need help; I need help."

"But I'm getting the raw end of this deal," Tommy said. "All you need is a red pen. I need tools and hard labor and what not."

"Oh, you know what else?" Jillian said. "We can start our text prayers back up."

The elevator reached the ground floor, and the doors opened.

Tommy looked at her. "Not if you can't up your limited vocabulary beyond two words."

Jillian walked past him. "Boy, hush . . ."

CHAPTER 57

OCTOBER

"Okay, sisters," Cyd said, "get comfortable because we're about to go deep." She sat on the edge of the sofa in her family room. "I've talked to each of you individually, and you've agreed to share matters that are private. So it goes without saying, nothing leaves this room."

"But I thought you were using this for a Bible study," Jordyn said.

"I'll be using pieces of your stories and perspectives anonymously," Cyd said. "But I loved the dialogue we had during Treva's study last year, so I wanted that same dynamic, especially for a topic like this. And you know I'm recording the audio for reference." She gestured toward Jordyn. "Jordyn is the inspiration behind this Bible study, both the content and the title. Living Water will produce it, and we're calling it *When I'm Tempted.*"

"So, question," Stephanie said. "You said you want real talk about temptation," she said, "and we wouldn't need all this confidentiality if we were talking about temptations like, I'm 'bout to eat this third piece of pie—which trust me, I could go there too. But if we're going *deep*, I'm thinking sexual temptation. So, umm —why are sister Treva and sister Cinda here?"

"You're trying to put me out?" Cinda said.

"I'm merely wondering," Stephanie said. "You know I've got nothing but love. Shoot, if that were the case, Cyd shouldn't be here either, except she's the one doing the study."

"So you'd be surprised if I told you I kissed another man two months ago?" Cyd said.

The whole room locked eyes on Cyd, but no one more than Stephanie.

"There's no way," Stephanie said. "I can't even see another man anywhere near your orbit."

"Micah Daniels," Cyd said.

"Oh my gosh." Faith covered her mouth. "Sorry, not judging, just . . . genuinely shocked."

Stephanie was still staring at her. "You're saying your lips physically touched that professor's." She shook her head. "I just can't see it." Her eyes got wide. "Does Cedric know?"

"He knows," Cyd said. "Now let's bring it back to the main—"

"Wow," Stephanie said. "Girl, I need a minute . . ."

"You're about to be the one to leave," Cyd said, "if you react like this whenever somebody shares."

"I know one thing," Stephanie said. "If Treva comes talking about what she did two months ago, I might *have* to leave. I can't take it."

Treva looked amused as she sat on the floor with a crawling baby Wes.

Jillian looked over at Stephanie. "Steph, we've been prayer partners for more than two years," she said, "and you've never asked for prayer in this area. So I'm wondering what *you're* doing here."

"If you want to know the truth," Stephanie said, "I'm wondering myself why I agreed. Girl, pray my strength."

"So just to set this up," Cyd said, "let's look at this word 'temptation.'" She had a Bible and notebook in her lap. "When we hear it, we tend to think of something negative. But temptation is not sin. It simply means to try or prove—putting something to the test. So"—she looked at Cinda—"can I use your case as an example?"

Cinda nodded.

"Let's say this guy approaches you," Cyd said, "and he's showing you all this attention. And he's popular, a lot of women want him. And you find that you're kind of enjoying the flirting and the attention—"

"How is this temptation?" Stephanie said. "Cinda basically dismissed Alonzo when they first met, even if she did enjoy the flirting."

"The guy in the example isn't Alonzo," Cinda said. "It's Donovan Shores."

"What?" Jordyn said. "I love his music. And girl, he's cute. Where'd you meet him?"

"At this birthday party I went to in LA," Cinda said.

"So in this example," Cyd said, "you can see how it could become temptation. The guy is flirting, you're sensing that you're beginning to enjoy it. But if you say to yourself, I'm married, let me move away and shut this down—the test just made you stronger. On the other hand, if you linger, extend the convo, maybe even exchange numbers . . . it's become a temptation that could lead to sin."

"Why is everybody looking at me?" Cinda said.

"You know why," Jordyn said. "What'd you do?"

"I landed somewhere in the middle," Cinda said. "These women were coming up to him, and he kept focusing on me, and I lingered longer than I should've. But when he asked for my number, I didn't give it to him."

"Girl, if you had given him your number . . ." Stephanie said. "You wouldn't even give it to Alonzo that first night."

"I know," Cinda said. "I don't even know why I felt that little pull to linger. It's so ridiculous in hindsight."

"That's the reality of temptation," Cyd said. "That's why it's so important to recognize it, especially in those 'little' beginning stages. Every day, we're tempted in some respect—to say the wrong thing, think the wrong thing, make the wrong choice. I plan to share in the study how I was tempted to back out of the debate because I feared rejection by colleagues and students. And I *knew* God was saying to do it."

"It comes up in so many scenarios," Treva said. "I'm glad the study will be speaking to those every day temptations."

Cyd nodded then glanced at her sister. "But Stephanie's right. I want to focus on sexual temptation too. Seems like we just don't talk about it until someone falls, and everybody says, how did that happen? And because we don't talk about it, we think we're the only ones dealing with it. Temptation *will come*. We need to know what it looks like and how to respond."

"It's so weird," Jordyn said. "I wasn't thinking about temptation before. Sex was just sex, no big deal. Now it feels like I'm *super* aware of just *wanting* to go there, then praying *not* to go there . . . which is actually sort of easy since I was embarrassed enough the first time Jesse put me out."

"Jesse put you out?" Faith said.

Jordyn nodded soberly. "I got in his bed and took my shirt off, and he told me I had to go." She blew out a sigh. "It was a blessing, though. That's the night I gave my life to Jesus. But I need this study because I still get tempted around him."

"What you said is awesome, Jordyn." Cyd turned a few pages. "I've got it here in my notes—Matthew 26:41. Jesus said, 'Keep watching and praying that you may not enter into temptation; the spirit is willing, but the flesh is weak.'" She looked at Jordyn. "You're aware of the temptation, which means you're watching. *And* you pray when you become aware. Praise God. That's real growth."

"You know what?" Faith had her eyes in her Bible. "That word 'keep' is jumping out at me. *Keep* watching and praying." She looked up. "I started out watching and praying when I would get together with Jesse. And I guess slowly, as desire built up, the watching and praying dropped off."

"Okay, Jesse is the man," Stephanie said. "He got *two* of y'all in here talking temptation."

Cyd threw a sofa pillow at her sister.

"What?" Stephanie said. "I'm just saying."

"That 'keep' is a good point, Faith," Jillian said. "I was just thinking too that there's watching and praying—then there's fleeing. I was seeing First Corinthians 6:18 in my sleep—flee sexual immorality—after what happened with Tommy."

"Umm, did I miss something that's common knowledge?" Cinda said.

"I don't know either," Jordyn said. "I knew you were going through something, Jillian, but I didn't know any details."

"Neither did I," Cyd said, "until Treva knew I was preparing this study and asked Jillian if she wanted to take part."

"That's so interesting," Jillian said. "I just knew when I did the video, people would put two and two together."

"I did, actually," Stephanie said. "The video plus Tommy leaving Living Hope *and* the two of you suddenly not speaking?" She gave Jillian a look. "Then you asked for prayer and confirmed it."

"So, Cinda and Jordyn, since we're here for real talk," Jillian said, "back in April Tommy and I were headed to a concert, stopped at his place to get tickets, and he found divorce papers Allison had filed. So there's all this grief and emotion, I'm telling him it's not over, to fight, that I'd be there for him, and he kissed me, very lightly. But that little spark lit a fire."

Cinda and Jordyn kept looking at Jillian.

"And yes," Jillian said, "we slept together. But there was this moment when things were getting heated and we paused, and he

said, 'I'm taking you home.'" She stared downward a moment.
"That's what haunted me afterward. I didn't flee. My flesh was
engaged, and I didn't *want* to flee." She shook her head. "If I
learned anything—and I'm still learning—it's that *nothing* good
dwells in my flesh—what verse is that?"

"Romans 7," Cyd said. "Wait a minute." She flipped to it. "7:18.
And Jillian, this is so good." Cyd looked at her. "This is the kind of
real talk I wanted—that sometimes you don't *want* to flee. I'm
doing a whole section on the battle between flesh and spirit. We
have to be so careful what situations we put ourselves in because
we put too much confidence in our flesh."

"I know I did," Faith said. "I thought I could stick to my
convictions about staying a virgin, but also flirt with how far to go
with Jesse. I really thought there were certain lines I wouldn't
cross. And you have no idea until you're *there* that your flesh is no
help. It's down for whatever." She seemed to think on it a
moment. "I needed to draw the line at—you're not coming in
my room."

Cyd nodded. "As you said that, Faith, I was thinking how we
can work against ourselves, making the way of escape narrower
and narrower. Which brings us to one of our main verses—First
Corinthians 10:13." She glanced around. "Can somebody read it?"

"I will," Jordyn said. "'No temptation has overtaken you but
such as is common to man; and God is faithful, who will not allow
you to be tempted beyond what you are able, but with the temptation will provide the way of escape also, so that you will be able to
endure it.'"

"Did you all hear the promises in there?" Cyd said.

"God won't allow us to be tempted beyond what we are able,"
Jordyn said.

"Hallelujah to that," Stephanie said.

"Also, that He'll provide the way of escape," Faith said. "And
that it's common, something others are experiencing."

"And that He's faithful," Jillian said. "I take that as a promise."

"Amen," Cyd said.

"Whenever I hear this verse," Treva said, "I can't help but think of a situation I got involved in."

All eyes focused on Treva.

"About nine years ago," Treva said, "we were living in Chicago, and I worked at a large firm downtown. I'd get to work early, leave late, work weekends. And I had this colleague . . ." She redirected Wes from a house plant. "He worked in a different practice area, but we'd run into one another. Then it got to where we'd get coffee around the same time. Then lunch a couple days a week. And since we worked late, lunch turned into an occasional dinner. It was this unspoken *thing*, like we were dating almost. And one evening in my office, we kissed."

"You never told me this," Jillian said.

"I never told anyone," Treva said. "But after what happened with Cyd, we talked, and I shared it with her." She sighed. "The kiss scared me. I said, what am I doing? I was a baby Christian, hardly ever prayed. But I prayed, asking God to help me get out of this situation. Then I got home that night, and Hezekiah had made dinner and cleaned the kitchen, and was helping the girls with homework or something. I felt even worse."

"So what happened, Mom?" Faith said.

"The craziest thing," Treva said. "Not long after, this colleague told me at lunch that he was transferring to the New York office. Now, I had prayed for help, but the first thing I thought was, *you're leaving me?*" She looked at Cinda. "How ridiculous is *that?*" Treva shook her head. "To this day I'm in awe of how God provided that escape. When I think of where that could've gone . . ."

"That's what shook me too," Cyd said. "The moment Micah and I kissed, I could suddenly see the path—how it could lead to more. And it had to be God showing me because it scared the mess out of me. That's what made me stop and take the *other* path, of escape."

"But how were you even drawn to him?" Stephanie said. "Seems like you and Cedric have such a strong marriage."

"I wish that was a guarantee that I wouldn't be tempted," Cyd said. "I spent way too much time with Micah, thinking it was fine because it was Bible study and we were colleagues. Never had any improper conversations, no flirting, nothing. But a connection was building nonetheless. I learned a lot, that's for sure."

"So if that happened to you when your marriage is on point," Stephanie said, "I'm not sure what to think about my situation."

Everyone focused on Stephanie, waiting.

"I love Lindell," Stephanie said. "I thank God for the mountains He's moved in this marriage. But our love life . . ." She shook her head, staring downward. "Despite numerous conversations, reboots, and prayers upon prayers, there's not much *life* in it. So I find myself thinking back to this one relationship and battling thoughts." She looked up. "And I know what you all will say, and yes, I cast out the thoughts, I pray, I try to think about what's right. But the *other* thoughts always come back."

"Steph, I didn't know you were dealing with this until a few days ago," Cyd said. "And I'm so glad you shared it because this is huge. This is where it starts, in the mind."

"I went through that when Cecil and I hit a dry season," Jillian said, "around year eleven of our marriage. Fantasies can seem so harmless. But I noticed I was finding comfort in the thing that wasn't real, and I wasn't focused and praying on the thing that *was* real, my marriage."

"That's good—finding comfort." Cyd wrote it down. "That's the thing about temptation—it makes its promises too. So for you, Steph, the thoughts promise to comfort, to satisfy, maybe even to bring a measure of joy. But it's all a lie. It's designed to take you out."

"Reminds me of James 1," Treva said, turning to it. "Verses 14 and 15—'But each one is tempted when he is carried away and enticed by his own lust. Then when lust has conceived, it gives birth to sin; and when sin is accomplished, it brings forth death.'" She looked at Stephanie. "You have to see these thoughts as poison. They're bad enough on their own, and it's not even the end game. You can be sure the enemy has next-steps in mind. Before you know it, this guy will be reaching out to you 'out of the blue'—or you'll be reaching out to him."

"So what do I do?" Stephanie said. "What's my way of escape?"

"Sometimes it's not quick and easy," Cyd said, "as you've seen. Look what the verse says—'but with the temptation will provide the way of escape also, that you will be able to *endure* it.'" She looked at her sister. "You have this underlying issue in your marriage. And as that's being worked out, you may continue to battle these thoughts. But the way of escape is to keep your eyes fixed on Jesus and on what's true. Believe that all things are truly possible with God, that He can heal this, that He *wants* you to have a thriving love life."

"Trust that God is always working," Treva said. "When those thoughts come, it's nothing but the enemy firing darts because he knows better than we do that God is always working. You said it yourself—God has moved mountains in your marriage. You think He can't spice up your love life?"

"I'll be praying for you not to grow weary," Jillian said. "Just the thought of having to endure is no fun. But keep going back to that promise—God is faithful."

"Amen," Cyd said. "I plan to do an entire section on endurance as well, because it's so key. Let's look at some of those verses . . ."

∽

Cyd's front door opened and closed, and voices filled the entry-way. The women looked up as they closed out three hours of study time.

"You've got company this evening?" Stephanie said.

They appeared one by one in the family room—Cedric, Lance, Tommy, Alonzo, Reggie, Lindell, and Jesse.

The women looked at one another.

"Hey, babe," Treva said, smiling as Lance picked up Wes. "What are you guys up to?"

"The guys have the evening session," Cyd said. "Cedric's going to lead it and record it, then have it transcribed—omitting names and other identifiers so I can glean from it. I really want this to include a guys' perspective as well." She stood. "So we need to leave and give them their privacy."

The women stood and packed up their things, chatting with the guys.

Faith looked at Reggie. "So what are you gonna say?"

Reggie put his arms around her and kissed her.

"That's not an answer," Faith said.

Cyd smiled. "Let's go, sisters."

Cyd pulled Cedric aside before she walked out. "Chase is at my parents' house, and you and I have a date tonight."

"But we probably won't get done till at least eleven," Cedric said.

Cyd gave him a quick kiss. "Perfect."

∼

Cyd came home through the garage entrance about ten-thirty and let the dog out, hearing the guys only faintly from the kitchen. When Reese was back in, she eased up the stairs and got the room ready as she waited for them to wrap up.

Close to an hour later, she heard Cedric's footsteps approaching.

"Sweetheart, sorry it took longer than—" He stopped at the doorway. "Wow."

Orange rose petals covered the landscape—on the floor, the

bed, the dresser and nightstands, even in their bathroom—along with orange candles lit around the room.

Cedric took a few steps inside. "Did I forget a special occasion?"

"No." Cyd sat against the headboard in a short silky orange robe. She stretched out her hand. "Come here, babe."

He joined her on the petals. "Where'd you find orange roses in October?"

"You're not the only one who's resourceful," Cyd said. "Since you wooed me with different colored roses, I'm guessing you know what these signify."

Cedric gave her a knowing look. "Passion."

"That very first weekend," Cyd said, "when I shouldn't have let you in my house at night"—she kissed him—"I felt the passion between us. It was totally physical, we hardly knew each other—"

"It was real, though," Cedric said, shaking his head. "And if I had seen you in something like *this*?"

Cyd nudged him. "I was thinking how, through the years, we've had that same physical passion. But more than that, you've shown a consistent passion for *us*. For our marriage." She looked into his eyes. "I don't know if I've shown that same passion. I get bogged down in so much that you probably wonder sometimes if I'm even thinking about us—"

"Babe, I know you think about us," Cedric said.

"I just want to be more purposeful." Cyd felt a rise of emotion. "I want you to know how much I love you. You are more to me than I could've ever imagined." She paused. "I just . . . I really don't know what I'd do without you."

Cedric looked into her eyes, tucked her hair behind her ear, and kissed her slowly. And Cyd melted in his embrace.

"I love you," Cedric said. "Passionately. And as long as we're on this earth, I will be all about you"—he kissed her again—"and me"—he kissed her once more—"and you in orange anything, every day of the week."

"I don't think orange is really my color, though."

"Oh, it's your color, baby."

Cyd looked into his eyes. "I'm feeling like I did that first weekend, tempted to take advantage of you."

Cedric chuckled a little. "Go with that feeling," he said. "I promise I won't put you out."

He kissed her again, carrying them away on a sea of orange.

READING GROUP GUIDE

1. Cyd almost backed out of the debate because she feared saying that she believed Jesus was Lord and Savior and the only way to heaven. She knew the truth would alienate some of her students and colleagues. Have you ever sensed the Holy Spirit prompting you to share truth about Jesus or the word of God—yet you were tempted to keep quiet because you feared rejection? What did you do ultimately?

2. Lance's mom Pamela asked him, "How is it the only time you think it's okay *not* to obey God is when He wants to elevate you?" When God calls you to do something, are you tempted to run the other way because you're too focused on self—your past, your abilities, your weaknesses, your resources . . . ? Do you recognize it as a temptation—and pray against it?

3. Alonzo had a very real issue with the *Greater Glory* project and knew God was telling him to turn it down. Yet Cinda tried to persuade him to do it because of the benefit she would receive. Have you ever been tempted

to pursue attractive opportunities, despite the godly cautions you encounter. Which path did you take?

4. Allison was discontent and struggling in her marriage because it wasn't what she thought it would be. She said she'd wake up "and all I could think was how much I missed the life I had before." Treva replied, "that's the enemy in your head, wanting you to be discontent, focus on self, dismiss the marriage vows you made before God." Have you ever been plagued by thoughts that you knew were not good, right, or pure? Did you agree with them? Or did you reject them by the grace of God and pray to have the mind of Christ?

5. In her video Jillian said, "Conviction and grief move me to repentance, so I can draw near to Him again. So I can cling to Him again . . ." When you sin are you quick to repent and draw near to God again? Do you sometimes believe the lie that He won't receive you? How well do you receive God's forgiveness? (Note 1 John 1:9—"If we confess our sins, He is faithful and righteous to forgive us our sins and to cleanse us from all unrighteousness.")

6. Both Tommy and Jillian prayed for the Lord to take away their feelings for the other. Do you submit your feelings to the Lord, asking Him to conform them to His will? Or do you tend to let your feelings take the driver's seat?

7. Jesse learned for himself that as a believer, he had the power of God within to resist temptation. Despite what he would have "normally" done, he cried out to God for help and walked in obedience. Have you seen God's grace and strength at work in your life in a strong way, in the face of temptation?

8. Cyd didn't see an issue with spending prolonged one-on-one time with Micah for Bible study—until temptation rose up when she least expected it. Whether

single or married, as a believer, what kind of boundaries do you draw with members of the opposite sex who aren't your spouse? If you're married, have you ever been surprised when, like Cyd, what you thought was nothing—became something?

ABOUT THE AUTHOR

KIM CASH TATE is the author of several books, including *Cling* (2017), *Though I Stumble* (2016) and *If I Believe (2017)*. A former practicing attorney, she is also a Bible teacher. She's been married to her husband Bill for more than two decades, and they live in St. Louis with their two young adult children.

Connect with Kim:

YouTube.com/kimcashtate
Instagram.com/kimcashtate
Facebook.com/kimcashtate
Twitter.com/kimcashtate

www.kimcashtate.com

CPSIA information can be obtained
at www.ICGtesting.com
Printed in the USA
LVHW112358261018
595028LV00001B/139/P